HOLIDAY MONEY

HOLIDAY MONEY

BEVERLEY JONES

A Cutting Edge Press Paperback

Published in 2012 by Cutting Edge Press

www.CuttingEdgePress.co.uk

Copyright © Beverley Jones

Printed and bound by in Great Britain by CPI Group (UK) Ltd, Croydon, CR0 4YY

PB ISBN: 978-1-908122-14-8
E-PUB ISBN: 978-1-908122-15-5

Chapter One

I had gone as far as picking up the phone to cancel the whole thing: the hotel booking, the flowers, the bloody pompous photographer, the silly, frilly cake.

I yanked open the pink, ribbon-tied notebook containing the precise operational orders for the big day, sending a sheaf of candy-coloured calling cards and glossy magazine cuttings spiralling in a vortex to the floor. For once I didn't mind the mess.

I was powered by the momentum of sheer rage, an unthinking primordial instinct that belonged in fire-dusty landscapes of smoking volcanoes and brittle, dark skies, a red and black urge to break, rend, destroy – quite at odds with the feminine-hued flowers and fancies. Slowly but deliberately my anger was condensing, winding in on itself, gathering like a rust-coloured tornado, ready to rumble unstoppably through the neatly planned progress of my life, spiralling chunks of debris, carrying all before it. If I was quick, and unrestrained, I might touch down and catch Daniel in the open, overwhelm him before he could bolt for a basement and seek cover.

I am whirlwind wife-to-be, hurricane bride – fear my wrath!

There had been a shuddering amount of neighbour-worrying yelling in the morning-verging-on-forever that had rattled by in the previous half an hour. It was accompanied by one thrown engagement ring (me) one hurled wedding manual (me) and an algebraically accountable number of expletives (surprisingly, me). For a while I could not spare the breath to cry. While Dan stalked off to the bathroom to cool down I retrieved the wedding manual from the back of the sofa, where I had just hurled it past the space occupied by his head. Then I dialled the first five digits of Blooming Marvellous. I could now tell that effete mincer Stanley that neither of his suggestions for silver stemmed, dipped irises or very on-trend 'crown of blooms' tiaras would be required after all, thank you very much! I'm sure you understand!

But then my dialling finger and my jaw began to wobble, my eyes began to blur. I realised I was weeping so much I would only have succeeded in snotting and gurgling at Stanley's haughty voice on the other end of the line, incapable of speech. I, me, about to be made wordless by the simplest of their sequences, by the memory of a most straightforward question: 'What would you like for a wedding present?' spoken by *that* woman, thirty minutes ago and counting.

Water surged from my eyes. My voice was drowned.

I let the hand holding the phone fall to the table top. I stood that way for what seemed like hours, just bringing forth water like Niagara Falls in high spring, bubbling saliva like snow melt. Then I lifted the handset and slammed it back on the cradle with a violence that ratcheted up my arm, jolting my whole body. That was better. It felt good. It restored my rage, kick-started the spiralling winds again.

I repeated the action from a greater and greater height until the handset shattered in a satisfying scream of plastic. I sniffed and then swallowed in the deeper silence that often follows on the coat-tails of carnage. The living room was holding its breath. Then I did something I had never done before. I exhaled and stopped thinking. I blew my nose on the corner of my cardigan, picked up the car keys and my ready-packed suitcase and walked out.

I still marvel at how it all happened so fast and so furiously. I was in the car and driving down the street, away from Dan, away from our house, before my brain had caught up. Up until that point in my life it really wasn't like me to throw a tantrum, make a fuss, lose my temper. It was very unlike me to raise my voice. And to swear? You fucking lying, waste-of-space prick, bastard! That was rarer still. I'd always prided myself on being an amenable person – self-possessed, reasonable, verbally elegant. I had taken myself by surprise in more ways than one.

I had always been known for my calm and composure. 'Easy-going' had been my mum's favourite adjective for me, from the time I was no more than a pink-cheeked, blue-eyed child. Twos? Terrible? Hardly! See little Jennifer playing contentedly on the rug with a cloth rag book depicting smiling farm animals. 'Placid' became the adjective of choice when I hit seven, and 'sensible' was the favourite when I turned into a teenager without any notable trauma.

These mild tributes were accurate if not inspiring; ranting and raging, indulging in hissy fits, was simply too embarrassing, too undignified. I never understood those girls at school – always bickering, going off into whispering corners, excluding others with their frosty, glance-askance eye-narrowing. Then there were the women at college and at work who seemed to spend an inexplicable amount of time locked in toilet cubicles in tears over men, cold-shouldering one another at the photocopier over some imagined slighting look at another's bum.

Perhaps I had been lucky to be surrounded by self-controlled people all my life. People who 'meant well,' people whose 'hearts were in the right place.' I came from a family of organisers not fighters – practical, friendly, uncomplicated, slow to anger – so I didn't think there was much that couldn't be resolved if you simply took the time to explain what you meant, to think about the consequences and consider what you thought could be logically achieved.

It wasn't that I didn't get angry sometimes, or there weren't a hundred things percolating in my head that I could have said. I just *counted to ten and thought again*, obeying my mother's sing-song mantra for sailing through daily life. Maybe I was bubbling a little underneath but I was smooth on the surface, placid as a windless day, thinking, 'What a *fuss* they are making,' and 'What's all the drama about? Honestly!'

Clearly, twenty-eight-and-a-half years of this didn't prepare me for the way I reacted on that seemingly ordinary Friday in October.

The day I became Hurricane Jennifer had started innocently enough. It was around 11 a.m. Dan and I had a long weekend off together. I was dressed and sitting in the living room reading the *Echo*. I was drinking my second cup of tea and eating my usual high-fibre breakfast of natural yoghurt, organic apricots and chopped banana. Sunlight slid in through the big bay window. The forecast in all senses was cool and dry.

Dan and I had had a disagreement the night before but he was deliberately avoiding any reference to it. Instead he was talking about the temperature and whether or not he would he need a thicker jumper in case the breeze picked up in the afternoon.

I knew something was going on, of course. He knew I knew but wouldn't acknowledge it. The hushed phone conversations at odd times of the night when he thought I was asleep. The sudden 'work conference'. The receipt for flowers I had not received.

Naturally, he had plenty of plausible ways to dismiss my questions, several reasonable explanations at hand. But I wasn't an idiot. I wasn't convinced. I fully intended to challenge him again. But the one thing guaranteed to put Dan on the defensive was an ambush over breakfast. Further badgering before coffee and toast would probably only result in his storming off somewhere, leaving me standing impotently and urging him to come back and discuss it properly. Besides, I didn't want a full blown fight before we left for the weekend. So I waited.

Dan was emptying coffee from the grinder and putting it into the machine's filter, dropping grounds all over the worktop in the process. When his mobile phone, plugged in and charging on the windowsill, began to ring, we looked at each other for a few moments with the, 'Who on earth is that now? Can't we ever get a moment's peace?' look.

'Leave it,' he said, fitting the filter paper into the coffee machine. 'It's our day off.'

But ignoring a ringing phone is almost impossible for me. With a sigh I got up and answered it for him, expecting a last-minute query from work or a telesales assault telling Dan he was the lucky winner of a luxury holiday if he just dialled a premium rate number.

But it was neither of those. There *she* was on the other end of the line.

'Hello?' I asked, with habitual, professional brightness in my voice, my calm, proficient, confidence-inspiring, non-threatening, work-day voice.

'Who are *you*?' she asked confidently, in response, not *May I speak to so-and-so*, or *Is that so and so's phone?* The emphasis on

5

the *you* implied surprise on her part. I was not the person she had expected to answer. She had some sort of accent – slight, modified, precise – but it was there. I pay attention to voices out of habit. Sometimes the tone, the inflection, says a world more than the words. If I had realised this single phone call would all but shift the gravitational axis of my world forever I would have made sure to pay greater attention and to take some notes. But I was impatient to end the interruption.

'Well now,' I responded, still bright and pleasant and going through the motions, 'Who is asking please?'

She didn't answer for a moment and then, cautiously, she said:

'Let me speak to Dan, please. This *is* his phone?'

The sudden politeness nettled me more than the initial cool confidence. It began to make me suspicious.

'*Who* is calling please?' I repeated, still polite.

'I probably shouldn't say,' she countered, the faintest trace of amusement surfacing. 'Who are *you*?'

'I'm his *fiancée*!' I responded with emphasis, a little more loudly than necessary. Dan, setting out the cups while the coffee bubbled into the pot, raised his eyebrows questioningly.

I hadn't really got used to the word *fiancée* in the last few months – I rarely used it. But a sudden premonition-like drop in my stomach told me this conversation was ping-ponging into unpleasant territory, very quickly, and an unusual proprietorial instinct overcame me.

After a moment of silence that was too long and too dense, the mystery woman laughed softly and said: 'Ah, that explains it. He clearly hasn't told you about us. That's a little hurtful but understandable.'

'Who *are* you?' I demanded, finally starting to lose my poise.

'You're his *fiancée?*' she continued. 'In that case perhaps I

6

should ask you what you would like for a wedding present.'

'Look, who is this?' I demanded.

Dan, looking anxious now waved his hand at me in a *give me the phone* gesture.

'I am Sophie,' she said lightly, simply and with finality, as one might say, I am the prime minister or I am David Beckham and clearly no further explanation would be required.

'Sophie?' We didn't know any Sophie, at least I didn't. 'Sophie who?' I insisted, a touch shrill now. 'What do you mean "us" . . . told me about "us"?'

'Perhaps you'd better ask Dan that.' I could not see her smile but I sensed it was there, sliding through the phone towards me.

For a millisecond I was baffled. I was standing in my living room, black suede boots planted firmly on the plum-coloured carpet, no need to worry about the stability of my footing. But then I looked at Dan and he looked so guilty, so horrified, so furious, that I knew at once what this must mean. I knew as the room around me receded and the floor dropped away, leaving my mind windmilling for balance. He knew who Sophie was, of course. And I knew what *'us'* meant.

Oh God, no! How awful. How twee. How predictable. How clichéd.

It took five seconds to process the information and one second more for my brain to short-circuit. The room returned to its customary proportions at dizzying speed. I bent my knees and reeled a little.

Quietly I ended the call and put Dan's phone down on the table. Then I took a deep breath and threw the wedding manual at him. I followed it with my engagement ring which rebounded off his cheek. Then I started yelling and I didn't stop.

He was understandably startled. He'd expected a plea for explanation certainly, followed by reproaches and, perhaps, tears. 'Who is that woman? Why Dan? Why?' but not this – my fail-safe rationality, my easy-going calm lost, and in its place a primal scream of unfettered outrage.

Oh, he tried to talk, he tried to tell me some cock-and-bull story and make excuses about the hotel receipt and the receipt for the twenty-seven lilies I had found. He tried to explain, retrieving my ring from the floor and pleading with me to *Just listen – please*! But the more he talked, and the more the lies were exposed in a little marching line, the madder I became.

That was when I exploded, split like the atom, mushroomed into being, arcing skywards, crowning through the clouds with nuclear ferocity. A moment later I was starting the car and pulling out of the street with Dan dashing after me from the bathroom, moments too late, then gesturing in a startled manner at the garden gate. The Cardiff suburbs, the M4, Port Talbot, Swansea: each location marker flashed past the windows of my Ford Focus like a back-projection in an old film, and all the time I headed west towards the Gower coast, cursing creatively, violently, and hitting the steering wheel with the heels of my hands.

Somehow I travelled for an hour without really knowing it, and then I was turning down an overgrown lane and rounding what I hoped was the final corner. All at once the land dropped away. The sea beckoned with salt fingers and the sky was shot with the last brittle gleam of the dying sun.

In front of me was my destination, so achingly pretty I had to stop the car, wind down the window and sigh into the breeze to clear the ghost of yelling from my scourged throat.

The Watch-house Hotel was perched on a cliff corner facing the water, above a sickle-shaped scoop of spray-wet shingle and powdery surf. Mist-bound and mysterious, it embodied a storybook location plucked from an old seafaring tale, perhaps, or a historical romance – all crooked lines and canting angles. A feather of narrowing smoke hovered above the chimney, scented with autumn. I was instantly enchanted.

Soft light bled from the wonky windows. The ancient wooden door stood open to reveal a fireside scene almost too tranquil to be true. Up under the eaves of the slate roof doves nested and cooed a welcome. It was perfect. Or it should have been. Dan had picked the spot for us from a review of boutique hotels in *Cool Cymru*, the glossy hotel guide featuring the best Welsh weekend breaks. 'Where Memories Are Made', it had proclaimed. The Watch-house had also featured in *The Times* travel supplement and *Elle* magazine, with its ten luxury suites, in- room spa service and a three-rosette bistro serving locally sourced organic meals.

The weekend was supposed to be a pre-wedding break, a chance to spend some time alone together, away from work and the immense project that the wedding had become. I had been even more excited about it because, as a rule, Dan did not 'do' romance. He was not the type to whisk me off anywhere or spontaneously buy a bunch of flowers. Usually he thought 'romantic gestures' were unoriginal and a 'conspiracy of mass-marketing hype'. So usually he did nothing – to be *individual*, I assumed.

But things had been tense between us for some time and the wedding planning was making it worse. The Watch-house was supposed to salve our irritation, pour aromatherapy massage oils on our troubled waters, apply balm to our bickering.

I had pored over the luscious-looking Henry Morgan suite on the internet once Dan announced he was 'taking me away from it all'. Being an old harbourmaster's house, all the rooms had seafaring themes; Henry Morgan of course, being the infamous Welsh pirate and governor of Jamaica. Other rooms included the Black Bart (or Barty Ddu, in the Fishguard vernacular), T*reasure Island's* Captain Flint suite and, rather oddly, to my mind, a *Marie Celeste* suite.

But there was no pirate-themed chintz to mar this 'rustic seaside idyll that breathes atmosphere and attentiveness' as the blurb had burbled. This was 'seaside chic at its most stylish'. I had eagerly anticipated wallowing in a king-size bath, up to my nose in luxury Molton Brown foam, after a day strolling by the crashing surf in Wales's 'hidden gem'. More than that, I had hoped Dan would remain unoriginal and fuss over me for three whole days with champagne and tender words, reminding me – or convincing me – that this wedding was still the right choice and not just the obvious one.

Yet there I was alone, on a darkening afternoon in October, in this picture-postcard pretty place, petulant, puff-eyed and abandoned.

Stoically I lugged my suitcase up to the front door but I almost had second thoughts. What on earth was I doing? Did I want to stay in a luxury suite that was a tortuous reminder that my former husband-to-be was a scum-sucking unfaithful liar? But where else could I have gone? I didn't want to see or speak to Dan. I didn't want to hear any more nonsense explanations and excuses. And the rooms *were* paid for – three nights' dinner, bed and breakfast and a complimentary bottle of wine. Maybe it would give me time to think – to breathe. I took a deep breath and headed into the glowing hallway.

The super-chic receptionist, perched on a high stool reading *Vanity Fair*, was elegantly dressed in a black polo neck and black trousers. Her hair was suspiciously raven coloured, cut in a razor-sharp, glossy bob. She was wearing the kind of natural-look make-up that I know costs a fortune at the Bobbi Brown counter. She closed the magazine discreetly, smiled automatically, then evaluated my red eyes and battered suitcase sympathetically. She refrained from alluding to the obvious gaping void at my side where a man ought to have been, while I signed forms, declined morning newspapers and was shown a map of the fire exits. Luckily I was able to check in early.

'The Henry Morgan suite really is our loveliest – such a romantic and intimate ambience,' she remarked, clearly quoting from the publicity release, before finally giving me the room key, which was tied to a piece of arty painted driftwood. Then she glanced away, sensing she may have been indelicate. 'Dinner reservation at seven for . . .?' The silence stretched out as her eyebrows stretched upwards.

'One, please.'

'Of course.' She smiled soothingly as if I had just said I was expecting the results of a cancer test, and steered me to the stairs. 'Let me know if you need anything. Just dial 0, ask for Vivi*enne*.'

The room *was* lovely – again canting and wobbly, but decorated in soothing creams, pale blue and dove-grey. A huge flat-screen TV floated darkly above an antique dressing table with an original art nouveau anglepoise mirror. The mullioned window with its window seat opened on to an expanse of heaving sea and empty dark sky. A large, soft-blanketed bed took up most of the space.

It *was* very intimate. *And* romantic.

Once I'd bid Vivi*enne* farewell I fell into the arms of the hand-spun Welsh wool throw blanket on the plush velvet chaise longue and wept salt water to shame the incoming tide.

Why Dan? Why? How could you? We should be here

together, I gurgled into the cross-weave. Now that I'd pulled the plug on my restraint, the rush was addictive. Perhaps I'd been missing a trick all along by being far too self-controlled.

After an hour of indulging in this tear-sodden self-pity I sat up, blew my nose and decided to crack open the complimentary bottle of plummy Merlot by the bed. Two glasses and six soggy hankies later I was surprised at the stern tone I took with myself, as if a voice originating somewhere outside my head – maybe based in a 1940s schoolroom, wearing a high-collared lace blouse – was speaking. It was unexpected but oddly reassuring.

You have two choices, it said starchily: lie here whimpering and wallowing– very unattractive, by the way – until you weaken, phone Dan, start being far too reasonable and believing his excuses. *Or* you can shower, get dressed, get something to eat and get a hold of yourself. Show some dignity. Let him stew for a while. Let him worry about *you* for a change. That lying, dishonest . . .'

I stilled the voice with a glug of wine. Then I downed the rest of the glass and undressed. Designer toiletries and a bath that would have accommodated Captain Morgan and half of his crew awaited in the beautifully appointed en-suite.

My instinct *was* to call Dan and beg him to say it was all a mistake, but for once I was counting to more than ten and thinking again . . .

I spotted *him* that first night after dinner.

I must have been more than a bit drunk, but feeling weird and woozy seemed par for the course since that morning's developments. I'd never rowed with Dan like that. I'd never interrogated a strange woman on the phone, thrown any household items or broken off an engagement, so how was I supposed to know I was not feeling normal?

An almost hysterically cheerful log fire snickered away in the grate beneath the ancient mantelpiece. It echoed the warming reds and chocolate browns of the Smugglers' Snug, otherwise known as the bar. I was self-consciously solo in a window booth, full to the brim with things I normally never ate because they are so bad for the heart, namely Perl Wen cheese-stuffed mushrooms, crayfish tails in cream sauce and homemade honey cheesecake.

Mournfully, I eyed the affluent-looking cuddling couples in their casual-chic sweaters. In the tear-halted hours after I'd checked in they had proliferated in the hotel restaurant and the Snug and were now one affectionate, shiny-haired, wine-sipping mass. The whispered miasma of their sweet nothings drifted through the evening candle glow. Two huge ginger cats were snuggled up together on the windowsill.

There was altogether too much snugness for a woman alone, I thought, though it would have been just enough for a cosy pair of lovers, in a snug, smug embrace. The night and the wine and the chattering fire enhanced the windblown romance of the place. The hour seemed to invite confidences and chance meetings.

I'd started reading Daphne du Maurier's *Jamaica Inn* upstairs and had brought it down with me. I'd found it, and a couple of nineteenth-century swashbucklers, tucked discreetly in the alcove of the window seat, alongside the obligatory Dylan Thomas poetry anthology and the collection of Welsh folk tales that is *The Mabinogion*. As a result, by my third glass of Merlot, I was eyeing the door, half expecting a rain-blown stranger to crash in, the start of a story on his lips that would rattle us to our landlubbers' bones. That would have been most welcome – anything to break the reality of being there alone and the actuality of what it meant. I should have slowed down on the wine. I didn't.

That was when I saw *him*, wedged in a nook at the end of the bar, engrossed in a novel. He paid no attention to the door or the limpet people entwined in corners. I couldn't make out the title of his book but I could tell from the binding and the layout of the type that it was a *real* book, not a *Bravo Two Zero*-style pulp military memoir or a sports biography. I'd stolen fleeting glances at him as he remained engrossed, occasionally pushing his floppy, sandy fringe back from his face.

He looked relaxed and a bit of an anachronism in the carefully contrived nineteenth-century fug of the Snug. He was surf-chic smart in faded jeans, a loose T-shirt, and with leather flip-flops on feet even more tanned than the rest of his golden skin. There were slight sun-crinkles around his eyes in defiance of the chilly reality of a Welsh October. He was sipping from a pint of real ale – not Stella, not Strongbow cider. These were promising signs, signs of a man of culture perhaps, a man of taste and depth, a man of parts.

He caught my eye once, causing me to flush a little. For around four seconds, the duration of the gaze, I'd forgotten about Dan entirely. That didn't seem like a bad thing at the time. If I tried harder maybe I could extend the four seconds to six and then twelve and who knows how much longer. I liked the curl of his hair.

He had smiled back quickly, warmly, when he'd seen my appraising glance but returned to his book just as quickly. I remember sliding *Jamaica Inn* onto the seat next to me and pulling out my other book from my handbag – the poetry of Robert Frost, angling the cover up a little so he could see it. I suppose I didn't want him to think I was some dippy reader of historical, bodice-ripping fiction. I was too sensible for that.

I was dignified and thoughtful, educated and interesting, and getting more drunk by the minute.

I half wanted and half didn't want him to look over again. Maybe he would strike up a conversation about how we were the only two un-snug singles in the snuggest bar in the world, curled up with only their books to hold close to our empty hearts.

Dan and I had been together so long I had no real idea what I would do if this man actually came up to speak to me. Blush certainly, babble possibly. But if I'm honest, I thought I felt something auspicious ticking in the dark corners of the Snug, echoing deep in my full stomach, in the bloom of my flushed cheeks: a chance meeting, a change of direction, an opportunity for rescue, escape, or maybe revenge. Something utterly unsensible. Something new.

A blustery night in an ancient pub, two eyes could meet and a story might be about to unfold . . .

But before I could explore this idea I realised I *really* needed the loo. After easing my wine-full bladder and popping on some extra lip gloss, I strode back to the bar, feeling ready for anything. But he was gone. I was surprised to acknowledge a flash of relief, but with it there was still a flutter of disappointment. Despite the anger and uncertainty I now felt towards Dan I'd responded to something in a stranger, however fleetingly, when yesterday it would never have crossed my mind. But then yesterday I had not spoken to *that* woman, and yesterday Dan was not the man he was today.

The hotel stairs seemed even more canting and wobbly as I negotiated my way back upstairs, the floor positively rolling, but somehow I made it into the outsize bed. I spent some time staring at the rafters of the Henry Morgan Room. The only visible nod to its fearsome Welsh namesake was a framed vintage poster of a 1940s advert for Captain Morgan's rum. I got up and helped myself to a couple of those from the discreetly concealed mini bar. I'd worry about my liver tomorrow. In one day I'd drunk more than I normally did in a week, maybe even two weeks. I was slightly impressed with myself.

Half-dizzy, half-nauseous, I flopped on the bed, seeping tears again, railing against Dan and what must have been the oceans of lies he had told me. Finally I fell asleep, succumbing to the confusing image of a tricorn-hatted pirate in flip-flops, a tanned hand pushing his sun-faded curls away from his sea-green eyes and advancing towards me through the sea mist.

When I woke in the weak daylight, the sound of skittering bird feet on the roof and the boom-boom alarm call of the morning high tide competed in my pounding head. Dan had left several voice messages and a text on my mobile phone. I did not respond.

My familiar frantic desire to make up with Dan and restore equilibrium to the world had not materialised with the return of daylight. Usually 'making up' involved me making the first move, most often saying, 'Please let's just be friends again, Dan, I can't bear it when we fight. It's not worth it.' Never adept at 'treating them mean', I couldn't hide my feelings. The sensation that chaos was about to overwhelm us if we did not reconcile and deal with the problem rationally was always stronger than my pride.

But that morning I felt cool-headed and blank. I savoured the novelty. I turned off my mobile phone again and left it in the hotel room. I realised my engagement ring was still sitting on the living-room table at home.

Seeing the sun had come out I decided to play *Sunday Times* travel supplement elegant short-break holidaymaker. I walked on the beach in my outsize cuddly cardigan, ate a locally sourced organic vanilla ice cream and poked around a tiny art gallery staffed by an aging hippy with dreadlocks. Then I ate a tomato bruschetta and drank cappuccino in the tiny beachside café, watching the breakers explode in the white, bright sea-light.

I fortified myself against the chill of the Atlantic with two large glasses of red wine in the seafront pub, followed by an Irish coffee. Afterwards, on the spur of the moment, I bought a new surf-style T-shirt top in a little boutique on the harbour, and some of those surfer-type coloured beads that you wear around your wrist.

My head was weirdly, widely empty, and the surf and shore rippled and rolled with the overhead skies. It was a pleasant change to have such a vacuum in my head that allowed the wind to whistle in, filling me with the sounds of the sea alone.

I was disappointed to see the hotel bar so empty that evening. I'd made short work of the Welsh lamb stew and delicious local cheeseboard and was ready to settle into the Snug with my book and another Merlot. But last night's air of romance and mystery had dissolved. The giant ginger Tom was spread across the bar, his partner departed. A wealthy silver-haired couple with 'we sail a lot' tanned faces were nursing coffees, huddled close in their matching Berghaus jackets, but no one else was around. After another glass of wine I decided it was time to strike out and explore the nearby pubs. Why not? I was a grown woman, and a capable one at that.

Wrapped in a long, stripy scarf of impractical proportions, I braved the unlit country road. It led a few hundred yards to the cluster of houses that marked the edge of the nearby village. Half a sandblasted castle tower loomed up out of the wind-crackling tree line, and the moon rode high overhead on the crests of the passing clouds. I remembered a school-taught poem by Alfred Noyes about a highwayman riding over the windswept moor to meet his sweetheart as just such a moon rode the stormy sky above. A highwayman would have been in keeping with the scenery.

It was wonderfully cold and blustery. Ahead on the right, tucked underneath the castle's solid flank, the coach lights of the Mochyn Ddu looked very inviting. This pub, too, had been reviewed in the *Cool Cymru* guide: 'upmarket gastro delights and local ales in a cosy, candlelit ambience'. It certainly looked magazine-shoot pretty, from the brass knocker to the Victorian stained-glass panels in the door. I hesitated on the doorstep. I had never gone to a pub alone at night before, unless it was to wait self-consciously for a friend who happened to be late. But I gathered my courage.

For a moment I had the distinct sense that if I edged over the threshold something would change. I would have accepted an offer from the fates, as the castle watched and the wind waited. Once upon a time Jennifer said – *To hell with it, what's the worst that can happen?* and she lived happily ever after on a distant shore without her rat of a husband-to-be.

Was that possible? What harm could it do to have one drink and then go back to my room for wine and weeping? What could possibly happen in so pretty a place on so beautiful a night to so ordinary a person like me?

It was very busy inside. Middle-aged couples and youngsters in their twenties were squeezed around little tables, gesticulating at the bar, laughing and talking loudly. As I elbowed my way through, ahead of me was Mr Literary Surf-chic – sweater, flip-flops and tousled hair intact. I was outrageously, irrationally pleased. I knew, of course, that this was the purpose of my visit. I'd been longing to see him again all day. Though I hoped my face revealed only a pleasant approachability, I was cart-wheeling inside, even more so when he flicked a smile of recognition my way. I smiled back at him and simultaneously smiled a tipsy thank you to the fates.

I saw myself advance in my mind's eye, windswept and smiling, in control, commanding his attention, scarf rolling behind me, a halo of sandy hair as my photographic backdrop, eyes glittering in the fire-glow –dramatic and daring.

A lot can change in one night. I was dimly aware of this fact. I wasn't scared of it. I wanted something to happen, something that was not the aftermath of *that* telephone call, the sound of Sophie's smile, and the look on Dan's face, something that was not expected and commonplace and predictable.

I got my wish – something did happen. And if I'd listened carefully I might have fancied I heard the fates laughing.

Chapter Two

'I grant wishes,' I replied, clicking into the daily log and calling up the latest incident on the screen. With my left hand I fiddled awkwardly with the buttons on the air con handset. It seemed to be stuck on 'full'. My fingers were like dry icicles. Soon I'd be able to see my breath.

'You do what?' demanded Jack huffily, on the other end of the phone, a note of surprise in his voice, already starting the ascent towards its usual indignant whine.

I paused, realising I had spoken aloud. There was no point in replying. Jack would be prattling again in a second.

'I'd settle for some common sense right now,' he blustered. 'I need the info a.s.a.p. I *am* on a deadline, you know.'

Of course I knew. There were constant deadlines. I lived by their deadlines. They were always *on* one.

I had come to loathe the clipped, 'let's get down to business, quickly. I'm terribly busy and by definition terribly important,' tone of Jack NewsBeatWales. His demands usually rattled thick and fast from the receiver three seconds after I had lifted it, one second after I'd spoken the corporate greeting for which I, and my colleagues, were widely scorned, 'Good morning, police press office.'

It was Thursday. I'd been back from the hotel for almost

a week and back at work for four days. That morning we'd had to deal with media enquiries regarding two sudden deaths, four car crashes, a gas leak evacuation, a freedom of information request about how much the police helicopter costs to run, and a big paedophile court case starting at 10 a.m. I had six other incidents to chase up for various journalists on my notepad list, all on deadlines, though not all imminent. Business as usual.

Two minutes before I voiced the errant thought about my wish-granting ability, Jack had called for the third time in half an hour to check whether or not a cause of death had been attached to the untimely demise of Craig Michael Brockway, aged twenty-seven, of Slipways, Cardiff Bay.

I already knew that Mr Brockway had hung himself in the wardrobe at the home of his partner Phillip. I knew he had used an old school tie and also that he played for the local rugby team. Drug paraphernalia, as the media like to call it, had been found in the room. It was a good story.

But Mr B's family did not know the details yet, not fully. It had only happened an hour ago. It seems they did not even know about Phillip, the *partner*. Even if they had known I would not have given any of these details to 'Jack NewsBeatWales.'

I told Jack, for the third time, that I was not able to confirm any details beyond the fact that a 27-year-old man had been found dead and an investigation was 'ongoing'. Yes, it was too early to say whether or not it was suspicious.

'But,' insisted Jack, 'we've heard this, and we've heard that and, blah blah blah, public interest, blah.'

'I'm afraid I don't know anything about that, Jack,' I countered, 'Sorry.' (I wasn't sorry but the subtext to saying it was , I say what I'm told to say or, I'm too lowly to be told anything.) And so round we went in a well-worn groove. I know, you know; you know, I know.

'But my deadline's in fifteen minutes!' whined Jack.

'No it's not. It's noon for the Valleys' final.'

'Yes, but for the website, the website! It's live time for the website.'

Now Jack was wheedling for 'off-the-record' guidance about the hanging element. I started to break open a packet of Rich Tea biscuits, the power of my silence expanding down the phone line creating a static fury I could almost hear humming in Jack's head.

I had never met Jack, though we spoke daily, and he cajoled and pleaded and sometimes flattered, demanded and sighed, probably sulked. In return I raised my eyebrows and smiled, or became stern and intractable, or doled out bits of sustenance and promises. In this way we behaved like partners in a long-term relationship that lasted for regular sections of every day, every week of the year. The only difference was that Jack would keep calling me back, no matter how the conversations ended or how mad he got, because I had what he wanted: names, dates, locations, quotes, statements, car models, weapons descriptions, suspect descriptions, family tributes, photographs of the dead and the damned, the shamed and the sentenced – the facts.

My voice was my power, the conduit via the telephone for the information that sat right at my fingertips in the sunny, whitewashed, air conditioned decontamination zone of the police press office, Southern Area. This was where information could be accessed at the tap of a keyboard, the blood and violence and sadness washed off and made clean and corporate and fit for publication, if I so chose. I did not choose to do so right then. Not for Jack.

I held the line as usual, upright and attentive in my chair. I was neat and smart in black trousers, a neat black top and smart cream cardigan, low heels, neat ponytail and smart lipstick. Never flustered, I was infuriatingly polite, dispensing wisdom to desperate journalists on deadlines, shaking my fair fringe from my fair face, espousing fair play. Refusing to lose my temper.

I'd only seen one photo of Jack from a picture byline on a tasteless article about teenage suicide he'd sold to the *Guardian* . He looked about thirty, handsome and cocky.

While he rattled on I gazed at the A5 photo print of a beautiful New England beach scene. It had pale yellow sand, dreamy blue sky and sea, a little white picket fence and a bone-white, blinding-bright lighthouse in the foreground. I had stuck it to the wall by my computer monitor. The sun on the late evening shore gave a warm glow at odds with the increasingly glacial chill of the office. I imagined myself standing at the waterline. I am smooth and serene as the water. Jack is in the water, floundering and thrashing for some reason. I simply watch his head slip lower and lower beneath the surface. I do not feel the urge to help him. I smile.

I often imagined that Jack's head had a little ill-fitting lid on top, like an old fashioned kettle. When stoked correctly, Jack might come to the boil. I believed I could hear a tell-tale pre-squeal, meaning a steam release was imminent. To add one extra degree of heat I said, 'I'm very sorry, Jack, but I can't confirm anything other than what I've been given. Try again later today, maybe after lunch.'

'But my deadline?'

'Hmmm, sorry.'

Then I heard the anticipated sound of a steamy little explosion.

'Then what are you people *for*?' There was spittle too now. 'Bloody press officers. What do you *do* exactly?'

I grant wishes, I thought again to myself – all your information-grabbing, hand-rubbing, sleaze-embracing, story-making wishes. There was no point in trying to explain, and there was no need. Jack had hung up. I put the phone down with a quiet smile.

'Was that Jack NewsBeatWales?' asked my boss, technically the media and communications manager, Nigel, un-technically 'Nightmare Nige'. The 'nightmare' part was a joke on the part of the press officers because Nige was possibly the nicest boss in the world, ever.

'Who else?' I replied, with mock resignation.

'Did he hang up on you? If I ever bump into him in a pub I'm going to fill him in, the arrogant little bugger. He didn't call you a bad name did he?'

A bad name, bless him! 'Nope, just the usual rant about our general uselessness.'

'He's got a nerve. Honestly, does he think we're here to furnish him with flippin' gory details for his rag? If he hangs up on you again I'll get that police klaxon and stick it up to the phone. That'll give him an earful.'

He beamed at his own gentle joke, pushing his trendy, square-framed specs upwards an inch on his narrow nose. That day he was wearing a pink and purple, Tom Ford-ish striped tie and a smart grey suit. Nige, six years older than me, was the best-dressed person on our floor, probably in the building, and he liked to experiment with ensembles from *GQ* magazine. He adjusted his tie carefully as he spoke. 'I don't know how you stay so calm and polite. You are too nice, Jen. Tell him to shove off.'

'I'm not nice. I'm just professional.'

'That you are. But you are too nice to *those* people. If he rings back, put him over to me. I'll sort him out.'

No Nige, you won't, because Jack would steamroller right over you in five seconds and I can handle Jack any day of the week. 'Will do.'

'All right. Can you go to Terrorism at eleven if you've done baiting the media?'

'Must I really?'

'Someone has to.'

'It'll be more obtuse nonsense. Like anyone's going to bomb Pontypridd train station or send anthrax to the Plaid Cymru office in Mumbles.'

'Yes, but it makes them feel all safe and warm to see us media professionals sitting there, hanging on their every word.'

'Well, ok, but Serian has to pick up the gas leak evacuation and the helicopter query.'

'Done! See, you *are* too nice. You could have held out to pass on the hanging, too.'

'Nice tie, by the way,' I added. 'And is that a new suit? It's a good colour on you.'

'That's what *I* said, but my wife said the tie's a bit . . .' He paused, and then mouthed discreetly behind his hand, 'gay'.

'I think it's cheerful.'

I grabbed my notepad and made for the door, picking my way past a collection of unopened paint pots and boxes on the floor. The station was undergoing a refit, starting with us and the top brasses on the top floor and working down, literally and figuratively, through the CID offices and scenes of crime suite, down to the PCs' parade room, the kitchens and storage, and finally to the cells in the basement custody suite. One day soon, station stalwart Sergeant Stan (I was never sure if this was his first or his last name) would have to give up his armchair in his subterranean hidey-hole among the shelves and boxes of the old evidence lockers and emerge blinking into a new world of low-energy light bulbs and ergonomically designed desks and chairs.

For the press office the revamp mostly consisted of a lick of paint, some new blinds and some 'storage solutions' as our office manager, Fat Paula, had snootily put it, casting a disapproving eye over the fire-hazard piles of newspapers, force magazines and little pots of free force key rings strewn across every surface. Sheets covered the workstations and our little seating area. Two blokes from Estates and Health and Safety were holding tape measures up to things and frowning into their clipboards.

It's amazing how quickly the day-to-day crawl of minutiae and bureaucracy reasserts itself when you've got urgent press releases to get out and you've just had *another* patient conversation with Fat Paula explaining how, no, I don't always have time to log it in the book every time I leave the office for five minutes, and no, running down to the CID for a comment that needs to be out five minutes ago doesn't constitute an 'agreed absence from the work area'.

Already, my weekend at the Watch-house seemed like a blip, a hiccup from a hundred years ago. I had pushed everything that had happened there deep down into my brain, tied it with tape and stored it like lost luggage belonging to someone else. I was back in the realm of reality, and all was continuing as normal. Well, almost normal. The smell of undercoat was making me a bit dizzy, and an unoccupied work-experience girl from one of the comprehensive schools was distracting me with her high-pitched prattling about *Gossip Girl*.

As Nige had requested I wandered over to the terrorism

update. This was held in the large conference room on the first floor, aka the Command Room, or Kelly's Kingdom, so known because Chief Superintendent Kelly Cavendish loved to call a Command Team meeting (comprising the area's senior officers) as often as most people like chocolate biscuits with tea. Despite being hampered by a girl's name and a comedy regimental moustache, he liked to play keeper of the kingdom in there, booming out orders and, in his hearty Yorkshire brogue, Henry the Fifth-style inspirational pep talks to grudging subordinates.

The room had big monitors that could be used to link up with the Gold Command room at HQ and the other command rooms for 'live hi-tech conferencing'. Cavendish was already there, deep in confab with someone from accounts who was inexpertly pressing buttons on the conference handset, trying to make the screen come on.

'Jen,' yelled Cavendish. 'Do you know how to work this bloody thing? We're trying to link with HQ. Steve and I are imbeciles with technology.'

'Sorry, boss, Behnaz usually sets it up. I can have a look if you like.'

'No, no, s'all right. Do me a favour, though. Run down to the CID office and see if the detective super's there. I know she's here today but she's not answering her mobile, probably knows it's me calling, but I'd like her in on this. Do you mind?'

'Sure thing,' I said, with a breezy smile. I was used to 'IT consultant' and 'general dogsbody' being part of my job description. I wandered down the hall to the CID room.

As I approached the door I heard a familiar voice say: 'The super wants the report from the PPU passed to the CPU so they can do the F1 on it and CSI get the stuff for the CPS.'

'What the fuck did you just say, mate?'

'The superintendent wants the report from Public Protection so Criminal Process can do the witness statement and scenes of crime can get the stuff to the Crown Prosecutor.'

'An F1 is a stop-search, dumbo!'

'Well, that's not what *she* said.'

'Obviously not, big brain!'

'Well, ring her and ask her what she wanted, then.'

'I can't ring the boss up and say, 'scuse me *ma'am*, can you tell me what you want me to do because my dopey colleague is thick as two planks!'

'Oi!' This last was accompanied by a stress ball streaking across the office and clattering into the air conditioning machine.

'Can I interrupt, gents? Or is this little conversation classified?' I enquired mildly. Bodie and Doyle grinned excessively and waved me into the room.

'Lovely Jen! Been looking for you!' thundered Bodie.

Bodie, aka DC Marc Ryan – definitely Marc as in Marcus Aurelius or other Roman, soldierly extraction, not Mark of the milk-and-water, Luke and John variety. (He had emphasised the spelling to me several times when I had put his name in press releases.) Indeed, I noted Marc seemed to be sporting a new goatee-and-sideburn combo. Added to his Julius Caesar crop and muscular physique, he bore more than a passing resemblance to Russell Crowe in *Gladiator*, albeit younger and more vocal, which no doubt was sort of the point, even though the film was already years old by then.

Doyle, aka Jimmy, DC Jimbo/Thin Jim Williams – smaller, slimmer, curlier of hair and twistier of smile, the speed to Marc's stature, the thinking woman's copper. The half-moon Harrison Ford-style scar on his chin came courtesy of a thug who'd made the mistake of trying to smash a pub window with skinny Jimmy's boyish face. He'd received an unexpected beating and three years 'over the wall' i.e. prison time, for his error. 'Speed of a rattlesnake, grace of a panther,' Jim had preened with a grin, proudly fingering the stitches, and no one had argued since.

Bodie and Doyle usually came as a pair and argued like husband and wife, in order, I suspected, to hide their deep, manly, platonic love.

'Come in, come in, then!' boomed Bodie with a force that almost caused my eyeballs to shudder with concussion. I thought I saw a quick tremor hit the rows of files and cuttings on the windowsill. He didn't mean to shout at me, it was just a CID thing. They all seemed to automatically lose volume control when they swapped police constable for *detective* constable. Technically, Bodie was an acting detective *sergeant* while the reigning one was on maternity leave, and his voice seemed to have gone up another notch in the last three weeks.

'Well, I don't want to interrupt you when you're clearly so busy.'

'Always time for you, lovely,' smiled Doyle. 'Just catching up on the old filing. Take a seat, take a seat,' he beamed, dumping a large pile of pending files the short distance from a chair to the floor to enable me to sit.

I always thought I'd make a good detective. From what I'd seen it wasn't really that hard. To be an efficient one you need common sense, an eye for detail and a hardy sense of logic. Nine times out of ten, crime isn't cunningly planned or well concealed. It's panicky and hurried or plain obvious. If you wanted to be an average DC you just needed patience and a tolerance for mountains of files and late nights; someone else would always help pick up the slack, someone who wanted promotion – someone like Bodie.

'Jen, Jen, Jen!' boomed Bodie. 'We need one of your inimitably styled press releases please, for a ne'er do well of the parish who has been turned over by his druggie acquaintances. Do say you can assist us.'

'I'm on my way to Terrorism but what are the details? By the way, the chief wants the super there right away. Seen her?'

'Yeah, she's having a fag out the back,' said Doyle. Having a fag out the back of anywhere had been off-limits since the smoking ban. Those who could not refrain were supposed to leave police premises. But it was damp and cold and the back of the boiler room would be warm and was not overlooked by civvies.

Bodie made a show of leaning out of the open-a-crack window, directing his sonic boom voice into the yard below. 'Boss! Chief Cavendish wants you, pronto! Terrorism!' I heard Superintendent Sue Seller's grit and gravel, too-many-Rothman's, Barry brogue say the word fuck fuck fuck in quick succession. I imagined her signature double thumbs-up gesture following it, and then the reluctant stubbing out of her cigarette. 'Job done,' beamed Bodie.' 'How's that for customer satisfaction? Jim-bob, you tell Jen about yesterday's action adventure, which shall henceforth be known as the Great Stella Heist of Twn Row.'

'I was just *going* to tell Jen about it if you'd shut your cakehole, *acting* sarge. It was a classic, Jen, a classic,' grinned Doyle, settling in for one of his colourful reconstructions. 'We got a code-one call from Twn Row about twelve noon from a *concerned neighbour* who says he's found a girl in the flat next door, knickers round her ankles, crying murder and holy hell. So we cane it up there and get to the flat, only to find it's our favourite crack-head slapper, Catherine Mansfield, in a pool of her own vomit, as usual. Mickey Ming Mong, our favourite prolific offender, is in the bathroom with a bloody nose, feeling really sorry for himself. Turns out he's been shagging Catherine, all relatively tidy, except she's currently 'dating' Mickey Half-Pipe, another ne'er do well of the parish.'

'They're both called Mickey?'

'Yeah, but don't interrupt. You'll ruin my flow. We search Mickey Ming Mong and find a load of heroin bags stuffed down his disagreeably skanky pants. Catherine's getting the Narcon from the first responder, that's her third time this month, mind you.' (Narcon is the 'miracle' injection administered to revive drug users when they overdose.) 'Turns out Mickey Half-Pipe has walked in on them going at it, given Mickey Ming Mong what for,' continued Doyle. 'He's gone off to get some *equipment* from his flat next door to complete Mickey's education in not knobbing his bird. She's passed out at this point, from the sheer excitement, we assume, and not the tonne of heroin she mainlined. In the middle of this, Mickey HP arrives with a baseball bat, sees us in the living room and legs it.

'Bodie's off like a shot, all Bruce Willis like, diving over car bonnets behind Mickey HP. He's legging it over the road and into the park. A bag of something goes into the bushes. I grab that, nice haul of pills and blow. A hundred yards later Bodie is flying through the air, tackles Mickey. Pow! They roll down the hill, right in front of the hairdressers, dolly birds and old dears inside screaming. Bodie whips out his handcuffs. You're nicked, mate!'

He emphasised this point by slapping his hand on the desk with undisguised glee.

'Best bit is, know what he said when we got him back to the flat to sort it out? I said, so Mickey, you beat Mickey up 'cos he was unfaithful with Catherine? He said, *Fuck her, he drank twenty of my Stellas and used up all my blow!* We found a half-kilo bag of heroin under the bed, and a Taser, yes an actual Taser, in the telly cupboard. Good day's work, by all accounts!'

He leaned back in his chair and laced his hands behind his head in a satisfied stretch that deliberately displayed several inches of toned lower midriff. 'Sadly, Catherine will live to shag another day, but we get both Mickeys for affray, possession with intent and resisting arrest.'

'And so,' he concluded, 'silence will fall on the suburbs of Cardiff and the good citizens of Twn Row can rest safely in their beds. *The End!*'

I was struggling hard not to laugh, in spite of myself. Even though I knew, since I was supposed to promote public relations, that I shouldn't condone this colourful and inappropriate retelling.

'Yeah, I was poetry in motion' added Bodie, giving Jimmy a short round of applause. 'You should have seen the look on Mickey's face when I tackled him. Good job I'm a textbook specimen of male physical perfection, isn't it? Feel my buns of steel, Jen? Go on, go on,' he urged, raising one bum cheek off the chair seat with a laugh, knowing perfectly well I wouldn't dream of such a thing.

At that point Dan walked in.

Bodie and Doyle's demeanour became stiffer at once and, to my amusement, Bodie jumped up into a smart, standing position, notebook in hand. A good little soldier.

'Gentlemen, are you harassing my fiancé?' asked Dan.

'Sorry, boss,' grinned Bodie, sheepishly. 'Getting a bit overexcited. Would you like a brew? Jim? Get the inspector a tea, you oaf. See what I have to put up with, boss?'

'I know you'll come through with flying colours, Marc,'

said Dan suppressing a grin. 'Can I borrow the press officer for a moment, if you've finished being politically incorrect to her?'

'How's my love?' he smiled, steering me off to the partial obscurity of the evidence racks at the rear of the room. 'Those jolly Neanderthals giving you trouble?'

'Naturally not,' I smiled back.

He gave me a quick, furtive hug, not wanting to be surprised in a clinch in the back office, even if it was with his wife-to-be. It just wouldn't be professional for a newly promoted middle-ranking officer.

There was an uneasy truce in operation between us. We'd had several heart-to-heart talks in the week since I'd returned from the Watch-house, sitting quietly in the living room and speaking for many hours. He swore he had told me everything – that it didn't change anything between us. That he wanted our life together to continue as we'd planned it.

But I had needed to hear Sophie say it. Not the details, the devil really can be in there, in sufficient quantities to start the brain reeling into an insanity of jealousy. No, I just needed to hear her confirm what Dan had told me – it was a one-time thing, nothing more.

She did tell me this, and she also told me she'd been just as surprised to hear of my existence as I was to hear of hers (though I thought this was unlikely and said so). Throughout this exchange, Dan had sat in the chair opposite me, his large fingers pressed anxiously against his mouth as if he was utilising them to physically prevent himself from interrupting. This by-proxy interrogation, this statement corroboration where for once he was not asking the questions, must have been uncomfortable, but he bore it silently.

Of course, he could have telephoned Sophie prior to that

and told her, or asked her, to say anything at all. It could all be lies. But her voice sounded genuine, businesslike – if she had felt any strong emotion I think I would have heard it. I think what I heard most was a touch of embarrassment.

I told Sophie I would expect her never to contact Dan or our home again. She said it appeared she had no reason to. Then I hung up the phone. I felt pleased with my ability to be so mature about it all.

Since then we had slipped temporarily into the 'giving it a chance' and 'trying our best to get on with it' stage. Dan was obviously trying very hard to convince me I was doing the right thing, hence his seeking me out in the CID office. Dan wasn't based at Southern, his office was in one of the sub-stations in the Northern sector, but business brought him down every so often.

'Want to meet for dinner tonight, Jen? I could get off early. I've booked us a table. Don't ask where, it's a surprise,' he whispered.

'I don't really like surprises, Dan.'

'You'll like this one. It's somewhere nice – honest, pet. You can dress up a bit if you like. You always say we never go anywhere different, so now we are.'

'Of course. All right.'

He gave my hand a little squeeze. 'I'll pick you up at the house at seven. I'll come straight from here. Right, lads,' he said, readdressing the suddenly industrious Bodie-Doyle duo, 'show me the sterling work you are doing to make valued members of our community feel safe on our streets and improve customer satisfaction.'

'Well, have you heard about the great Stella Heist of Twn Row, boss?'

'Oh God, yes, thank you very much, from the DI already

– twice,' said Dan with mock alarm, stalling another retelling with a raised hand.

Dan had been Jim and Marc's sergeant when they were all in uniform, and they all got on well, even still having the odd pint together. But Dan had his shoulder pips now, and an invisible chasm had opened between the men who once wrestled burglars side by side.

As Dan prepared to beat a hasty retreat, his eye caught the screen of the computer by the door. As soon as it did the inspector knew he had to speak.

'Marc, lock your PNN session, mate.' (The Police National Network holds the names and personal details of criminals.) 'I've told you before, password and security lock, every time,' said Dan, clicking the 'close' key. 'Oh, and your NOMAD application is open too, and any old fool can breeze in and access it. Lovely! Come on! Get on your game, Marc! '

'I know boss, sorry! I keep forgetting. It's the refurb. I'm bouncing from desk to desk while they're painting my office.'

'You're a DS now. Hardly an excuse, is it?' said Dan, properly pulling rank for a moment. 'Data protection? Security? I know you've heard of those. Set an example!'

'Will do, boss,' nodded Bodie without malice. He knew how the game worked.

'Naughty, naughty!' mocked Jimmy as Dan retreated.

'Piss off, *detective,*' said Bodie, good-naturedly. One day soon he'd be pulling rank properly on Jimmy, and they both knew it. It was fine.

Turning to me with a smile, Bodie said, 'So you're doing one of your excellent press releases for us on our arrests, right? Make it sound all professional-like.'

'Well, not today. I've got Terrorism.'

'But you could squeeze it in for us, couldn't you, for

tomorrow's papers? Fighting the good fight against the evil world of drugs, and all that.'

The deadline would be at five, and it would take some time to pull out the facts from Jimmy's colourful story. Half of it couldn't be told at all because court cases would be pending, and the rest would need to be sanitised considerably. The usual sort-and-shuffle process would hone it into the acceptable format: outcome at the top – what had happened, where it happened, who it happened to and when – names, ages and addresses, arrest and court information, quotes, contact numbers. Clean and tidy.

The press release would ultimately be unrecognisable from Jimmy's tall tale but it would be the truth, the bare facts – as much as the reporters and the public really needed to know.

'I'm not sure I'll have time today, I've got loads on,' I protested.

'But you are *so* kind to us. You always make me sound articulate,' wheedled Bodie, seeing I was weakening.

'And crime-fighting is a 24/7 commitment,' deadpanned Doyle. 'Your old man will understand – you'll be *setting an example*.'

'Kit-Kat in it for you,' said Bodie, waving the bar in front of me with a magic-wand flourish.

'I don't eat chocolate,' I smiled. 'But all right. As it's you two.'

'We take advantage of you, don't we?' grinned Bodie. 'We'd like to do it more often.'

The press release *did* make me late. I had to finish it between writing an arson update for one of the inspectors and trying to arrange a photo of the new Pontypridd community policing team with the local paper. On the way home I had to collect

Dan's suit from the dry cleaners and get some cash out to pay the milkman, who always called on the last Thursday of the month. At ten past seven I was trying to powder my face and put on some lipstick in the car en route to the restaurant. Dan was fiddling with the iPod again – trying to get it to link to the radio so he could regale me throughout the journey with whatever he'd downloaded from iTunes.

iTunes was his new obsession. He was fond of his 'shiny kit' as he called it and had an impossibly space-age phone with Wi-Fi. (I could just about text on my mobile as long as the predictive thing was off.) His state-of-the-art iPod was always with him, though the selection was usually something old fashioned that I didn't like.

I had never been deeply into music, not 'into' it as a lifestyle choice. You know, as in, 'What are you *into*, Jen?' as the kids at college had asked, like it was a test of social temperature, cool or uncool. Say Coldplay and it was into the instant permafrost. As a general rule it was 'glamorous indie rock and roll' for me, as the Killers had pointed out. I'd always had a good eye for the up and coming. I'd been listening to the Killers a full year before hysteria officially broke out, likewise with the Kings of Leon before they won all those Mercury and Brit awards. But of course, overnight, everyone was 'into' the Kings of Leon, old and young alike, so now they were almost anti-cool. Tepid, possibly. It was positively embarrassing to pass the station post room and hear Tony, the assistant business manager, with the proto-comb-over and slip-on brogues, serenading the photocopier with an off-key version of 'This Sex is on Fire'.

Dan, on the other hand, generally felt all music after 1995 was pointless and self-consciously 'retro'. To my unspoken exasperation he was partial to a bit of heavy-duty synth,

Depeche Mode, Peter Gabriel and even a bit of ska. Most alarmingly, he'd recently swung towards 'classic rock' which caused a shiver of embarrassment if we happened to be driving with the windows down and stopped at some traffic lights. It was like performing in one of those Father's Day *Dad Rocks* CD adverts, even though Dan was only thirty-two.

Still, Dan really *was* making an effort to work things out so, as usual, I didn't complain when he put on Peter Gabriel. In the week since 'the phone call' as we now referred to it, he had been extra attentive. There'd been an impromptu bunch of yellow roses, two unsolicited mugs of evening hot chocolate and an attempt to watch an episode of *Lost* with me without continual interruption and scorn.

I think having to come and retrieve me, tipsy and sullen, from the seaside, had given him a bit of a scare.

He'd booked us a meal at the Pomegranate, the best restaurant in Cardiff Bay, as a romantic peace offering. I didn't like it much. Glistening in glass and steel on the watery edge of the docks, it took the idea of minimalist to almost antiseptic lengths. But I didn't want to be seen to criticise a gesture when I had been complaining he never made one. At our candle-lit table, before the gaping windows facing the twinkling lights of the barrage, our talk naturally turned to the wedding plans.

'I know the last week hasn't been easy but I still want you to be my wife, more than anything,' said Dan. 'I know you'll look beautiful.'

I wished he wouldn't gush like that in the impersonal hollow of the restaurant. There was some irritating ambient jazz playing in the background but only a low murmur of voices from the other couples who seemed cowed by the uncomfortable, trendy, tubular metal furniture. There was a crash and a muffled flurry of activity as someone dropped their butter knife onto the cold, tiled floor. Idle, white-shirted minions dashed to assist, seemingly glad of something to do.

'You do believe what I told you now, don't you, Jen?' continued Dan, undeterred. 'I never wanted to hurt you. I never really wanted anyone but you. No more secrets between us from here on in, ok? Believe me?'

No more secrets, yes, right. I did believe him. At least I believed that he believed it. But deceit is the hardest thing to overcome. The acknowledgement of lies alters the space between two people. Lies have a way of working their way into the corner of every conversation and every caress, creating more and more questions, not fewer. And I still had a lot of questions. It's true that many of them I needed to ask myself, not Dan. But I wasn't ready for the answers. So we ate.

By the time the main course had arrived, the chatter of diners, now well into their bottles of overpriced wine, was growing tinny and overpowering. I prodded at my crusted hake with cucumber coulis, wishing there were some chips with it rather than three tiny new potatoes. Suddenly, I really wanted a large Jack Daniels with coke and ice, but thought it would seem uncouth to order one with the main course. I gulped some more wine.

In low tones Dan was excitedly telling me about an upcoming police operation to arrest two big drug dealers. It was very hush-hush, he said, as if he needed to. I tried to look interested and to look as if I was enjoying the meal – it *was* pretty expensive. Dan had always trusted me with secrets – secrets from work, confidential operations. He knew I was trustworthy, that I understood implicitly that the power of the secret is in the keeping. He knew I would be watertight, would never gossip, chatter, natter – words exclusively applied to women, meaning they were leaky as sieves in the secret-keeping sense.

Not me. I was a stone at the bottom of a sea of discretion, tight-lipped, as silent as the grave. Normally I was flattered to receive Dan's confidences, but that night they seemed hollow. I had taken it for granted that his truth-telling had carried over to all parts of our lives. But while he felt he could tell me about confidential work shenanigans he hadn't been honest with me about Sophie, had he? At no point had he felt the overwhelming urge to confess about that.

Part of me could see why – why he'd thought there'd be no need to make things complicated over something that was over so quickly. But he'd done extraordinarily well at keeping it on a 'need-to-know' basis. Dan – open-book, community-radio-style, confessional Dan, *had* been able to keep a secret from me. How could he now say 'no more secrets' so easily? How would I know, anyway? I hadn't before.

While we toiled through our dinner, my mind was running riot, backwards. All those long nights he had spent on late shifts gave way to dalliances with lip-sticked harlots in the back of panda cars, seats slippery with illicit sweat, then on to other imagined scandals, unwise bets on sure things at the bookies leading to disreputable dealings with loan-sharks, wrong side of the sheets, back door, mixed-race babies living in council flats with mums called Chantelle or Kylie. Other wives, other lives, other names, well-played games and I the unwitting loser in each one. How was I supposed to live with that?

The neat little timeframe imposed by the upcoming wedding wasn't helping. Part of the problem was that I hadn't been a very good bride-to-be before that phone call from Sophie. Right from the moment we had set the date I felt like a woman playing at planning a wedding, and I think Dan knew it too.

Women are supposed to want to marry, aren't they? They are supposed to dream of dream weddings. My colleagues and friends had always had clear ideas of what they wanted on their 'big day', seemingly since they were old enough to play with pink-as-a-religion Barbie.

When Dan proposed to me I had been disconcerted rather than delighted. Why? was my immediate response. We'd been together eight years, lived together for five; what difference would that slip of paper make, except to remove any option of retreat? And, if I'm honest, I like to know where the exits are. I'm the kind of person who, when staying in a hotel, checks the location of the fire escape immediately after unpacking. You never know when it might get too hot for comfort and you need to flee.

My indecision wasn't helped by the fact that it wasn't exactly a bells-and-whistles proposal. He asked me after a night in the pub, walking home. He hadn't bought a ring or anything. It didn't seem like he'd made much effort to make it a special occasion. Didn't he think I was worth it? But not having any good reason *not* to get married, and of course, loving him – because I did love him – I had agreed the following day.

I was astonished by people's reactions to the simple statement that, yes, WE ARE GOING TO GET MARRIED. *They* added the capital letters, each woman bordering on hysterically enthusiastic.

'Congratulations,' they cooed, 'How wonderful! You must be *so* excited,' as if I'd just revealed I was being awarded the Nobel Prize for Literature or perhaps, more in their line of reference, won the *X Factor* final. All the hyperbole came out at once in a dizzying torrent: 'Marvellous, fantastic, fabulous, joyous, wonderful.'

I think their 'joy' was also tinged with just a little touch of relief. Clearly I was still the same capable, no-nonsense Jen that sat at my desk in the press office, but now I was imbued with what I had previously lacked – girlishness and glamour, innate femininity, natural superficiality. Something they could relate to.

So I didn't watch soap operas or reality TV? I would rather tear out my own hair strand by strand and eat it than watch the *Sex and the City* movie? I never got a spray tan or a manicure. But I was a *girl* underneath, after all.

'So tell us, then,' they demanded, gathering round in an alarming high-pitched gaggle, 'Church or civil? White or ivory? Sit-down reception or buffet

Disco or band? Bridesmaids? Pageboys? Matron of honour? Fruit cake or chocolate cake, or no cake and lots of little cakes piled up in an improbable pyramid?'

Valium? Lobotomy? said the patient voice in my head. I hadn't anticipated that getting married would necessitate multiple-choice questions being fired at me at the speed of a semi-automatic. I hadn't even known it was a test. If I had, I would have revised for it.

In every wedding magazine article I read after that, the words *'your big day'* – always italicised, sometimes with *exclamation marks*! – was a cause for intense alarm. It wasn't that I didn't want to look nice and wear a stylish dress. It wasn't that I didn't like smart clothes. I wore wear make-up and owned high heels. I just happened to think that less would be more. I didn't have the facials, soft furnishings and fairy dust gene that seemed to afflict other women and made two hours discussing colour schemes and throw cushions seem not only palatable but essential.

But by October the invitation cards had gone out naming the day the following June. I couldn't keep putting the details off forever. Sooner or later I had to sit down and strap in for the ride.

As it happened, Dan and I had an appointment with the hotel wedding planner on the forthcoming weekend and I could already envision, 'Call me Luella' approaching at frightening speed, a frothy executioner bedecked with lace and wearing a teeth-aching sugar smile, her eyes glazed with pound signs, wielding lethal, suffocating chirpiness. I would need lots of back-up to face her.

So I was less than pleased when Dan told me, through a mouthful of gingerbread cheesecake, that he wouldn't be able to make it because he was covering an extra shift for the football match. He had the good grace to be intensely apologetic. He knew I wasn't in my element, he said sheepishly, but I'd manage it wonderfully. I was so organised, so practical. I could always take my mum along for moral support.

I instantly wanted to throw the sloppy remnants of my poached pear in cinnamon at him. I had a sneaking suspicion he'd told me in the hush of the restaurant, rather than at home, so I wouldn't be able to make too much fuss.

I wanted to say, 'After the lies you've told, you can't even find the time to come to see the bloody wedding planner with me? What does that say about your commitment to this relationship? You're supposed to be sorry. Does this seem sorry enough to you? Bailing out on me when I need you most? On second thoughts, why get married anyway? What's the point now? This is insane. I am insane.'

But I didn't say this. It might have made me feel better, it might have been more honest, but it wouldn't have been very helpful. So I bit my tongue to stop it lashing out and nodded resignedly. I didn't want this to turn into another *issue*. There were enough of those already.

Dan patted my hand with relief. 'I'll make it up to you, pet,' he promised.

I finished my coffee, wishing I was in the pub with my glass of JD, and wishing that Dan realised that.

As Dan was helping me into my coat my work phone beeped, announcing a text. I frowned. I wasn't supposed to be on call. It was Serian's week to get phone calls from nervous inspectors wanting guidance about incidents in the middle of the night, or press releases drafted at six in the morning.

All it said was, 'How're the wedding plans? Lots to do?' It ended with a kiss.

I didn't recognise the number.

'Control room?' queried Dan. 'You're not on call are you? Aren't you next week?'

'Yes. I mean, I'm on call next week. It's not the CR. Don't recognise it. Maybe it's Becky's new phone.' My friend Becky was always 'upgrading' her phone. God knows why she thought she needed a Bluetooth when she worked in a newspaper sales call centre selling obituary space. She was going through a sticky patch with her current man, Stephen, and had taken to texting me little updates on the current state of play. 'Why don't people put their name at the end of the text instead of assuming you know who they are?' I moaned. It was one of my constant grumbles.

'Because most people assume you know how to work the phone book,' said Dan.

I ignored him and texted back: 'Beck? All under control. Jen x'

Then I forgot about it.

A few days later the first email arrived.

Chapter Three

Initially, I'd had no reason to be suspicious of yet another email. My inbox was awash with a steady flow of them, peaking like monsoon rain at around 3.30 p.m. as the last dash of the news deadlines really began in earnest.

For a brief moment I thought it was one of Bodie and Doyle's 'jokes'. I'd been down in the CID office earlier that day answering their summons. When I popped my head around the door the two of them had been watching some CCTV footage, huddled round the battered portable TV, arguing over who got to hold the remote control for the ancient VHS. Anyone under the illusion that policing is high-tech these days need look no further than the eighties electronic shrine that is your average CID room. Look hard enough and you'll find a well-used fax machine lurking in a corner and probably a hand-cranked copying machine.

Bodie's back was to the door, and he was making a note of the time signature of a particular sequence on his pad. The pair were not laughing or saying anything remotely lewd but I could detect a definite air of unspoken snigger about them, an odour of nudge-nudge, wink-wink.

'*X Factor* highlights again, gents?' I asked, deliberately loudly.

'You know your PNN is open *again,* acting DS?' I rapped my short nails on his monitor.

'Jen! Christ!' started Doyle. 'You're like creeping Jesus. You're worse than Dai Hard (DI David Harden or Dai Hard-on, currently chief thief-taker and enthusiastic motivator of slacking CID minions).

'Shit!' harrumphed Bodie, bounding over to the computer and security-locking it immediately. 'That bloody machine. Sorry – language. I'm an uncouth yob. Good job you're not your old man, eh? Come on in and have a shufti at this. Jim's had the CCTV from the shop across the road from the St David pub. It's a cracker.'

Jim cued it clumsily to the right time code. 'Watch the bird by the railings, absolutely rat-arsed.'

As I watched I could see a girl of about eighteen in a very tight vest top, receding mini-skirt and skyscraper heels, leaning over the railings at the side of the road, almost to the point of tipping over. She had that limp-limbed look that goes hand in hand with the treacly speech of the seriously drunk. Her handbag was on the pavement beside her and she seemed to be leaning down to reach into it. After some effort she retrieved what looked like a mobile phone, only to drop it into the gutter.

At this point an ordinary-looking bloke approaches her.

'This is the bit, this is the bit,' said Bodie eagerly.

After a moment the man kisses the girl, not violently – she's clearly too drunk to protest. Her head lolls in a way that suggests she's probably not able to really see him. She obviously can't feel it as he slides his hand up her leg and under the scrap of skirt into her crotch. It's clearly a deliberate gesture. He shields this action from the bouncers on the door of the pub a few feet away. Whatever he's doing he's doing it quite urgently for several minutes, before sliding his hand into his own trousers, briefly. Then he zips up his fly and lowers the girl to the kerb into a sitting position. She seems to be trying to speak but you don't need sound on the images to see she's struggling to form any words. The man walks away, unhurriedly, into the main street.

'Believe that?' says Jim. 'Perfect end to a perfect night, or what? Her father came in this morning saying her bag had been nicked. He found her like that, on the pavement, about half an hour after this. This morning the aforementioned victim, who's only sixteen, by the way, wakes up complaining she's a bit sore *down there* and there's some blood in her pants. She can't remember anything much after nine pm but Bodie here, ever diligent, roots out the CCTV from the Bargain Booze and spots this lovely little short film.

'Superintendent Sellers just showed this to the girly. She has no idea who this bloke is. She burst into tears when she saw it. Not surprising, mind – finding out the day after the fact that you've been felt up by some random perv would be a shock. But what do these girls expect when they're too slammed to see, let alone say fuck off, mate! Sorry, *language*. She says her drink must have been spiked because she can't remember much. If I had a pound for every time someone said that! She was just shitfaced. The mate she was with, who went off with some bloke and left her at 11 p.m., says they drank half a bottle of vodka in the park before they even got to the pub and then drank some more shots. We'll do an appeal for the guy now, of course – good chance we'll get him when we show the pics to the doormen, but that's one lucky little madam. Never even knew Bargain Booze had new CCTV.'

'Community intelligence. Got to keep abreast of it. That's

why I'm a sarge and you're the foot soldier, mate,' ribbed Bodie.

'Yeah, but like Will Smith says, I make this look good. Look at this, Jen,' he grinned, offering me a squeeze of the bicep that suddenly sprang to life beneath his shirt sleeve as he flexed his arm. 'Impressive, eh? Like boulders under a bedcover, but I won't ask you to feel them, not with Bodie here. He'll get all jealous.'

'Let me know when you want to appeal then?' I countered with a patient smile. 'Can we get a still of the less graphic bit with a shot of his face? We'll blur hers out, of course. We can't say anything that would ID her, because it's a sexual assault.'

'Will do, press lady! We're on it. Will email it a.s.a.p.'

'Great. Actually it's good timing for the Christmas anti-rape and alcohol campaign. You know, the one we do every year with the posters? 'Know Your Limits', and so forth. It's launching next week for the beginning of November.'

'Course, yeah, that'll keep the super happy. Crime prevention and all. Give us a mention, though,' said Bodie.

'Yeah,' said Doyle, clearing his throat and assuming a serious tone. 'DC Williams says, We urge women to be aware of the amount of alcohol they've consumed as they risk making themselves vulnerable to this sort of crime. To enjoy your night out without problems, please plan your journey home in advance or 'take a taxi you can trust.' You know – like it says on those cards we stick out with the Community Support Officers.'

'Yeah, yeah. DC Williams means, "Slappers – stop getting lashed!"' added Bodie.

'I *will* quote you on that,' I smiled.

'It's too busy to see who might have half-inched the bag,'

added Doyle. 'Black patent bag, pink Playboy purse inside. Classy – stick that in, too.'

What is wrong with young girls these days? I'd mused, meandering back to the press office, already drafting the release in my head.

Chaos reigned in the press room. Nigel's half of the office was filled with a collection of chairs and boxes as the new cupboards were being assembled. They stood in pieces waiting for the workmen to finish their lunch trip to Gregg's. Nigel stood in the middle of the room, talking exasperatedly into his mobile. Two newly arrived wooden paper racks, the kind you see in libraries with folded-in-half papers draped over them, were standing in the corner – the storage solutions.

All the phones were ringing at once.

After picking up the nearest one and dealing with a call from Jack NewsBeatWales about a post office robbery in Grangetown, I checked my email for the sex-assault CCTV stills. When I clicked my inbox the mail icon was blinking and there was a new attachment waiting. There was no title. It just said 'footage of interest'. It had overloaded my email storage. I sighed with frustration. This happened a lot, thanks to the antiquated IT system.

Nigel finished his call, which turned out to be from the Control Room, notifying us of another multiple collision on the M4 – that explained the ringing phones. I detached the email file and saved it in my Footage folder without looking at it. It wasn't until 4 p.m., after I'd dealt with the collision, drafted a media strategy for an attempted murder and released a couple of ASBO photos, that I remembered the CCTV appeal.

For the first few seconds I thought it was a joke. It looked like a home video of a couple having sex, with the naughty bits and the faces blurred out. I frowned with distaste. My first thought was how did this get through the firewall? The security filter was unpredictable, but anything with flesh on display, even photos of kids in football kit for force cheque presentations and so forth, often got flagged with a warning of 'inappropriate content'.

But there it was – full screen and full frontal.

I expected some stupid message to come up – a joke or punchline. I expected Bodie or Doyle to poke his head round the door, smirking, at some point. This is taking a joke too far entirely, I thought.

Then I thought, 'That girl's got the same birthmark as me. What are the odds of that?'

It took just a few seconds for me to look again at the shoulder-length sandy hair and the coloured surf beads on the wrist to release something was horribly wrong. I felt my cheeks flood with shame.

Instinctively, I clicked 'minimise' and reduced the image. There was no audio, as we set our machines to default mute. My desk wasn't directly overlooked that day because of the new cupboards, and only Nige was at the other end of the office, seemingly deep in a phone conversation with Anne Nolan from the *Chronicle*. I assume it was her. He kept saying, 'Now Anne, that's very misleading, don't you think?' I sat numb and dumb and pink-cheeked for about fifteen seconds as my stomach rose up and lodged in my chest. Then I realised Nige was staring at me.

'You ok?' he mouthed, phone crooked into his neck, typing at the same time.

'Hmm, mmm,' I nodded, swallowing and swallowing in the hope of stopping the tea and multi-grain snack bar I'd eaten a few minutes earlier exploding from my mouth. I clicked the video again. This time I could see quite plainly that it was me on the screen, and what's more it was *the cottage*. The cottage where I'd spent the night with Justin.

Justin – that was him in the image, wasn't it, on top of me? The hair was right, and those were the frayed little blue and green surfy wrist bands he'd been wearing.

Oh dear God! What is this? Some sort of joke, some sort of fake Photoshop or video equivalent thing? But how could it be? I recognised myself and that room, the one with the heavy orange curtains and the old Welsh dresser.

'That Bodie's CCTV tart?' asked Serian, materialising over my shoulder, manoeuvring past some paint cans to her desk with a coffee for us both. 'Looks x- rated, the pervs,' she observed, with relish rather than offence. 'They were in here earlier going on about it. Bodie's pretty cute, isn't he? Don't you think so? He's got a hot body. Shit!' This last as she stumbled on an extension cable and slopped some coffee on her hand. 'Nige! I thought Estates were sorting this mess out? How can we work like this?'

I clicked the screen off at once. Luckily, Serian was too busy mopping her keyboard and calling Estates filthy names to be interested in what was displayed.

With what seemed like glacial speed, I grabbed a memory stick and hit buttons to save the attachment, deleted it from my email inbox, deleted it from my deleted items folder and sat there sickened and painfully aware that I was not breathing.

'You sure you're ok?' asked Nige coming over, smoothing down his lilac shirt and cornflower blue tie. 'You look a bit flushed.'

I knew I was supposed to speak but it took some effort to form the words.

'Actually, I feel a bit fluey.' I knew I was speaking too loudly.

My voice sounded forced and theatrical, as if I were an inexperienced bit-part actress delivering a line. 'I wonder if I might nip off early?'

'Sure thing,' said Nige. 'Not feeling swinish are you? Short of breath? Fever?'

'Trotters?' added Serian.

'No'. The effort of the word was almost too much.

'Scary, this swine flu thing, isn't it? Julian from business development has supposedly got it and I had a coffee with him yesterday,' added Serian with a touch of alarm.

'Well, it's been a busy one,' said Nige. 'Pop off while you can. Have a quiet evening with the old man. You look harried.'

Harried. That sounded civilised. Nige often used refined vocabulary like that. Harried, discomfited, disconcerted. Harried sounded better than horrified, hysterical, hyperventilating, so I went with it and made a dash for my car.

So how did I get from the pub to Justin's bed?

I asked myself that question a million times in the days after I returned from the Watch-house and I asked it another million times on the drive home from the office that day. What had happened to make me do something so utterly out of character? Why had I slept with a man I had just met and knew nothing about?

The root of the answer was to be found well before the night I spotted Justin in the Snug, even before '*that* phone call' from Sophie, though I hadn't admitted it, even to myself. I'd been too afraid. To verbalise it would have made it real, the speech once issued into the air causing the breath around me to crystallise into solid form, the words 'Is this wedding a mistake?' dropping icily into being before me. Then I'd have to pick them up and acknowledge their cold and burning presence.

How could I explain myself? How could I distil something as amorphous as the ticking, prickling dissatisfaction I'd begin to detect each morning, first sitting in the bottom of my stomach, then marching its way along my forearms, up to the back of my neck, like a thousand little solider ants, itchy, irritating?

So I thought Dan's taste in music was embarrassing? Why did he only drink beer, never wine? How come he never took me out for a romantic meal or bought me flowers? Why didn't he read any of the books I liked? Why couldn't he be more spontaneous, more thoughtful, less insistent on leaving dirty cups around the house and his boots in the middle of the living room? Why did he think graphic print T-shirts were the height of cool?

It sounded pathetic even to me – vacuous, trivial, surely not enough to break an almost nine-year relationship in half over?

But a woman called Sophie? That was a different matter. She was concrete. She was solid. When she called that morning I'd realised, perhaps in the fractured and glittering second I hurled the wedding manual, or when I threw the engagement ring, that I was intensely relieved. I now had a get-out clause, a get-out-of-jail-free card, a reason to sound the alarm, initiate the hotel fire escape plan! Twenty-four drunken hours alone in a luxury boutique hotel and Justin had been standing right under the flashing exit sign, extending his hand towards me. Or at least he had suggested the cessation of the countdown now ever-present in my head – that inexorable progression towards posies and place cards and 'The Best Day of Your Life' in silver copperplate writing. And towards the word *wife*, possibly the most boring and predictable word in the world.

All of this had been bubbling under the sloshing layers of red wine when I'd sidled up to Justin at the bar of the Mochyn Ddu, when he opened a conversation that would alter my life forever.

'Hi,' he'd said. 'Watch-house just a bit too snug for you?' with a smile so twinkly it rivalled the Milky Way. 'Down for the weekend?'

'Just a few days,' I'd replied, shyly. 'You live here?' I managed to add after a moment.

'Yes, in town. It's very nice, isn't it? If you don't like the bright lights, that is. '

My tongue felt thick and I felt stupid. I wanted to say something witty, to make an impression. I failed. 'You're a surfer?'

He had laughed, smoothing his sun-bleached mop. 'How can you tell? I'm a writer too, if that makes me sound less of a slacker.'

'Really?' the interest must have shown in the leap in my voice. Thank God, he's not a total bum. 'How interesting.'

'Not as interesting as it sounds – short stories, a novel once, but I make ends meet with stuff for travel and surfing magazines.'

'Well that sounds interesting to me,' I answered honestly. 'I love books – well, novels, poetry. Anything, really.'

'Ah yes, Robert Frost wasn't it?' He'd noticed. '"The Road Not Taken" – I love that poem.' My heart somersaulted upwards, spun in mid air and landed in a perfect dismount back in my chest. 'I get what Frost was saying. I've tried, too, to take a different path,' he continued. 'Try a new way of my own. Been around the world a bit, here and there. But somehow I still ended up back here in Gower, thirty-two years old and still scribbling. But it could be worse, it could be Porthcawl.'

I laughed. 'What's wrong with Porthcawl? I have fond memories of the pleasure park.'

'Yeah, but that was fifteen years ago, before the McDonald's and the pole-dancing place round the back of the old Woolworth's.'

'Is there really a pole-dancing place?' I knew I looked aghast.

'No, not really,' He laughed at my disgust, but I didn't mind. He had a nice laugh, deep and warm.

'Wanna sit down?' We were getting bumped and jostled at the bar as a pack of local student types poured in.

'Er, sure, for a bit,' I replied. Why not? I thought.

'Carl, mate!' he shouted over the hubbub, waving his hand at a tall skinny chap in a goat herder-type hat with ear flaps at the other end of the bar. 'Good lines today?'

'Sure, mate,' shouted Carl with the glazed good humour of the chemically relaxed.

'Baked as usual, same story since we were sixteen. Let's sit over here so he won't come and regale us with surf stories of great slowness and dullness.' He ushered me to a corner table. 'I'm Justin, by the way. Justin Reynolds.'

'I'm Jen Johnson.'

'So what do you make of the Watch-house?'

'Nice beds,' I said, then I blushed, first because it sounded unsubtle and then because I had been embarrassed by something so innocuous. I was out of practice when it came to talking to men. Actually, I'd never had any practice.

Justin grinned. 'Indeed. What brings you here? It's mostly a chic retreat for couples, isn't it?' Or, you know, girls there for the spa indulgence.'

'That's exactly what the guidebook said.'

'Yeah, I should know. I wrote it. Whatever pays the bills, right?'

'You wrote the review?'

'Yes, I do quite a few round the country from time to time. I'll be trying to sell another one on the Watch-house soon. You here alone? I didn't happen to see any boyfriend last night.'

'No boyfriend.' Keep it casual, I told myself. It's just a drink.

'No boyfriend or just no boyfriend *here*?'

'Er . . .' I didn't want to lie, give the wrong idea outright, make it seem like I was out to pick him up. I wasn't wearing my engagement ring. It was still on the living-room table. 'Not actually sure at the moment – maybe both.'

'I *see*. In these cases I find wine helps immensely. Not with making a decision, of course, just to forget what you were trying to think about.'

'Here's to that, then.'

And from that point the night and the chat rolled on.

It was going well – spectacularly, irrationally well. He was so nice and attentive and also playful. We'd laughed and joked and talked about books and music. He liked so many of the same things I did I was starting to think our meeting was fate. Love the music of Elbow? Sure! Currently my favourite band in the whole world. Like me, Justin had all the albums, even the early ones, well before the Mercury Prize made them popular. He had even been to the concert at the Cardiff Arena that Dan had refused to come to. I'd gone with Becky, who hadn't enjoyed it much. Justin must have been in the crowd that very night. What a small world.

'Normally I don't like big gigs, too many idiots, but the Arena's just right – you can really hear the music,' he said. My sentiments exactly.

David Mitchell fan? Read *Cloud Atlas*? Of course, but *Ghostwritten's* still my favourite too. Love Thomas Hardy? Hate D.H. Lawrence? Thank God someone agrees.

Love to visit Italy? Wouldn't we all? Who doesn't fantasise about the Uffizi, the Vatican museum, the Sistine Chapel? The 'Birth of Venus', 'La Primavera', those hideous but mesmerising Bosch visions of hell and damnation stalking on twisted legs, God and Adam on high, a spark of divinity breaking between their fingers.

I told him about my university exchange trip to Siena, how much I longed to go back to Tuscany. He'd spent a summer in Italy touring and writing reviews for holiday magazines. How wonderfully envious and impressed I was.

And so it went on.

It seemed easy, comfortable. I even spoke to him a little about Dan. Not everything, just the main points of the row and the engagement. He seemed easy to confide in. He seemed to have been sent to listen.

After an indeterminate number of drinks had vanished, and hours alongside them, he suggested we go on to a party that some of his friends were having in a nearby cottage.

I hesitated for a minute, aware I didn't really know him, aware that I never did things like this. Chatting in the pub was one thing, but a party was different and potentially treacherous ground. Did it suggest a receptiveness, a willingness to move things on between us into more intimate territory? But the momentum of the night seemed right. I didn't want it to end. I didn't want to be the one who stands sensibly back, takes a piece of chalk and draws an unwavering line across the room saying, I think that's enough. More than anything I didn't want to return to my king-size bed in the Watch-house and let this exciting evening fade into sleep and then into the inevitable dawning of an uncertain new day.

I was busy convincing myself it was destiny. It was ordained. The row with Dan, the hotel, Justin – the first man I'd felt any explosive connection with for years – it couldn't be just a coincidence, surely? Someone was sending me a sign, a signal. I just had to be smart enough to decipher it and everything would be different.

Seeing my reluctance, he'd immediately been chivalrous. 'No, of course not. You don't know me. What must you think? I'm sorry, Jennifer. I just, well it seems like I was meant to meet you tonight and I don't want to go home just yet.'

I was already sold, though I made a show of slight reluctance anyway as I allowed him to guide me along the bumpy lane that formed the short walk to the cottage where the party would be starting. It was midnight-dark and he clutched my arm to steady me. As we stumbled along I inhaled the soft salt-smell of his jacket and the warmth escaping at the nape of his neck. And I thought, What the hell are you doing, Jen?

The cottage's low lights beckoned through the chill, and there it was, thatch-headed squat and whitewashed. But inside it was quiet. No sign of a party at all. Not even voices.

'They're not back yet,' said Justin, taking my coat. 'Well, never mind. I can have you to myself a little while longer.'

I was flattered and more than a little drunk, and I felt daring and grown up and free and impulsive. But still I said, more for show than with conviction, Perhaps just one drink and then I *must* be going.

In no time at all Justin got the wood-burning stove crackling and smoking. We huddled in front of the growing flames, cupping our wine glasses and chattering easily. The wind tried to join our conversation, muttering under the eaves.

It seemed easy to explain to him some of my doubts and fears about the future. It was a relief to tell someone how scared I was that I might be making a mistake. The more I unburdened myself, the more relieved I felt, the closer I leaned towards his warmth. The night started to grow a little hazy round the edges at some point. I hardly noticed that we were not joined by any other friends as we talked about anything and everything. Justin talked about his writing, his travels, and I thought for a moment there might be a place for me on the road by his side.

Yes, there was wine and firelight and music but it didn't have the feel of a concentrated seduction. I felt safe. There was no sense of urgency of his part. He was nothing if not gentlemanly. But I was not surprised, nor alarmed, when he leaned over to me and said, 'I'd really like to kiss you.' And he did, and every nerve ending was soon blistering with sensation, soft and measured. I'd forgotten this. How could I have forgotten this?

We must have stayed that way for some time, engaged in the kind of childish, exploratory kissing that teenagers savour, when every flutter of contact is new.

'I'd really like you to stay,' he said.

'I don't think I can. That is, I don't think . . . I don't usually do this sort of thing.'

'Neither do I, ordinarily,' he said. 'But this doesn't feel like an ordinary night, does it?'

I remember standing over the white enamel bathroom sink, staring into the tarnished mirror at the girl wavering within, swaying more than a little, asking myself, 'Do you really want this? Do you?'

And the girl within was braver than me. The only answer she gave was Yes, oh yes. When I finally emerged, Justin was standing in the bedroom door and candlelight flickered behind him. He held out his hand and I walked towards him. Outside I could hear the distant sea.

*

Next morning I woke with a brain-cleaving headache. It took a few moments to remember where I was. I couldn't really remember much at all – Justin at the door of the bedroom, then maybe a confusion of images, red and black and warm in the wine-drowned dark.

Since I was naked and my clothes were scattered on the floor it seemed fairly obvious what had taken place.

I wish I could say I was horrified or that I felt guilt. But that wasn't the case. I felt a bit embarrassed, but I was snug in the sheets, still warm from him. I listened to the sounds of the cottage, its creak and settle as the wind passed by, listening for sounds of his returning to bed. I was smiling more than anything, inside and out. I lay there for some time before I realised the house was completely silent. No toilet flushing or water running. No slip-slap footsteps on the wooden floor.

Tentatively, not to tax my aching head, I swung myself upright and planted my feet on the floor. I was a bit wobbly but ok, so I dressed hurriedly in the shiver of the morning.

Two torn condom packets lay on the floor at the foot of the bed. Two? Crikey, that was heavy going. Dan and I might sometimes manage it twice a week, but only once a night. The thought of Dan stilled me slightly, momentarily, as it slid its fingers around my neck, but I shook it loose. I was on the pill, of course, but at least I knew we'd been careful.

The fire was out and it was cold. There was a note on the kitchen table. 'Surf's up. Call you soon. Have some tea. J x.'

Smiling, I did just that. The fridge was completely empty, save for the last dregs of a pint of milk, but there was a half-eaten packet of Rich Tea on the table, so I sipped and crunched and tried to replay the events of the night in my head. But no matter how much I concentrated, a blank wall reared up every time I thought of what had happened after

I came out of the bathroom. It wasn't like me to forget an evening, but then I had been drinking almost all day, for almost two days.

After my second cup of tea I mooched around the cottage living room. It didn't give much away. It was very functional, probably a man's cottage, with not much in the way of personal touches. Whoever Justin's friends were, they liked James Bond paperbacks and oddly, Barbara Cartland and Catherine Cooksons too.

I waited until ten o'clock before I started to get impatient. Where was Justin? The shine of the morning was starting to tarnish. I was chilled and hungry. My self-generated air of imagined bad girl was dissipating. I wanted to speak to Justin. I wanted to hear him say that he wanted to see me again.

Take your time, Jen, take your time, I told myself. Nevertheless, when I thought of Justin there was a little bit of glee inside, turning like the bright centre of a star. Eventually, at around ten-thirty, I decided to go back to the hotel, freshen up and change my clothes. I wrote a note with my phone number on it, left it on the kitchen table and wandered back to the hotel, still upbeat.

Then I showered and waited.

He didn't call.

I drank tea and waited some more.

No call.

Puzzled, I decided to go to the Mochyn Ddu for lunch. I was beginning to get a bit annoyed. Why hadn't he called me? All the signs had been positive last night. He'd seemed keen. We'd really connected. The kitchen note had seemed promising.

After I'd finished my smoked salmon and watercress sandwich I went up to the bar to pay. On the spur of the moment I thought maybe I'd check one of the beaches, see if he was still surfing, so I asked the landlord, 'That guy Justin, do you know where he surfs?'

'What guy?'

'Justin, lives here. His mates have a cottage down the lane.'

'Don't think so.'

'Tall guy, sandy hair.'

'No, I mean, don't think he lives there.'

'Well, maybe one of his mates does?'

'No, I mean no one *lives* there, love. It's a holiday let – no one there this time of year, though.'

'Holiday let? What? 'But you *know* Justin?'

'Don't think so.'

'He was in here last night. We sat over there – tall guy, surfy hair.'

'That's half the people who come in here, lovely. *Surfers.*'

'But he's a local, comes in here all the time.'

'Sorry love, don't think so. I know the locals.'

I went back to the cottage. To my surprise it was shuttered up. I peered in through the half-closed curtains of the kitchen window and my note had gone from the table. Actually, in the daylight the place had the deserted air of off-season emptiness. That explained the empty fridge and the discarded novels.

But surely there was some mistake? Justin would call. He would call me.

I spent an hour wandering around the beach, kicking at shells. Maybe his phone had no signal. Maybe he'd lost the paper with my number on. As time passed I was beginning to feel increasingly foolish, but my brain wouldn't allow me to acknowledge the rational explanation for his absence, the one that was scrabbling along the edges of my awareness.

Cutting through the goose grass dunes to the quayside I

suddenly spotted Mr Sherpa hat from the night before. Craig, no Carl, I think Justin had called him. He'd hailed him over the pub din, asked about 'lines' or something. He was wearing a wetsuit and booties (and the Sherpa hat) and was crouched out of the breeze, rubbing wax on a magnificent-looking surfboard. It was covered with an intricate lacquered Polynesian design, set against a background of exploding bougainvillea blooms in improbable primary colours. On the underside, as he twisted it to steady it in the wind, I could see a transfer of a Jaws-like shark mouth, teeth cutting through the foamy surf.

''Scuse me,' I said. 'Just wondered if you'd seen Justin today? Thought he might be surfing.'

'Hi there,' he said, looking up, not in the least startled by seeing a strange girl in the dunes so late in the season.

'Don't know a Justin, darling. Sorry.'

'But sure you do,' I persisted. 'Justin Reynolds? It's Carl, right? He waved at you in the pub last night, the Mochyn Ddu. I saw him. He asked you about surfing, about waves. You know, about lines?'

He looked glazed. I expected he often looked that way. His eyes fixed on something in the middle distance and he said nothing for at least ten seconds. Just when I thought he wasn't going to speak at all he said:

'Oh, yeah. Yeah, right. Tall dude.' He spoke with a Welsh accent but the intonation was oddly half-local, half-Californian. 'Nah, don't really *know* him, just gave him some directions yesterday. Wanted to know where to park his camper van. Old girl was giving him some trouble. Those original beauties always do, unless you love them real regular.'

'You don't know him?' That didn't make sense. 'You mean he's not from here?'

'Nah, darling. Like I said, he had this rad camper van and

he wanted to know where he could park it up safe for a few days. Nice van – oldie but a goody, you know, burning some major oil or something though.'

'Then how did he know your name? He called you Carl in the pub.' I was sure of that.

He thought for a minute, going through the same trance-like sequence of horizon gazing before turning round slowly for my benefit. 'Carl' was stitched in red letters across the back of his suit.

I stared at it stupidly. 'He, er . . . did he say anything else?'

'Just that he liked my ride – nice, ain't it?'

'Yes, it's very . . . colourful.'

'Yeah, cool dude in Nottage does it. You know, down the Vale. Rad, eh? Good surf down there if you can take it, this time of year.'

'Yeah, I bet. Ok, thanks.' Feeling increasingly foolish, I turned to retreat.

'This guy owe you money or something, darling?' asked Carl amiably.

Then I had a thought. 'No, no . . . Eh, look, Carl, where did you tell him to park his van?'

'Down by the side of the harbourmaster's shed on the front, never get a ticket there. Traffic wardens can't be arsed to walk all the way out there in this weather.'

I'd passed that area earlier and there had been two, or maybe three, old fashioned two-tone camper vans there. I must have looked hopeful,

'Great – thanks.'

'No point in going though, love. Looked myself this morning. Wanted to show Dominic,' he gestured to a black shape cresting the distant waves on a surfboard far down the shore, 'the cool shark he had on the side. Same guy did it as did my board, I reckon. He has this smooth style, but it had this cool seal in its mouth. I'd like to get one like that for my buggy. Was gonna check it out with him but he was gone. Sure he don't owe you money?'

'No, it's no big deal. Thanks.'

'Hey, no probs. Come down anytime you'd like a ride on my Beast.' He laughed at my startled expression and pointed at the board. 'Everyone loves the Beast. One of a kind.'

I dragged my feet through the rough sand, back the way I had come. So it seemed Justin really didn't live in the village. But it could still be a mistake of some sort – he could be visiting family for the weekend, his parents or something, and be living elsewhere.

There was little for it but to go back to the hotel. The hotel! All at once my ego offered me a lifeline – maybe he's gone to look for me at the hotel! Of course, that would be it. He wouldn't expect me to *still* be at the cottage or tramping the beaches. He might even be staying there. I'd first seen him in the Snug, for God's sake!

Eagerly, I trotted up the lane and into the hotel lobby but he wasn't there, neither in the reception nor the Snug. As a last resort, I asked the receptionist Vivienne, Sunday-chic now in camel cashmere sweater, if a Justin Reynolds had a room. But of course there wasn't anyone of that name checked in. And 'No, there have been no callers and no messages,' she'd said, eyeing me with professional sympathy again. 'Can I do anything to help?'

I checked my mobile. Dan had left two more messages, the last one sounding quite concerned. I went up to my room, lay down on the bed and fought back the tears.

Finally, dusk rose murkily off the water, and I slumped in the window seat staring at the heaving grey sea that matched my mood. I had to admit the run-of-the-mill truth. I was a one-night stand, nothing more.

I'd never been or had a one-night stand before. Dan had been my first date and my last.

I was humiliated. But more than that, I was disappointed. Everything about Justin had seemed so perfect.

I was starting to wonder just how I could have been so gullible, so unguarded, when Dan pulled up in his car. Unshaven and clearly shaken, I saw him dive into the lobby below, and two minutes later, while I was trying to marshal my thoughts, he was knocking with restraint on the room door and asking quietly and calmly to come in and talk.

I was wary. Was this just a prelude to a 'storm off', his customary tactic when he said I was making his brain overheat with my argument and he couldn't think straight? Was he just getting the upper hand back so he could walk out on me? But it seemed not. He'd come to bring me home, he said. And it seemed he was also willing to plead and promise and explain, wonderfully without losing his temper. This was something I'd never expected. Dan was reasoning with me. Not setting his mouth, shaking his head and withdrawing, but reasoning.

My reserve broke at the sight and sound of his apologies. In the time it took to inhale just once, the hurt and the need rushed back into my chest like the autumn tide. I sat shocked and stiff on the bed, pushing away thoughts of the previous night, of Justin, concentrating solely on Dan's lips pleading with me to come back and try again.

In a second he was kissing me and I was kissing him and we were both crying. How treacherous is the familiarity of someone's face and the warmth of their hand as they smooth away your tears? How gratifying to be pleaded with and needed and told it? There was a lot to say but we needed time to say it, and after nearly nine years we had to give each other that chance, didn't we? he cajoled. Yes, I thought. Yes. And no. And, everything's still wrong, and maybe. And also – what have I done?

At once I realised I had agreed to go home with Dan, as I'd known I would if, even once, I heard his voice on the phone. After that, all that remained of that bruising, confusing forty-eight hours since Sophie's call was a vague half-vision of an indiscretion that writhed in the corners of my recall, just out of reach.

But then there it was, resurrected and restored in full colour on a home video – a matinee show to jog my memory. The images writhed on the computer screen in front of me – in my own study now, with curtains closed – in slightly grainy format, blow by blow, thrust by thrust, large as life and twice as sweaty. I could hardly bear to look at the thing with the churning arms and legs, the creative geography of the movements, the entertaining evidence of my infidelity.

I couldn't understand what was happening. It was bad enough that Justin had run off and left me in bed that morning, discarded like an old hanky as soon as the fluids were wiped up, but this?

'I'll be in touch,' the email text said. Just those words. No name. But it had to be Justin, didn't it? Who else could it be? Be in touch about what? Remember our fond night together? Fancy a replay? Why the hell had he sent it? Why and how had it come to my *office*?

I hoped it was all a misunderstanding. But why did those three little words, 'I'll be in touch,' sound so much like a threat?

One thing I knew for certain – I couldn't let Dan see it, or let him know about Justin. Not when he was trying so hard to make things right. He might be six feet tall, proficient with a metal baton and know several ways to disable a man with his bare hands, but it would break him in half to see this.

'No more secrets', he'd said that night in the Pomegranate. It had never even occurred to him to ask if *I* had any to share, to ask what I'd been up to in the two nights I'd been at the hotel. It had never crossed his mind that *his* Jen might be bedding some stranger she'd just met in a pub. That wasn't the woman he was about to marry. She was sensible and practical and faithful. And until now he'd been right.

But it *had* been me that night and now there was evidence to prove it.

I waited a week for another email to arrive, for the sender to 'get in touch' as promised. It was an agonising time for me, fearfully scanning my computer every few hours for any further contact, while Serian and Nigel and painters and carpenters milled around me. Snatches of sentences about rawl plugs and court cases and vanilla-cream skirting board whirled over my head as I tried to think about anything but *that* night. I concentrated on writing tributes to dead people and press releases for stolen motorbikes and of course, dealing with anti-social behaviour issues around the Halloween weekend.

At home it was worse. I steadfastly avoided Dan's gaze, busied myself with chores and went to bed early when I could no longer maintain the muscles of my face in a charade of a smile that suggested normality.

The worst thing was feeling so helpless. So unable to do anything but wait.

After ten long days another message arrived at work.

'Wouldn't want Dan to see your close-up, would you?' Just that. That night an email was waiting on my home computer. '£200 for the copyright. Details to follow.'

So it was down to business, then.

I gaped at the message in a state of disbelief. I was still speechless ten minutes later when it was followed by a text on my work mobile.

'Don't spoil the wedding.' That was all it said. I sort of recognised the number. I remembered the night at the Pomegranate, the text about the wedding plans. This time I knew it wasn't my friend Becky.

Chapter Four

Why was Justin doing this? Why had he targeted me? I hadn't done anything to him. I wasn't rich. I wasn't anything special. How could anyone do something this horrible, this depraved? These were the thoughts that played on a loop all of my waking minutes, while I waited for the next email or text to arrive, from my drive to work in the crawling traffic to the in-and-out-of-office appointments and the lunch hour spent stewing in the memorial garden eating my sandwiches.

My pride was the main casualty. *I* knew that what I had done with Justin that night was so out of character as to be schizophrenic, but he had probably looked at me and thought I'd be just as easy as the next girl. And he'd been right. It wasn't fair. I had slept with only one man in my life other than my husband-to-be, and now that man wanted to literally make me pay?

I wanted to be incandescently angry, but in the first few days all I could feel was sorry for myself, struck dumb by confusion, disbelief and the great throbbing hole of hurt where my stomach used to be. Once the shock had subsided I did what I think anyone in that situation would have done. I tried to contact Justin.

I replied to the email first, asking him to call me so we

could talk and sort it out properly. I had to speak to him to make sense of all this. But there was no reply to any of my entreaties. Then I called the number shown on the text. As I'd half expected it went straight to answerphone. It went straight to answerphone the next dozen times I called over the following eight hours of that day. In the end I wanted to take the phone and smash it to pieces on the floor. In desperation, I eventually left a voice message. 'Justin,' I said, trying to sound in control, though I could hear the tremolo in my voice, the prelude to the surfacing panic. 'If this is you . . . Look, I don't know what this is about but we can talk about it? Just call me, ok? You obviously have my number, just call me.'

There was no response for two days. When it came it was in the form of a text to my personal mobile, two words: 'Just pay. x.'

That was it. No discussion.

How dare he? I thought. How dare he treat me like this? I won't let him get away with it.

The next day, on my lunch break, fuming in my car, so no one could overhear, I telephoned *Cool Cymru* magazine. Justin had told me that he'd written the Watch-house review, that he wrote lots of travel reviews. I found the editorial number online and asked if I could speak to Justin Reynolds or if they could tell me how to get in touch with him. I was holding the hotel review he said he had written in front of me.

The woman who answered told me there was no such member of staff. Their reviews were written by regular contributors, that particular one by Mr Donald Towers. I asked if Mr Towers was thirty-ish with sandy hair. I slumped when he was described as sixty-five and bald. Then I straightened my back and tried *The Times* travel supplement next, then the

Mr and Mrs Smith hotel guide and even *Elle*, asking to speak to him, asking the same questions. Their answers were the same – an irritating wave of 'You must be mistaken, sorry.'

But I *had* to speak to Justin. If I could speak to him then I could work this out somehow, I was sure of it. He couldn't really intend to blackmail me with that video, surely? Things like this didn't happen to nice people, decent people, like me. I didn't deserve this. I had swung from shock to self pity to outrage. Now I was simply determined not to let him hide from me. I was in pursuit, fuelled by indignation alone. I would run him to ground one way or another.

The next day I tried Googling 'Justin Reynolds'. Then I put his name into Facebook and Twitter. I was amazed I hadn't thought of this sooner. I didn't use Facebook myself, I'd never seen the attraction, but I knew a lot of people were obsessed with posting the minutiae of their lives on it. Serian, a devotee with over a hundred 'friends', had helped me set up an account I could use to check what was being posted for work purposes. Reporters were just getting wise to what an amazing, untapped resource this so-called 'social networking' was. It was a free source of information they could mine for personal details, for stories. And remarks and gossip posted on the sites by friends and family could be used as quotes without reporters ever having to come through our office. Usually they used it to download photographs or mawkish comments about dead people without family approval, 'Miss you, babe – forever in heaven with the angels,' that sort of thing. But when I tapped in 'Justin Reynolds', I didn't get any matches.

I tried a different tack. On the internet I found a company that rents character holiday cottages in Gower. I found the right one, the one I had spent the night in, by going through a few dozen thumbnail photos of properties. It was called

Hope Cottage. I called them to see if they had any forwarding details for that week's rental in October. I told them Mr Reynolds had left me his number but I'd lost it. An officious woman told me they couldn't give out details of clients but there must be a mistake because that particular cottage had not been rented since August, and that had been to a family of four.

Well that's that, after all, I thought. Then I burst into tears.

This, in itself, was almost as humiliating as my failure. I'd never been much of a crier. I was certainly not one of those women with a high water content, the sort that spill over at the sight of a baby in a plant pot dressed as a sunflower or a cute puppy in a Santa hat. As far as I was concerned 'reduced to tears' meant the reduction of your self-respect, the loss of your dignity. But I supposed I'd already lost that when I'd allowed Justin to film me naked and on my back.

I slumped on the study table, my chest hitching with frustration at my own powerlessness. I felt my face crumple in on itself.

'Is this actually happening?' I whimpered, dribbling tears and saliva into my cardigan sleeve.

Maybe it's Justin's idea of a joke, I rationalised. A sick, perverted joke, admittedly but a joke nevertheless. Maybe he would call any minute now, laugh and say, I had you going there, didn't I? Admit it, I had you going?'

But if it wasn't a joke, what should I do next? If I paid the money perhaps he would go away. Instinct told me that if I *didn't* pay he would go through with his threat to somehow show Dan the video.

I considered the coolly calculated way he'd sent the emails and the texts to me – not all at once, but drip-fed, over days. Teasing, letting me know he could get in touch anywhere –

at work first, then at home and then on my mobile. The added last 'x' at the end of his order to 'Just pay', was a parody of a kiss, a calculated cruelty, a sneer in a single letter.

But how had he done it? How had he found me and my contact details when he was so hard to trace? I hadn't given him my work email or phone number, but I *had* told him I worked for the police. I suppose it wouldn't be that difficult, knowing my name, to find me. How he'd done it didn't matter at that moment. I had to limit the damage, and I needed to do it quickly.

The next day I went to my bank account and withdrew the £200

'What do I do?' I texted back.

A week passed.

'I'll let you know soon,' was the reply

I waited.

Chapter Five

Dan and I were late for the Divisional Christmas party. It was always held very early in December, before the real Christmas party season. Naturally, police officers tend to be busy during that time. At 7 p.m., after a mountain of press interviews about another pile-up that had closed the M4 for three hours, I was in the press office loo, hastily changing into jeans and what I hoped was a festive green silk T-shirt top. In my purse was a heavy pair of onyx teardrop earrings I would put on at the last minute. I'd picked them as my birthday present from Dan. He was hardly ever organised enough to get to the shops between shifts. They were beautiful, but weighed a tonne.

I added just a little black eyeliner and a slick of Berry Fool lipstick. I felt that if I forced myself to go through the motions of being festive I might succeed in deluding myself that everything was all right, for at least this one evening.

Christmas had never been my favourite time of year. Between Dan's shifts and my on-call duties (yes, nervous officers like to have one of us at the end of a phone twenty-four hours a day, even at Christmas), opportunity to celebrate was rare.

Dan usually went for a few beers with his work mates in one of the quiet pubs in Cardiff, well before the real fun began on the last Friday before Christmas, 'Black Friday' (or Bleak

Friday, as the politically correct brigade were now telling us we had to call it.) He would return home, smiley and hug-generous, to fall asleep on the sofa with Brains beer and curry on his breath.

I would attend the communication department's turkey meal and invariably returned from an afternoon of listening to people moan about their children and watching them trying to get off with each other in the toilets – tipsy, irritable and swearing this year would be my last.

If we were lucky, Dan and I would go to the pub together at least once. I would wear a new top but with flat boots and a woolly parka, 'so we could walk home if we couldn't get a taxi and you won't be cold,' as Dan always asserted, ever practical. Then, if we were lucky, and the God of the Rotas was smiling, we'd have Christmas dinner or Boxing Day dinner together, never both.

In addition to these variable delights, Dan and I tried to do our duty by attending one of the Divisional or Area work dos. It was more as a gesture of goodwill than any enthusiasm on my part. I would rather have lain on the settee eating rationed-out segments of Chocolate Orange, watching classic movies, but I went along to smile, be polite and make a good impression as 'the girlfriend'. That way no one could say Dan's missus from the top floor was a stuck-up *piece*, too snooty to show her face with the likes of us. It would be mainly the women who would say this, naturally.

It was also a good opportunity to see which senior officer might go crazy and perform an impromptu strip tease on the dance floor, or maybe end up smooching with a senior/junior colleague who was married. Sometimes one of the PCs ran an unofficial sweepstake on the latter.

Dan always appeared to have a good time at the dos,

probably because everyone loved Dan. People always seek him out to chat about nothing in particular, ask his advice, tell him their problems. The rank and file men love him because he's a no-nonsense, straight-up-and-down, none-of-that-poncey-senior-officer-crap kind of guy. The senior officers like him because, despite the above being true, he's articulate, reliable and would dissuade them from getting their shirts off on the dance floor, or at least ensure all the mobile phone photos were deleted immediately.

The office girls and young female PCs particularly love him because he's athletic and handsome, and is very skilled at giving the impression of being deeply interested in their inanities and nonsense. They gravitate sinuously towards him like snakes to the charmer – eyes wide, lips parted.

It has always been this way since the first night Dan and I met at a Christmas party while we were at university in Cardiff. I was in the first term of my first year, straight out of school. Just out of the bag, bright and clean, uncreased, unsmudged, unfrayed, inexperienced.

He was studying for his MA is social and political science, and was four years older – a rowing, running, athletic, *Sunday Times*-reading postgrad. He was rather dashing.

He jogged in the park, past my halls of residence, wearing tight red shorts that were well known to the second-year girls and, unofficially, a popular local attraction three times a week around 5 p.m., if it was dry.

I'd watched him surreptitiously, with stabs of shy longing before I'd ever dreamed of speaking to him. Tall and lean, smooth in motion, he was quite mesmerising. But he was also so much a man, rather than a boy, that the girl in me slightly feared the backwash of his easy physical energy, his solid presence which seemed to fill so much space and time, so easily.

Then, on the night of the athletic club Christmas party, the inexplicable occurred. He excused himself from the side of a model-perfect Nigerian girl and a pretty hennaed redhead wearing a Santa hat, sidled over to the corner I was sitting in and starting talking to *me*. At first I was baffled as to why he would show an interest in me when all the rah rah, 'I say, Victoriaaa', athletic clones with abs of steel were becoming more scantily clad by the minute. Henna girl and her friend were positively astonished. I was pretty enough, easy on the eye in a low-maintenance, shiny-haired, Doc Marten boots and indie girl T-shirt way. But though I didn't wear glasses or flowery skirts I had the air of the geek, I think. Something of the scent of a wallflower clung about me, but maybe of one who was waiting, wanting to bloom, and would do so if watered and placed in the sun.

Dan asked me to dance. His voice was softer, less strident than I had imagined, his hand on mine heavy but gentle. The gimlet eyes that flashed from all the girls in the room as his arm slid around my waist were wonderful to behold. In that moment, revolving under the lights, in his arms, the world faded out and I was somewhere else far better. I could have stayed there forever. I could have died there.

We left the party soon after and sat in a quiet bar where we talked until closing time under the glint and glitter of the Christmas tree lights. Then he asked me on a date. He actually seemed to think I might say no, asking the question almost shyly, as if he was used to refusal. But that couldn't be possible, surely? Anyway, there was no question of my refusing. I'd been rehearsing a cool fantasy acceptance speech in my head since we'd left the party, never thinking I'd get the chance to use it. When the time came, and he looked at me expectantly, I grinned like an imbecile for far too long and said, 'Yes, ok. Pasta sounds nice.'

With his nippy red Fiesta and Oakley action-man sunglasses, Dan was far more glamorous than anyone I'd encountered at my little village school, peopled as it was by would-be farmers, arc welders, car mechanics, beauticians, teen mothers and hairdressers. Not that there was anything wrong with this, but it just wasn't for me. I already wanted much more.

It's fair to say that, from that very first date, I believed I fell drastically in love with Dan, with his old-fashioned manners and willingness to eat Sunday lunch once a month with my mum and dad. But something inside me always held back. There was a sliver of restraint, a shard of self-awareness beneath my composure that stemmed from my keen awareness that we didn't really have much in common.

Dan came from London and had no real family, no grandparents, just an elderly, doting and enviably wealthy great-aunt Alice, who had passed away in his first year at college. She'd raised him after his mother had died in a car accident when he was ten years old. She'd instilled in him the value of education, thrift, hard work and the benefits of vigorous regular exercise for a strong body and mind. I imagined her as a Lady Bracknell-type character from the *Importance of Being Earnest*, but kindly underneath, not so snobby. If we had ever had the chance to meet she would not have disapproved of me. She would have been dressed in Burberry, perhaps, or Christian Dior, and offered me slices of Madeira cake or scones and jam, with Earl Grey tea. She would own sugar-cube tongs.

Dan had never really known his father, who he said his aunt had described alternately as 'a big noise in the city' and 'a nasty piece of work when in drink'. There had been some sort of unspecific 'unpleasant business' that had caused his mum to sever all contact. Then his dad had died of colon cancer. Dan did not like to talk about it, which was a shame because it seemed terribly interesting and romantic to me.

I loved my dad, but he worked as an accountant for a firm that made plastic containers and was one of the most easy-going men on the planet. I loved my mum, but she was first a devoted housewife and mother, and then a primary school assistant. Neither was great romantic, epic material.

On his aunt's death Dan had inherited the nice Victorian three storey semi-detached house in Chelsea that had trebled in price by the time he graduated. He'd sold up, and invested the money wisely, learning along the way to save a lot, spend a little and be a jolly team player of sports.

I, on the other hand, had grown up in a neat terraced house north of Pontypridd, in South Wales, with a good-natured, nosey collection of easy-going extended family nearby. Despite thrift and hard work there was never much money or much privacy, but there was a lot of 'counting your blessings' and 'counting to ten'. It was only natural for them to live in a gaggle of noise in each others' front parlours and back kitchens, and in each others' business from dawn till dusk. So, though I loved them, it was only natural for me to long to be somewhere quiet and calm and, one day, to get a good job and a bigger house.

Our annual family holidays were taken in rickety self-catering flats and caravans up and down the Welsh and Devonian coasts, where vast communal teas were served on windswept beaches and everyone talked at once about cake recipes and football scores.

Instead I dreamed of the South of France and Rome in early spring. At night I studied the illuminated globe I'd begged my mum for, for my tenth birthday, spinning it to the places

I would visit and then reading about them in my illustrated atlas.

How could I not be mesmerised by Dan and all that he represented? He had a *past*. He knew his way around London. He had attended art galleries, been to the opera, visited Berlin with his politics course, spent a week in Milan on a student exchange.

He listened to my feminist analyses of the novels of Virginia Woolf and Charlotte Brontë without sniggering, asking pertinent questions. He liked classic movies and old science fiction films, not just *Star Wars*, which all boys liked, of course, but the real fifties and sixties classics which he said reflected the political paranoia of the era. And he appeared to genuinely hate football (an inestimable bonus).

He seemed to understand many of the issues involved in the conflicts of the Middle East, as well as military history, a topic I was interested in but ill-informed about, and a lot about current affairs in general. He had *opinions* about things and a self-motivated, can-do attitude. And he was kind.

But surely it was only a matter of time before he would see through my carefully constructed air of studious, good-natured calm and find someone better, someone prettier, cooler, sexier, more exciting, more sophisticated, more confident?

It was only as the months passed and we became a real couple that I realised Dan really *didn't* want what the other twenty-something boys appeared to venerate in women – tight tops and exposed cleavage, acres of lip gloss and coy, appreciative giggles.

In the beginning I would occasionally ask him, 'How come you're with me, Dan?' gesturing to the bevy of pretty, sporty little things making cow eyes in his direction. 'You could have any girl you want.'

He'd look perplexed, annoyed that I could even ask such a thing.

'Why would I want one of them? I detest those girls. They're just shallow – all cleavage and hair. You're *naturally* pretty. And I like my girlfriend to have an IQ bigger than her bust size, thank you. They talk so much nonsense. They drive me nuts. They watch soap operas, for Christ's sake. And they can't be relied on! *That's* why I'm with you, my sweetheart. I can *talk* to you. You think about things that matter.' Then he'd tuck me into the crook of his rowing-toned arm, snuffle a kiss into my hair and I'd fill with warmth from the tips of my toes to the crown of my head.

Soon, without warning, or any obvious increment of days passing, we'd been together nearly nine years. Everything was different. We were GOING TO BE MARRIED. I was a well-paid press officer who had swapped sneakers and jeans for smart shoes and trouser suits. He was a newly carded police inspector on the accelerated promotion scheme. We lived in a semi-detached Victorian house in a nice part of the city.

But one thing that hadn't altered was that we still attended parties where I watched lipsticked lovelies chancing their arm with my man.

Almost as soon as we arrived at the Area do at the North Road working men's club, Dan was trapped in a corner talking to the firearms manager, and a scenes of crime girl with over-enthusiastic fake eyelashes was batting them at him with blurry, butterfly-flapping determination.

He ignored her and tipped me a little wink as I stood at the bar with Serian, sipping a glass of red wine. Ordinarily, I would at least have had a mild, repressed urge to go over and pull the eyelid wings off CSI Barry girl, but all I could really think about that night was Justin. Why hadn't he texted about what he wanted me to do with the money, and what would he say when he did? I couldn't help pulling my phone out of my pocket and checking it every so often, just to see if I had missed a message.

Meanwhile, Serian was ordering me an unsolicited sambuca shot, of all things, and babbling about her plans of conquest for the night. I liked Serian, but sometimes she seemed to have only half her brain engaged at any one time. She was younger than me, only twenty-two, and was 'sort of' going out with an amiable lad called Rees, who worked in the post room and took her to gigs at the students' union every Saturday night.

Secretly she had her eye on one of the DCs from Cardiff Central with a fancy Mercedes. She was alternating between telling me about Rees's plans to take her to Glastonbury that summer and agonising over whether or not DC manhood-over-compensation-car would turn up. Should she go over and talk to him if he did? Would that be too obvious?

Serian, usually fairly sensibly attired in Top Shop Office mix and match, was obeying the whore-code rules of the work Christmas party. Her leopard-skin top was slashed almost to her belly button and she was covered in more fake tan than Jordan. Her usually sleek black hair had been hot-tonged into a mess of hairspray-crisp ringlets, and she perched atop a pair of what could only be described as red, seventies-hooker platform shoes. 'Obvious' seemed to be a given.

'For God's sake, stop playing about with your bloody phone, Jen,' she snapped, downing her shot. 'Should I make a move on DC Wilkins or not? He definitely doesn't have a girlfriend, right?'

'That's what Bodie says, and he's the oracle when it comes to who's getting what with whom,' I replied.

'Oracle,' she said, puzzled. 'Like those things they make down Carmarthen?'

'Noooo, I think that's a *coracle*, Ser – it's like a little boat. Never mind. I just meant he's "in the know".'

'What if he doesn't come?'

'This is the Area do, 'course he'll come.'

I hovered on the edge of the bar while Serian chatted to a girl from accounts, trying not to catch the eye of pervy Oliver from Force Policy, who was hovering close by. The problem with being a civilian staff member at these things, if you don't wear a boob-revealing top and come-hither panda eyeliner, is that you slightly scare people. You don't really belong with the uniformed staff who do the real dirty work, or the top brass who think they do, until some of them get drunk – then they want you to realise that they're ok guys, really, especially the older ones.

When the superintendent of Serious Organised Crime comes up to you, tipsy, wearing stonewashed jeans and his 'I'm off duty now' stud earring, it's a bit like attending a school youth club disco and being accosted by your maths teacher in a 'cool' denim jacket, wiggling his hips to the 'hit parade' to show he's down with the kids.

Luckily, Dan came to my rescue. 'Can I pinch my girlfriend for a minute?' he beamed as Oliver arrived at my right shoulder and opened his mouth to speak. Dan handed me another small wine and I pushed the sambuca away down the bar. Someone would appropriate it. Luckily, Oliver was already distracted by Serian who had flown on to the dance floor and was gyrating with gusto to Beyonce's 'Single Ladies'. The slash-fronted leopard-skin top was coping woefully with the challenge.

'Listen, pet, I've been having a word with Phil and he's

offered me a couple of weekends deputising on the public order exercises coming up,' said Dan, steering me off to a corner. I knew the force had been planning emergency exercises at key locations in the coming months. They held a few every year with the police horses and the support teams in their riot gear. This year would be the flu pandemic scenario. The press office would be involved with the 'public reassurance' aspect, glossing over any alarming suggestions of crowd-control measures in the event of service disruptions, and absolutely not mentioning the locations of leisure centres and offices that were designated as temporary morgues.

'It'd be good experience for me,' continued Dan, keenly. 'Bit of hands-on experience will look good, and it'll be some extra cash for the wedding.'

'Well, when is it?'

'Planning on the fifteenth and sixteenth of January. January twenty-first and March third for the scenarios.'

'But Dan, we've got the meeting with the wedding planner on the fifteenth of January and on the twenty-first we said we'd talk everything through with the photographer.'

'Did we? Is it then? I didn't realise.'

'I told you to put it in your diary about a hundred times.' If it wasn't in his and my diary it didn't exist in the real world. It was in my diary.

Dan had the good grace to look apologetic. 'We could rearrange, couldn't we? It's not like they can rearrange the exercises. It's months till the wedding anyway.'

'Don't disappear on me like this, Dan. I can't do all this stuff on my own,' I said sulkily.

'Course you can, multi-tasking is your middle name, my capable, beautiful fiancée. And your taste is much better than mine.'

'That's not the point, is it? We barely spend any weekends together as it is. Now you want to spend three running around playing Survivors.'

'Look pet, I know. It's just a good chance to get my face seen. If I turn down the chance they may not ask again – you know how it goes.'

'And you'd be "under the thumb" if you said you'd promised to arrange your wedding with your fiancée?'

'Don't make it sound like that. It's just a good chance. Is it ok?'

'Yeah, I suppose so.' There's no point in having a row about it when you've made up your mind already, I thought. I also thought: right now, I don't actually care that much.

'You'd better make it up to me with a dance, then,' I said, trying to make light of it. 'They're playing our song.' It wasn't really *our* song. It was Whitney Houston's 'I Will Always Love You'. It was the first song we'd danced to, that night at the Christmas party years ago, and we often joked, because we both detested it but hadn't wanted to say so then, that we should have it as our first wedding dance.

But Dan was distracted. 'Not to this. Not here, Jen. You know I hate to dance.'

'You didn't used to,' I retorted, rather huffy all of a sudden. He *didn't* used to – we'd always get up for the slow ones. He'd put his hand on my waist and take my other hand in his, pulling it in to his chest, gently. I couldn't remember the last time we'd danced.

'Well, not in a place like this,' he countered, with the determined look that I knew meant he wouldn't be persuaded. He untangled his arm from mine. 'Look, I need to talk to Phil and the sarge, sort this stuff out. Catch up with you in a bit. Buy you a cocktail, ok?' Now *he* was trying to make light of it.

How determined we were not to fight.

'This is a working men's club, Dan. A vodka and coke is a cocktail.'

'There you go, then – bargain.' He grinned and pecked me on the head before bounding off.

I fished in my pocket for my phone and glanced around for Serian, but instead there was Bodie, looking, I must say, beautifully honed in a slightly-too-tight sports T-shirt and expensively cut jeans, heading towards me.

'Old man too busy hob-nobbing to dance?' he grinned. 'Looks like I'll have to dance with you. It's my duty as the next most senior officer.'

I smiled patiently, about to say something nice before sidling back to a safe vantage point, but Bodie was decisive, removing my wine from my hand and twirling me in a single motion onto the dance floor. It's hard to demur when six feet two inches of Max-Muscle protein powder-enhanced bicep is doing the steering.

'Marc slides into action and they're away!' he grinned. He was happily, foolishly drunk and pleased with himself, so I couldn't help but smile. He whirled me round with surprising coordination as the DJ entered the seventies cheesy section of his playlist. His infectious cheer was difficult to resist and so I joined in the spirit of the thing, waggling exaggeratedly in time to ELO's 'Mr Blue Sky'.

'That Dan bloke should not have passed up the chance to dance with the prettiest lady in the room,' he leered good-naturedly into my face, sliding his hand on to my hip.

Dan was standing by the cling-film covered buffet, smiling at me while talking to the superintendent. Sometimes I wished he would experience just a pang or two of jealousy. It wasn't the first time I'd been ambushed by someone at a works do.

It wasn't that I wanted Dan to stride over and say *Get your hand off my bird*, or anything like that. That would be immature. I just thought it would be nice if he so much as frowned occasionally.

At that point Bodie's hand slid up to my waist in an attempt to pull me closer. 'Marc,' I began, putting my hand on his to remove it with a smile.

'Shush now, shush, the Marcus is making a serious declaration of "like" here,' he continued. 'I was about to say you are my favourite press officer in the whole world.'

Right at that moment my mobile phone vibrated and fell out of my jeans pocket. Loosened by Bodie's twirling, it clattered to the floor. Bodie stooped to pick it up from between his boots at exactly the same time I did. We almost head-butted each other and I had to perform a sudden pull-back swerve.

Holding the glowing phone up to his eyes in drink-related myopic concentration, Bodie focussed on the words. 'Get on the train to Swansea at 6 p.m. tomorrow,' he read aloud. 'Oh, who's this? Your fancy man?' he cooed in mock horror. 'I have a rival? The blackguard! I'll lay the man out. Who is he?'

'Ok , tiger,' said Jimmy, appearing at his shoulder, 'Give the nice press lady her phone back and let go of her before she asks me to arrest you.' I kept a vacant grin on my face.

'Sorry, Jen,' said Jimmy, placing the phone in my hand, then making the universal gesture for 'he's had a few' as he firmly took Bodie by the shoulder. 'Come on, *Sarge*. Bedtime for little girls.'

Bodie looked at the phone and then at me. He did look a bit like a little girl who'd had her dolly taken away. Jimmy grinned. 'Don't worry, I'll see him safely home.'

I made the face of the graciously rescued heroine and waved them goodbye.

Then I stumbled straight to the toilets, gestured vaguely at the three receptionists refreshing their eyeliner in the mirrors, and bolted into the nearest stall. I reread the message on the phone while swallowing down my heart.

'Get on the train to Swansea tomorrow, 6 p.m.,' as Bodie had said. 'It also said. 'Last carriage. Alone.'

An hour later Dan and I were in the back of a taxi, sliding through the night streets. 'You looked really pretty tonight, Jen. You made me proud,' said Dan, cuddling his arm round me and kissing my brow.

Pity you didn't spend more than two minutes with me, since I only went for your sake, I thought. I hadn't even had my promised 'cocktail'.

I leaned my head against his in reply. I was a bit drunk and a bit queasy. There was a faint scent of cigarettes and sick in the taxi. Dan was practically sober. He didn't drink much at work dos.

'Did you see the state on some of those women?' he ran on. 'Call themselves officers? You'd think they, of all people, would know better. There'll be some stories tomorrow I bet . . . Probably at least one tearful complaint that someone grabbed their tits or overstepped the mark because they can't explain how they ended up in the toilets with someone other than their other half.'

'That's a nice way to talk about your colleagues,' I sighed, even though I usually agreed with him.

'You said yourself – Serian looked like an East End tart.'

I *had* said that, so I said nothing.

Serian texted me to say she was in the DC's flash car heading for his home.

'Take care,' I texted back, wishing I had given myself the same advice when it would have mattered.

*

Luckily, Dan was on nights the next day so I didn't have to explain what on earth I was doing leaving work and getting on a train with an envelope full of money.

It was raining heavily, but I was glad because everyone was wet and grumpy, with hoods up and umbrellas over their faces, and less likely to pay attention to me or anything else.

I'd forgotten the ordeal of the evening train between Cardiff and Swansea, the commuters crammed in like cattle as the carriages swing westward, out of the capital and on to the end of the line. The 6 p.m. is the London train that starts at Paddington and passes through Cardiff. There was a fug of steamy heat, wet umbrella and damp wool in the carriage. Everyone's hair looked rain-spoiled. Half of the last carriage was empty – a lot of passengers tend to spill out at Cardiff – the rest was taken up by the zombified businessmen in suits who, after one or two stops along the half-hour route past Bridgend, were sleepily head-lolling in time to the train's rhythm.

Every so often the jerky, slumbering atmosphere was broken by a gaggle of women on their way into Swansea city centre for a 'session', talking at the tops of their voices about the beery exploits to come. They all looked the same: stringy haired and pallid beneath the patchy, gravy-stain fake tans and lashings of over enthusiastic kohl. They pushed their way into the empty seats next to the tie-encumbered businessmen and purse-lipped business women. An air of sickly-cheap cider, cigarette smoke and hairspray lingered in their wake.

Fortunately, I was seated next to a bright-eyed granny with an industrial-sized bag of mixed sweets. She wore a neat button-up princess coat in pale grey. What could only be described as an enormous sherbet lemon-coloured muffler was wound round her neck. A little lemon felt hat sat atop her blue grey curls, fixed by a pearl-topped pin. She did not appear to be damp in any way. She was reading Stephen King's *Misery* through little wire-rimmed specs with a look of intense concentration and delight on her face.

She frowned with exaggerated disapproval at each of the cackling groups of girls, offering epithets such as *Very common*, and *Shameful lack of decorum* in a strong Welsh accent without lowering her voice.

About two stops from the city, my mobile beeped. It was a text: 'Go the rear of the carriage by the toilet.' Here we go, I thought. Would Justin be waiting nearby? Was he watching me now, as I got to my feet? Was he on the train? Would I suddenly see his face as I remembered it? What was I going to say to him? Would I rage at him or would I plead? Would I hand him the envelope or hurl it in his face?

My heart was clattering around in my ribcage, I was breathing too heavily. Bumping my way past the hairspray harpies I made it to the where the toilet was, at the end of the carriage. I waited.

New text: 'When the train pulls out of the next station, toss the jiffy bag out of the window when you get to the end of the platform,' it said.

'What?' I exclaimed aloud. Christ on a bike! This was getting daft.

'Christ on a bike,' was a favourite phrase of my mum's. By the mother-child osmosis gradient it had passed from her stronger element to my weaker one sometime around my twelfth birthday, along with a dislike of people who spit on the street and a hatred of dirty cups that lie around the living room. My mum never resorted to profanity (it's pure laziness, Jen) but she'd never minded this odd circus-invoking bit of bicycling Christ blasphemy.

I liked the bizarreness of the image. Our Lord, on a bike –in my head, a seventies-style Chopper – sandals struggling on the pedals, robe billowing out behind him. It seemed to fit the bizarreness of the situation too – me on a train to Swansea, throwing blackmail money into the bushes. I scanned the station platform warily as we pulled in. It was only a little, unmanned stop with a plastic shelter. Just one young couple got off, hooded and huddled against the flurries of sleet that was trying to be snow. A car was waiting for them. Its headlights streamed out across the car park at the rear. I couldn't see anyone lurking in the shelter, or any other vehicles parked nearby. Was Justin hiding, watching?

This was it. I'd come this far. It occurred to me, as I threw the little jiffy bag out of the window, that Justin, wherever he was, was having a damn good laugh. This wasn't a joke but it *was* a game, wasn't it?

But it was also quite clever. He hadn't given me a chance to confront him or connect him to the money. No one had seen us together on the train. He could easily retrieve the bag unseen from the spot he'd chosen. It wasn't covered by the CCTV cameras, by the look of it, and I couldn't make it back in time to stop him. Even if I'd told someone in advance – Dan, or the police – chances were they couldn't get to the spot in time from the road or the platform, not in the dark.

I got off at the next stop and caught the connection back in the opposite direction. As the train passed through the dark station I couldn't help myself from looking out at the spot where I'd dropped the cash. Naturally, there was nothing to see.

I got home, wet and cold, to an empty house an hour later, after a delay outside Cardiff Central. I was in bed long before Dan came home. I was glad of this. I didn't want to look at him, or him to look at me. But at least it was over. That's what I thought to myself as I curled up under the duvet trying to warm up my cold feet and hands. It's over now.

The next day I bumped into Bodie at the morning tasking meeting, back in the office after a day's leave. He was his usual bluff, joke-cracking self as we trawled methodically through the incidents of the previous twenty-four hours and the tasks were assigned. Everyone was still talking about Wednesday's do and the extent of their hangovers. Apparently, it was all around the station that Serian had spent the night with the DC. She had told me as much, in lurid detail, but I had kept it to myself. Clearly there'd been no need. Everyone but post room Rees, tucked away downstairs out of chatter range, now seemed to know.

'Sorry if I was a bit of a twat at the do,' said Bodie, looking sheepish, as we filed out next to each other once we had been dismissed. 'I didn't mean anything by it. You're not offended, are you? You didn't say anything to Dan or anything? He's a good mate. I wouldn't want him to get the wrong idea. I don't want things to be weird between you and me either.'

'Don't know what you are talking about, Marc,' I said dismissively 'I was too drunk to remember.' I patted his impressive bicep with a roll of my eyes, and he smiled with bearish gratitude, giving my arm a little squeeze.

That afternoon Dan and I hurried to make the last appointment of the day with the local registrar of births, deaths and marriages. The office was housed in a wing of the former town hall. Built, like all good Victorian architecture, from austere grey stone with high, narrow windows, The formality of it all was immediately sobering as we trudged up the steps. Even Dan seemed uncharacteristically cowed by the stern portraits of the Victorian town elders glaring down at us from their gilt frames in the reception, demanding humility before the mighty edifice for which they had stood.

We were there to formally register our intent to marry. I think it was dawning on both of us that this was official now. We waited twitchily for the great mahogany door to swing open, and to be called into the inner sanctum for the process to begin.

Dan, constrained in his uniform, was tugging at his tie in the stuffy, overheated air, yawning repeatedly behind his hand. The radiators were on full blast. Tiny beads of perspiration were gathering along his hairline and upper lip. He looked every inch the reluctant bridegroom, even if it was I who was the one fighting the urge to flee back onto the street.

'What are we actually doing today?' Dan asked me, for the third time in twenty-four hours.

'Just registering the marriage and the date and place and what-not, as I told you. Then they ask us some details and then they post the banns.'

'Right. They still do that? Post the banns?'

'Yes, though it's not like it's announced in the streets with someone ringing a bell or anything. It just goes on a board somewhere in the public view. Here, look.' I pointed to the wall opposite where little typed sheets of paper sat under glass on a noticeboard. 'Chantelle Williams is due to be married to Shawn Jones on 24 July 2010, blah blah, dates of birth etc. You know my birthday – right, Dan?'

'Of course!'

'I was born in Pontypridd cottage hospital?'

'Of course.'

'My mother's maiden name was Jenkins, right?'

'Yes. What, they're actually going to ask us stuff like this? Don't we just fill in the forms?'

'Yes, but I think we go in one at a time and they ask us each other's details. I think it's so they know we're really a couple, though it's hardly rocket science to fake it if we were getting married for money or a visa or something. They need the parents' names for the certificates and such like, and the legal records. Your parent's names were Alice and John Collins?'

'Yes.'

'And your mother's maiden name was Lancaster?'

'Yes. No, Selford.'

'What, I thought you said Lancaster?'

'Did I?'

'Yes, when I asked you.'

'Right. No, I must have got confused. It's Selford.

He sounded a bit uncertain.

'That's what's on your birth certificate, then? I thought you were going to check this, the details.'

'Yes. I couldn't find it.'

'I told you to dig it out and check the details. How can you not be sure? We need to get this right today. I told you this at the weekend. This is the legal bit. You have to be sure.'

'I am sure.'

'Ok, then. You've got your passport too, for the formal ID?'

'You already asked me that in the car. I'm not an idiot.'

'Ok, just checking. I don't want to have to try and make another appointment if we miss anything today. It took me a month to get this one scheduled with your shifts, after you *forgot* to turn up for the last one.'

'I said I was sorry about that. I didn't *forget*. It was the firearms thing, the negotiator was late. I couldn't leave. It's all right, this is just going through the motions, filling in the forms.

We'll be in and out. It's not a problem.' He yawned again.

After a moment or two I said: 'You're right. Let's hope it's quick then we can get home and get something to eat. I've got some of those lamb chops you like thawing out.' Dan was always crotchety when he was hungry and he'd been up since 5.30 a.m. He reached out his hand and gave mine a little squeeze that said, *I'm sorry to bite your head off.* Then a little buzzer went off and the registrar, a grey-haired woman in her middle fifties, emerged with funereal sombreness and beckoned from the mahogany door.

Dan went in first. While I sat and watched the dust playing in the swathes of light and listened to a computer keyboard clacking somewhere down the hall, I thought, this is it – this is a formal declaration of intent in the eyes of the law.

After a few minutes a young, heavily pregnant girl and a sallow-faced lad, both wearing tracksuits, arrived and took a seat opposite me. I tried to avoid catching their eye. I was too tired for small talk, but it was no use. The girl, perhaps eighteen or nineteen – pretty, but in the way that wouldn't last long into her twenties – was just dying to share her excitement.

'This is pretty scary, ain't it?' she said with no trace of discomfort. 'I'm so excited, I can't wait. When you doing it?'

'Er, in June,' I smiled. 'When are you?'

'Soon as possible. Well, before the baby comes, if we can.' Her partner patted her bump with obvious affection.

'When are you due?'

'Ten weeks.'

'Gonna be a boy. Little Jayden,' said the lad.

'Brooklyn,' insisted the girl playfully.

'Like fuck!' replied the dad, and they both grinned.

'Nah, it'll be Jayden,' confirmed the girl. My mate Gemma's boy is already called Brooklyn.'

I looked at the clock and listened to the low murmur of Dan's voice responding to inaudible questions through the door. I wondered if I should just get to my feet, smooth down my trousers, pick up my handbag and walk calmly out into the tea-time sunlit street. I had the car keys. I could get in, turn the engine over and drive. I don't know where – anywhere. All I would need was my credit card. Who knew where I would be when darkness began to descend softly and the night grew cool.

I didn't do that, of course. Dan came out of the office looking relieved, then it was my turn. Twenty minutes later we were walking to the car, with the promise of documents in the post and eternal wedded bliss.

Chapter Six

Soon it was Boxing Day. Christmas had all but crept past for another year. I had only three days' leave and meant to make the most of them by doing as little as possible. Dan was sprawled across the armchair reading Antony Beevor's *D-Day*. He liked Beevor's military books. I had bought Dan a military-themed book every Christmas since our Christmases had begun and this was no exception. He'd read *Stalingrad* and *Berlin* and *Paris* and other conflicts by big-name historians. Dan liked to read about war. Mostly he concentrated on World War II and Vietnam, but also, with the changing times, Iraq and Afghanistan.

It wasn't that I didn't find these things interesting; I found a lot of things interesting and read about many of them. But Dan never read anything but historical memoirs or analyses. Where I had once found this impressive, in the last few years I'd been finding it more and more annoying. If I'm honest, I'm suspicious of people who never read any fiction at all. I don't understand them. If I don't have a novel by the side of my bed, and also one in my handbag, I feel a physical surge of panic at the absence of that paper-solid rectangle, as one might feel the absence of a limb long after the loss of it. Contemporary fiction was my favourite obsession that year, with a big dose of the classics old and modern, anything but chick lit (enough said) or crime (well, there was no point in reading about crime when you work for the police and get the real thing).

If I didn't pop into a Waterstone's bookstore at least once a fortnight for a quick hit, I would experience violent, anxious withdrawal symptoms. Even as a child I'd always 'had my nose stuck in a book', as my mum used to say. The phrase makes perfect sense to me. It was always the book smell I found so tempting, the tangible sense of the paper and print. The nose senses the unveiling of what is between the covers, inhales it, sucks it down, the promise of the pages, the tantalising glimpse on the outside of the world waiting to be unwrapped inside – a universe of stories waiting to be told, lives to be lived, emotions to be explored.

Before I began to buy my own novels, childhood Christmases were synonymous with new books. My mum would order a whole array of annuals and Ladybird classics for me, and story compilations such as *Tales from the Arabian Nights* or *101 Ghost Stories* from the newspaper shop in the village. Mr Lewis would let you pay so much a week from June onwards so you didn't need to pay all at once in December.

My excitement would be uncontainable on Christmas morning, sitting Buddha-like but very un-Zen at the centre of a fan of titles, hard- and soft-backed. I would run my hands over the covers of the *Twinkle* or *Mandy* or *Girl* annuals, the *Grimms' Fairy Tales*, abridged and illustrated historical classics like *The Three Musketeers* or *Lorna Doone*.

My favourite stories always contained blue-blooded babies who had been accidentally given to the wrong families at birth. In many well-rehearsed fantasy scenarios I too had been given to the wrong family at the Valleys cottage hospital where I had been born. At any minute, without warning, my *real* family might arrive in a gold-liveried carriage, or as I grew a little older, a jet-black limousine. It would cause quite a stir in darkest Pontypridd when these sleek chariots slid up outside our house and the feather-headed footman or velvet-clad valet alighted. My real mother, a beautiful and regal member of the Italian or maybe Swedish aristocracy, would then embrace me as I hurled myself into her arms.

Naturally, adult Christmases did not have that same sense of storybook excitement, but there were still three novels from my mum, a reference book about art nouveau icons from my dad and an unexpectedly lovely illustrated copy of Italian Renaissance art from Dan, lying unwrapped at the foot of the settee. I just couldn't quite bring myself to read them yet. While Dan Beevored away on the beaches of Normandy I channel surfed and ate another Brazil nut for the selenium and essential fatty acids.

I was deliberately not looking at the pile of wedding magazines and folders of information sitting truculently on the coffee table by the window. I was trying to relax.

It had been a month, more or less, since my theatrical little train payment to Justin and there'd been no further emails or texts. I had started to hope I could type *incident closed* beneath that humiliating period of my life. I had been busying myself with doing wedding-type things. This included reviewing possible dinner menus, visiting the chocolatier with my mum to look at wedding favours and keeping a fixed grin on my face.

At five o clock on that rainy Boxing Day afternoon my main concern was simply surviving a turkey sandwich tea with my parents. I also had to defend my Trivial Pursuits champion's title. I had been the first to collect all the little coloured pie wedges for five years in a row and I think my dad had been swotting up to mount a challenge. He was always very serious about quizzes. Twice a week, from the age of eight or nine, the world would cease to rotate for thirty minutes while he and I sat together on the sofa and watched *University Challenge* and *Mastermind*, sometimes *Blockbusters*.

I knew my dad had been putting in some serious preparation behind the scenes. How strange it is to think that there was once a world where something like that, winning a quiz, seemed important.

When my phone beeped I thought it would be my mum texting to say they were trapped at Uncle Owen's under an avalanche of mince pies and fruit cake. But this time I recognised the number as soon as I saw it.

It said, 'Your Xmas donation was much appreciated. Another for the New Year. Watch this space.' Fourteen words to end a world, or open a door into a new one.

Nausea surged over me, accompanied by the ding-a-ling of the doorbell. A moment later I heard my mother hallooing Happy Christmas through the letterbox on full volume, the festive spirit party-bright in every syllable.

Oh, dear God! I can't deal with this now. Not now, I screamed inside my head, so hard I felt my eyeballs might burst. This is my *home* and it's *Christmas*. Dan slowly roused himself from the blood-pink waters of Sword or Juno beach and the squashy grip of the armchair, grinning. With mock-seriousness he snapped the book shut and said:

'Well, here we go then, ready for the fray? You've a title to defend, Miss Brainiac.'

'Dan!' I burst out. 'There's something . . . I mean, I don't know if I can . . .'

'Hey, petal,' he soothed, patting my head from his full

standing height as if I were a puppy. 'That's ok. Don't feel the pressure's on. It's just a game.'

'It's not that, you idiot, it's . . . sod the Trivial Pursuits. It's . . .' *Don't say it, don't say it, don't say anything. Don't be a coward,* ordered the voice in my head.

'Hey,' said Dan, gently, pulling me to my feet. 'Don't worry about your mother. I'll get her drunk on Martini Rosso like last year and have her eating out of my hand by seven. She'll be as good as gold.' He gave me a good, solid vice-tight hug, hard muscle and soapy shower smell combining in an overwhelming wall of reassurance.

'I love you, Dan,' I managed to say, squeezing my voice out between my crushed ribs. Make it better for me, just for once. Make it go away for me, I begged, silently.

'Once more unto the breach!' he said theatrically, releasing me and trotting gamely to answer the door. 'Shakespeare and me, you see? Not just a dumb copper.'

'I just need to check my emails,' I muttered.

'Now?' he looked faintly annoyed.

'Just be a minute.'

Sure enough, when I logged on to the PC, a new video was demanding to be viewed. It was the same sequence of film as before but this time it showed my face, a bit blurred, but identifiable to anyone who knew me. I gazed at it in growing disgust, mesmerised by my mouth opening and closing in rhythmic fish-like gasps, approximating wet and wild passion.

'Oscar-worthy performance for the internet? The force website? Price of fame?' it said. 'Drive westbound on the A436, towards Cardiff Airport. January 15th.'

Airport? I was surprised to hear a strangled snort of laughter, then I realised it had come from my mouth. The airport? Oh,

God! What was he going to want me to do this time? Charter a plane? Drop the package over the sand dunes of Ogmore-by-Sea? Parachute it on to the deck of a waiting ship at the dark of the winter moon? Hysteria lurched up into my mouth, a rictus grin stretched my lips back over my teeth. This really was a game now, right?

Downstairs, I could hear my mother layering strangle-hugs and kisses on Dan, then the clink of glasses meeting bottles.

'Where's my daughter, then?' she called, shouting from the approximate area of the living room, diaphragm fully engaged. 'You can't sit up there in the bedroom all afternoon. I've got more presents for you and your lovely hubby, and there's this wedding stuff to show you.'

'Wedding stuff, oh God.'

I hurriedly clicked off the laptop . A moment later she burst in through the spare bedroom door. With the sequins of her smart red Marks and Spencer Christmas cardigan sparkling, she brandished a sheaf of magazines and brochures in one hand, and seemed determined to smother me in a hug with her free arm.

'Look . . . Look at this, Jen,' she said, bubbling excitement from her neat greying hair to her sensible Clarkes pumps. She pointed at the John Lewis and Debenhams glossies. 'This is the dress one, and this is the underwear one. They've got *lovely* 'mother of the bride' stuff too. I might have one of those feathery fascinator things, so much more delicate than a full hat. I've folded down the page for you, for the bride's underwear where they have those lovely bustier things and those "shaping" corsets, maybe even a garter?'

A corset? A garter? Are you insane? I wanted to say. Are these nuptials now in fancy dress? Am I starring in the matrimonial version of the Moulin Rouge? I had a sudden flashback to the time one of the police community support officers had thought it would be hilariously funny, and not at all slutty, to have a Moulin Rouge fancy dress hen party. Cue wandering the pubs of Cardiff, bosoms on shelves, in fishnets and frilly knickers. I had tried to get into the spirit of the thing and turned up as the Master of Ceremonies in a three-piece suit and dickey bow with a top hat.

'Haven't you missed the point a bit, Jen?' asked Allyson the bride-to-be, she and her cleavage jiggling in unison as she bounced on the knee of a meathead she'd met in Wetherspoons.

There was a plastic willy attached to her dress and an L-plate on her back. 'You're so serious, you should have a bit of a laugh, you know. Loosen up. People will think you're a lesbian.'

With my mum now enthusing about weddings and white silk stockings in the same breath I could stand it no more.

'Stockings? Garters? Is this a wedding or a bloody cabaret?' I shouted. 'Will I be expected to do the cancan? Am I a bride or bloody call girl? Can't we have one day off from talking about this bloody wedding nonsense? Christ on a bike, is it all we ever have to talk about? '

'Oh, fine, fine, Miss Grumpy,' said my mother airily. 'I just thought as it is a *special* occasion you might want something *feminine*. I'll leave the brochures for you downstairs. Auntie Anne says she could make the wedding cake, if you like. And let me know when you want to talk about the wedding photos and the wedding video. Uncle Owen's mate does them now. He says he'll do you a good rate.'

Wedding video – no need, I thought. I've got a beautiful little ninety-second highlight right here. I'm sure you and the other guests will *love* it.

I burst into tears again.

'Oh goodness me, Jen, what *is* wrong with you?' she asked good-naturedly. 'Anyone would think you didn't want to get married.'

Patting me on the shoulder (why were people patting me like a bloody poodle all of a sudden?) she beamed at Dan who appeared in the door with a Martini Rosso. It was the one day of the year my mum permitted herself more than one glass of alcohol and he intended her to make the most of it.

'Come and see to your fiancée, officer,' she said, beaming at the very sight of him, as usual. 'She's a bit *highly strung*, because of the *wedding*,' she mouthed in a theatrical whisper, while I just sat there brimming over and gulping the words, 'Can I have a large Jack Daniels, please?'

'Since when do you drink Jack Daniels?' asked Dan, seemingly surprised.

'Since as long as you've known me.'

My dad won the game of Trivial Pursuits.

Chapter Seven

It was 28 December. Doyle, DI Harden and Laura from the Crown Prosecution Service were perched on desks, surrounded by paint pots and chairs under sheets, giving their updates on the voyeurism case for the following Tuesday. I had drafted the media statement, to be approved in advance, so we'd be ready for the inevitable queries as soon as the court sat.

Mr and Mrs Taylor had contacted us the previous February after discovering that their electrician had put a hidden camera in the smoke alarm he'd been asked to fit, right above their bed. He'd been filming the bedroom 'activity' for almost a year using a little transmitter to send the images to his home computer. Their electrician also happened to be their best friend, Rowan, whom they'd known for ten years.

They'd found out by accident when Mr Taylor, responding to the fire service's stern TV pleas to test your smoke alarm now! Don't wait! had been puzzled to find the alarm wouldn't sound.

Rowan had been using the disks 'for his own gratification' and quite possibly sharing some choice clips with one or two close personal friends via email. The Taylors, a prosperous and reserved couple in their early thirties, were naturally mortified. The court date was set for 3 January. CPS Laura said there was a strong probability that Rowan would plead guilty, sparing the Taylors the ordeal of giving evidence at a trial and the necessity of a jury hearing and seeing the evidence.

I'd strongly advised the couple to stay away from the courthouse. As victims of a sexual crime, they'd get anonymity in the press. But the reporters would still know who they were, would badger them for reactions and comments, maybe even ask if they'd like to participate in a 'sensitively written' feature about their 'ordeal' and 'how their trust was betrayed', where they could be photographed or filmed in shadow to protect their identity.

Jack NewsBeatWales had got wind of the case and was already sniffing around for an interview. I had prepared the basic press release to the effect that there'd be no comment.

'Everyone's going to hear about this, aren't they?' said Mrs T, when I briefed them on the media interest and what they should do to minimise it. 'People will know it's us, the people in the court, the lawyers. People locally will know. You know how this sort of thing gets around. They'll all know. You can't imagine what it's like, something so private, so intimate. We thought he was our friend, and all the time . . . Your officers have been marvellous. Detective Ryan and Detective Williams have been so wonderfully considerate and kind. But it's so *humiliating.*'

I felt deeply sorry for her, pale and teary, being comforted by her grim-faced husband, but of course I was mostly thinking about myself and how I could avoid being in the same awful position, how I could stop anyone else ever seeing my own pornographic debut.

I've always thought pornography has an odd place in relationships. Some people want to pretend it doesn't exist, some want to enjoy it quietly, some want to make their own and even show it to their friends. Before I joined the force my knowledge of porn had been limited to one instance after Dan and I moved in together, and we had finally succumbed to the march of progress and had the internet connected at home.

Whenever I poked my head around the study door enquiringly, offering tea or a sandwich for supper, Dan appeared to be looking at police kit or research papers, as he said. But, one day I accidentally clicked on the Google history and the recently browsed sites popped up. A visit to something called 'Homemade Hotties' and one to 'Busty Babes Next Door' were on the list, below 'Mountain Bike Mania' and 'Sportshoe Warehouse'. At that point he hadn't discovered the 'delete search history' tab.

At first I wasn't sure how to react. I had only 'sort of accidentally' clicked on his browsing history. Ok, I'd been poking around to see what he'd been up to, so, even though I was shocked and displeased, I still felt like a snoop. People who listen at keyholes seldom hear good of themselves, I heard my mum's voice say. But I was curious.

Furtively, I'd gone onto the 'Homemade Hotties' site. To my relief, it didn't seem to be anything out of the ordinary, or what I imagined to be out of the ordinary. There were no sadomasochistic rape fantasises or people weeing on each other. In fact it was a bit banal, mostly guys having missionary or rear-entry sex with young, but not too young, pouting girls in crotchless pants and stockings. Despite my involuntary blushes it was unexpectedly educational. I hadn't imagined that double penetration was actually possible.

'Busty Babes' did what it said on the tin, but new to me was the idea that these sites seemed to feature *real* girls on home webcams who 'lived next door'. I remember thinking – they're not even that pretty, and, I'm fitter than her (though less busty).

Also, 'What if your dad saw that, or the milkman?'

I was relieved that at least Dan wasn't a closet pervert. Though energetic, he was a conservative and considerate lover. He'd never asked me to dress as a nurse or a call girl. He'd never even tried to handcuff me, which might have been a logical first step, considering their availability and his profession.

After being shocked for a while I didn't say anything about it. If I had I would have had to admit that I had been peeping into his internet browsing and nosing in his emails. Surely it was a short step from this to rummaging through his pockets and checking his mobile phone every night. If I had to go picking through his private business like Sherlock Holmes with PMT then I had more serious problems than the odd bit of porn. All men do it, I told myself. So even though I would have preferred him not to do it, I tried to be sensible and went back to the business of ignoring its existence.

Now the tables had turned in an alarming way. I wondered if Dan ever went 'accidentally checking' in my emails? What would he say if he saw my video? Or Justin's little updates? Even worse, what if Justin lived up to his threat and emailed it to him, or put it in the public domain somehow – on the force internet, a social networking site or linked it to a chat room?

What if Dan stumbled across my video, on the YouTube equivalent of reader's wives, a 'Homemade Hotties'-type site, and thought, hmmm, that appendicitis scar looks familiar? How would I explain that away? Especially because what we were doing on that video looked far dirtier, more animalistic, than anything I'd done with Dan.

I couldn't hold the moral high ground like the Taylors had. They were an unusual example of this type of case because they had been completely unaware of their situation, and Rowan was clearly guilty. But more often than not, these cases weren't so clear cut and were nothing like as easy to prove.

A suppressed groan would pass between the CID officers when they were handed this type of complaint. I could sense their dread and frustration in the barely perceptible slump of their shoulders, the dip of the chin. It was an acknowledgement that, nine times out of ten, it would be a waste of their already thinly stretched time and manpower, manpower they'd much rather spend out on the streets, tackling drug dealers or arresting the yobs that harassed the local shopkeepers.

Complaints, sadly becoming more and more regular, mostly consisted of calls from unfortunate women who wanted their ex-boyfriends arrested because they'd posted naked mobile phone pictures of them on the office noticeboard, or shared them with their mates in revenge for catching them in bed with someone else. More and more they seemed to involve a woman or girl who had exchanged revealing pictures online with someone she'd met on Facebook, then seemed surprised that these images were doing the rounds among her ex's 'friends'.

Other women had made sex tapes during drunken encounters, only to find they had got into the hands of others, deliberately or accidentally. Most worrying were the reports from distraught mums and dads of teenagers who'd been persuaded to get drunk and take their tops off for all of Year 12 on a bedroom webcam.

The trouble was that, in ninety-nine per cent of these cases, it was a lengthy process to prove who had posted the pictures and that it had been done without consent. Unless, like Mr and Mrs Taylor's mate Rowan, you had the wires and the access, and the warrant turned up trumps with a stack of videos, you were often stuck to the 'he said, she said' statements and one person's word against the other's.

So, dear God, how could I even think of raising my current problem with any police force and hope for a result that would yield anything but utter humiliation?

What if they were to see my starring role in its full-colour glory? My Oscar-worthy performance? I'd wither into dust from shame because, all at once, I'd be another stupid slapper who had got drunk, couldn't keep her knickers on and had been caught out by an opportunist.

Not to Bodie and Doyle, of course, who I knew would fly to my defence if someone so much as looked at me wrong in a pub, but others, other DCs, in other stations, sitting and silently sniggering over the moving image of my round white backside in its gym-shaped but proto-cellulite glory.

I couldn't delude myself it would stay a secret – word always gets around in the force. Not deliberately or maliciously usually, but it would be impossible to keep an investigation like that confidential. Besides, what would I say? What information could I give them to investigate with? The more I thought about it, the more I realised I knew nothing about Justin Reynolds. He didn't seem to exist, so how could he be found and challenged?

The email address he was sending the clips from was just a Yahoo one – accessible through any PC, internet-based. I couldn't remember what had happened that night in the cottage. I had only hazy, fleeting recollections of the actual sex, then waking the next morning with a killer hangover and great blanks in the previous ten hours. That wouldn't inspire sympathy or confidence in the CPS, or anyone else.

It didn't look like anything other than sex on the tape – he obviously wasn't forcing me or anything. Could it be rape by non consent, if I was too drunk to agree? Could it be voyeurism if you were in it? Was it an offence to video or record someone without their consent?

Demanding money was blackmail, of course, but how could I prove that had happened? I didn't have any written or hard evidence. Out of sheer panic that Dan would see what was going on, I'd been systematically deleting the texts and emails. It did cross my mind that I should be saving them, but the idea of them incubating like a virus in my machine, or saved on a memory stick somewhere, felt like a violation. I hadn't wanted their taint anywhere near me.

I had the phone number he'd been texting me on. But it wasn't enough to find a mobile phone, especially if it was a pay-as-you go phone, not a monthly contract. Even if you did, it was difficult to prove who had sent the text.

The same applied to a computer. If even one other person had access to it you could say you knew nothing about it and the onus was on the police to prove you had done it. It works for paedophiles – they use this defence all the time when indecent images are found stored on hard drives.

Even if the police could find Justin, was it worth it to be humiliated? I could never face anyone again without wondering what they'd been told or even if they'd had a preview of my adult debut.

Was it worth it to humiliate myself? To humiliate Dan? Oh, God! Dan would probably leave me, and he would have to leave the force for sure. How could he turn up on a Monday morning and expect to wield any authority, or command respect, after everyone, including the bloke who cleaned the toilets, had seen his slut wife doing it doggy style with another man? Well, it's the quiet ones you have to watch – snigger, snigger.

I thought about for a long time, then I made up my mind. I suppose I just had to do it. I had to find Justin myself and make him listen to me. And make him stop.

Chapter Eight

I waited until the middle of the afternoon when I knew Bodie would be in the afternoon briefing. I'd already tried to sneak into the CID room twice that day but DI Dai Hard had been in there, typing what appeared to be an interminably thorough witness statement. Each time I'd checked I just ended up waving at him through the open door and strolling by. But when I walked past at 2 p.m. the room was empty.

I hovered in the deserted corridor for a few moments, making sure no one was nearby. There was no sound of voices approaching, no crescendo of footsteps or chatter.

It had taken me twenty-four hours to pluck up the courage to try and do what I intended to do. Notebook in hand, I counted backwards in my head from ten to one, an old habit for readying myself. On the zero I slipped inside and seated myself at the computer. Sure enough the system was switched on, and Bodie's PNN session was open. It was not security locked, despite Dan's warning and my warning, and no doubt countless other people's warnings.

This is how it works. Officers have passwords for the Police National Network. It contains details of anyone who has been convicted of an offence or involved in one. Because Bodie had logged in with his own password, I didn't need to enter a password again to run a check, which was just as well because I didn't have a password. Civilian staff are not meant to have access to the PNN unless they work specifically with offenders, but from Bodie's machine I could run a search and it would not show on my ID. Jennifer Johnson, Force Number 2234 was still innocently logged on to her own machine upstairs, in the press office, exactly where she should be.

Even if you had a password you needed a specific reason to conduct PNN searches. I would not have a good reason to run a random search for Justin Reynolds, just as I'd have no good reason to look up my neighbour out of curiosity because he played loud music at night or had screaming rows with his wife.

PNN information is confidential under the Data Protection Act, and the force was absolutely paranoid about it. Though the odds were against getting caught fiddling about where you had no business, there were random checks. People had been disciplined for misuse and sometimes fired. I knew of one officer who had searched a street where he wanted to buy a house, checking the neighbours, looking for anti-social behaviour hotspots. Another had looked up his seventeen-year-old daughter's would-be boyfriend to check he wasn't a psychopath masquerading as an unassuming apprentice paramedic. Both had been quietly 'asked to move on'. Others had even ended up in court, one with a suspended jail sentence.

But I told myself I didn't have much choice. I had to find Justin Reynolds. His address and contact details might be inside the machine, ready to spring out at me at the touch of the keys. A search under Bodie's ID, Marc Ryan: Force Number 89963, would give it to me, and if I was quick and cool no one need know.

I typed in the name. In a minute or so I'd know if Justin Reynolds had ever been in trouble with the police. Briskly, alert for any approaching feet in the hall, I clicked *execute*, and the little egg timer began to whir along with my quickening pulse. I tried to slow down my breathing.

It seems odd now that I worried so much about this little bit of technical law breaking, but at the time it was the most illegal thing I'd ever done. I'd never even left a restaurant without pointing out they hadn't charged me for the second bottle of wine or had forgotten to include the price of the dessert. I didn't have a speeding ticket or a single point on my driving licence. I'm not sure this official lily-whiteness was directly down to unbridled honesty on my part. Probably it was more to do with the fear of being challenged or the embarrassment of getting caught. But in this case I considered it an emergency, and worth the risk.

The computer was processing very slowly, as was often the case. The longer it took the more jumpy I became. I felt sure my heart was bombulating like a gong that would call every officer and staff member on the floor to the scene of my transgression. But the corridor remained step-free.

After a minute or two the computer pinged and the search field flashed up negative. Negative? Nothing! Damn it! So Justin had no criminal record. Next stop NOMAD – the local list of incidents and calls logged throughout the force area each day. Unlike the PNN it holds contact details for every car theft, assault or complaint about anti-social behaviour within the force boundary. The caller's details would be recorded, as would the victim of the crime (the 'injured person' or IP) and any witnesses and suspects, even if it had never got as far as an arrest or a court appearance.

I had my own password for NOMAD. I needed to be able

to find information to update the journalists when they called with queries. But again, our searches were supposed to be confined to work-related issues. I put in Justin's name. The egg timer whirred again as I glanced at the door, hoping no one in sneakers was approaching stealthily, preparing to leap upon me.

Bugger! The search was also negative. Justin Reynolds had not made any complaints to the police. He had never reported a car theft, a burglary or a lost wallet. He had never been spoken to as a witness to a crime or received a penalty ticket for parking or speeding.

Last chance – the DVLA database link. Again, the slow, agonising hum of fibre-optic thinking stretched my nerves to snapping point. *Negative.* There was no vehicle registered to Justin Reynolds anywhere in the UK. There was no registered address for him in the police area.

I sat back, puzzled. This didn't *definitely* mean he wasn't living in the area, of course, just that he'd never come to police attention, been the victim of a crime or legally owned a car. Or more likely, as I'd begun to suspect, that he was here somewhere but had given me a false name. If I was going to try and commit blackmail, I wouldn't be daft enough to use my real name either. And it would explain why there was no trail, no sign of him. Everyone casts some sort of electronic shadow, it's unavoidable.

Hurriedly, I closed the applications, cancelled the search session and restored the screen to Bodie's last official search. With a quick check of the corridor I scuttled back to the press office, exhaling with relief that I had not been caught, but also angry that I'd been defeated at so early a stage in my search, when I was sure it would yield something useful.

Who are you Justin, and where are you tonight? I thought.

Though at this rate I knew where he'd be on 15 January. Somewhere near Cardiff Airport, driving off with another envelope full of my money.

That night was mine and Dan's ninth anniversary – nine years since we'd met. I could hardly believe it. The specific day was actually two weeks earlier but Dan had been on a full set of double shifts then. We'd shunted it forward and now I had to endure enforced nostalgia on the worst night of the year – New Year's Eve.

Our anniversary was always a delicate time. I would spend agitated weeks wondering if Dan would, maybe this year, whisk me away on a surprise treat or finally buy me something I wouldn't have to hide my disappointment over when I opened it. Sometimes he'd double up and combine an anniversary and a Christmas present, which irritated me on principle. I felt cheated, as I imagine children whose birthdays fall around Christmas feel when they receive only one set of gifts.

It wasn't so much the amount he spent that mattered, but I wanted him to think I was worth the effort, worth a bit of thought to make a present personal, even if it was just a £5 book of poetry. That year I'd bought him a rather smart leather wallet to replace his battered one.

This time I was actually quite pleased with the lace trimmed silky pyjamas he bought me. Clearly, since the Watch-house mission of recovery, he was raising his game, showing he'd paid attention to my grumbles and was trying to adapt. Hence the accompanying attempt to 'do' the whole romantic dinner thing as well. Of course he'd left it too late to book us a table in a restaurant anywhere. But he'd cooked me a meal with dessert and bought wine. He'd laid the table properly, with tablecloth and place mats, and lit some tea light candles in an attempt to create a romantic ambience. The lamb was a bit overdone, and the potatoes were steam-in-the-packet from Sainsbury's, but since it was the first meal he'd cooked in years, I was touched.

It's not as if *I'm* a whizz in the kitchen. I mean, I always made a dinner for him every night. I used to boil potatoes and roast chicken or fish, steam vegetables, even stretch to the odd curry and stir fry, but nothing fancy. Dan had never complained, though. He ate anything I put in front of him, and always said it was great. So this time I followed his example and confined myself to compliments.

'I know things haven't always been the way you wanted but I will try from now on,' he assured me. 'Try to be a bit more romantic. You know I love you to death, I just sometimes forget to be organised enough to do something to show it. Work is so crazy. I'm just rubbish at multitasking like you. That's not an excuse, it's my failing, but I'm working on it.'

It was a shame all I could think about was the message from Justin about the upcoming money drop. It arrived by text as Dan was serving up the raspberry panna cotta. '£250. Head for the airport. 7 p.m.. Wait for my instructions.'

The rest of that night saw the performance of my lifetime. I was the perfect girlfriend – grateful and pleased and without a concern in the world. We'd promised to pop in to the New Year's Eve party in Gee Gees bar, where most of the not-on-duty coppers would be, before making a hasty retreat to the pub by ourselves. But how I immediately wished I would not have to spend the rest of the night looking at Dan's cheery face, knowing I was lying to him in so many ways.

It was also the worst party I had ever been to. Everyone was really drunk and having a great time. There was a lot of boisterous dancing and pawing at each other in the dark sticky corners that Gee Gees was known for. Detective Superintendent Sue Sellers cornered me in the loos to tell me, in a drunken, throaty slur that I was damned lucky to have a bloke like Dan.

I had never wanted to be out of anywhere so badly, away from the people laughing and screaming, bumping groins and locking lips, under stupid New Year's Eve hats trailing tinsel and glitter. I wanted to be in a quiet corner of an old fashioned pub with Dan, drinking and talking and laughing like we used to when we first met.

So we headed for the Old Station pub before midnight and squeezed into a booth next to a man dressed as Ronald McDonald and a woman dressed as Batgirl. When the countdown reached zero and the jukebox rattled out 'Auld Lang Syne', Dan, buoyed by a few pints of Brains, grabbed me in a firm hug, took my face in his hands, as he used to when we were fledgling lovers, and said, 'We're going to be all right now, Jen. I know it. We've come this far and we'll never let anything get in our way again.' Then he kissed me gently, with infinite tenderness.

All at once I found myself clinging to him to hide the fact that I was cracking open inside, suffocating from holding back a now familiar sea of tears.

Later, I was curled up in bed in Dan's arms. Snow had begun to fall. He nuzzled into my neck like he often did saying, 'I've missed this. This is the best bit of the day. Of any day. Happy New Year, my love.'

In moments he was asleep. I lay awake for many hours, but I didn't want to move from his circle of warmth.

Late the next day, while Dan reluctantly went to work for the afternoon shift, beer-groggy and still sleepy, I took my car to Porthcawl. I had fifteen days before the next payment was due. Fifteen days to try and find Justin, make him listen to reason, face to face.

While lying awake, listening to Dan's slow and contented breathing, I had decided to try something a little more hands-on than computer searches and Google. I had begun to realise that I *did* know several things about Justin that I hadn't taken into account, things he and other people had said that weekend at the Watch-house.

Constantly working on the phone and dealing with comments, quotes and facts, meant I was uncannily good at remembering conversations, what people had said to me and what I had said in return. When it's a matter of law or of someone's public reputation, your information has to be accurate. Also being around police officers had given me an advantage. I knew how to process the information by doing what they did – asking questions and methodically working through the possibilities provided by the answers.

In other words, I decided to start treating the business of finding Justin like a press officer (or a police officer), not like a victim. I didn't want to be a victim. I'd dealt with enough of those.

I took stock of what I knew. I'd met Justin at The Watch-house in Penallt, in the Gower. He'd told me to take a train to Swansea for the first cash payment. The looming money drop at the airport in the Vale of Glamorgan, outside Cardiff, suggested a general area of familiarity at least, a sort of turf triangulation. More than that, Justin had said he was a surfer. He had mentioned the seaside town of Porthcawl once or twice that night at the pub, and Carl, the Sherpa-hat surfer dude had said his 'Beast' board was made in Porthcawl. Everyone loved the Beast, right? Maybe everyone wanted one.

If Justin was a surfer, might he not be following the waves too? There was a hard-core surfing crowd at several beaches in Porthcawl where the tides were notoriously high – the second highest tidal range in the world, in fact, second only to North America's Bay of Fundy, or so I'd read somewhere.

Justin also drove a distinctive van, didn't he? A surfer van with a painting of a shark on it? Carl had said so.

These were slight tapering threads on the tail of a probable long shot but it was worth a try. I had to start somewhere, or sit back and wait for Justin for take my money, or worse. I kept telling myself, over and over, that this approach was logical and sensible. I think I genuinely believed I could get him to listen to reason, or make him take pity on me, prick his conscience. Either way I knew I needed to be face to face with him at least once more – to pull out what had happened between us and untangle it all, in the open, where I could try to understand it, shape some sense out of it.

Porthcawl's Coney Beach looked more tired than usual in the low, grey light of the January lunchtime. As I pulled up on the promenade it seemed to be suffering a New Year's Day hangover like everyone else. Last night's snow had died out after a few flurries. The sky was heavy and grey, but it was dry.

The tide was full in on the big sweep of sand, bounded at the far end by the headland known as 'the point' with its cement lifeguard tower. The pleasure park and fairground idled in the foreground, a faded, peeling, former splendour of carnival colours washed out by the rain. The flags still streaming from the turrets at the top of the rickety rollercoaster, and Big Bump Super Slide, were rag-edged and stained, whispering remnants of dimly remembered sun-bright summers.

I walked along the prom, past the pepper-pot lighthouse on the sea wall, standing stubbornly against the wind-whipped sky above and the coffee-froth breakers below. Six seagulls, fat with feather-fluffing, huddled by the steps to the beach, waiting to peck children and steal snacks. There were only a few tourists on this forlorn New Year's Day, cupping teas and sugary doughnuts in the lee of Dolly's Tea Cabin, shouting at children to watch out for the puddles and the patches of ice.

It was a far cry from the fond memories of seaside trips when my family got together for high-energy social chaos on the beach. The memory was warm, even in the freezing-cold breeze. First a scratchy blanket and stripy windbreak would stake out the territory, then Uncle Owen would be in charge of cooking the sausages on a primus stove, and slapping them, steaming hot, into finger rolls. Auntie Non and Nanna Jenkins would sit in their deckchairs, still in their support tights and wrap-around cardigans, despite the thick shimmer of summer heat, complaining contentedly to one another. Once they had tea and biscuits inside them stories of their teenage times 'in service', in the big boarding schools on the south coast of England, would trickle out. These tales always contained doodle bugs and cheeky American airmen called Joe or Brad, unpleasant poker-backed matrons, polishing brass, baking bread and lighting enormous and temperamental cooking ranges.

Nanna's tall, exotic tales, delivered through slurps of weak tea, could last long into the afternoon. Even at the age of nine or ten, Nanna's life had seemed exciting and just a bit risqué to me, because she had had quite a lot of boyfriends by the sound of it, and each one had bought her wonderful presents, frivolous and impractical gifts that had to be bought *for* you, a testament to your exoticism, like a hat with fancy red cherries on it, or an alligator-skin handbag with a diamanté clip.

Dan had bought me a North Face rucksack one Christmas – I used it for the gym.

'More nanny, tell me more stories,' I would coax, cross-legged and rapt on the sand.

Now, above where we used to sit, where the sandbanks once swelled above the high-tide line, a clutch of burger vans and a pinball arcade squatted on a recently added concrete walkway. Sure enough, despite the cold, there were about half a dozen hard core surfers in all-season suits, booties and black beanie caps, floating in the water in front. Occasionally one or two would pick up a peeling breaker, leaving the rest bobbing like big black seals in the swell. A short line of candy-coloured camper vans were parked up at the sand edge on the double yellow lines.

I drew in a vast, cold breath and tried to steel myself. I eyed the vans keenly to see if I recognised any of the people hovering around, making a subtle pass, first down one side of the walkway and then the other. None of them bore a shark painting or motif, though. I suppose that would have been far too easy.

A bunch of smiley young surfer dudes were gathered round, sipping coffee and eating hotdogs, still in their wetsuits and woolly hats. I supposed I had to start somewhere. I'd come prepared to ask questions, even if I wasn't sure what else I was prepared for.

Striking up conversations with strangers in person, without the buffer of press officer or official spokesperson, was largely virgin territory for me. I was an ace on the phone, of course. I could ask all sorts of questions then. It's much easier to stay calm and firm when shielded from view and judgement. I was used to taking cues from people's voices, reading inflections and tone to placate or insist. But there was always a prescribed pattern of professional behaviour to adhere to and limits to what you could say or do.

This was different. I was making it up as I was going along and had almost decided to give it up entirely. Then I thought of that video. Something clarified in the front of my brain and solidified in my chest. I counted down from ten to one. I clenched my hands, let out a breath and identified the young man who looked like the alpha surf-dude among the group.

He was easy to spot, sitting cross-legged in the open back door of the camper van, wetsuit unzipped to his waist, a woolly hoody over his top half. His hair was so summer-blond and elegantly surf-streaky I immediately suspected he used Sun-in highlights, or something similar, to get the carefully balanced, careless effect.

One of the other lads was handing him a hot drink and a chocolate digestive, which he accepted as if he was used to such services. Two other lads were cross-legged on the kerb, laughing while he related some surf adventure, no doubt. They looked like the kind of healthy, wealthy, wiry students or postgrads who were probably public-school educated. Their camper van was pristine – a recent two-tone cream and blue model with all the trimmings. I didn't know much about cars, but even I could spot a tonne of money on four wheels.

'Excuse me, guys,' I heard a relaxed voice say. 'Sorry to bother you, but I'm trying to track down an old mate. Don't suppose you know a bloke called Justin Reynolds, do you? He surfs down here, so he said.'

King Surfer interrupted his story and fixed a beatifically white and welcoming smile on me. That was some expensive dental work. I realised he wasn't very old, twenty-one or twenty-two maybe.

'Hello, hello,' he said. 'And who is the lucky guy that has you searching him out?'

I was right about the public school bit. He had so many plums in his mouth he was practically dribbling jam.

'Just an old friend,' I said neutrally. For all I knew they could be Justin's best mates. He might be in the van now, out of sight, pulling off his wetsuit or getting a hotdog from one of the kiosks.

'An old friend, or an old *friend*?' said Surf King, with a meaningful twinkle in his eye.

'Let's just say I lost his phone number,' I replied, with an attempted twinkle of my own (Oh that was good, I thought – flirty, non-committal. I'd surprised myself, pleasantly. My confidence surged a little.)

'You can have my number instead, if it makes you feel better,' he offered, with another flash of the high-wattage smile. I couldn't help wishing I'd been that unselfconscious, that sure of my entitlement to my place in the world, when I was his age. Or right then, for that matter. *Don't spoil it by blushing like an imbecile*, I said to myself as I felt heat rising to my cheeks, but hopefully it passed as the glow from the winter wind.

'Well that's the best offer I've had today,' I rejoined, as playfully as I could.

'Stick around, the day is young,' said one of the other wetsuits on the kerb, grinning shyly, prompting alpha-surfer to chuck his booties at him. Everyone chuckled pleasantly.

'Well, how welcome you're making me feel,' I said. 'But I do need to find him. Justin Reynolds? '

'Sorry angel, don't recognise the name,' said the king. The others shook their heads. 'Does he owe you money or something?'

'No, he doesn't owe me money. I'd just like to look him up.

He's got a lovely old camper van, old fashioned one. Maybe you've seen it? Has a great shark painted on the side?'

I drew the line at saying a 'rad' van/shark like Carl had. There was only so much pretending I thought I could pull off. I hadn't seen the painting myself, but on a hunch, thinking of Carl's surfboard, I added, 'Lots of swirly flowers round it, like Hawaiian flowers or something. Don't suppose you've seen it?'

'Sorry, not ringing any bells. You surf round here? Don't think I've seen you. You must go up to Rest Bay then, right? With the out-of-town crowd?'

I'd worn my jeans, Converse trainers and one of Dan's semi-surfer looking fleece jackets he used for hiking on holiday. I'd put on a bobble hat and the surfer wrist beads I'd bought in Gower. When I planned this information-gathering exercise I had wanted to look like the kind of person who hung out at the beach, who might spend time catching a few waves, the sort of person who might have an entirely innocent reason for searching out a surfer and his van.

'Sure,' I heard myself lie, 'though just a beginner, really, a year or so. I was up at Rest Bay earlier but it was closed out today, too bleeding cold anyway.' *Closed out?* That seemed like a stroke of instinctive genius, even as I spoke the words. I'd just heard a surfer chick say it to her friend, on the walk over from my car. I didn't know what it meant – but it popped out as confidently as if I'd said I was popping into Sainsbury's to buy a loaf of bread. I waited to see if I'd put my foot in my mouth and lit a giant neon 'faker' sign over my head without saying 'rad,' but the king just grinned and said:

'Yeah, it's dropped off down here too now, no good rides. It's nobbling as well. Me and the crew stayed in till our gonads were like blueberries and then bolted.' The crew chuckled a bit. Then I spotted a beautiful painting of a whale on his surfboard, propped upright against the driver's door of the van. It looked to be in the same style as Carl's 'Beast', florid pattern and all. He saw me looking.

'You like my whale?'

'Definitely. My mate Carl has got one like that, only his is a shark.'

'Yeah, I know that dude, that's Carl from Penallt, yeah?' He couldn't quite get his tongue around the Welsh pronunciation of the double 'l'. 'He loves his boards, man. Bit flaky, but the older dudes are. Too much . . .' he mimed the universal smoking gesture, while approximating a stoned expression. 'He's taken so much shit he's California dreamin' all the time. Gotta take it easy – pace yourself, I say.'

'Know what you mean. Gotta keep it in check,' the surf chick now inhabiting my mouth said.

'You are right,' said the pavement suits, nodding ruminatively.

'You, er, get your whale in Nottage too? Carl got his in Nottage, he said. Think I'd like to get one for my board.'

'Yeah, Santos in Nottage does all the great ink. He'd do you a cool one, just make sure you haggle, man. He thinks he's an artist. You can't have a whale though – that's mine.'

As if used to explaining why there was a monopoly on whales, one of the pavement lads pointed to his boss and said, 'Jonah'.

His companion pointed at the board and said, 'And the whale.'

'But this time I ride the whale, it don't swallow me, you see?'

'Your name's Jonah?' Christ on a bike, definitely too rich for his own good, I thought. Bet Mummy and Daddy wish you'd get a haircut, and a job.

'Hey,' continued Jonah, 'Maybe Santos knows your shark van guy. He does quite a lot of sharks.'

You don't say? I thought. So there is a light on in there after all. After a bit more flirting, I was getting into it now, relaxing. This investigative business wasn't so hard after all. Jonah wrote down the information about Santos and directions to his surf shop.

'Don't suppose you wanna do some weed, do you?' he said languidly, handing me the piece of paper.

Do I look like I might want to do some weed? I thought. Really? Cannabis is still illegal, you know, it's up to five years for possession, fifteen for dealing, and it messes with your head, said the press officer struggling with the surf chick. 'I'm great, thanks,' came out of my mouth.

'Don't suppose you want to sell us any grass, then?' he twinkled.

'Sorry, I'm, er . . . I'm out.'

'Yeah, that's cool. Never mind.'

I turned to make my exit. 'Cheers, fellas, see you again.' But Jonah called me back.

'Hope you find your man. But just in case . . .' He gave me another slip of paper with a mobile phone number scrawled on it. Cheeky bugger, I thought, rather flattered. I accepted it with a smile.

Strolling back up the prom to my car, I was quite pleased with the way the little encounter had gone. It had been easier than I'd expected. I was a bit shocked by my apparently natural instinct for convincing lying but no one had ever given me their phone number before, so that was rather nice. Buoyed by my performance, I jumped back in the car and headed straight to Santos's place in Nottage, five minutes down the coast, on the trail of the shark painting.

Santos's shop was situated next to the greengrocer's, in the tiny row of shops behind the picture-perfect village green, with its Norman church and single storey Georgian-fronted pub. Dan and I had been there once, seeking a quiet drink on a balmy August evening, after a day trip to nearby Ogmore-by-Sea.

Ogmore has the largest natural sand dune system in Europe, and with the sun shining, and Dan not working a Saturday for once, he had suggested we take a walk and explore them.

Dear God, it was a hot, sweaty, grit-in-the-eyes three hours of up and down effort. I'm not averse to outdoor exercise – I'd even walked up Pen Y Fan, the highest peak in the Brecon Beacons with Dan once, and enjoyed it. But it was twenty-six degrees on that August day and I really fancied sitting in a café bar somewhere, in sight of the sea, sipping a cold white wine.

Dan, however, had been working three weekends in a row so it seemed only fair to let him have his wish to 'get some air in our lungs and some daylight for a change'.

He had come prepared with a full rucksack, toted easily on his broad back, filled with sun cream and sun hats and, to my surprise, very welcome cans of cold Orange Tango in a coolie bag. (He knew it was the only soft drink I drank, but only rarely, because it's bad for insulin levels and for the teeth.)

Still intent on getting my glass of wine before the end of the day, we headed over to the Squire in Nottage before the drive home. Dan had a Coke because he was driving. But our visit had coincided with the annual local lifeguard clubs' Aussie barbecue party event. The village green was swarming with buff guys in hula shirts and Hawaiian shorts, good-naturedly clinking Fosters cans together and shouting g'day to each other.

A freakishly tanned guy, with a pair of DJ headphones

bisecting his woolly sun-whitened afro, was playing a mixture of the Beach Boys and ravey club tracks from a set of mobile decks on the back of the surf rescue truck.

'Jesus, are we still in Wales or have I got heat stroke?' said Dan irritably.

We left after just one drink. I'd thought it would be quite good fun for a summer's evening, well at least for an hour. I wanted to stay and watch the dancing and maybe even drink a can of cold lager, lying on the grass with my shoes off. But Dan was convinced that the combination of beer and sun would result in fighting.

I recognised Santos as the barbecue DJ as soon as I walked into the shop. He still had the wild, whitened afro and Ronseal tan. The shop walls were filled with amazing shots of guys cresting terrifyingly large but terrifyingly beautiful waves, not quite like the silty estuary waves around Porthcawl, but there's nothing to stop a guy dreaming. The floor space was filled with expensive wetsuits and Billabong and Reef casual clothing. Through to the back there was a separate room stacked with surfboards of all sizes and colours.

'Hey, babe,' called Santos. 'What can I do ya for?'

It occurred to me that I had been called babe, sweetheart, angel, darling and God knows what else, by more strangers in the last few weeks than ever before in my life. Ordinarily, I didn't like it. I had a name and I liked people to use it. But I chose to take these honorifics as pleasant rather than patronising, the friendly feminine equivalent of 'mate'. Inspector Karen Smart was the only person I knew who called women or girls mate. I rather liked it when she did.

'Happy New Year!' beamed Santos.

'And to you,' I beamed back. Close up, I could see he was older than I'd expected – early fifties, maybe. He was perched on a stool by the till, drawing something on an A4 sketch pad. I could see familiar swirling flowers and leaves and a busty looking female in a hula skirt taking shape.

'Can I help you with anything, then?'

'Actually I'm looking for you.'

'Oh, what trouble am I in now? Do I owe you money?' He smiled.

What is it with these guys and owing money? I thought. 'No, I'm interested in your designs, actually. I'm looking to get something done and someone recommended you.'

'Who was that, then?'

'It was bloke I met down in Gower. You did his camper van for him. A shark? He said you'd remember. Maybe you'd do something like it for me?'

Santos thought for a moment. 'Yeah, I remember, blue and white VW, right? He's been in a few times. Don't do many vans, mostly boards. That was tricky but it was one of my best pieces. Paul something, his name was, but I told him not to go blabbing it round. See, I run a surf shop. The artwork is just a favour for a few friends, you know. If I was getting *paid* for artwork I'd have to declare it to the tax man.'

'Oh, I see,' I said, cottoning on. 'Might you consider doing me a favour, then?'

'Well, I'd have to know you better first, lovely. We're not *friends* are we?'

A small silence threatened to expand and push me out of the shop. Just as I was trying to think of how I could ask about Justin (or was it Paul?) without seeming too obviously nosey, Santos casually slipped an A4 sheet of paper out of the back of his artist pad and slid it across the counter. It had a little chart on it with a price written next to a sample design. I moved to take it but he kept his fingers on it and shook his head. Clearly it was for viewing in-shop only.

'Friend of mine does these, though,' he continued. 'He's the er . . . *professional* artist. If you were interested he might be able to do you a deal, if I set you up.'

'Right,' I said, nodding exaggeratedly. 'I might like that.'

He winked. 'Great, anything else then? Special on sex wax today.' To my relief he plonked a pink cake of surfboard wax in front of me.

'Cheers, but I'm all waxed up.' That was the surf chick again, rallying to the call.

He grinned. His look still managed to convey the sentiment, 'You don't know one end of a surfboard from the other, do you sweetie?' but he didn't seem to mind that. I got the impression there wasn't much that Santos minded.

'Say, I don't suppose you kept contact details for Paul, did you, seeing as he's a mate?'

'No, lovely, I'm not big on paperwork. Why?'

'He said he might be thinking about selling his van. He gave me his mobile number, but God knows where I put it,' I shrugged my shoulders in an 'I'm such a bimbo' gesture.

'Sorry,' he began, but then rethought, and fished about in the counter drawer. 'Hold on, you might be in luck.' He pulled out a loose page of a notepad that carried what appeared to be an illegible scrawl. 'That's right. *Now* I remember. He's coming back a week Friday afternoon to collect his new surfboard. Ordered it a few weeks ago for some big trip abroad he's off on, lucky bastard. Newquay's the furthest I get nowadays.'

My heart spasmed. It couldn't be that simple could it? 'He's coming here to settle up next Friday,' I repeated.

'Nooo, to get the board. I get the money up front nowadays

– not daft, am I? There's lots of Shysters out there. Half their brains are fucked on weed. That's not what it's supposed to be about. It's about the wave, right? You know what I mean.'

I nodded in wholehearted agreement. 'Well, thanks Mr Santos. I'll have a think about the, er . . . friend's stuff.'

He laughed. 'It's just Santos love, not Mr Santos. My last name's Protheroe. 'Course, technically my first name is Don, but it hasn't really got the right *vibe*, has it? Been Santos since Hawaii, 1976. By the way, have one of these.' He handed me a business card from his pocket with 'Don's Disco' written on it. 'Never know when you might need a mobile disco. I do weddings, pub nights, golden weddings. Classic rock, dance, golden oldies. Anything like that, Santos is your man.'

'You do discos too?'

'Yeah, for the extra cash. There's better money in it than this, unfortunately. We all need the green eventually. My boy wants to go to uni in Swansea next year,'

'Really?' I was surprised at the thought of Santos having a son who wanted to study at uni.

'Don't they do that new degree in surfing down there?' I offered clumsily, for something to say.

'Yeah, that's really taking the piss, isn't it? A bloody surfing *degree*! But Dean wants to do law and not be a fuck-up like his old man. Who can blame him? Let me know if you want the ink.'

Friday. The word echoed in my head as I waved goodbye. Justin was collecting his board next Friday.

That was still ten days away. Somehow I'd have to force myself to wait again. And find an excuse to leave work and be there on that Friday afternoon.

Chapter Nine

'So, I said to the old witch, for God's sake, she's only little. Give her a chance to acclimatise. She looked at me like I was dirt but I'm not having that old bag tell me my daughter has behavioural problems.' Becky was on a roll and it would have been foolish to try and impede her forward momentum, so I stayed silent.

In addition to having boyfriend trouble, my friend Beck was now also having some trouble with Izzy, her three-and-a-half-year-old. Izzy had started school in September and was still not very happy about it. She couldn't seem to grasp the fact that it was a permanent arrangement – well, as permanent as I imagine anything is to a three-year-old, even one as startlingly bright as Izzy. She continued to cry and cling to Beck's legs every Monday morning with alarming determination, as Beck was explaining at length while trailing her hand wistfully along the dubious silk and taffeta confections frothing out of every corner of the Beautiful Brides gallery (note *gallery*, not shop, as the over-solicitous assistant had emphasised on arrival).

It was a Thursday, so I assumed Izzy had been deposited successfully at school for today at least. Not that I don't like Izzy. She's funny. She has mad, curly red hair like her mum and asks awkward questions far beyond her years. She came to mine and Dan's house with Beck around her third birthday. Our house, being old and Victorian, and belonging to two housework-avoiding, childless people, was clean enough but hideously un-child friendly. As soon as Izzy set foot over the door it seemed to be precipitously full of sharp, sticking-out, eye-endangering edges, wobbly shelves, dubious wiring and radiators missing valves ticking away at third-degree burn level. Basically everything that we never quite got around to adding to the fix-up list.

It also had absolutely no toys. Izzy hadn't minded, though. She'd sat in a very grown-up fashion on the lounge armchair, eating some Parma violets left over from trick-or-treat visits at Halloween and putting knots in the fringe of my scarf.

Since the wedding invitations had gone out I was doing my best to involve Becky (and Izzy) in the planning for the big day. I'd just bought her coffee and cake in town and given her my best advice to temper Stephen's seeming addiction to online poker. If truth be told, I felt I was constantly making up to Becky for past transgressions in our friendship, mainly my less than helpful reaction when she had told me she was pregnant with Izzy.

She had been twenty-five at the time. David, her on-off boyfriend was a complete idiot. He was what my mum would call 'shiftless,' my dad would call 'bone idle', and the epitome of the 'currently between jobs, I'm trying to find myself' postgrads that Dan despised.

David worked in the ticket kiosk at the Chapter Arts Centre and cinema in Canton in Cardiff and wore a lot of black and army surplus clothes. Beck said he wrote poetry and was making a short film about the bittersweet life of an alcoholic guitar genius who lived in the back of Cardiff Central bus station.

When Beck said she was pregnant, only eight weeks after they'd started 'dating', my instant reaction was, 'Christ on a bike, aren't you on the pill?' and then 'Do you want me to come with you to the doctor, help you arrange it?'

She'd stared at me as if I'd just said I was intending to climb the north face of the Eiger naked. 'No, I'm keeping it, Jen!' she replied firmly, when her astonishment subsided.

I'd been dumbstruck. It hadn't even occurred to me that she wouldn't have an abortion. 'Are you nuts?' I'd blurted. 'You've said yourself, David is a tosser! You can't have a baby. You live with your mum.'

'Lots of people are still living with their mums after uni,' she said defensively. 'You live in a council house.'

'Yeah, well, we do own it.'

'What about your career?' Becky had got a job at the newspaper obituary office after uni to raise some money while supposedly looking for a job in event planning. But she'd never actually got around to looking.

'I'll get maternity leave,' said Beck, as if I were a moron. She made it all sound so simple, so practical.

'But Beck, what does David say?'

'Dunno, he's upped and gone. Said something about going to Brighton to make a documentary about gay modern art.'

'Well then, you can't keep the baby, Beck.'

'Jesus, Jen, lots of people are single parents. Not everyone's doing an interesting job and living in a nice house with a great guy like you. It's not like I planned it, but I can't get an abortion. I can't do it.'

Is that how she sees me? I thought. My great guy? My great job? My desirable life?

'Why not? Why can't you get an abortion?' I maintained.

'You're not Catholic. Do you really want to raise a shiftless, artsy-fartsy poet-child in Newport?'

I can't believe I actually said that to her, about the artsy fartsy poet-child. I think I said it because I wanted to shock her into accepting that having a baby at twenty-five was a truly terrible idea.

I wasn't sure why I was quite so horrified. It wasn't as if she was fifteen. And her mum's council house *was* very nice. It had a Habitat-style kitchen and a roomy double garage.

I suppose I just thought she was letting the side down early. I had thought we shared a vision of the future that didn't include being single mums or living with our parents when we were approaching twenty-six.

A baby for God's sake! I just didn't seem to have that tick-tock baby-clock countdown that everyone talked about. I had a vague notion of maybe hearing it 'when I was older' and was perfectly happy to be vague. Just like getting married, it would happen one day, of its own accord.

'I hope I can get married one day,' moped Beck, now pulling another floor-length, ivory thing with a tulle train and a skirt you could hide a family of four under, off the rack. 'Not everyone can be as lucky as you and catch a Dan.'

'If you don't put that back right now I'm going to strangle you with that tulle, Becky Benton,' I said with mock seriousness. 'You are being no help at all. I *told* you, something plain and simple.'

'Ok, Bridezilla,' laughed Beck. 'But for that I think we're in the wrong shop.'

'Gallery,' I corrected with over-inflected gravitas.

My smile was fixed in place, my manner light, but my heart was sinking. I had hated the sight of every wedding dress in every one of the six shops we'd visited that afternoon. I had known I would. I didn't believe Beck would understand why. Yes, I had my man, my enviable fiancé. But did I want him enough? Was what the future offered enough? Why was I so ungrateful? Would Justin ruin everything anyway, long before I got the chance to say 'I do'?

'Let's blow this joint,' said Beck. 'I want pizza.'

I want it to be tomorrow, I thought. Tomorrow I have a date with a certain surfer at the seaside.

But tomorrow took forever to emerge from the long haul of that shopping session. There was also a great deal of empty time after Beck departed at 8 p.m. I filled it as best as I could going through the motions of routine, showering, ironing clothes, taxing Dan's car online because he'd forgotten to do it, *again*, and all the while thinking what I would say to Justin if he emerged from Santos's shop in twelve hours' time and we were face to face once more.

The urge to see him had become almost unbearable. The energy that I'd felt between us had been real, hadn't it? Surely he couldn't just have felt nothing at all? Even in the light of what had happened since, that feeling had been real – it must have been, or why did I do what I did?

I wanted to believe it was all a mistake, a misunderstanding. If I could *talk* to Justin there'd be an explanation. There was always the faintest chance that the texter and emailer wasn't Justin at all, wasn't there? What if he was as innocent as me? What if he knew nothing about the whole thing? It could be some other nutter, right? Some other guy had made the tape and taken the money? I mean, the CID had just dealt with a case of a landlord who'd put cameras in his holiday rental cottage to film the holidaymakers showering and yes, enjoying themselves in the bedroom. What if Justin was oblivious to the video? What if he was being blackmailed too, and there was a third person in play that I didn't even know about?

If so, and Justin and I could sort out the problem together, maybe he would confess that, even though he had left me and not called me, it had been because he was confused, there had been an urgent crisis or he had lost my number and didn't know how to find me.

Some part of me was clinging to these tiny shreds of explanation, these cobweb handfuls spun into skeins of hope, insubstantial as they seemed. That's why, on the Friday afternoon, I was sitting in my car, on the corner near Santos's shop, trying to stop my brain consuming itself with unanswered questions, trying not to wring my hands into shreds and telling myself it would all work out.

It was 2.20 p.m. I'd been there for three hours. Santos had said Justin would collect his new surfboard in the afternoon, but not knowing if that meant 12 noon or 5 p.m., I hadn't wanted to take any chances on missing him. I had told Nigel I had an appointment with the orthodontist at the University Hospital of Wales to get my wisdom teeth X-rayed. That would account for a good few hours of absence.

I was carefully scanning the street when I saw a blue and white camper van drive up the narrow road, leaving a little trail of black smoke behind it. It pulled up outside Santos's and Justin got out. Just like that, nothing dramatic. He simply stepped out of the van and onto the street.

I couldn't quite believe it. There he was, tall and tanned and laughing into his mobile phone. I think I'd built him up in my mind into super-human proportions, a man radiating golden Hellenic charm, with a stride like an Athenian god, the motion of his passage creating winds that would blow into weather systems miles wide. But on that Friday afternoon, in the drizzle, he was just a man in a rather tatty sweater, albeit a striking one.

Without a hint of warning, part of me contracted inside. I think it was a sense of longing. Not specifically desire, just the suggestion of what he promised, there in the flesh, full of life, floppy hair blowing – a reminder of what he had seemed to promise that night in the pub and the cottage.

I sat motionless, my hands magnetised to the steering wheel, just watching him walk unhurriedly into the shop, my mouth sandpaper-dry. Now the moment had come, what was I actually going to say?

Ten minutes which seemed like a decade ticked out on my watch before he came out with a new surfboard under his arm. He was fishing for his keys in his jeans pocket when I found myself out of the car and standing on the road a few feet behind him saying the words, 'Hi, Justin.'

He turned automatically, and then he smiled.

But in the moment, just a flicker of a moment, really, between his eyes fixing on mine and the formation of the easy smile I remembered, there was a crack of something indefinable in his face – shock, displeasure, panic maybe – that made me realise this was not going to go well.

I think he was debating whether or not to acknowledge that he recognised me. His gaze fluttered over me and back along the street. Then, realising that I was alone, that there was no fuming boyfriend concealed in a nearby car or doorway, he relaxed slightly and said, 'Jen, this is a surprise. What are you doing here?'

He almost managed to make it sound breezy, casual, but I noted his hands were gripping the surfboard tightly.

'I wanted to talk you,' I said, dismayed at the already pleading note my voice carried. I had hoped to appear nonchalant, until I knew what was happening. But that was very unlikely now.

He paused for a moment then stared down at the pavement, resting his board on its end. 'Then why didn't you answer any of my calls?'

For a moment I was blindsided. Perhaps it was the baleful look in his blue eyes, the tight sound of hurt in his voice. My brain staggered slightly.

'I . . . you never called,' I blurted, as it readjusted. 'I woke up alone. You never rang me back.'

'I did try,' he said, looking at me now. 'When I got back that morning from the beach I tried, and I tried later, but . . .' He let the last word trail away into nothing, apparently leaving it to serve as a metaphor for the subsequent days – implying a wistful regret, something reluctantly lost. Nice try, said the small part of my brain that was evidently working and sending impulses to my mouth.

'You didn't leave me a message,' I insisted.

'Well, I thought I'd better not. I mean, with you being *engaged* and all. I didn't want to cause any trouble. When you didn't call me, well, I took the hint.'

A noble hurt filled his eyes. He pushed his hair back from his brow and gave me an achingly sad smile that could quell legions.

'I didn't *have* your number,' I offered.

'Sure you did. I left it by the bed.'

I thought back. Could I have missed a number by the bed? But I hadn't missed any calls. And there had been no number.

'You didn't call,' I said after a moment. 'You didn't try. But I got your email, and your texts. Of course you already know that, Justin.' Then, on a hunch, I said, 'Or is it Paul?'

Something focussed behind his eyes when I said that name.

141

It made me press ahead, to see where it would lead.

'You don't even live in Penallt, do you? You certainly don't work for *Cool Cymru*.'

He stared intently at me. I could see he was now wondering, for the first time, exactly *how* I happened to be standing outside Santos's shop on a damp Friday afternoon, miles from where we had met.

'You're right. I didn't call,' he said after a moment, still patient, but I could detect a note of caution in his voice, and a note of excuse. 'I got back with my ex-girlfriend, ok? I know it was a shitty thing to do but I was mixed up too. And you were getting married. I thought it would be better all round if we just let it go.'

He hesitated, looked at the ground, then glanced up at me through his fringe. 'It was special though, wasn't it?'

Fingers of torn emotion were scrabbling up my chest and fixing around my windpipe. Yes, it was special. It was special for me, I wanted to say. I wanted to shout so loudly he'd have no choice but to acknowledge it. There really was something between us, wasn't there?

But at the same time, without the fug of wine that had blurred the edges of our pub meeting, our night together, something about him wasn't convincing. I'd seen that under-the-fringe eye play before and I could see the cool edge of something appraising working behind them. Minute cogs and gears were shifting back and forth between a number of possible responses and he was making anything but a random or honest selection. He was using strategy to gain the upper hand in this game.

In the back of my head I heard my mother's voice say, 'Fool me once, shame on you. Fool me twice . . .' Painfully aware that I did not want to be made a fool of again, I decided not to play back. Just don't cry, I ordered my eyes, don't you *dare* cry.

'Do you really need the money so much?' I asked. My voice sounded harder now, a lot harder than it felt. 'Was that all it was to you, or was it a kinky thing? Is that how you get your kicks?'

As I'd anticipated, he replied, 'I don't know what you mean. What money?'

'You mean you haven't been sending me copies of a little video taken on that night. You and me . . .' I wanted to say *making love*, that's what I usually called it, when it was with Dan, but it was hardly that, I was beginning to realise now. 'You and me − screwing,' I concluded, spitting out the word with the distaste I felt.

'What are you talking about?'

'The two-minute highlights of us in bed that arrived on my email, at my *office.*'

'I don't know anything about that. I don't know what you're talking about.' But he didn't sound very outraged. Even more telling was that he didn't immediately ask what I was talking about. Most guys would have been at a bit alarmed, surely? If they were innocent. If they really didn't know what I was talking about they'd say, What video? Or, oh my God, someone videoed us? Then he seemed to realise he hadn't thought quite fast enough and said:

'Look, I'm sorry this didn't work out, Jen, but that's the way it is. I have to go.'

'I'm not paying you any more money,' I said, firmly, though to my horror I could feel drops of water forming again behind my eyes.

'I don't know anything about any money,' he said with infuriating calmness.

'You know, the *blackmail* money you've taken off me, you lying useless *fucker*!'

The fury of the last profanity came out like a whip crack and I saw it strike Justin as an almost imperceptible narrowing of his eyes. He recoiled slightly. He was about to retreat. But I couldn't let him run, not after all this. Not after all I'd done to find him.

'I've told Dan,' I said flatly. 'So it's over. The police will be knocking on your door any day now.'

Justin put down his surfboard and leaned it against the side of the van. After a moment he walked over to me in a careless way.

'I don't know what you are talking about, sweetie. I think you need some help,' he said, his face a perfect approximation of concern. He put his hand on my arm, casually, as if to offer reassurance. But, while still smiling, his grip tightened, making me wince.

'Sounds like this little video isn't something you'd want anyone to see, if you ask me, though. I don't think you'd want your fiancé to see something like that. I don't think you'd want the police to see it either. You could tell the police, of course, but that would be very embarrassing wouldn't it? A little starring role, an Oscar-worthy performance. No, if I were you I wouldn't do anything too hasty. Sounds like the kind of person who would do that would be the kind of person you wouldn't want to mess around with.'

His grip tightened further, as a full stop to the sentence, then he dipped towards me, kissed my temple and let his hand drop. He smiled.

To anyone watching we were two friends ending a personable chat, then saying a customary goodbye.

'It was fun,' he added, his smile breezy but the centres of his eyes were nail- sharp.

He picked up his board and slid it into the back of the van. Then he got in and turned on the ignition. I was still standing in the middle of the road, rain beading on my hair and lashes, long after the van's rear had disappeared from view.

Now I knew what sort of man I was dealing with. There was no confusion. Perhaps, without realising it, he had used the exact turn of phrase he had used in the text to me. 'Little starring role. Oscar-worthy performance.' If I needed final proof that Justin was responsible, that was it.

But I hadn't needed proof. I'd known it all along. I just hadn't wanted to believe it.

Why had I been so stupid? I demanded of myself, as I sat shell-shocked in the car. It's not as if I had been wrapped in cotton wool all my life, not in my line of work. Until that moment, it had all seemed like a bit of a game, a bit of drama – tortuous drama, indeed, but one which could still have had a positive resolution. I had indulged in a little personal detective work, a little dress-up-undercover-pretend. Deep down it was a temporary inconvenience and I had been sure that, somehow, I would resolve the situation rationally and logically, like I did every day at work, then I'd go home and forget about it.

But how could I deal with the supreme indifference Justin had shown? He clearly didn't care enough to need to consider anything I said, or the effect what he was doing would have on my life, on the people around me. He didn't need to be reasonable or even to show pity. He had the power. I had none.

This isn't fair! It's so unfair, yelled a shrill, childlike voice in my head.

He had laughed at me too. I didn't like to be laughed at. I really didn't like it.

Worse, I had to make the second payment at the airport or risk the consequences.

In that instant I really, really wanted to talk to Dan. Ordinarily, in the face of any issue or dilemma, he was the first person I turned to for advice. I realised quite clearly, driving home from Porthcawl, squinting through the metronomic swash of the windscreen wipers, bemused and blank, that he was the *only* person I confided in.

Radiohead's 'The Bends' was playing on the radio, Tom Yorke raging about how the girl in the song has no friends she can turn to over the wail of electric guitars.

That song had always made me uncomfortable. Now it seemed to lash out at me through Radio One's digital broadcast clarity, flagellating my already torn ego and inflaming the red welt on my upper arm that would leave a hand-shaped bruise.

It was true. I *didn't* have any real friends. There was no one I could talk to about this.

Beck would not understand. She was raising a child alone, working a crappy job and living with her mum. She clearly thought Dan was the incarnation of the Perfect Man, shining bright and unblemished. How could I, earning three times her salary, in my own home, planning a wedding, tell her what I had got myself into and expect her to be sympathetic? It sounded absurd, even to me. I even suspected she might be secretly satisfied at my descent into tawdriness; it would bring me down off my high horse a bit, wouldn't it? Reverse our roles for a change.

There was Serian, I suppose, but we were the kind of friends who went for a quick glass of wine together after work, or a hasty lunchtime trot to a café for a moan about Fat Paula, rather than confidantes. She, too, adored Dan. And Serian could never keep a secret.

I could totally rule out speaking to my mum. I had never been able to speak to her about my doubts about the wedding because I already knew what she would say. 'Count your blessing, my girl. You've got one of the good ones.' Dan could do no wrong. She would accept it reluctantly if I told her he had slept with someone else, he was a *man*. But I was easy-going, practical Jennifer and I did not do such things, I had no reason to be so ungrateful, so selfish, so undignified.

No, it was always Dan I would turn to if I had any real problems. If I had a disagreement with Fat Paula about her obsession with the signing-in book, or filling in my time sheets, Dan would listen to my monologue of disgust then suggest ways to forget about the old dried-up bag. If I had a confidence crisis about a big meeting, or a less than genial encounter with an arrogant officer, Dan would see me through. If I disagreed with my mum he would take my side. Even if I was just down and grumpy for some reason and wanted someone to offload on, he was always there, ready to listen with tea and reassurances.

But now I had no friend to seek advice from. I was alone in my own head and it was a vast, echoing warehouse of self-pity and confusion. I did not know what it was like to have 'the bends', but if it was anything like the surging nausea and panic-dizziness welling up inside me I wouldn't wish it on anyone.

Except Justin. I'd wish him a lot worse.

I thought about not paying him, I really did. It wasn't the money that mattered so much. I simply couldn't bear the thought that he would follow through with his threat.

*

On the night of the designated money drop I drove to the airport on the road the text had specified. Luckily Dan was due to be off playing Survivors on the pandemic exercise until the early hours of the morning. As instructed by the next text, which arrived as the air traffic control tower rose above the fields ahead of me, I pulled in at the designated bus stop, dropped the envelope of cash into the yellow grit bin behind it and drove away. I had no choice.

That was twice I had lost my nerve, twice that Justin had got the better of me. I didn't know how yet, but somehow I was determined that there wouldn't be a third time.

Chapter Ten

I pulled on my leggings and hooded top, tied on my trainers and went out running. Running was good. Having never possessed the patience to be a great team-game player, I had first started to run with a nervous Scottish girl called Pam from my English class at university. Unlike the other girls, we couldn't master the complicated combinations of aerobics or tolerate the gee-up, shouty, *work those muscles* encouragement compulsory with the instructors.

I'd probably run a hundred times the circumference of Cardiff in the years since then. I didn't run for distance, or for time, or for calorie burning. I didn't compete in fun runs or half marathons. I wasn't part of a running club. Three times a week, or thereabouts, I just put my trainers on and ran.

In summer, in shorts and T-shirt, I ran through the parks in the evenings, along the Taff Trail by the river, watching the seasons parade their wares. In winter, in running trousers and a long-sleeved fleece, baseball cap and gloves, I strode through the dim and quiet evening streets, glistening and glassy with departed rain. I didn't mind the cold or the dark; I preferred it, preferred the anonymity. The quieter the route the better, though I always kept my phone in my little pocket pouch and a close eye on any walkers, ready to flee if I sensed anything out of the ordinary, any threat.

I also never ran with an iPod which someone might want to steal, or which could prevent me from hearing a sudden tread behind me. I'd released far too many crime prevention press releases in six years to be caught out like that, though mostly I ran without music because I liked the silence.

The sound and feel of the pound-pound of my feet, the controlled suck-blow of my breath, speeding up as my muscles warmed, my lungs filling and the perspiration starting to flow, was the best sensation at the end of the day. It was a way to clear the noise pollution, the prattle of continually ringing phones, strident journalists' demands, radios crackling and words reeling in and out of people's mouths into handsets and keyboards, an infinity of click-clack-cackle-rattle noise, cleaning it out of my head, stilling and emptying it with the rhythm of the purely physical.

Then, if necessary, there'd be time to think.

I had gone running after Dan had proposed to me, before I finally accepted him.

I had also gone running after I spoke to Sophie that second time, on the day I returned from the Watch-house. I hadn't really felt like a hypocrite at that point, even though seventy-two hours earlier I'd been in bed with Justin. These were exceptional circumstances. If Dan hadn't lied in the first place, if Sophie hadn't phoned and I hadn't learned about his unspeakable deceit, it wouldn't have happened at all.

Feet pounding, running, running, I had visualised Sophie getting smaller and smaller in my mind's eye, then blinking into oblivion with a tiny pop, winking out of existence like the last seconds of life in a dark and destructive supernova. There had to come a point where I took Dan at his word, didn't there? When he said he loved me more than life, and that he wanted to be with me only?

Justin didn't figure in the equation at that point. He was already consigned to the past. Our wedding was still eight months away. That had seemed like a long time. There was still time.

Three months later, I was still running, but now it was only five months to the wedding and everything was different.

I tried to empty my head, to immerse myself in the winter scene that spread out before me instead. The immaculate white ground, frosted with overnight snowfall, glittered under acres of piercing blue sky as I hit the playing fields and headed for the river trail. It was beautifully calm and snow-quiet. The day had already taken on a pre-sunset softness as I headed across the rugby pitch and into the woods. I was temporarily delighted by the explosive crunch of my feet on the un-trodden snow. As I approached the river path, winding into the copse of naked trees, I thought of Robert Frost's 'Stopping by Woods on a Snowy Evening'. In the poem a rider longs to linger in the snow-bound woods but must keep his promise and complete his journey before he can rest. The poem was a metaphor for the journey of life and ultimately, the sleep of death at the end. I remembered how I'd taken the book of Frost's poetry with me to the Watch-house. Justin had commented on it – 'I've tried "The Road Not Taken". I love that poem,' he'd said, 'But I still ended up back here in Gower.'

All at once I found myself visualising Justin's face, grinding it beneath my feet, mashing it to a pulp, watching his cheek bones fracture first, then the blood gushing out of his smashed nose socket. He was making whimpering noises and flailing his arms while I continued with my blows, long after his mouth was just a bloody mess of teeth.

My lungs filled with cold, crisp air and I heaved out some of the sick hatred that had been popping and hissing inside since my trip to Porthcawl and the ride to the airport. As the miles paced out under my feet, I had to think what to do next.

So far I'd used my savings to pay him off, twice. I had some money left but it wouldn't last long if Justin kept making demands at this rate. Dan would soon get suspicious if I began pleading poverty or asking for loans.

But, practicalities aside, something indefinable was setting in my jaw. Something dark and sticky was coalescing in my chest, dripping down from the back of my throat, settling in the pit of my stomach. I directed it into my stride, waiting for a burst of clarification and direction to come.

As I arrowed out of the trees and approached the ice-capped fishing lodge on the riverbank, a group of teenagers were making snowballs on the steps.

'Run Forest, run!' yelled one teenage boy, chuckling to his mates.

I'd seen them there before. This was one of the more polite comments I received when running. *Nice arse, love,* and *Fancy sucking my dick?* were other favourites. They couldn't have been more than thirteen. I ignored them as usual, because the alternative was to shout obscenities back, which I felt would lower me to their level, and probably make them worse, or to run somewhere else, and I was determined not to let a bunch of prepubescent wankers literally run me off.

Something went click in my head at that moment. In fact, I wasn't going to let anyone run me off, I thought – quite the reverse. Perhaps I should try to make Justin run instead.

In that instant my lungs opened with a burst of oxygen, endorphins coursed through my veins and clarity exploded in my skull. I ran three times round the playing fields, then headed home with an idea of what to do next.

The snow only lasted twenty-four hours, but the following morning I still ended up having to sit in on a lengthy operational debrief that followed the closure of the M4 (again), as well as the closure of a number B roads after a dozen accidents overnight.

Jack NewsBeatWales had phoned four times before 9 a.m. for a 'round-up' of *snow related chaos*, as he called it. It hadn't been that chaotic, I'd tried to tell him. I couldn't give him specific details of every little RTC (road traffic collision) that occurred in twenty-four hours. No one was dead or likely to die but he wanted to know things such as car makes, damage details, number of occupants, their ages, towns they lived in, which hospitals they'd gone to, their injuries.

I did my best, but the systems aren't always immediately updated for non-fatalities. Jack wasn't very happy with the generic stuff I emailed across but he'd have to lump it. I could feel a headache forming above my eyes and round the back of my head. I rarely got headaches. I hoped I wasn't coming down with a cold as I took my seat in the weekly Proactive Tasking meeting, wishing lunch would come so I could try and get to Bodie's computer and access his PNN again.

I sat, tired and bored, as the uniforms droned on and on about partnership working, promoting good news and keeping the local councillors happy by publicising community initiatives. When I had started the job it's not as if I thought it would be terribly exciting or worthy, but I had no idea it would be full of so much bureaucratic nonsense.

I applied for the post, more or less straight out of uni. It was supposed to be a stopgap job . I hadn't studied anything media- or PR-related at university; my degree was in British and European history and English literature. At the time I loved the simplicity of knowledge for knowledge's sake, the acquisition of information, fusing with my wider longing for the escape of fiction. I'd loved the synthesis of facts and events merging with the wider tapestry of stories behind them that this most classical combination of subjects provided. It hadn't exactly equipped me for any particular line of work but that hadn't mattered at the time. I was sure I'd discover which career I wanted to pursue along the way, just as I was sure that, at the first opportunity, I'd be moving out of Wales and would live elsewhere in the UK, maybe even outside the UK.

I ended up at the police press office almost by accident. I met Dan.

Dan had been finishing his MA at the end of my first year and was accepted onto the police training scheme at the end of my second year. He was soon working nine to five and then learning the reality of horrible shifts. By the time I graduated he was qualifying as a constable and wanted us to buy a house together. 'Renting is a waste of money, Jen,' he'd been saying for two years, 'just cash down the drain and nothing to show for it in the long run.'

He would have liked me to move in with him before I graduated. He meant to save *me* money, knowing I didn't have much. He would not have expected me to go halves on the rent. He would be happy to pick up the cost alone, he insisted. But I resisted with equal stubbornness, saying I needed time and space to study, and it wasn't fair on either of us, our lifestyles were too different.

Once I graduated though, top in all my classes, with a hard-earned first-class degree, and an indolent summer and autumn had passed, I had to earn some money. My mum and dad had scrimped and saved diligently to help me get through the last three years. But I was weighed down by loans like everyone else, and also by the problem of having little specific notion of what I actually wanted to do.

At that point Dan succeeded in persuading me to buy a house with him. When the job at the force press office came up in the February and the salary they offered was pretty good, Dan said:

'It'd be experience, look good on a CV, and it would help you pay off your loans. You could just do it for a year while you decide what you really want to do. You're so smart, you could do anything you turn your hand to.'

That had almost been my point. How hard could it be to shuffle out press releases? Besides, buying a house *and* working for the police seemed rather final, rather too grown up. But since I had no cash to swan around with, debating the application of my life to something more rewarding, I did the practical thing. I filled in and posted the application form.

Nightmare Nige had taken my interview, with Fat Paula sitting in from HR and one of the chief superintendents.

'Ordinarily we wouldn't take someone without a related discipline in the field,' Nigel had said, when he called to tell me I'd aced the interview. 'But you were head and shoulders above the other candidates. We were very impressed with your obvious maturity.'

The job *had* seemed worthwhile at first. At least it was a role that affected the lives of real people, I told to myself. That had to be better than manning a phone in a call centre somewhere. I was interesting in policing and its history. Dan and I regularly discussed subjects such as 'institutional racism', Home Office interference, the effects of lack of funding, the efficacy of anti-social behaviour orders – all the related political and social issues of policing in modern-day Britain.

Dan came home every night with stories that the public wouldn't believe and didn't really need to know about – horrific, sad, humorous, heart-warming stories. I imagined the drama and excitement of being involved in *incidents*, or even *emergencies*, donning my hat and coat and rushing to a scene to 'facilitate' interviews while the media flashbulbs exploded around me.

There was an element of this of course, but there was also a tremendous amount of statistical malarkey, target chasing and political jockeying to contend with. And meetings, endless meetings.

Normally I survived these by switching off the higher functions of my brain, thinking about somewhere pleasant and what I knew about that place, for example, drinking a Bellini (white peach juice and Prosecco, invented in Harry's Bar in Venice in the 1930s, frequented by Noel Coward, Truman Capote and Ernest Hemingway), in the sunshine of St Mark's square in Venice (which Napoleon called 'the most elegant drawing room in Europe') in the shadow of the Campanile (where Galileo had mounted his telescope, and propounded the Copernican view that the earth revolved around the sun.)

But that day, behind my practiced smile, I had no time for the daydream game.

As soon as the meeting closed I hardly hesitated as I ducked into the CID room and called up the search field on Bodie's NOMAD. I had to be quick about it. Soon the CID would return from a stabbing in Splott and the room would be full of detectives ousted from the other offices because of the refurbishment, bickering who got to use the computers first to write up their reports.

As it happened it looked like the redecorating was almost finished. I'd spotted Sergeant Stan's lumpy old sofa in the back yard by the recycling bins that morning. The last rolls of carpet were waiting by the door to the custody suite. Soon Bodie would be back in his office upstairs, with his new desk and flat-screen machine, which meant it would be possible, but trickier, to find a time when his computer was free and unobserved.

Of course there was still no Justin Reynolds on NOMAD. That wouldn't have changed in the last few weeks. But NOMAD holds registration numbers of cars that have been in reported accidents too. I typed in the one I was interested in.

When I'd encountered Justin at Porthcawl I'd automatically memorised the licence plate of his camper van. Excellent recall and police habit had served me well. Last time I'd searched on Bodie's PNN Justin Reynolds had not appeared on system, or the DVLA database, as the legal owner of any vehicle. But the man calling himself Justin Reynolds had been driving the camper van. Enter the registration, find the van and find the name of the man. Maybe . . .

The machine beeped. There was a match. It was an oldish hit but a hit nevertheless. Eight years ago. I scanned the jargon of the incident report with practiced speed, one ear cocked for approaching intruders. It looked as if the camper van had been involved in an accident with a Land Rover and a post office van in 2002. The Land Rover had skidded across the road, by the Village Stores shop, on the B234 in Aberthin, hit a post box and clipped the post van. The camper van, which had been travelling behind, had stopped at the scene but, since there was no damage, it had left before the police arrived.

The postman had taken the number plate in case he needed a witness to back him up with his bosses, so the log said. A check at the time had shown the camper van was registered to a 57-year-old Michael Mathry from Pennard, and all the insurance was in order. When the statement was taken from the owner of the Village Stores, he had confirmed that he knew the Mathrys, and that they had a caravan pitched at the nearby caravan park. Their son used it a lot and drove the van, but the shopkeeper wasn't sure of the son's name.

Since the driver of the Land Rover was three times over the alcohol limit, and the Village Stores shopkeeper was an independent witness, the police officer had never bothered to chase up Mr Mathry to take a statement.

I searched hurriedly for Michael Mathry on the DVLA link on the PNN. Sure enough, Michael Mathry was still the registered owner of the camper van. The insurance details on the system were old. But sometimes the system isn't updated. And sometimes when people sell their cars, especially privately, they forget to contact the registration bureau and transfer the details to the new owner. The only way to be sure if Michael Mathry still owned the van would be to telephone the Insurers' Bureau, but I could hardly find a legitimate pretext to do that.

But then, I might not need to – there was an address in Pennard for the Mathrys. There was even a phone number.

I had realised while I was running, running, running, the night before, that I still didn't even know Justin's (Paul's?) real name. I needed to know who he was, because Justin clearly knew far too much about me. He knew my name and the where, when, what, how of my life which had enabled him to set the speed and the conditions of our little game of tag. All this time I had hung on the end of my phone, waiting for the next instruction, the next little threat, dangling on his hook between emails and text messages, dancing to the ring tones and the ping of *message received*.

He had counted on my confusion, my disbelief, my panic. He had counted on me playing along, blindly.

But *I* was supposed to be the one with the inside track – the information, the facts, the details, and the choice of how to dispense them. These were for me to bestow on others, my wishes to grant.

These facts were the constituents of my daily life and the basis of every press release I ever constructed. I needed to know the who, what, when and where about Justin, starting with his real name. These facts might help me find out what his secrets were, his weaknesses.

I'd obviously startled him by tracking him down to Porthcawl, and I'd seen in his face that it had thrown him off balance. Being confronted by his victim was clearly not part of the plan. Now I had to disrupt it a little more. I needed some leverage. Leverage for when the next video update arrived, as I was now certain it would. At the very least I might be able to make him think it might be too much effort, or was simply too risky, to keep up this game with me. Knowing who he was, and where he was, might be the way to get Justin on the run.

And I had made some definite headway. The Mathrys owned, or had owned, the camper van. The Mathrys had a son who often drove it.

As I contemplated this I heard the sound of the stairwell door bumping open down the corridor and the hearty voices of the returning detectives. Hurriedly, I restored Bodie's computer to the default screen, and was heading out of the door when Fat Paula barrelled into me. I should point out that Fat Paula wasn't actually fat at all. She was one of those skinny women who are as sharp at the hips and shoulders as they are sour in the face. She was only called Fat Paula because she continually lamented that she was putting on invisible weight, ostentatiously refusing office cakes and sweets because she was on a permanent diet of some sort – Atkins, Weight Watchers, you name it, she had tried it.

We assumed she was less than sweet-tempered because of constant low blood sugar. For some reason she seemed to be saving her particular sourness for me at that time.

'Ah, there you are. I've been looking for you *everywhere*, Jennifer,' she announced theatrically, barring my way with an upraised hand as if stopping traffic.

'Do you want something?' I asked, with as much politeness as I could muster.

'Yes, to find you. I was looking for you *ages* ago. The DI asked for you. No one seemed to know where you were. You have to be available, you know, accountable, from nine to five. We've discussed this before. You can't just *disappear* from your desk willy-nilly.'

'I was in the Proactive briefing.'

'That was finished more than half an hour ago.'

'I went to get a coffee and then came here.'

'There's no one else here.'

'I can see that. I was looking for the DI.'

'I've told you before, Jennifer, for absences from the office, or for meetings or otherwise, you need to sign the signing-in-and-out book. We need to know where you are.'

'Nige knew that I was in Proactive.'

'Half an hour ago,'

'I know this is a police station but I wasn't aware it was a police *state*,' I answered coolly. 'My job is very busy, Paula. I'm running around here like an idiot, chasing people up, people who never answer their phones, so I have to speak to them in person. I've been in Snow Gold and Proactive Tasking and ten other places this morning. It's gone two o' clock and I haven't even eaten my sandwich. My mobile's on. If I'm in the building and you can't find me, ring me like everyone else or use the Tannoy.'

I was surprised by my little speech. Normally I just looked at her as politely as possible and told her I would try to do better, then made a face behind her back. But my patience was wearing paper thin and my blood was rising.

Paula was more than a little taken aback herself, and said nothing for a moment. Then she opened her mouth, probably to give me the HR rulebook speech, but luckily, Bodie came round the corner at that moment with DI Harden.

'The lovely Jen,' Bodie bellowed. 'Been looking everywhere for you. We need your excellent advice on a racist assault appeal.'

The corridor reverberated slightly with this declaration. He beamed at Paula, though I knew he thought she was as big a waste of space as I did. 'This one's our girl. What would we do without her, eh?' He beamed again, giving me a hearty shove.

'*Dai*, I've been trying to find you,' I said, deliberately not using the inspector's title.

'Ships passing in the night as usual,' boomed the DI.

Paula looked as if she had just sucked a sour raspberry. Not only had I given her an uncharacteristically defiant earful, she had never liked the fact that I was on first-name, and obviously friendly terms with most of the senior officers in Southern. In her department of cowed admin assistants and file clerks, no one was on first name terms with anyone above PC level, and jokes, or even smiles, were regarded as probably detracting from workplace productivity.

Paula also didn't like banter. She liked it even less when

Bodie or someone called me 'lovely', or complimented me, but she was also a little afraid of the hearty lads of the CID, so she bit her tongue.

'Yes, well, remember what we talked about please, Jennifer,' she said, bustling off with a head-mistressy bob of her chin and a toss of her lank brown hair.

'What did the old witch want?' asked Bodie, grimacing. 'She was down here earlier, asking if anyone'd seen you.'

Was she really? Now why was she sneaking about down here? She'd almost caught me about my illicit business on PNN too. I'd have to watch out for her, I noted.

'She has a bee in her bonnet about me, that's all,' I shrugged.

'Because you don't click your heels like a good soldier? Bloody Nazi,' he remarked, doing a Hitler heel snap and salute, finger-moustache under nose. 'If she was actually fat maybe she'd develop a bubbly personality. Probably needs some good lovin', but I'm definitely not offering. Be like making love to a drawer of knives and forks.'

'Marc. Enough,' said the DI with required, senior disapproval. Then, to me, 'Come on in and advise us, Jen, before I have to put Bodie on report.'

Half an hour later I wandered back to the press office after I'd been briefed on the 'racist' incident. It wasn't exactly what the race legislation was designed for. A drunken English bloke had called a man in the Wetherspoons pub an ugly fucking sheep-shagger. The man had promptly responded by calling him a useless English cunt. A fight had ensued, then a trip to the hospital for both. It was the work of ten minutes and a bit of sanitising to draft an appeal for witnesses.

I was more concerned about Paula. If she had caught me on Bodie's machine it would have been difficult to find an explanation for what I was doing. Also, she'd surely have it in for me now that I'd stood up to her.

I grabbed my chicken salad sandwich from the fridge. It was already 3 o' clock. In addition to the racist assault release I had to brief the chief super about a complaint against one of our officers and write a 'good news' strategy before I could go home.

As soon as I was back in my seat, Serian was quick to tell me that Fat Paula had been on the warpath about my apparent absence all morning.

'She's been in three times asking for you, naughty girl!' she crowed, slapping the back of my hand and pulling off a good approximation of Paula's disapproving school-marm scowl. At this rate I envisaged Paula's obsession with me turning into a Benny Hill-style comedy pursuit sketch, she bristling after me as I ducked into doorways and behind drinks machines, while I performed an exaggerated tootley-too-musical jog.

'Yeah, I saw her downstairs,' I admitted.

'I tore a strip off her for hassling you,' called Nige, across the room. What he meant was, as my manager, he'd told her he was perfectly satisfied I was somewhere working but he'd remind me about signing the book for *prolonged* absences.

'Thanks, Nige,' I smiled.

'Just to keep her happy, though, could you try and sign the book extra carefully for a few days – red tape, but it keeps the pencil-pushers smiling.'

'Anything for you, Nige.'

Then he proceeded to tell me about the latest outrage by a reporter who had called from The Sun. I nodded my head in an approximation of interest but really I was thinking that I needed to take a little fact-finding trip to Pennard.

*

'I think I've found a nice little resort in Greece,' called Dan, as I staggered in through the door at 7 p.m. that night, dizzy with exhaustion. He had two days off before his night shifts began again, and he appeared to be cooking something. The smell of tomatoey pasta sauce and garlic bread wafted from the kitchen to greet me.

'Oh, and your mother rang, something about wedding invitations really needing to be confirmed for the seating. And someone from the florist's rang – camp sounding bloke called Stanley?'

Dan emerged from the alarmingly steamy kitchen, looking damp-faced, a tea towel slung over his shoulder, a spoon dripping lumpy red, sauce on the wooden hall flooring. I put my bags down wearily and waved a hand at the errant globules of Bolognese.

'Oh, shit,' he acknowledged, dipping down to wipe up, then pecking me on the cheek. 'You look zonked. Busy one? There's tea in the pot. I'll pour one for you. Food'll be ten minutes or so.'

He retreated into the kitchen and I could hear things being clanged about while I heaved off my coat and shoes. Sky TV news was blaring from the living room and I went in to turn it down. My head was already pounding at a high frequency. I gathered up two used cups and a Snickers wrapper with one hand and Dan's discarded work boots in the other, then headed back to the kitchen.

It was hot as a spa bath inside. A pall of ghostly pasta steam hung a few inches below the ceiling, undulating lazily in the updraft from the gas hob.

'Put the extractor thingy on, Dan,' I said to his busy back, pulling out a chair and sitting down before a pile of open holiday magazines.

'It's still broken,' he reminded me, throwing open a window instead. I resisted the urge to hover around behind him, wiping the food-splattered surfaces and putting dirty things to soak, as it only irritated him. And I was almost too tired to move.

'Look at that one there, on the top,' said Dan, waving at the magazines. 'It has a fabulous pool. You can hike in the hills if you get bored. It's miles from anywhere, no crowds or lager louts, guaranteed. Flights from Bristol.'

Impossibly blue seas and pristine crescents of sands shimmered before my eyes. I was hot and lightheaded.

Since we had set the wedding date Dan had kept going on and on about booking the honeymoon, like a man possessed. I still hadn't got round to arranging half the essentials of the wedding (Stanley wasn't the only one chasing me for the deposit and confirmations) but Dan seemed intent on getting the honeymoon sorted out. You'd think it would have been easy to choose a honeymoon destination. There were so many places I'd longed to visit that it should have been a cornucopia of choice. But holidays were one of the primary things Dan and I had always disagreed on, and suggestions for honeymoons had been no different.

Dan's idea of a perfect break was a beach or a pool with some hiking thrown in. Anything outdoorsy and quiet with a perhaps a low-key taverna or bar to provide beers and snacks in the evening. Cue the Balearics, Portugal or somewhere similar.

But ever since I had goggled at those Christmas morning atlases, I wanted to wander the stone rim of the Coliseum, marvel at the ceiling of the lofty and divine Sistine Chapel, drink from the fountains of the Alhambra, plant both feet firmly in the middle of the Brandenburg gate, climb the art deco wonder that is the Empire State Building – you get the idea.

I had always wanted to share these things with Dan, and I imagined us strolling hand in hand among old yellow stones amid the scent of freesias, drinking one of those Bellinis in Venice, or some other preppy, buzzing European bar, kissing under a crown of stars, just like lovers.

But it was not to be.

Our first joint holiday had not been a success. It was a short break during the summer vacation before the start of my second year at university. I had dragged Dan to Amsterdam, convinced he just needed a nudge or two to appreciate my more sophisticated take on holidays, and warm to the attractions of a more urban experience. Flights had been cheap, and Amsterdam had seemed like a rite of passage for students. But the only part he'd really liked was the Anne Frank house, because it had to do with war, I suspect.

He'd been uncomfortable in the extreme passing the doorways of the pot cafes. That was understandable, I suppose. He was due to sit his police entrance exam at the time. He had an irrational fear that he'd have to do a drug test, and somehow he would have passively inhaled invisible whiffs of weed. And he said the cafes were full of layabouts and lazy pricks.

'Layabout' or 'lazy bugger' was Dan's highest form of insult, even then. Lazy pricks were beneath contempt.

He'd refused point-blank to even walk through red light area (which was a bit of a relief).

I thought maybe the location had simply been a poor choice, but Dan equally disliked the idea of visiting of Copenhagen (too cold and apparently not *wonderful*), Prague (too full of stag dos and pickpockets), Paris (too clichéd) Rome (a tourist trap, overpriced, dirty and covered in graffiti).

Various Valentine's days, birthdays and anniversaries passed without any hint of a surprise romantic mini-break. Then during the summer, at the end of my second year, when fellow students seemed to be packing rucksacks in readiness for travel to all sorts of exotic climes, Dan and I spent ten days in Portugal – the Algarve to be precise. It was a nice, classy hotel, secluded, tasteful. Dan had tried his hand at windsurfing and snorkeling. We both swam in the sea. I read a lot on the beach. It was nice enough. I was bored, fidgety and lonely.

On the flight home Dan was already suggesting the Balearics or somewhere for the following year's break.

So, right at the end of my third year, when he was graduating to full PC and pressuring me to buy a house, I was determined to go somewhere interesting even if I had to go alone. In a rare burst of truculence that terrified my parents, and if I'm honest, myself, I organised a lengthy holiday rebellion. I enrolled as a counsellor on the Camp America programme.

It was nine weeks on a camp, in the middle of the raccoon- and chipmunk-infested Massachusetts woods, looking after kids. But I also signed on for an organised camping trek at the end, which would whisk me on a whistle-stop tour through New England. I was still just young enough to qualify.

Dan had been baffled and annoyed when I'd waved the application forms in front of him, muttering, the War of Independence, the Boston Tea Party, Salem witch trials, the beaches from *Jaws*! He was positively hostile when the acceptance documents came through and I showed him the camp brochure.

'Those things are pretty much slave labour, you know. It'll be full of layabouts. You won't like it,' he'd insisted.

What he meant was, it wasn't like me to be so adventurous, not to be dissuaded by his reasonable arguments that I hated kids, that it was dangerous.

'I won't know where you are day to day. I won't be able to get hold of you,' became his familiar refrain. Granted, it was long ago before the era of the ubiquitous mobile phone, but I assured him I'd call from every pay phone I encountered, and he'd have the addresses of where we were staying.

'It's all a bit "studenty", isn't it? It'll be expensive,' he warned, when he could see I didn't mean to back out, to relent, as I usually did before his calm but sustained verbal assault.

What he meant was, he wanted us to get settled and proceed with the *nice little house* idea so he could crack on with climbing the career ladder.

But I was only twenty-one.

Armed with my guidebook and essential local literature (an anthology of Robert Frost's poetry and Nathanial Hawthorne's *The Scarlet Letter*), I loaded my rucksack with shorts, T-shirts and sun cream and boarded the plane. Four months under an old New England blue sky, among the trees and ripple-stroked swimming lake of Rock Shore Summer Retreat, was exhilarating in terrifying and unexpected ways.

It's true I was almost always exhausted, and the kids got on my nerves. They were boisterous and affectionate gangsta-rapping, finger-clicking, black and Hispanic girls, all under twelve, from the 'projects' of Bosto, understandably amused and confused by the very white, very proper British counsellors.

The counsellors were pretty irritating too, though, mostly filthy rich and bumming round on Mummy and Daddy's credit cards.

But even though I spent most of the time not knowing what the hell I was doing, I actually quite liked it. Sometimes, on our weekends off, the other counsellors and I would hide out in the staff hut drinking weak and warm Buds and Jack and coke, against camp rules, flirting clumsily, dancing to whatever was playing on the crackle-and-pop radio. Once I took a puff of a joint – just one puff. I wanted to take more because I knew Dan would disapprove, but I didn't like the taste.

There was a benevolent and bearded ex-hippy called Joe who drove the kids around in his school bus. He took a shine to me and told me stories of the sixties and seventies, or what he could remember of them. He owned a tattoo parlour in the nearby whitewashed town of Orange, next to the white clapboard church and the Porky Tum pizza shop. He offered to tattoo a bluebell on my shoulder, because, he said, *it's exactly the colour of your eyes, man.* The Doors played long into the firefly-speckled evening.

How I loved that surreal story-book confection of a land where everything was coated with a glaze of extra bright colours and topped with extra fries and coffee refills.

I missed Dan, but not as much as I'd expected. It had been harder on him, of course, at home, jobbing along, finishing his probation, in the usual routine without me.

The camping trip took us up through Boston, then up into the towns and villages of Vermont and Maine and back into Massachusetts. We eventually pitched up on the beach in Cape Cod, tanned, road-dusty and barbecue ready. Way out there on the shifting fringe of that vivid blue sea, on the edge of the once New World, something shifted inside me.

I breathed deeply inside my globe of sea and sky with the little white wooden houses at my back, the bone-white lighthouse, gulls reeling above and eternity opening in a hundred shades of blue and grey ahead.

Within the sound of the stiffening breeze was the rag-tag whisper of blissful uncertainty. I wasn't nervous or afraid of it anymore. The salt-tang taste on the wind was a little like that of blood. For a moment I felt I might find my feet freed from the damp sand, my body circling skyward, breaking off into the evening sun, invisible wings rattling behind me.

In that second I had been sorely tempted to stay with my new-found travellers, to run off for weeks or even years, decades perhaps. I could disappear into the expanses of the American heartland, vanish TV *Fugitive*-like, roaming from town to town, working at bars and diners, becoming involved with unlikely people and having alcohol-soused road-trip adventures, Jack Kerouac style. All this, secure in the knowledge that I could move on and out whenever the urge to become attached to any place or person started to work its way under my skin.

But then, in the front of my mind, was Dan, the tie that bound me to reality. I could already hear the metronomic certainty of the tick of our days at the end of the rapidly decreasing miles, now leading back to Boston and then a 747 to the oblivion of home. That was the first time that I felt a surging resentment towards the man I loved, as I stood by that surge-slow sea, with its water-light, Massachusetts sun, that humming, singing sun.

Inside, in a cooling place in my chest, while I fingered the small silver heart-shaped pendant Dan had given me at the start of the trip, so confident of my return, unchanged, unspoiled, I knew I could not run away. I didn't have the courage or, deep down, the true ability to say I didn't really love him. Because I did love him. He was right about that, at least.

Once the hugs and kisses of an airport reunion were done, and we were again riding home in Dan's little red car, what I felt most keenly was a sense of loss. I had left a part of myself on that already long-ago shore and exchanged it for a stone that sat below my heart, weighting me in place. It came with a memory of sifting light and receding possibility – a guarantee, good for at least ten years of asking 'What if?'

I'd gone home, we'd looked at houses, spotted the police 'stopgap' job, and in a split second it was the end of anything 'studenty', aka irresponsible.

It was an age of reason.

It became all too easy to stop drinking Jack Daniels in favour of wine, to start taking holidays that Dan liked, to stop saying that I'd prefer to listen to something else on the radio. These were little things, tiny things. They didn't even seem like enormous sacrifices at the time. It just happened, drip by drop in the ocean of everyday compromises, so what I thought inside I just didn't say anymore. What was the point of making an *issue* of something that wouldn't change?

The point was that none of this had mattered very much while I thought I knew who Dan was – while he was solid and reliable and fixed as true north. I knew where we stood and what we stood for, and I knew there were worse places to be standing.

Then there was *that* phone call – from *that* woman. *Sophie*. And all at once Dan wasn't any of the things he had appeared to be. He wasn't staunch and reliable Dan – honest, truthful, Dan. The ground had shifted under me.

All the hopes and desires I had shuttered away had sprung out through the crack in my heart. Foremost was a tumble of 'Whys?' and 'Do I's?' *Why are we getting married? Why are we together? Do I love you enough? Do I have to settle for this?*

With these questions circling vulture-like in the offing, I had got into my car and driven to the Watch-house with my copy of Robert Frost. I remembered the smell of the wood smoke and sea salt as I pulled up outside the hotel, the wonky little windows glowing from the fire within.

When I started from my dark reverie, Dan was saying something about Zakynthos, draining tagliatelle. He was talking about lagoons and parascending as he sloppily dished wet strings from the colander onto some plates.

I stared at the magazine and the honeymoon-perfect photographs before me. He was waiting for me to answer. To give my opinion. Greece might be ok if we chose the right spot, I thought – there are temples, that's good. Greece was good enough for Homer and Virgil.

'Do we have to do this now, Dan?' I sighed, an aeon of ancient weariness weighing me down in my seat. 'I'm just too tired.'

Undeterred, he picked up the brochure, pointing at a modern-looking five-star hotel.

'You don't have to decide now, pet,' he placated. 'I'm just saying, take a look at it. We don't have forever, you know. There's *still* all the wedding stuff to get straight. Your mum sounded stressed on the phone.'

'*She* sounded stressed?' I was instantly defensive.

'I just mean we have to think about it *some*time. It's already February.'

'I know that. Of course I know. I *do* have a real job too, you know. I don't have endless time to deal with all this crap.'

He put the pasta down on the table in front of me. He looked hurt. I instantly felt like a shrew. I hated to see that wounded look in his eye. It wasn't really his fault I felt like this. It was mine. He knew what *he* wanted, after all.

'Thanks for the dinner, Dan,' I said, relenting an inch, then a yard. 'It's a nice surprise.' I took a bite. It actually tasted good. 'It's really nice.'

'I just thought I'd save you cooking for a change,' he said, prodding at his meal sadly.

I'd done it again. I'd ruined his mind's-eye scene of domestic dinner bliss, his simple offer of food. He'd only wanted to do something nice for me.

'I'll look through the stuff this weekend. I promise, pet. I'll ring my mum later.'

'I love you, Jen,' he said.

'I love you too,' I replied.

'I'm off tomorrow. I could come and meet you at Southern. We could have lunch. You never take lunch. I bet they could spare you for half an hour, for a change.'

'Sorry, love – I'm up to my neck in stuff tomorrow,' I replied truthfully. 'I won't get the chance to get away. Another time, though, promise.'

The map of west Wales and the Gower in my bag loomed large in my mind.

Chapter Eleven

As good as my word to Nigel, I signed the office book very carefully that morning when I left. I'd already updated my online diary to say I was paying a visit to the Swansea neighbourhood policing team. In brackets I put 'proactive publicity strategy' as added evidence of my diligence. Let's see Fat Paula complain now, I commended myself. Then I set off for Aberthin in search of the Mathrys.

In theory I could pop in and see PC Dick Thomas and his new probationer PC, Rhian something, at the community office on the way. We could have a half-hour chat about upcoming local events to cover my tracks, then I could make the all-important detour of my own, to see a man about a camper van, and a caravan. The caravan site was marked clearly on the west Wales area map.

Unfortunately, when I had rung the Mathry's phone number that morning, the one that had been listed against the address in Pennard on the PNN incident, I was informed by a crackle-voiced, ancient-sounding woman that the Mathrys had moved out about six years ago, to the Uplands area of Swansea.

I was disappointed, but not deterred. People down west like to hang on to their old caravans (and their old camper vans, which are often considered collectors' items.) Maybe they still owned the caravan at the Aberthin site, near to where the road accident had occurred. Maybe they still owned the camper van. Someone down there might know them or where they'd moved to. Perhaps the camper or the caravan were still used by a son who liked surfing and internet sex games.

If they were nothing to do with my Justin, and Mr Mathry had sold the camper van and not updated the DVLA, they might remember who had bought it. It was a process of elimination.

What raised my hopes was that Aberthin was only about half an hour's drive from the Watch-house hotel in Penallt. That seemed too close to be a complete coincidence. I'm on your trail, Justin, I said to myself as the sea appeared ahead of me. Just you wait and see.

If you didn't know exactly where to find the Aberthin caravan park, you could pass within twenty yards of it and still miss the entrance. Though it was only fifteen minutes or so from the main road, that part of the coast is riddled with country lanes, woodland and scrub, a twist-around maze of tracks and trees and turnings that are all alike, leading to lonely stretches of sand and pebble bays.

After expecting to be lost, I suddenly realised I had been there before, a long time ago.

It was the row of landmine warning signs that jogged my memory. I'd once spent an illuminating holiday at my friend Wendy's family caravan on the site when we were sixteen. Their dilapidated 'shed on wheels', as she affectionately called it, was permanently anchored there, usually ankle deep in mud. But that summer we, and our mate Shirley, had been allowed to stay there by ourselves, and the lack of glamour didn't deter us.

The caravan had been untouched since the dawn of caravan-making time, the décor, consisting mostly of orange and brown plastic, suggested circa 1970. The roof leaked and the chemical toilet was always a last resort, but it was a first taste of freedom as we bobbed adrift, in a sea of grass, blissfully parentless.

On the single day it did not rain we cycled recklessly through the meandering country lanes, dodging hails of water from the overhanging trees. And just beyond the entrance turning was the first sight of the battered signs bearing the skull and crossbones warning of submerged and slumbering World War II mines. We had shivered at the thought of their corroded presence, skulking beneath the tufty, green-black, seaweedy crust off the road. Why in God's name anyone would want to invade via back-end-of-beyond Aberthin was a mystery to us , but it made for a good salty, shorts-and smiles-photo.

For the rest of the week we had taken shelter in the caravan, one blonde, one brunette, one redhead, eating jam on toast and fried egg sandwiches, drinking weak Ribena, sitting cross-legged on the scratchy upholstery. Finding a space between the various pots and pans co-opted as water catchers beneath the leaky ceiling, we read with glee through a pile of Wendy's mother's Mills and Boon novels, while the wind and water seemed to surge sideways from the nearby bay.

Every few minutes one of us would burst into fits of laughter and read the others a particularly overblown paragraph or slice of flirtatious conversation. How we laughed over the repetitive scenarios, the frequency of Lucindas, Charlottes, Felicities, Chads, Armandos and double-barrelled thingummies who were fashion designers, PR assistants, photographers, Swiss bankers, freelance journalists or oil magnates. My favourite Mill's and Boon tale was called *Mistaken Love*, because it featured

Stein Wallbeck, a man one small step away from being a rapist, who kept pressing his manhood up against young virginal Felicity, the photographer, and wrestling her on various pieces of garden furniture.

Henceforth, any over enthusiastic individual would be referred to as 'a bit of a Stein', with knowing grins. But I knew then that, though we'd laughed with genuine hilarity, we were discomfited by the feelings this aggressive sexuality had awakened in us. No doubt three teenage girls fell asleep under the eiderdown, top-to-toe, in a row, with similar unresolved thoughts about Mr Wallbeck, that night and the nights to come.

Well, twelve years later I *was* working in PR and Justin had turned out to be more of a Stein than Stein – how ironic. How sad.

I didn't want to attract too much attention when I arrived, so I parked my car up on the grass verge around the corner and walked the rest of the way from the little cattle grid onto the site. Bodie had often told me that a lot of police work involves watching and waiting, looking to see who does what, how many times, with whom, without them knowing it. If you are lucky, at the end of it you might get to wrestle with someone and take them for a ride in the police van.

The aim of this exercise, of course, was not to be caught in any situation that would require wrestling. I wanted to find out if the Mathrys had a son who still had their camper van.

I'd changed into a fleece and jeans in the car. I didn't want to look too obvious – a woman in trousers, a suit jacket and heeled boots in the middle of a mud-streaked caravan park in February would look nothing if not notable.

It was sad to see how much the site had declined since my last visit. Quite a few of the old caravan plots were empty.

The bare concrete hard-standings were cracked with weeds. With one or two exceptions, the caravans still in place looked tatty and untended. All in all there were about thirty of them. There were a few cars parked outside the ones at the sea end, with fleeting suggestions of life in the shadowy windows.

There was no obvious sign of a camper van parked up anywhere.

There was a little site office at the side of the entrance track, near the gate. It was more of a concrete pill box, with a melamine counter cutting it in two and a drinks machine on one wall, but it was locked. There seemed to be a chart of caravan plots on the wall that I could just make out through the window dirt, but I couldn't read the faded type to see if Mathry was one of the names. I didn't want to just wander up and down the rows in case Justin was inside one of the caravans and suddenly looked out.

I pulled the peak of my baseball cap down slightly and eased my collar up. It was breezy and cold enough for this not to look conspicuous. There were a few people wandering back and forth. An old couple, in their early seventies, also in fleeces and baseball caps, were sitting under a plastic awning outside the door of their caravan. They looked like the sort of cheery busybodies who keep an eagle eye on all comings and goings. Their van was near the bumpy track, so they'd see all the car and foot traffic along it.

Their caravan had new tyres and there were plastic flowers in pots in the rear window, which was clean and not rain-streaked. The triangle of grass beneath their camping seats was cut short and bounded by white, painted beach pebbles. A little kettle was bubbling towards boiling on a gas stove and the pair were eating flaky pasties out of paper bags. This was probably my best opportunity to ask some questions.

'Hiya,' I said with a wave, affecting a slightly thicker Welsh accent than my own. This was something I did at school when I wanted to blend in. Then it was a defence mechanism, now it was a tool of trust and partly of disguise.

'Sorry to bother you, but I don't suppose you know where the Mathry's caravan is do you?'

'You looking for someone, love?' asked the old woman.

'Well, yes, Michael Mathry? I used to come down here as a kid. Him and my dad were friends, like, and I used to play with his boy sometimes, but it's been so long I can't remember which end it was. That's if they still come here, of course – it's been a long time.'

'Mathry? Well, of course I know. Been here longer than we have, eh Len? His boy'd be Paul. Be 'bout your age, maybe a bit older.'

'Aye, Paul, that's him,' I nodded enthusiastically. *Paul.*

'Aye, well. The caravan's just behind that one, love. That one there with the shed, on the end.' She pointed to one further down, on the left. 'Lucky having that shed, I always said, for the car or their van. We wanted that plot but they already had it and wouldn't sell it, see. Can't say I blame them, though. It's a good plot, off the track and back from all the toing and froing.'

She looked around as if she expected to see a convoy of sun-hatted holidaymakers pouring down the track, buckets and spades at the ready. But the only thing moving was a muddy cocker spaniel with a plastic ball in its mouth.

'Nice van that,' said the old guy to neither of us in particular.

'That's what I said, Len, nice van, nice plot.'

'No, I meant the camper van, Gwen. That old fashioned one. I had one like that when I was twenty-five. Had some good times in that.' He gave me a little wink. 'I got rid of it, though. They burn oil something terrible.'

'You were never twenty-five, Len. Besides, she don't wanna know about the camper van. She wants to see the Mathrys. Sorry love, but they don't come down no more. Well, the boy comes down now and again. At least we see the light on sometimes, though he ain't exactly chatty. Old man was nice, always said hello, stop for a chat, but the youngsters now don't know no manners. No offence, like.'

I just smiled.

'Place has gone down a bit a now. Not what it was. Not the same old crowd, you know, the old bunch. Browns now, have gone, sold up,' she pointed at the dilapidated van next door. 'Polly and John from two down, they went five years ago. Lots of the vans are empty. But rain or shine we're here every weekend, and, if the sun's out, in the week too.'

'Mathrys might've moved now. Gone to Uplands somewhere, I think. Wasn't it Uplands, Gwen?' put in Len. But Gwen was still continuing her previous answer and had merely paused to take a bite of pasty.

'We get the tea on, get the pasties and the fruit cake out. Sea air and peace and quiet, then a walk on the beach with Ernie.'

She gestured to the cocker spaniel, now digging at something by the wall of the site office. 'Beats the telly any day. Best place in the world, I says. Don't I, Len?'

'Aye, you do – all the bloody time, girl.'

'Husht now. Go and get the milk before I die of thirst. The tea's up.'

With another wink at me, Len lifted himself out of the chair with surprising agility and pottered inside.

'You've been here a long time, then?' I asked, more for the sake of keeping the conversation going then out of interest, but Gwen didn't need much prompting.

'Oh aye, 1967 we bought this 'un, well not this 'un – this one we renewed in '87. Not many people have renewed, as you can see, gone downhill. But we're happy with this 'un now. We'll stick it out until we're in our pine boxes. Good butties, were you? With the Mathrys' boy?'

'No, well, I haven't seen him since I was a teenager, like, but I've come back to the area now and thought I might just say hiya to some of the old lot.'

'Well, there was some fuss with him, you know,' she said, conspiratorially, leaning towards me and away from the caravan door where I heard the distinctive pressure-pop of a fridge opening. 'Back about ten years now. We weren't sure like, but there were rumours he'd been mixed up with the vicar's daughter from up Pennard. Father Miller, I think. We didn't know them lot personally. I think the girl came here a few times. Skinny girl, black hair. Shy, like. 'Course, Paul was older by then, and my girls were off at uni, and it wasn't like it used to be when they were all kids and would play together.

'Well, I expect he got her in trouble or something. *You* know, not married or anything like, and the vicar's daughter. They moved off to the Highlands, I think. They never said anything for sure. They hushed it up, like, said it was a nervous breakdown, change of scene. My sister Carol used to know the woman who used to clean at the Sunday school and she told her. Well, it might have been that. Anyway, the boy went off travelling or something, and then there was a fuss with him running up a big debt on the old man's cards.

'Old man Mathry used to come down here every weekend before that, then he mostly stopped coming. Just glad my girls turned out good as gold – both got babies now. Still I shouldn't be saying it, should I? It was a long time ago.'

'I can hear you, you know, Gwen. And no, you shouldn't

be spreading dirt you don't know nothing about, and never did,' said Len's voice from inside. He was making his way out with milk and sugar on a little plastic tray decorated with the official photo transfer of the royal wedding of Lady Diana Spencer and Prince Charles.

'Well, like I said, I haven't seen him since we were little so it doesn't mean much to me. And I guess there's no one here anyway. Well, thanks for your help.'

'Would you like a bit of cake?' asked Gwen.

'Thank you, but I'd better be off.'

'Nice cuppa tea? It's Tetley. Len only drinks Tetley. He says it's the best and the only, don't you Len?'

'I do Gwen, I do.'

'Thank you, but I must get going. Thanks again.'

'What's your name, love? If I see them I'll tell them you was looking.'

I said the first name that came into my head. 'Anne Nolan.'

'Like the Nolan sisters, right?'

'Yes, that's it.'

'Want to leave your number?'

'No, it's all right, I'm in the book. Thanks again.'

I had to get back to the office, of course, before Fat Paula became suspicious. I also had to check that Justin was one and the same as Paul Mathry. Santos had called Justin Paul, and it seemed the Mathrys might still own their camper van. I knew I would have to come back soon and check out that caravan properly. And that shed. It would be better to do it in peace and quiet, and in the dark.

Chapter Twelve

In contrast to the cool reserve of the Cardiff registrar, the registrar in the Vale of Glamorgan was neat and plump and radiated cheery jollity from the moment she set eyes on us.

Dan and I had dashed over from Cardiff after work, in separate cars, from separate stations, and met across the road in the old Italian café, but we hadn't had time to get a coffee. Dan had been waylaid by a firearms incident in Roath. The Glamorgan registrar, not particularly put out by our moderate lateness, would be conducting the wedding ceremony for us, as the hotel we had chosen was in her area.

A roly-poly ball of smiles, she ushered us into her newly built, airy office in Barry, congratulating us on our upcoming wedding and, seeing Dan's uniform, asking him how she might find someone to do something about the yobs that kept graffiti-ing the bus stop near her house.

Once we got down to business she repeatedly warned Dan and me about the strict 'no religious inferences' code for our civil ceremony, but other than that she treated the whole thing as if we were preparing for lovely big party together.

She talked us through the booklet containing the ceremony running order and the choices of wording for the vows. Then she wryly passed us leaflets containing suggested poetry we might wish to use to punctuate the official exchanges. Her 'let's not make too big a deal of it' approach seemed to rub off on both of us and within a few minutes we were fairly relaxed.

I was overcome by the urge to laugh at the appalling bits of sentimental greeting-card guff in the suggestion pack. Mostly it was pieces of doggerel about how love is 'giving not taking, mending not breaking' and about the joy of walking long roads side by side in the glow of eternal sunshine and togetherness.

'Some people write their own verses, of course,' smiled the registrar, as if she herself couldn't quite believe anyone would sink to such depths of sentimental exhibitionism. 'You can have any poetry you like a long as *there's no religious references*,' we all chorused together.

I couldn't understand how this twee rubbish was supposed to capture a sense of genuine love and attachment, something as intensely private as what is shared in the most cloistered and intimate moments of your life, spoken in front of dozens of people waiting for the free food and wine.

Part of me wanted to bolt for the door and part of me wished Dan and I could just elope and do the whole thing with no one ogling and watching the exhibition of staged affection. Even worse, it seemed like a sham event anyway. I couldn't see how we could make it to the wedding now, not with Justin lurking on the sidelines. He'd sent me another tantalisingly cruel text a few days before.

'Get ready for your Easter cash instalment,' it said. 'Video update to come.'

I wasn't surprised. I'd known it was just a matter of time. Sooner or later this was all going to explode in my face. Smiling and chatting with the registrar I felt like a woman stubbornly laying out a tablecloth on the garden grass for a picnic, setting out the cups and plates, sandwiches and cupcakes, even though the Met Office had issued a severe weather warning for the day.

'We won't be having any poetry or verses, thank you,' I'd insisted politely. 'We'd like it simple and straightforward, as little fuss as possible, just sincere.'

'Oh, thank goodness,' beamed the registrar, or Claire as she'd insisted we call her. 'I've been doing this for fifteen years and you wouldn't believe the tosh some people want to spout. It's as if they're trying to outdo every other wedding they've ever seen. They're getting more sickly and tasteless by the year, I'm afraid to say. Sometimes it's all I can do to keep a straight face. Same goes for the music. Lots of people go for things like that God-awful wailing woman from *Titanic*, or Whitney Houston warbling "I Will Always Love You-ooooo"!'

'Really?' I blurted with horror, and she laughed again.

'Oh yes. Once I had a guy whose mother played the *Titanic* song on a harp in the middle of the ceremony. It was awful. It was so warm in the room the strings were all flat but this little woman, in a monstrous purple hat, with almost a chicken's worth of feathers on the top, gamely persevered until the end. Don't you worry though – we'll make it lovely for you. If you don't mind my saying so, you seem a lovely, down-to-earth couple.'

I smiled at that, and so did Dan. Then, unexpectedly, he blushed – a truly alarming shade of pleased but embarrassed red.

'I don't need to spout a load of sickly stuff in public to prove anything,' Dan said to me, giving my hand a little squeeze on the way back to the car. 'It's too private. I'd rather tell you when we're alone. No one needs to hear that. It just makes it seem false.' This was one topic that, for once, we agreed upon.

'By the way,' he said. 'I've got a surprise for you this weekend.'

'But I'm on call, and you're on nights,' I replied, thinking I had to try and find time to get back to Aberthin and to the Mathry's caravan. 'I'm bound to get called away.'

'Wrong on both counts,' he said mysteriously, and would say no more.

I rolled over onto my back and stretched out my legs. It was light outside but dim in the bedroom, and I was reluctant to throw back the quilt. I'd always liked the gap in the morning before getting up, the gap that belongs neither to the night before or the day to come. I liked to spin this out as long as possible, especially if it was a weekend, a little cosy space out of time that had nothing to do with the trivia of going to the office, getting the milk in, arguing about who washes up, putting a load in the washing machine, picking up a spare light bulb, paying the credit card bill.

Dan didn't seem to mind getting up as much as I did, except when he'd worked a lot of nights or long overtime stints, which was more and more often since his promotion. On these occasions we'd lie in bed together in the morning drowsiness, neither wanting to be the first to get up and admit the snooze was really over. When it seemed we couldn't delay any longer one of us would reluctantly say,

'All right, let's do The Count.'

Then we would count backwards together from ten to one, slowly but steadily, the intention being that when we reached zero we would both sit up and slide out of bed at the same time. Inevitably, one of us would fail to rise at the last minute, then the other would flop back on the mattress too. There'd be indignant rib-poking and chuckling and we'd begin The Count again. It had been Dan's aunt who had introduced him to The Count, to help rouse him on cold, dark winter mornings ready for school. He had introduced it to me and we had adopted it as our own. I, of course, had taken it up elsewhere, a mantra to steady me for anything I was reluctant to begin, or disliked the thought of doing.

Dan had got up early that morning, and I was alone. If I did The Count alone I always got up at zero, or started whatever was at hand, otherwise there'd be no point in doing it. I lay there a little longer listening to Dan boiling the kettle in the kitchen, whistling what sounded like AC/DC's 'Highway to Hell'. I listened to the murmur of Sky News from the living room. I listened to him opening a cereal packet and the contents tinkling into a bowl and, I think, on to the counter top. I suspected, from the intermittent muted clattering, he was also digging his thermos flask out of the kitchen cupboard. He'd said something about *coffee for the journey*.

In two hours we were taking a trip to a boutique hotel from the *Cool Cymru* brochure. It was Dan's surprise, an attempt to make up for the ruined weekend at the Watch-house. He had chosen another intimate little nook to fuss me in. But I wasn't sure I wanted the day to start. I didn't know if I could bear to be with Dan in a romantic hotel when all I could think of was that *other* hotel and that other night.

But the possibility of being able to do anything other than accept was very remote. Dan had surreptitiously swapped his weekend shifts with one of the other inspectors and had even asked Serian to swap her on-call weekend with mine so he could organise the surprise. Eventually, I began The Count, elevated myself out of bed on the exact beat of the zero, and put on my clothes and face for the day.

Three hours later we were sitting outside a pretty-as-a-painting Georgian townhouse hotel, gazing across the rippling swathe of harbour to the Regency pastel-hued homes across the way. Sheep bleated on the lee of the swarthy hill opposite, its stubby trees bent away from windward. A collie dog raced up and down the steep fields, its occasional determined yaps snapping across the valley. The only other sound was the lapping of the water on the seawall and the fleeting melancholy calls of seagulls.

As if we had ordered ahead, the sky turned a beautiful paint-pot blue and the sun revealed itself from behind the clouds. I was sipping a glass of red wine, and Dan was doing the same from a pint of local golden ale. A lunch of Perl Wen cheese and leek tartlet and Welsh Black beefburger sat comfortably in our respective stomachs. If there was a spot where contentment was meant to be born and bloom it was on that wooden seat, wine-warmed and peaceful, with Dan's hand on my thigh – a stolen silent season in the sun.

On our arrival at the Aeron Inn, the chic receptionist (glossy blond bob, glossier lips and immaculate white shirt) had shown us to the gloriously chic Queen Aeron Suite. It had a gasp-inducing harbour panorama, a super-king bed with Welsh woollen throw blankets, an immense roll-top bath and underfloor heating. All the rooms were named nostalgically after the smacks and schooners that had been built in the harbour's heyday.

The hotel bar, with its driftwood counter and cosy velveteen nooks for intimate supping, was peopled in chattery fashion by pleasant young couples and well-to-do locals. We were an hour or so past Penallt, northwards up the coast on Cardigan Bay, but I had to conscientiously fight the flicker of familiarity that was disturbing my equilibrium. I'd done this before –

except of course, this time Dan was beside me, where he ought to have been the first time.

Dan seemed to be relaxing. He was working his way through the ales and bitters at a hasty pace but I didn't comment on his thirst as I might have done previously. He needed the break. By my third glass of wine I was starting to think the surprise had been a really good idea. I wasn't even annoyed when my phone rang and, before I'd even had a chance to say hello, Bodie's voice bellowed, 'We've got a suspicious death in Port Talbot. How quickly can you be over here?'

Amused and a bit tipsy, I was not sorry to hear his voice. 'And why would I care about a suspicious death, Acting Sergeant?'

'Because you're on call. You have to care.'

'I'm not on call.'

'Yes, you are. You're on the rota. Control room said so. The DI wants you at the scene, pronto.'

'How demanding of him,' I laughed, aware I was slurring slightly. 'But it's Serian this weekend. We swapped. The control room just probably forgot to amend the rota again.'

'Well, if you're not on call where are you, then?'

'Not that it's any of your business, but I'm in a hotel, in Cardigan Bay, drinking wine.'

'Are you pissed?' asked Bodie with amusement.

'I certainly hope so. If not, I will be in half an hour.'

'Oh, right! Well, it's all right for some, by the sound of it. Sorry to have ruined the mood. Enjoy your dirty weekend, you lazy, drunken slacker.'

'Yeah, love you too!' I smiled and clicked off the phone.

'Who's that now?' asked Dan, a ruffle of exasperation breaking through his ale-induced calm as he carried another tray of drinks and a little bowl of pistachios to our table.

'No one – just work,' I said, shoving my phone into my bag. 'I forgot to knock it off.'

'Give it to me!' he insisted, hand out.

'What? Why?' A sudden twinge of alarm spiked in my stomach.

'Just give it to me.'

How could I refuse? Reluctantly, I did as he asked.

He switched the phone off and, with emphasis, tucked it into his fleece pocket. Then he pulled his own phone out of his jeans, switched it off and put it with mine.

'No phones,' he said. 'No work, no queries, no road accidents, no dead people. No call from your mother, no wedding budgets. Just you and me. As it was meant to be.'

'It's a deal,' I grinned with dizzy relief. 'Let's drink to that.'

For the rest of that day, though I knew it was only an illusion, I felt like a woman released from the shadow of an uncertain future. There, by the water, out of our own police area in Dyfed Powys, and surrounded by polite and friendly people, it seemed as if the whole Justin affair was merely part of a tedious television drama I had decided to switch off. It could have no affect on me unless I let it. And the wedding would still be there on Monday when I had deposits to drop off and lists to double check. For that moment at least there was a slice of relief in being away from home and just being with Dan.

In the late afternoon we strolled around the town admiring the beautiful Regency houses, and restored cottages. Snowdrops were peeping from grass verges, the air smelled of wood smoke and salt water. I pointed out antiquated wonders such as metal boot scrapers beside the front doors of the oldest houses and hitching posts for horses near the village inns. It was like landing in the middle of a Jane Austen novel. Young mums strolled by with grinning, chuckling toddlers and august, grey-haired town residents strode or hobbled back and forth with shopping bags and rolled up newspapers, nodding 'Good afternoon' to anyone who happened to be passing.

At one point a wizened but smartly attired old chap, walking his dog, pottered past us as we peered into the window of an old-fashioned chocolate shop.

'Good afternoon,' he said, and to my delight tipped his little trilby at me.

'Good afternoon,' chorused Dan and I, with a grin at each other.

'God, I'd love to work up here,' said Dan. 'Bet the most trouble they get is the odd bit of sheep rustling and incorrigibles peeing on the post boxes after too many real ales.'

After that we wandered along the quay and ate ice cream. We even held hands.

'Look, Jen. I was thinking – about the honeymoon,' said Dan that evening in the restaurant. 'I really don't mind where we go, as long as we're together. Wherever you want is fine with me. I guess I've been a bit selfish about going somewhere quiet and remote. Getting away from it all. You've never wanted a big, expensive wedding, so you should get whatever you want for the honeymoon. That's only fair. You deserve it. I know the last few years have been about me and work and my promotions and so on, but it doesn't have to be that way now I'm getting established. You could retrain or something, if you like. We can do anything we want. When I come to a place like this it makes me realise there are lots of better things to do and better places to be.'

'I'll drink to that,' I said, raising my glass of Merlot, my voice suddenly thick with a thousand emotions I did not want to name. Instead of speaking I put out my hand and cupped his cheek. He took my hand and kissed my palm.

We fell asleep that night, curled around each other, to the sound of the cables clinking on the moored boats on the bay and the occasional hoots of barn owls somewhere in the black depths of the old west-Walian night.

Chapter Thirteen

It wasn't until a week after our seaside interlude that I had the chance to get down to Aberthin again. There'd been a couple of rather public suicides in the force area that week, and the search was also on for several missing people. All in all we were kept busy in the office during the day and then wedding planning ate up my evenings with ravenous haste.

First my mum had 'popped over' for half an hour on the Tuesday night to show me the dark turquoise dress with velvet wrap and matching shoes she had bought for herself at John Lewis. She had gone with the 'fascinator' headdress idea rather than a full hat, and showed me how the feathery and silvery beaded thing on a headband completed the whole ensemble *perfectly*. Actually, she was right. Still slim, and relatively wrinkle-free, she looked very smart, very chic and very excited.

I still had not bought my wedding dress. It was almost March. On the Wednesday evening I had allowed Becky to drag me to two more wedding stores after work, before digging my heels in and insisting – No more! I'd get a dress from an ordinary shop. Becky had picked up a nice navy silk cocktail dress and cardigan for herself though.

'Navy's not too dark for a wedding is it, do you think?' she'd asked. 'It's more a darkish blue than actual navy, isn't it? I mean, I like it but if *you* don't, if it doesn't go with the colour scheme, I'll change it'.

I reassured her that there *was* no colour scheme, and she could wear what she liked as long as she came along and enjoyed herself.

I could tell she was pleased. 'You must pick something for yourself soon though, Jen,' she'd emphasised with quiet concern, 'It's getting closer by the day.'

I knew she was right, but right then I had other priorities.

Thursday was Dan's early shift and he was home by five, so I had no chance to sneak out. Then the weekend came and Dan was off work.

But on the Monday night, to my great relief, the evening was my own. At around 8 p.m. I waved Dan off with a lunch box full of chicken noodle stir fry and rice – I had never liked to think of him doing a whole twelve-hour nightshift without a proper dinner inside him. An hour later, I was heading to the Aberthin caravan park.

I parked my car, as I had before, around the bend, just off the road from the cattle grid. I had cross-checked my information as soon as I'd got the chance by running a quick PNN search on the name Paul Mathry. Unfortunately, there'd been no one on the system that tallied with my information. There were only two other Mathrys in the South Wales area (apart from Michael Mathry) and they were twenty-two and forty-seven, in jail and in Newport, respectively.

I put Paul Mathry into Facebook, just in case. There was one registered in South Wales but there was no photograph, just a thumbnail stock photo of a surfer cresting a wave. The details were sketchy, occasional updates about good places to surf or trips taken in the last few years, a mention of a holiday being planned in August. There weren't many 'friends' listed on his profile – just a few with surfer type-nicknames like Board-boy and Wave-rider. None appeared to use the site regularly.

But it seemed to add weight to my theory that 'Justin' was really Paul Mathry. Added to what Gwen had said about there being some trouble with a girl, it made me think I was on the right track. Gwen had said the caravan was used by Paul from time to time, or at least that she'd seen the lights on there.

I needed some sort of confirmation about Justin, an X that would mark the spot of his existence so I could start digging for something more useful. Time was moving on, not just to the wedding day, not just to the Easter payment demanded, but to the point where Justin would push this game too far.

There was clearly no one at the caravan. There was no sign of life in the hour I'd been patiently watching. It was heavily, inkily dark, and no light had come on inside, no tell-tale TV flickered. I was glad the previous week's snow flurries had retreated and we'd had seven days of dry, cold weather. Snow illuminates too much, refracts light and shadow, sucks in and stores footprints. I wanted to leave as little trace of myself as possible, for obvious reasons.

The caravan site itself was all but abandoned to darkness. One van at the far end showed a dim lounge light, but the only other illumination was from the grimy, widely spaced lamps along the access track and a dim arc light on the little locked office.

I padded quietly to the Mathry's shed, the peak of my baseball cap pulled down, and peered in through the water-warped wooden panels. It was padlocked with a newish lock which looked serviceable, but there was no camper van in there. I crept round the outside of the Mathry's caravan, listening carefully for any sound, peering in through the frosted window of the door and the gaps in the side curtains, carefully scanning the field for any emergent activity, dog walkers and so on.

As I'd thought from my previous visit, it was the medium-sized static kind of caravan, rather than the towing sort. On the off-chance, I tried the door, but it was locked, naturally. The windows were all fastened shut too.

But it was very similar to Wendy's old caravan – which was exactly what I'd been counting on for the last week.

I'd come prepared. I was going to break in.

I didn't use that exact phrase when the idea popped into my head. I told myself I was on reconnaissance, intelligence gathering. I wasn't going to steal anything, just see if I could find out if Paul and Justin were the same person, and if so, if he had anything to hide.

I admit I almost lost my nerve when I heard a guffaw across the field, a gang of teenagers at boisterous play. I heard one youngish male voice laughing and yelling, 'Fuck *off*, you prick,' more laugher and what sounded like a bottle breaking.

Crouched in the shadow of the caravan, hands clenched, I contemplated bolting for the car. But after a few minutes of tense listening, silence had resumed. Sucking in a great breath I counted down from ten to one, exhaled, then got to my feet.

It was do this or do nothing, I reasoned. Go home, give up, keep paying and keep praying that Justin wouldn't premiere his film and smash my life to pieces with one callous click of his index finger. The thought of this filled me with steely purpose. The unexpected weekend at the Aeron Inn had clarified something for me. I might very well be questioning whether or not I wanted the life I had with Dan, but it was *my* life. I might *choose* to abandon it, but that would be *my* decision. Justin couldn't just bowl up and decide to steal it away.

A surge of renewed outrage pushed me forward – that and the fact I happened to have an advantage that made the prospect of getting inside the caravan surreptitiously and quickly, fairy simple, *if* it worked. When I had stayed on the site with Wendy and Shirley years before, one of us, each blaming the others, had locked the door key inside the caravan. Wendy, unconcerned, had shown us a solution her family used in just such lock-out emergencies. It was simple if you knew how, a trick of the trade, gleaned from many a family's arrival, all the way from home only to discover someone had left the caravan key behind on the kitchen table.

It was a stroke of luck that the caravan was on the end so that the rear and one side were overlooked only by the thick hedge. Heading round to the oblong side window I pulled out Dan's Swiss Army knife. The big front windows of those old caravans are solid, fixed glass. But the side windows and little bedroom windows are hinged on ratchets that allow them to slide and tilt open, bottom outwards.

Wendy had explained that most were only secured by a flimsy central catch. If you applied a blade between the window and the window rim and pushed upwards you could pop the catch easily. Then all you had to do was slide your hand in, click the sliding arms out of the teeth and lift for entry. The bedroom windows were too small to allow entry, but the side window was man, or woman-sized.

It was just as absurdly easy twelve years later. After a moment of exploratory poking with the knife blade I felt the edge of the metal catch inside the rim. It was a bit sticky but, with a flick, it popped easily enough. A few seconds later I was hoisting myself up on my gloved hands (no harm in taking precautions against leaving finger prints) and swinging one leg onto the cushioned bench beneath.

Cautiously, I pulled the window closed behind me. I couldn't believe it had been so easy. I couldn't believe I was actually doing it.

Exhaling heavily, and still listening for any sounds of movement outside, I remained motionless, waiting for my eyes to adjust to the dark. Right away I detected the familiar caravan smells from my youth. Damp, mildew, old seat cushions, a faint whiff of grease from fried eggs or bacon cooked on the little stove. But winding through these historic base notes was something else: fragrant, herbal, like the smell of the CID evidence room when it was jungle-deep with seized plants after a cannabis farm raid.

Slowly, things emerged from the interior gloom. The caravan, upholstered with the familiar plastic and polyester browns and oranges, had certainly been well used, but seemed fairly clean and tidy. There were signs someone had been occupying it, if only intermittently, fairly recently. Copies of the *Mirror*, two or three months old, lay on the seat before me. I could make out a packet of Tetley tea bags by the sink and an open box of Pop Tarts. A fairly new portable TV sat on the side unit.

Careful not to disturb anything, I rose and padded, in the dark, through to the bedroom at the back, and the little bunk bedroom next to it, just to convince myself there was no one lurking there. But all was quiet.

Carefully, I switched on Dan's old Maglite torch (good job he had all this handy bloke stuff lying around in the room under the stairs), taking care to keep my hand cupped over the light. I didn't want anyone to see the glow of a torch on the closed curtains. I wasn't sure what I was looking for exactly – proof of identity, something incriminating. Maybe a laptop and discs containing that hideous video that I could steal and smash and regain my freedom, but I knew that would be hoping for too much.

I started my search with the kitchen cupboards but there was nothing much inside except the expected collection of mismatched dinner plates, bowls and cups, and odds and ends such as a few boxes of sticking plasters and a roll of bandages. In the kitchen drawer was a stash of the sort of junk most people absent-mindedly hoard: rubber bands, a novelty bottle opener, money-off coupons cut from boxes and packets, take-away menus, screws and nails in an old, lidless tobacco tin.

Under the bits and bobs I found a couple of crayon-scribbled child's drawings showing bright, waxy, seaside staples: wavy-blue-line sea, sandcastles, a triangular-sailed boat riding the horizon. Also there were some old photographs – the little square kind that were developed from cameras in the seventies and early eighties, when cameras were still something of a novelty, and the photos came in a half-flap paper envelope from your local chemist's shop.

There were several of a stern-looking, middle-aged man in neatly pressed shorts and short-sleeved shirts, probably Michael Mathry, and a woman in a variety of flowery dresses – Mrs Mathry? There was one of what was clearly a much younger Gwen and Len with a cocker spaniel (though presumably not Ernie, rather one of his predecessors), grinning from deck chairs with two little mop-topped, sunburn-pink girls.

And there were several of floppy-haired, skinny young boys, maybe eight or nine years old, in Hawaiian shorts with fishing nets, plastic tennis rackets, or snorkels in hand, holding up crabs and starfish, one thumb aloft.

Justin? I wondered, but there were too many years between the children and the man – the boyish frames had not yet filled out into muscle, the faces were pink and still girlish.

There were more photos in the small, bunk-bed room, taped to the wall alongside the bottom bunk. Most of them showed a girl, in her early teens, pretty, skinny, pale-complexioned, dark-haired. She looked a bit sheepish, as if she hadn't wanted to be snapped at that moment. In almost all of them she was wearing a little gold crucifix that glinted in the sun.

Skinny, dark hair . . . Gwen had mentioned her – the vicar's daughter?

In a box under the bunk were more photos in a cardboard folder inscribed 'Suzy'. There was the girl, perhaps seventeen now, in various beach settings, paddling in the white-topped waves, hair half blown across her laughing mouth in black streaks, white skin, eyes raised shyly at the camera; or cross-legged in the sand, earnestly waving the camera away; or tugging at the flyaway skirt of her sundress, barefooted.

Interspersed with these were concert ticket stubs, birthday cards, teenage keepsakes. And then I found what I was looking for – a smiling, arm-around photo of her with Justin. They might have been sixth-form sweethearts or students. Justin looked younger, his hair longer, a little darker, but the same clear blue gaze, those storm-cloud eyes, arrowed out of the picture. And in the background of the shot was the sea, a strip of sand and the blue and white camper van.

I grinned in the darkness. 'Hello Paul Mathry,' I whispered, saying it aloud to sound it out, the new name on my tongue. But I couldn't get used to the idea that he was now Paul. He was still Justin to me.

I pocketed the photo. I knew it was a risk but it didn't look as if anyone had touched the box for years. And I wanted proof that Justin existed. Until now he was almost a phantom inhabiting my mind, seen by few, known by none, indeterminate, untouchable. But now I had his photo and his name. It was an identity at least, a fixed point, so much more than I'd had before.

I continued my stealthy search, feeling vindicated. In the main bedroom Justin had stored a stash of essentials: two sweatshirts and a pair of jeans hung in the narrow wardrobe, socks and pants lay in a neat pile on the unit top. A clean towel was folded beside them. There were some interesting items in the bathroom, mixed in with the expected toothbrush and razor, soap and bottle of shampoo. There were several old bottles of Prozac, pharmacy dispensed, several bottles of Valium, Tamazepam and Ibuprofen – your basic Prolific Priority Offender's stash.

There were also twelve unopened three-packs of condoms.

But I was hoping for something more. I knew I had smelt weed in the caravan lounge. I could still smell it faintly. Maybe Justin had something more notable hidden away. He'd hardly be likely to keep drugs like that in the bathroom cabinet, and I couldn't exactly go riffling through the caravan, overturning seat cushions and pulling off wall panelling like a TV CSI, in the dark. But I was convinced there'd be something more interesting here somewhere.

If I were Justin, where would I hide the stash? Not in the toilet cistern or the tea caddy – too obvious. Besides, he wouldn't be primarily thinking he'd need to hide it from a police search. Why would he? He was more likely to think about preventing anyone who was likely to break in from finding it and thinking it was worth stealing.

Then I thought back to a box of tampons I'd seen in the kitchen cupboard with the plasters and bandages. The box was quite old. Why would Justin have tampons? Sure enough, inside was a little plastic bag of loose weed, what looked like a little plastic bag of heroin and a couple of what I took to be Ecstasy tablets wrapped in a piece of cling film. There were some others – white ones and little blue ones, unmarked. I wish I'd paid more attention during our police 'Know Your Drugs' demonstrations, the ones we did at schools and open days for the kids.

Most interesting of all was the little blister pack of unmarked red pills. I knew what they were immediately. We'd done a press release on this type of drug as part of the 'Know Your Limits' alcohol safety campaign every Christmas for five years. It was always entitled, 'Don't take your eyes off your drink!' There were two blister packs in the box, and it looked as if one or two strips were gone.

Rohypnol.

The implications of this little find made me freeze. I pulled out one of the silver strips. Six of the tablets were gone from the first row of eight.

I took a step or two backwards, leaning against the little table, deep in thought. But my weight made it wobble and, as a result, half a dozen magazines piled haphazardly near the edge slithered to the floor. I picked them up, anxious not to leave anything out of place. Nothing should give away the fact I'd been there.

As I gathered them up, I realised they were travel magazines – two or three surf glossies and a couple of UK travel guides. The current and two previous editions of the *Cool Cymru* hotel guide had fallen out of the middle of the pile. There appeared to be some scraps of notepaper spilling out that been tucked between its pages. There were all sorts of scribbles on the papers, mostly nonsense, innocuous things like date and time reminders, or phrases like 'buy milk'. But there were also scrawled album titles, telephone numbers, what looked like hotel names and travel information, high tide and low tide times, website addresses.

I skimmed through the recent *Cool Cymru* booklet. Some of the pages had been turned down at the corner. One of them was turned to mark the Watch-house. Someone had circled part of the review. The other two hotels on turned-down pages were in North Wales.

On instinct I flicked through the *UK Top 100 Places to Stay*. It was a few years old. Six pages were turned down marking four hotels in the south of England, one in Northumberland and one in Norfolk.

I looked back at the paper scribbles: hotel names, album titles, girls' names, phone numbers, website addresses.

While I was pondering this jumble of information, acknowledging the crackle in my head as neurons jumped to connect with each other and see the pattern in what was before me, I heard the slow bump-crunch of a vehicle outside on the track.

A few seconds later a flare of expanding headlights lit up the curtains around the front. Someone was driving up to the caravan.

Chapter Fourteen

At the sight of those headlights I solidified, stone-still, for a split second that expanded like a crack in the fabric of time. The notepapers were clawed in my left hand, my limbs locked in the flash of the car headlights. I saw myself from outside, suspended in the freeze-frame, caught in the act.

But then a startling flight response coursed through my bloodstream. I was moving without thinking – swift and calm. At double speed, I shuffled the magazines back on to the shelf, placed the box of drugs back in the cupboard, closing it quietly. I doused the Maglite and stuck it in my fleece pocket. My head snapped around looking for an escape route.

The headlights came to a stop at the front of the caravan. They flicked off but the engine was still running. Carefully, I moved to peer through the curtain to make sure I really was in as much trouble as I suspected.

A youngish looking man with flyaway, surfy blond hair occupied the driver's seat of a Land Rover parked outside. It was the old olive-drab army kind with canvass side flaps. The man was lighting a cigarette and apparently fishing for something below the dashboard.

It wasn't Justin.

It was obvious however, that, whoever he was, he was headed

for the Mathrys' caravan. Any minute now he'd turn off the spluttering engine and step out. The caravan had only one door. It was too late to bolt and make a run for it. As soon as the man got out of the Land Rover he'd be in full view of my exit. He turned the ignition off and fumbled on the floor, for what turned out to be a battered kit bag.

I took in all this detail in a hair's breadth of a second. Just as quickly I realised there was only one thing for it, one way out. I had to hover by the side window and wait. I had let it drop closed but had not latched it when I had pulled myself in. Yes, it was in full view of the Land Rover *now*. But if I waited until he, whoever he was, reached the caravan door, it would be out of sight. As soon as I heard the key in the lock I could lift the window, slide out and drop to the ground. If I was lucky the sound of the door opening would cover the sound of my drop as he stepped up and inside. The caravan was dark, the door was tucked in the recess behind the kitchen unit. It might be just enough to cover my exit.

It would take the man a few seconds at least to register that anything was wrong. In those few seconds I'd already be running, full steam, around the side of the caravan, towards the tree-lined lane twenty yards away, where he couldn't see me.

Crouched on my tiptoes on the settee, I placed one hand on the rim of the window which was open just a tiny bit. Every sound, every breath was distilling down to one precise moment of action – I had to move at just the right moment.

As I heard the man's approach, I registered the sound of a mobile phone ringing.

'What?' said the man, rather impatiently, from somewhere near the Land Rover. Then, 'I'm here now, as it happens.' Pause, 'I said I would, didn't I?' Pause.

Closer now, 'Yes, of course I know that . . . Nah it's the arse end of beyond, you know that. There's no bugger for miles.' Pause.

Closer still, but not quite at the door, not yet. 'You're just repeating yourself, mate. Take a Valium, for fuck's sake.' More silence. 'Nah, of course not, what do you think I am, stupid? Yeah, yeah . . . For God's sake, I know!'

I heard the call end, a sigh and then the muttered word 'Prick!' I heard the man shift his bag up onto his shoulder as he approached the door, fishing in his pocket now, a silvery jingle of keys. The key in the lock. A click.

My timing was perfect. The window opened out as the door swung in. With his step inside, I was dropping out. But at the last second the leg of my jeans caught on a piece of loose window trim, slightly throwing my landing off. I fell on to one side with a thump. I heard the window bump shut.

There was a moment's thinking silence before I heard the click of the light from within and at once I was illuminated from above. I didn't look up or wait to see if the man had heard or seen me. I was already on my feet, legs and arms firing in unison.

There were a few seconds' silence, and then, in what seemed like vivid, ear-shattering stereo, I heard the shout, 'Oi, you fucker!' issue from the caravan, followed by the caravan door flying open. Purposeful footfalls advanced over the gravel and on to the grass.

But I was already out of his sight, hidden by the hedge. My legs pumping strongly at full pelt, hat still down, I hoped I was gaining enough ground. I thrashed around the lane corner like the very devil was on my heels, and perhaps he was. My first thought had been not to be caught in a caravan I had broken into. But then I realised I would soon be in the coal-black woods surrounding a deserted caravan site, with almost no one around to hear or intervene if I needed them. And someone who knew Justin was running after me.

Of course he couldn't have seen who I was. It was too dark. The most he would have registered was a figure in a hoody and baseball cap, fleeing into the dark. The obvious assumption? Some scumbag burglar or druggie.

The memory of Bodie's story about the Stella Heist pursuit of Twn Row flashed back to me, as I shot for the cover of the trees in a breath-bursting sprint. If testosterone-fuelled, sprint-ready Bodie had been on my tail at that moment I think I would have had almost no chance. In seconds I would have felt that solid wall of muscle-man in motion crashing into me, flopping me to the ground, flat and stunned like Mickey Half-Pipe. Or Mickey Ming Mong? One of the unfortunate Mickeys, anyway. But this man was not so pursuit-ready. And I wasn't making the same mistake as Mickey. I wasn't trying to outrun him, just out-distance him. Because between fight and flight there is always *hide*.

I had six or seven seconds head start and lots of Cardiff-centred foot-miles behind me. Almost without thinking, I'd measured the distance from the caravan, to the corner of the lane – within a moment of sparking synapses I was off the track, into the scrub and flat on my stomach behind the bushes.

Six seconds later the man rounded the corner at something like a full run, but already panting heavily, his gait uneven. Ten paces or so past where I lay, slowing my breathing in the winter-crisp leaves and brambles, he staggered to a stop, still staring off to where the road wound out of sight.

'What the . . .? Fucking hell,' he managed to gasp after a second, bringing forth a tremendous barking cough of breath and spittle.

Dropping his hands to his knees he surveyed the empty lane. Then, in unexpectedly timely fashion, came a repeat of the earlier sound of breaking glass and teenagers shouting and laughing, sputtering towards us down the lane. Never have I been so grateful for the sound of anti-social behaviour in full swing.

The man, alone and winded, was obviously thinking twice about continuing the pursuit. After a second's consideration he called, 'Yeah, just keep on running, you prick!' at the empty lane, before staggering back in the direction of the caravan.

I didn't move for what seemed like forever. I wanted to be sure he was really gone. I remembered how Justin's hand had gripped my arm in the street, the bruise it had left. This guy was big. Not fit, obviously, but big. And he had reason enough to be annoyed. Staying on the ground seemed safer.

Perhaps half an hour of listening later I pulled myself to my feet, brushed the twigs and earth from my clothes, and crept to the bend in the lane. The caravan light was on. The sound of the portable TV ebbed in and out.

I should have just crept away then and there. That would have been the safest thing to do. But I was curious to see what this guy was doing. I suspected it was Justin who had called him earlier, who had been on the other end of the phone clearly questioning him, giving instructions. But instructions about what? Had he sent him here to do something specific? It had sounded that way.

I tiptoed towards the drawn curtains. They were open just a fraction, daring me to peek in. I put my eye up to the sliver of light. The man was slumped, lying chest up, head thrown back, on the bench seat beneath the window. There was a greyish haze hanging in the air. In front of him, on the table, was a large bong or drug pipe of some kind. The window I'd made my escape from was still open just a fraction – he hadn't secured it. Perhaps he hadn't realised what had happened, exactly. Through the gap I could smell weed and something else – something fragrant, much stronger.

The man's rucksack was on the bench opposite him, and the magazines and papers I'd examined were now poking out of the top. There was another carrier bag of what looked like papers, or perhaps photos, next to it. Open on the table was a laptop. That's where the sounds were coming from, not the portable TV.

Shifting to get a better view I could see blurry images running on the screen. It was immediately obvious that it was porn. I realised at the same time that the guy's trousers were unzipped and a clutch of crumpled tissues lay on the table. I could see the banner at the top of the site running on the screen. It said 'XXX Surf Sluts. Hot and Wet!'

It looked like a homemade video of amateur scenes just like the ones I'd stumbled across on the 'Homemade Hotties' and 'Busty Babes' site. Saliva trickled in my cheeks and I fought the sudden urge to vomit. I managed to stop at a dry heave. It wasn't so much what was actually on the screen. It was just moving flesh. From the angle I couldn't make out much more than the site name and the male and female figures. There was nothing specific to see, but I had a hollow and bitter feeling that that might not always be the case - the performers could easily change.

At that moment the man's mobile phone started ringing again – a shrill, repetitive beeping that pulled me from the little join-the-dots process unfolding unbidden in my head. Whatever the man had been smoking or inhaling, the phone didn't seem to penetrate his slumber but I didn't wait to see if it eventually would. I backed away. Then I hugged the edge of the field, following it away from Justin's van, past the caravans to the other end, before heading back up the track from the opposite direction, towards the entrance road and my car.

By the time I fumbled with the lock and fell inside I was shivering and exhausted, the adrenalin seeping out of my system. I forced myself to put the key in the ignition and drive. As I met the main road minutes later and the glow of the street lights signalled a return to civilisation, I caught a sudden glimpse of myself in the rear-view mirror. On my right cheek was a livid scratch, brown-red with crumbling dried blood. A pinkish, thumb-sized bruise was already forming beneath it, along the cheekbone. Max Factor concealer wouldn't cover that, I mused. It must have happened when I'd hurled myself into the bushes, but I hadn't felt it.

Spitting on a tissue recovered from my pocket I wiped my cheek clean as best as I could. It wasn't too bad. It wasn't deep. It would heal in a day or so, I told myself. It could have been worse.

I drove mechanically, automatically, carefully. Though I was tempted to floor the accelerator and shoot home, I didn't want to get caught by a speed camera or stopped by a police officer so far from home, with a bruised face and mud-streaked clothes. *Everything's fine officer, no problem here!*

When I finally closed the front door of the house behind me and slumped to the floor in the hall, the telephone message light was blinking.

There were two messages from Dan. The first said he was just ringing to see if I'd had a good day, and that he loved me. The second said it was a quiet night and to call him if I got the chance, before I went to bed. The last message had been left two hours ago.

I didn't return his call. I knew, without attempting it, that constructing a coherent sentence would have been impossible just then.

It wasn't until I pulled off my muddy jeans to throw them in the wash that I realised the strip of red pills was in my pocket with the photo of Justin and Suzy. And Dan's Maglite was nowhere to be found.

Chapter Fifteen

I was running. I was running fast and hard, breathing harder. At first I didn't pay much attention when I spotted a man in the distance, running towards me from the direction of the playing fields. He was a hazy shimmer of indistinct motion as I sped on, undeterred, but then he seemed to deliberately increase his speed as he got closer. I tensed as he accelerated towards me, sidestepping to allow him to pass with unspoken runners' courtesy, but he matched my motion at the last minute, stopping suddenly, blocking my path. I weaved to avoid him, shoes sliding on the leaf-littered path.

He pulled his hood back and I realised it was Justin. His face wore a triumphant slash of a smile. His eyes expressed nothing at all. I opened my mouth to speak, but all too quickly he had knocked me to the ground with a single sweep of his arm. The force startled and winded me, giving me no time to react before he was on top of me, trying to pin me down. I was thrashing and writhing, hopelessly. He was too strong.

'If you don't give me my money, you'll have to pay your debt some other way,' he snarled. I wanted to scream but couldn't. I wanted to fight but I couldn't.

Dan! Dan! I screamed in my head, help me! But no sound escaped into the air. Then I realised the hand on my arm *was*

Dan's, and I was thrashing against our king-size duvet and woollen bedspread, which were wrapped around me in a stranglehold.

Slippery-slick with cold sweat, my eyes swam through the swallowing darkness until I finally made out the familiar appearance of my bedroom. The glow of dawn filtered in through the curtains.

'It's ok, Jen. I'm here,' murmured Dan sleepily. 'You're safe. You're safe. You're just dreaming.' He stroked my hair, instinctively, very gently, slowly, like he often did when I needed soothing or when we were cuddling and he was telling me he loved me.

I lay there breathing fitfully, letting myself shake off the dream, the memory of Justin's grip, mingled with the memory of the flight of the night before. Both seemed equally as real and equally as terrifying. After that, sleep was all but impossible.

At around 7 a.m., as I lay groggy and stomach-sick under the covers, fitfully dozing, the beep of a text message sounded from my mobile on the bedside table. Dan lay snoring beside me. It was another text from Justin.

'I called last night,' mumbled Dan, from somewhere only just this side of sleep, sliding his hand across my waist.

'I went for a long run,' I whispered, turning away from him, one hand on my phone, hiding Justin's now familiar number, hiding my bruised cheek in the pillow in the day-tinged gloom. I could tell Dan how I got it later. Not the truth, of course, but a good excuse. 'Go back to sleep.'

'It's early. Who's messaging you at this hour? Are you on call?' he murmured.

'Yes. Go back to sleep,' I repeated. Luckily, he was already asleep.

I took my phone to the bathroom and saw that this time Justin wanted £300. Calm and direct, just like before.

'Fat Paula's been looking for you again,' said Serian cheerfully, as I arrived in the office two hours after Justin's text. She handed me a sheaf of papers and a coffee. She eyed my cheek. I hadn't tried to cover it with make-up. That would only have made it look like I had something to hide. 'What happened? Lost a fight?'

'You should see the other guy,' I replied benignly, as I already had several times that morning.

It's amazing the way people look at you when you are a woman who appears one day with a facial injury, especially if they are police officers. I told Serian what I'd told Nige, and the front counter clerk, and Superintendent Sellers and Kirsty from file preparation. 'I tripped while running.'

This was simple and convincing. And it was sort of true, though I still sensed people regarding me with concern, as if I'd said, 'I walked into a door.'

I was half expecting one of the domestic violence team to approach me, subtly, quietly, in the corridor, to tell me, sensitively, considerately, that if there was any problem, I could speak to them, privately, confidentially. But since Dan was an Inspector they showed uncharacteristic restraint (or maybe it was cowardice) and bustled by, eyes downcast.

'Old man socked you one?' asked Doyle with a grin, as I ducked into the monthly CID briefing to avoid the imminent approach of Fat Paula, who I had spotted lurking down the corridor. I ignored the surreptitious stares of the company at my purple-coloured cheek and took my seat. I saw Fat Paula come to a halt and then hover in the doorway. Thankfully, Superintendent Sellers was just closing the door, and Paula didn't quite have the courage to interrupt the meeting. Whatever she wanted, I didn't want to hear about it that morning. I hardly heard a word the superintendent said about drug raids and intelligence packages either, except that there was a dead baby involved somewhere – a Methadone overdose, I believe.

All I could do was stare into the dark realm inside my head, reliving the night before and what I had seen and done. Before I had collapsed into bed I'd tried to check the internet to search for the 'Surf Sluts' site. My stomach repeated its heaving motion every time I thought about it. I just couldn't banish the question, *What if I am on that site?*

It was more than possible, wasn't it? What if that was the place it would start, where my *debut* would be posted, before the video of Justin banging away at me hit Dan's email, or the email of my friends?

Unfortunately, there'd been no network connection. I'd tried to log on three times without success. The whole search system seemed to be down, the message, 'Access to this function is unavailable at this time – please consult your internet provider', flashing up stubbornly every time I clicked on the internet tab.

All I could do was wait for the problem to resolve itself, but the waiting was soul-crushing. Unseen, unnamed, these horrors were on a recurrent loop in my brain and I had to try and short-circuit it before my nerve endings disintegrated in full view of the senior CID staff.

I tried to distract myself by attempting to mentally clarify what I had learned. I knew Justin's name now. That was the key fact that might enable me to open him up, like an old fashioned can of corned beef, first peeling back a thin strip around the outside of who he was, then taking off the shell to reveal the soft pink weakness underneath.

But I hadn't really found out anything I could use against him, any leverage. I'm not sure what I'd hoped to find at the caravan – child porn perhaps, imprisoned illegal immigrants, handcuffed Polish prostitutes, a crystal meth lab. There *had* been some drugs, but nothing that the Crown Prosecution Service would find criminally significant.

However, the red pills I'd stuffed into my pocket when the headlights startled me were significant in other ways. Rohypnol. The perfect incapacitant, dissolved in a drink it is tasteless and odourless. Easily available on the internet, following ingestion it quickly renders a person unconscious, or close to it, and, the next day, leaves them with memory loss. It's the perfect date-rape drug.

Date rape: the first word innocuous, full of promise, the second holding connotations of violence and violation. Put them together and the result is a hybrid of male-female interaction and coupling since time began, but in a neat, media-friendly term.

I kept thinking back to the moment I had stood in the cottage bathroom in Penallt that night, trying to pin down the last things I truly remembered. But all I could summon was a woozy montage of indistinct images and the glasses of wine Justin had given me shortly before.

There were ten red pills missing from the box. Twelve packets of condoms in the bathroom cabinet.

All along I'd assumed that Justin had targeted me, perhaps opportunely, or out of malice, but ultimately specifically, singly. But a whole box of Rohypnol, ten missing from the box, and twelve packets of condoms? That would add up to a lot of lost memory, a lot of unremembered sex, more than one night could account for surely?

There had been a lot of girls' names scribbled on the papers I had seen in the caravan. Many hotels had been marked in *Cool Cymru* and in the UK hotel guide.

It also made me wonder again what exactly had happened to Suzy, the vicar's daughter? Was she one and the same as the girl in the photos I had found, the little crucifix glowing at her throat? Was it as simple as an unwanted pregnancy and a scandal, as Gwen had implied? Or was it something worse? There she was, in the photo with Justin. She had known him, and something had gone wrong for her. Sex had featured in there somewhere, surely – didn't it always?

As soon as the briefing was over, I slipped downstairs to the CID room while they all went to get lunch. Bodie's machine was not security locked, naturally. I ran a search without a second thought. But there was nothing on the system for a Susan or Suzy Miller. I wasn't really surprised. If it had been something that had come to the attention of the police surely Gwen and her sister's church-cleaning friend would have known about it. It was almost ten years ago, too. If there had been some police involvement but it had been privately resolved, it might not have been transferred over to NOMAD.

Reluctantly, I made my way to the canteen for a coffee, thinking perhaps Suzy Miller might know a lot about Justin if I could only find her. I needed to consult someone who knew more than NOMAD did, and had a longer memory. The person who immediately sprang to mind was PC Dick Thomas, in Swansea.

Dick was one of my favourite coppers– a career PC, as they are known. They are among the number of slowly dwindling old hands who remember the old days and are nearing their long-awaited retirement. Over the decades they've accrued more knowledge and experience than half the senior officers put together, but for one reason or another have never wanted, or managed to gain, promotion. Every station or area has one (Southern's was Sergeant Stan in the basement). The great thing about these guys is that if you treat them nicely, indulge them in the retelling of their old stories, and take them a packet of biscuits from time to time, they'll be the best contact you ever make in any police force, an untapped seam of everything that never made it into the official police records – gossip, hearsay, rumour and sometimes truth that no one could prove.

It was Dick and his new community partner Rhian I'd visited, as a decoy for Fat Paula, on the day I'd first visited the Aberthin caravan site. I was already in his good books for taking along a packet of Bakewell tarts. He seemed a bit surprised to see me again so soon, but I had a good cover story. I arrived at the station after lunch with a big box of newly printed community meeting posters we were in the process of issuing to all the out-stations.

The station was really just a three-room community office in a converted bungalow. Its opening, six months previously, was part of the plan to make officers more 'accessible to the community' as the Home Office had decreed. The force had also opened several little offices in comprehensive schools and some of the big supermarkets. Local community meetings were supposed to be the new way of 'engaging' with the public and also, I suspected, a way of distracting the same public, and the media, from the fact that hideous budget cuts meant old-fashioned stations were closing by the dozen.

Dick's station/office was always immaculately neat and

businesslike, as was Dick himself – shirt smartly ironed, grey hair smartly cut.

'Crikey, walked into a door, did you?' he asked with his twinkly-eyed smile as I arrived at the counter.

'Fell. Out running.'

'Oh, well, exercise does you good, mostly. You should try that, Rhian, moving around a bit. Be a novelty for you.'

Rhian, the new PC, was lounging on a chair, tie undone, hair in a scrappy ponytail, reading a copy of *Heat* magazine and looking even younger than her twenty-one years.

'Bugger off, Dick,' she said pleasantly. 'Hiya Jen, back again?'

'Put that away, will you love?' Dick asked Rhian, motioning to her magazine. 'Make yourself useful and put some tea on for the press officer. Then start writing the time and date on the posters Jen's brought so we can get them up around town a.s.a.p.'

Rhian obeyed – good-naturedly, if slowly.

'No motivation, these kids,' whispered Dick as he offered me a seat 'God help me, she's willing enough, but dumb as an egg.'

'Dick?' I began, settling into the chair, nursing a steaming cuppa. I broke open the packet of chocolate digestives I'd brought along and pushed it towards Dick. When he'd started to munch on one I said rather absently, as if it had slipped my mind and I wasn't terribly interested, 'While I'm here, I wanted to pick your brains. Do you remember a bit of a scandal down here, a few years back now, about a vicar called Miller and his daughter? I seem to remember someone talking about it when I was down in the village last year, for the charity fun-run with the community team. I only ask because we, well some of the bosses in HQ, are thinking of doing a 'stop child abuse' campaign with local churches across the force area.'

(This much was almost true. A few weeks previously there'd been an arrest involving a vicar who'd allegedly sexually assaulted two young boys in Swansea. That, and the ongoing revelations of the child abuse scandal in the Catholic Church, meant many church organisations were keen to increase their community activities with the police.)

I pressed on. 'I have this vague recollection that someone in Child Protection said something about the vicar up in Pennard maybe being a bit dodgy, and there'd been a scandal, something about his daughter being involved. Obviously, we wouldn't want to put our foot in it, if it's a bit of a sensitive issue. You know what long memories these villages have, and the relatives might still be around. I thought you'd know, being the expert on this patch and having the memory of an elephant and all.'

Dick grinned, flattered as I'd intended, and said, 'Well, I do say, no one's had more time on the beat in this area than me, and I do like to think I have golden recall. Can't much remember where my car keys are in the morning, mind you! But if it happened down here in the last twenty-five years, I always say I probably had something to do with it, or knew about it.'

He thought for a moment, and then he said: 'Milland, that was it! Father Milland, like Ray Milland, the famous Welsh actor? Though probably you wouldn't remember him. Too long ago.'

'*The Lost Weekend*, right?' I offered with a smile.

He jerked his head over at Rhian in delight, 'Hear that, Rhian? Wish you knew a bit about something other than *Hello* magazine! Jesus, you are a sharp one, Jen. How does someone your age know about that?'

'I had a nanna who liked old black and white films and I'd watch them with her on a Sunday afternoon.'

'Bloody marvellous!' I'd obviously just gone up another notch in his estimation. Between that and the biscuits he was eating out of my hand.

'Anyway, Father Milland,' he said, thoughtfully fingering his tie. 'Now, I recall there was nothing wrong with that man. A proper old fashioned gent, he was. Who said there was any funny business with him? No, it was the daughter there was some business with. That's right, I remember now. She'd got pregnant, I think. And, that's right, she said that she'd got pregnant because she'd been raped. Well, *she* didn't actually report it, it was one of her friends who did that. The girl had just gone to university at the time. I think there'd been some family ruckus about her being away at uni and going out drinking or being with boys, usual student stuff, but like I said, the father was old fashioned. What would you expect from a vicar?

'Well, the allegation of rape was made and I think Inspector Keith Cottle dealt with it. He's gone now, of course.'

'He's dead? When did he die? He was only in his fifties.'

'No, not gone from this world, you daft bugger, just gone to Hull, but that's almost the same. Anyway, it wasn't like it is now with all the rape suites and dedicated officers and so on, and it was a couple of months after the fact so there wasn't any evidence to get. But it didn't matter because when we spoke to her about a proper statement she withdrew it a few days later – said she'd made it all up to her friend because she didn't want her dad to know she'd been with a guy who'd done the dirty deed, knocked her up, sex before marriage and all that.

'It was a shame because she'd been such a nice, tidy girl – quiet like, studious. I remember her when she was younger, about fourteen or fifteen, always round the church up there when I'd do my rounds. Black, black hair she had, jet black, and little glasses – really pretty in a nice way. The family wanted to keep it quiet, obviously, so they moved away. I think she had an abortion or maybe put the kid up for adoption.'

'So there was never any rape investigation, then?'

'Nope.'

'Not even the basics?'

'No, like I said – no evidence, and she withdrew it. Probably nowadays we'd look into it a bit more, to make sure, like, but then, well, no complaint no case. Tragic, though.'

'Tragic? How?'

'She killed herself.'

'What?'

'Yes. She killed herself, down in Carmarthen, about eighteen months later. They'd moved there, and my cousin Alun who's in the job down there, well, he was at the time, he runs a B & B now, retired three years ago, but he told me about it because he knew they were from my patch. Apparently, she walked out onto the viaduct one day and jumped off. Only twenty-one. A tragedy, really.'

'And there wasn't anything suspicious about it?' I asked, trying to get my head around what he'd said.

'No, nothing funny. A clear-cut suicide, he said. Some said it was because she'd got rid of the baby, or given it away, I forget, and couldn't forgive herself. Though there was something about her going off the rails before that, drink and depression. If memory serves me right there was something about topless photos floating round, or turning up somewhere. That was a bigger deal then, like. Don't suppose anyone'd care much now. You see more boobs being flashed on a Saturday night down the Kingsway, I guess, pardon my coarseness.'

He fell silent, and so did I.

'Probably all that strict upbringing,' he resumed after a few moments and a couple of bites of another biscuit. 'Once that straight-laced type loses it, you never know what they'll do. It's the quiet ones you've got to watch. The old man had a massive heart attack after that, Alun said. Sad, all in all. You have kids and they're the death of you. Not mine, of course.

'Did I tell you my oldest, Sally, is expecting her first baby? I'm going to be a granddad. I'm going to love that – best time in the world is when they're little. I'll be off in six months, officially retired, and then its baby on the knee, walks in the park. No more pickpockets, dole scroungers and domestics. Sally'll probably go back to work. She earns good money now, at the solicitors, environmental law, that's the ticket nowadays, ain't it? I've told her and Bob I'm happy to watch the little mite. I'm only too glad to get out of this game anyway. It's not what it used to be.'

He eyed Rhian mournfully, as, with great care, she felt-tipped the date and time of the meeting into the box on the first poster, her tongue sticking out of the corner of her mouth.

We chatted a bit about the weather then, about their upcoming charity car wash with the local school and the fire service. As usual I told him to let me know the details and I'd bash out a little piece for the local paper.

Driving back home an hour later I couldn't get the image of Suzy Milland and Justin out of my head, or those photos of her on the beach, carefree, hair blown softly over her face, skirt clutched above the waves. Had Justin (or Paul , been the father of her baby? Had there been a rape, a rape that was hushed up? Or was it something else? Had that been where Justin had first got the idea about the power of blackmail? The topless photos, taken willingly or unknowingly? Surely it couldn't be a coincidence? Was Suzy his first victim in one way or another? If so, Justin had started his games young and now had ten years' practice, ten years' more practice then I had.

Clearly, I couldn't find Suzy and ask her what had happened. She couldn't give me my leverage because she'd taken the truth with her off that bridge.

Chapter Sixteen

'What the hell happened to your face?' asked Dan with alarm. He was pulling on his tunic, ready to go to work as I opened the front door and put down my bag. I'd hoped he would have already left so I wouldn't have to explain anything. I'd almost ceased to register that our lives often seemed only to bisect at certain coordinates, the same spot in space and time for days on end, at the front door of our house, our bed in the small hours of night, the occasional office at Southern. Recently this had been working in my favour, helping me guard my secrets.

'Oh, I fell while out running,' I said.

He came up and cupped my face, surveying the bruise. 'I rang last night.'

'I know,' I said, pushing his hand away and pecking him on the cheek. 'I didn't hear the phone. I must have been in the shower. By the time I picked up your messages I thought it was too late to call back. I was knackered.'

'You fell?' he asked uncertainly, still eyeing the bump.

'Yeah, tripped, whacked it on a branch.'

'I've told you not to run by the river. It's too lonely. What if you'd fallen and knocked yourself out? No one would have known where you were. *I* didn't know where you were. Anything could have happened to you.'

'I had my phone.'

'You can't use a phone if you're *knocked out*. I wish you would text me if you're going to go off on your own when I'm on nights. No one would know there was anything wrong. Someone could have jumped you, or mugged you, or worse.'

I think the 'worse' has largely already been done, I thought.

I said, 'Ok, ok – please, not now. I'm too tired to argue.'

He was annoyed. I could see it. But I knew it stemmed from concern.

'Bloody hell, Jen,' he said, touching the bruise tentatively with his fingers. 'People will think I've been giving you the old back-hander.'

'They already do. But they're too polite to say so.'

'Does it hurt, sweetheart?'

'No, it's ok. It looks worse than it feels.' If only I could say the same about everything else, I thought, burying my head in his washing-machine clean, work- ironed shirt. He clasped me in a hug.

'Is everything ok, Jen?'

'Sure it is.'

'What will you do tonight?'

'Just sleep, probably. Read, then sleep. What did you get up to yesterday?'

'Oh, just spent half the night trying to find a missing old lady from Grangetown. Well, she'd been missing for three days. Ninety-three years old – dementia, you know – walked out of her sheltered accommodation in her dressing gown and slippers.'

I did know. Her name was Iris Fellows. Serian had been dealing with it when I had left for Swansea.

'Found her last night. She's fallen down the railway banking by the bus stop, by the looks of it. Something had eaten off a couple of her fingers – a fox, more than likely – but her wedding ring's gone. Looks like she died of hypothermia. It's so sad.' He sat down heavily on the stairs. 'She might have been lying down that banking all night – injured, unable to attract anyone's attention, all alone. These ones never get any easier. We'd had the helicopter up, and the search and rescue out, but we were looking on the wrong side of the cutting. I can't help thinking that if we'd started on the right slope, not the left, maybe we'd have found her in time.'

'You can't think like that, love,' I said, reminded of how much he took these things to heart, how he still managed to feel sadness even after the fiftieth or hundredth missing person turned up pale and puffy at the foot of a cliff, on a river bank or in a filthy flat with a needle in their arm. So many police officers lost that, that compassion, and the victims became a string of details and incident numbers, another task to be completed. It's not callousness or complacency, it's a defence mechanism, a necessity for dealing with the daily death and personal tragedy so many members of the public are blissfully unaware of.

Even I was guilty of this, moving swiftly through the motions of the 'last seen wearing' variety, compiling facts for missing-person appeals with cool precision, filing the photos of the absent in my 'Book of the Dead', the macabre-sounding but banal black A4 file that I kept next to my computer. In it I always filed the original appeal photos, in case the family wanted them returned, then added the name, age, address and description of the person pictured with the incident number. A life reduced to a footnote. Often I didn't even feel any sympathy.

I leaned over and kissed Dan's forehead.

'Don't fret, sweetie. It's nobody's fault. Someone's always dying somewhere, as we well know. You can't dwell on it.' When I said this it was a truism meant to comfort him. Later I would remember these words and realise I had been right in a wider sense. Someone was always dying somewhere. But I was wrong about the part of it not being anyone's fault.

I cuddled Dan for a minute or two, then he left with a chicken curry ready meal I'd grabbed for him in Tesco on the way home. Two minutes later I was ready to try and log on to 'Surf Sluts'. The network connection was back up. There was also a new email from Justin, sent around 7 a.m. that morning, the same time I'd received the text. It contained the same demand for £300, the same threat of exposure, the promise to be in touch.

With dread mounting in my heart, I put 'Surf Sluts' into Google. This was not something I ever thought I'd be doing, trawling for porn, but I was getting to the point where nothing was that surprising anymore. A deluge of hits appeared in the search results list. The word 'slut' was obviously a common denominator, along with the word 'slit', which was included in the 'did you mean to search for slit?' alternative option box.

There was only one 'Surf Sluts' that specifically stated 'amateur'. An array of options popped up on the front page, where a naked girl on a surfboard bent away from the camera, pushing her buttocks towards the screen, leaving nothing to the imagination.

Fearfully, I clicked on the images indicated. It was clearly homemade stuff. The clips and videos were all similarly graphic: blowjobs, handjobs, doggy-style sex and some more creative positions. In some of the clips the girls were panting

228

and pouting at the camera enticingly. In some the girls' faces were in shadow or out of shot, just the anatomy in full-frame glory. The main difference between the amateur and 'professional' sites seemed to be the prevalence of pubic hair.

I picked my way through the highlights offered. 'Horny hottie pleasures randy plumber. Sex-pot girlfriend gives good head.' I couldn't see any too familiar flesh on there, thank God. But I did see something else familiar. The guy from the caravan was in one of the videos, having sex with a girl with long blond hair. She seemed drunk or maybe, possibly, in the light of what I suspected, drugged. She was not completely out of it, not totally insensible, but she was not far from it. I couldn't be sure – it was dark – but the background looked like the orange and brown inside of Justin's caravan. The clip had been uploaded a few months ago and had had 297 hits. Review ratings ranged from 3 to 4 stars.

The title read 'See Annaleigh take it in the Ass'. Hadn't the name Annaleigh been scribbled on one of those bits of paper in the *Cool Cymru* guide? I couldn't be sure, it had all been so hurried, but my stomach churned anyway. I clicked off the site.

Minutes later I was running again, hard and swift in the fading light. But this time it wasn't working, the longed-for calm was not coming. I was striding out, faster and bolder, flying over the leaf-strewn ground, over puddles and fallen branches, waiting for my body to trigger that burst of adrenalin-fuelled release and activate the white-out in my head.

Please, God! Don't let me be displayed like that, like a lump of meat, I begged. It had been bad enough seeing the video of Justin and me out of context, in private. But on that site, or one like it, it was doubly degrading. I would be just one in a range of faceless fucks. This was not a world I inhabited. I was not one of *those* women.

My head was addled with images of body parts and fluids, images swirling murkily, a churning oil and water mix, sloshing noisily back and forth in my skull. I ground to a halt outside the cricket club, panting, coughing and suddenly dry-heaving. I wobbled to a sitting position on the edge of the pavilion steps, ignoring the bunch of teenagers lurking on the bench at the other end, smoking fags, hoods up against the chill of falling darkness.

There was some nudging and sniggering occurring. After a minute or so one boy, around fourteen or fifteen years old, shouted, 'Hey love! Give you £5 for a blow job.'

In what appeared to be just one second I had covered the distance across the grass in fast-forward time, a burst of adrenalin fuelling muscles that a moment ago had been trembling with exertion. It took me a moment to realise I had grabbed the boy who had spoken by the front of his parka jacket and pushed him back against the seat with a short, violent jab of my other hand. He gasped, eyes saucering with surprise. His friends fell silent. I leaned in close.

'Don't ever speak to me, you little prick,' I snarled, spittle flying from my lips. 'Don't *ever* speak to me again, you useless fucking chav, or I'll wipe that fucking smile off your face with my foot. Do you understand?'

The look of horror on the faces of the boy's friends was gratifyingly simple and rewarding. The boy stared into my face for a moment and then nodded jerkily that he understood. I let him go and he cowered back, tugging at his twisted coat.

'Fuck's sake, lady,' said his mate, sulkily. 'It was just a joke.'

I wiped my hand across my mouth, stood regarding them

for a moment. 'Do you see me laughing, you piece of shit?' The boy looked as if he was about to cry.

I resumed running without another word. I was hoping, as my mind steadied a little, that I wouldn't now be arrested for assault on a minor. But for a few seconds I actually felt better than I had in months.

Then a memory flickered back into my head and ruined it again. Two condoms. Two condoms in the cottage that morning. Two condoms.

Chapter Seventeen

The ring of the phone had started to drill a hole in my forehead. It was a small hole at first, but it quickly opened up into a fissure, emptying most of my skull. My clarity had increased to the point where it seemed my brain was a clear morning in the nineteenth-century Midwest, where the sun rises slowly over the cooled plains and the air is so sharp you can see hundreds of miles to the horizon.

Who would have guessed this was the head of a 28-year-old woman in a flattering wrap dress, sitting among the starched white shirts and epaulettes of the senior officers of one of the largest police forces in Britain?

From my distant, desert vantage point I watched the men in shirt sleeves, gathered soberly around the chief super's conference table, wielding their pens with practiced authority, playing with their hats, sipping coffee. Some were grey-haired, quiet and well-intentioned, some positively prickling with ambition and youthful hubris. None seemed to have any relation to me or my life anymore.

The reason for my distress was that Bodie had pushed into the weekly tasking meeting at the request of the DI to give a quick update.

'Been a fire down at a caravan site in Aberthin,' he whispered, in response to my raised eyebrows. 'Media are making a nuisance of themselves.'

I had to sit in the meeting for an entire half hour thinking, what the hell is this now? Aberthin? There's only one caravan park down there. That couldn't be a coincidence, surely?

As I learned later when Bodie gave his update, Justin's caravan and the two nearby had gone up in flames in the early hours of that morning. Ordinarily Aberthin would have been out of Southern CID's patch, but the detectives down in Swansea West were tied up with the vicar abuse case and a nasty murder, and our team had been drafted in to help start things off.

Likewise, ordinarily the Southern press office probably wouldn't have dealt with the media for a local issue like that, but the Swansea area press officer was on long-term sick with some sort of stress, so it fell to us to fill the gap.

It was hard to stop the surge of alarm that shook me as I realised my private ordeal now seemed to be connecting, unbidden, with my daily work. The last thing I wanted was my colleagues climbing all over that caravan site and asking questions.

Reading the brief preliminary incident report it appeared Gwen and Len's caravan was the seat of the fire, which had then spread to two others, the Mathrys' and the immediate neighbour's. It was being treated as a possible arson.

The fire service was carrying out a joint investigation with us, their guys sifting through the charred and smoking debris, our guys taking statements and speaking to the owners. The fire dog had already sniffed out the presence of a possible 'accelerant' of some sort, possibly petrol or gasoline. But of course, lots of old caravan cookers run on gas bottles. Luckily, it seemed no one had been injured.

NewsBeatWales and the *Chronicle* had evidently been pestering officers at the scene, trying to cross the police tape at the edge of the site, and talking to the usual gaggle of onlookers. One male reporter had been caught trying to take photos from behind a hedge in the nearby lane, inside the cordon. He'd been *escorted* from the scene.

A brief media holding statement had been issued via the control room at eight that morning but it said little, and everyone knew we would need to get a proper statement written quickly.

'I want to be kept informed of any potential media problems or community impact,' intoned Detective Superintendent Sellers, inclining her head pointedly at me.

'As you know, normally this kind of thing is insurance-related,' Bodie explained to me afterwards, as I sat in the CID office, pen and notepad at the ready, though anything but ready to hear what he might have to say.

'There's something a bit odd with this one,' he continued. 'I've been taking an initial statement from the old couple who owned the van that the Trumptons think was the seat of the fire. They're adamant that someone has specifically targeted them. It seems there's been a bit of palaver over the last year with the owners of the adjacent land, the caravan park owners and a development company. Most of the plots have been empty for years. It's pretty run down. Charles Weaver, some Swansea businessman, has made an offer to the farmer of the adjacent land to build a luxury holiday village there, or something. But the caravan park is in the middle of the plot fronting the sea and has the road access.

'There's some clause in the contract that says the caravan owners own the plot of land itself, not just the caravan that's on it. The administrators of the caravan park own the club house etc but not the plots. This old couple, Gwen and Len

Nash are the fly in the ointment. They just don't want to sell. Fuck knows why, but they love it there so much they've refused to budge for nearly two years. 'Course, that hasn't gone down well with some of the other people who own the plots and want to sell out. They fancy a nice little windfall, but it's no-go until the oldies agree.

'Turns out, without the caravan field and its access, the deal's off. Parts of the area on either side, fronting the sea, are covered with landmines left over from World War II. It would cost a fortune to try and clear them. The national park and heritage coast are on the other side, so it's the caravan park and its access or nothing.

'The old couple reckon they've had people nosing around there over the last six months. Their caravan window was smashed last August. They've had silent phone calls, that sort of thing. They say someone tried to poison their dog. They do appear to have reported some incidents of harassment in the last six months. The one with the dog is on record and the phone calls, but to be honest, the local response team hasn't done much with it. 'Course, it's all hearsay at the moment, but it is rather convenient, isn't it?'

I struggled to take all this in, realising I'd soon be expected to ask pertinent, media-related questions.

'So the Nashes, that's the oldies, right? Their caravan is now a write-off, I take it?'

'Dust and ashes.'

'Right. But wouldn't they just buy another caravan for the plot if they're that adamant to stay?' I asked, as I would had I known nothing about Gwen and Len at all, as if forty-eight hours earlier I had not been breaking into a caravan next door or hiding in the bushes.

'Probably they would if they had insurance,' explained Bodie.

'But they haven't had any for a few months now. The wife says they've been meaning to get round to it but they've had trouble finding a willing company because the site is up for development.

'We're still trying to get hold of the other two caravan owners. Neither caravan has been in use much over the years,' he said, consulting his notebook. 'Mathry and Smith are the names we've got from the site records. Jimmy's on it now. I'm going to do the statements from the Nashes formally, at 1 p.m. Got to have a few hours kip first, I've been up all night. But the trouble is, one of the reporters from NewsBeatWales. He's got on the site and spoken to the Nashes and they've spilled all this stuff about the sale of the land. Now this Jack fella's badgering the cordon officers for comments as to whether it's a 'line of investigation'.

'Seems like the Nashes have been in the local paper before – last year, campaigning to stay. They had a few other people supporting them then who didn't want to sell either, but one by one they've changed their minds. The Nashes say they've all been threatened but could be the others just got a better offer and thought, Sod it!

'It's been a local issue under the radar for a while and now it's big news all of a sudden, everyone whispering about how shady it is and so on. There's certainly a lot of money involved. What do you reckon we should put in the press release, Jen?'

'What?'

'What should we say to get the media off our backs for a bit?'

I was trying to make my brain click into gear, so I could make myself think of this as another story with its sequence of facts, but I was finding it hard to believe the fire was unrelated to Justin and my adventures of two nights ago. Bodie was looking at me expectantly though, so I said:

'I'll start drafting the basic details for you to look at. We can do an appeal as usual. We should leave this development business out of it entirely, until we're sure it actually *is* arson. Let this Weaver guy comment if he wants to.'

'That's what I told the DI. See, great minds think alike,' he beamed.

'Time frame for the fire?'

'Last night – well, this morning around 1 a.m.'

'Estimated cost of damage?'

'I'll get Jimmy to get back to you.'

'Right, if you get back to me when you've spoken to the Nashes properly, we'll see where we are with the statements.'

'Sure thing. Chief Inspector Davies down there is getting in a right tizz because his chief's on holiday in Mauritius and his super's supposedly got swine flu. He's in the big chair and the press are calling his office directly. He wants to do some phone or one-to-one interviews to address the "community tensions" and provide "reassurance" etc. The usual crap. Will you ring him and talk it through?'

'Yes, of course, right, I'll do that.'

That was the problem with this type of issue. It starts out as a simple fire, then the rumour mill gets going and the press blow it up into a 'community issue'. They know they're supposed to direct their queries through the press office but they always try it on with the inspectors. The inspectors panic, moan to the top brass, and before you know it, every senior officer wants to be a spokesman, and be seen to be doing something 'reassuring'.

'By the way, Jimmy's got some bits for the appeal he's emailing over to you now,' added Bodie. 'Apparently, for a couple of nights, there were teenagers hanging around the site, drinking and so on. The site office was damaged and some bottles were smashed in the lane. Could be connected, a prank that got out of hand or something, who knows?

'Also, Mrs Nash, though she's mad as a fruit bat, says there was a woman who came round three days ago asking a lot of questions about their caravan – how often they stayed there, if they came down on weekends and so on, if the caravans nearby were used or empty. She's given us a description, a pretty good one. Odd thing is, the woman said her name was Anne Nolan but that must have been false because Anne Nolan is a reporter with the *Chronicle* and it just so happens she was doing an interview with the local Assembly Member at the time. Jimmy checked with the editor and the AM's office about half hour ago.'

Christ, they had been thorough for two guys who had been on shift since 2 p.m. the previous day, I thought. It was sometimes too easy to forget that, despite his manner, Bodie wasn't an acting sergeant at twenty-eight because he was careless or unmotivated.

'Bit of a weird thing to lie about, isn't it?' mused Bodie. 'It might be nothing but it could have been someone casing the site, someone looking to see when the area was likely to be empty.'

I looked at the printout of the description that Bodie was handing me. Of course I knew what it would say but I made a show of reading it carefully anyway. The suspect was: white, five feet seven inches tall, in her late twenties, slim build, wearing jeans and a black fleece jacket, blondish hair tucked under a blue baseball cap with a red 'B' stitched on the front. Local accent. Yep, that was about it. That was me.

'She's working on a bit of an e-fit too,' continued Bodie.

'As I said, mad as a badger, but we all know nosey old dears like this can be useful if you can get them to focus. By the way, I asked her if she'd be prepared to give some quotes for the papers for the appeal, give it that "human interest" angle you're always on about.'

He looked pleased with himself. He had taken note of my usual pleas for comments when we did appeals together and pre-empted me, trying to show he was willing to learn and had paid attention to what I had advised.

'Might be better to have her on side, and at the same time gently warn her to keep her gob shut and not to go off half-cocked again talking to any reporters about the details, eh?'

Again, in his words I recognised my own approach from previous incidents, reflected in Bodie, the keen and appreciative pupil.

'Can you ring her, Jen? Here's her number. I couldn't stay to sort it out but I said you'd call and talk her through the usual stuff.'

'You want me to ring her directly?' I stuttered, startled. 'I don't usually speak directly to IPs, Marc, you know that. I get the statement via the officers.'

'I know, but the DI's asked if you could *please* help us out this time because we've so much to do with that attempted armed robbery in Roath as well. The chief's getting his knickers in a twist because he's getting angry calls from the local councillors down there, who he knows from his golf club or something, and calls from the AM about public safety and antisocial behaviour round this caravan thing. It's all electioneering of course, but you know Chief Cavendish. He'll want to smooth the waters himself, show he's in control.'

So it had started already, then. There was no point arguing with the DI if he had the chief on his back.

'Ok, just this one time,' I assured Bodie. 'Let me know what develops.'

I returned to the press office and slowly readied myself to ring Gwen, or Mrs Nash, as I now would refer to her.

The fire couldn't really be a coincidence, could it? Not now? Obviously there was some background to it with the development thing, but the timing was suspicious to say the least. The Mathry's caravan had just happened to burn down too? Of course, there was nothing for it but to carry on as normal, do my job by following the same steps as usual, pretending I wasn't in the strange and unexpected position of having to make a media appeal for myself.

Why had I told Gwen my name was Anne Nolan? Because she was one of the reporters who called most regularly and it was just the first name that had popped into my head. I hadn't expected Gwen to remember it, or the fact I'd been wearing my baseball cap, the one I'd bought in New England on that trek after college. The red 'B' for Boston Red Sox was stitched into the front.

I was glad I had automatically used my heavier Welsh accent when I'd spoken to Gwen and Len on my visit. At least that meant she was unlikely to recognise my voice on the phone now I had to call her and pretend we'd never met. I made a point of emphasising my clear and precise telephone manner just a little more than usual, just to be sure.

It was a taxing conversation. It was difficult to keep Gwen on the point as she veered off tangentially, talking again about the good old days of the caravan site and also the infernal developers. She was obviously genuinely distressed that her caravan had been destroyed. Her love for the place had been clear enough when I'd met her, and it had been elevated to mythic status now that it was in ashes. Every damp summer spent eating pasties in the awning had become halcyon and sun-kissed, and every neighbour was an old and trusted friend with a smile as wide and generous as Swansea Bay itself.

But what I really had to ask her about was her visitor. The mysterious girl.

'Oh yes, she was very *sly*,' insisted Gwen, sniffing morosely out of the receiver.

Sly? *Really*? Surely not? I'd gone out of my way to be open and pleasant.

'She asked a lot of questions, you know, about how long we'd had the caravan, when Len and I came down, how long we stayed, would we stay here into our old age.'

Actually, I remembered Gwen had volunteered all this information and a lot more besides. She also said the visitor had asked if any caravans were for sale, which I patently hadn't. But I couldn't correct her.

'Then I saw her the next day, hanging around by the lane with a big bag on her back and talking on a mobile phone,' continued Gwen, he voice lowered slightly, mysteriously.

'Pardon?'

'Oh yes, the next day, same girl, only this time with black gloves on and a big bag. I thought the gloves were weird, 'cos it wasn't that cold since the snow had melted, and the big bag seemed odd. It wasn't a rucksack or a handbag-type bag, it was like a black sort of tool bag.'

This was starting to get weird.

'You're sure it was the same girl, Mrs Nash? The next day?'

'Oh yes, I'm sure,' said Gwen confidently, though obviously she was mistaken about several things. I don't think she was deliberately lying. I think that's how she remembered it. Maybe she'd mixed up the days and seen someone else with a black bag, for all I know. It's a known fact that eye witnesses are notoriously creative and unreliable. Ask two people who saw the same incident to give a statement and their accounts will often vary wildly, though both believes what they are saying is the God's honest truth as it happened. Black gloves, though?

Luckily, Gwen seemed to have forgotten, or at least omitted that I had specifically asked about the Mathrys. Not that it would have made much difference, but until I knew what was what, it was better for me if the Nashes were the focus of our officers' *and* the media's attention.

'I should've known it was funny though,' continued Gwen. 'What was a girl like that doing wandering round an old caravan site? She didn't want to give her name like, you could see that. Kept looking about, like she was, you know, expecting to see someone. But you trust people, don't you? You just assume they're genuine. And she had such a nice smile. You trust a nice smile.'

Indeed you do, I agreed silently. It's the smile that first pierces your defences then renders you helpless, how well I knew that.

So I took down the details and prepared to present them as fact without being able to say, I didn't say that, and I didn't refer to that, and I was not there with a bag on Thursday. I had to put this information into the appeal, of course. How could I not? Her account made it sound far more suspicious than it had been. The newspapers would love it. But, in a way, the misdirection might be a blessing for me.

After much discussion, Mrs Nash and I had agreed on a quote for the appeal that I could attribute to her without inviting slander charges by accusing the developers of being lying, threatening arsonists.

Doyle appeared an hour later with a printout of the e-fit of me. I was glad I had worn my baseball cap because it made the face on the paper more generic. Usually, these things either turn out bland and forgettable or barely human looking, a caricature of a shady character if ever you saw one. But this one was pretty good. It actually looked like me, or maybe like a sister of mine, a passing resemblance, but not quite the same. She'd made me a bit younger and a bit thinner, but the likeness was pretty close.

No one noticed, naturally. Why would it even cross anyone's mind that the person we were appealing for was the person making the appeal? This irony wasn't lost on me as I issued the information to Jack NewsBeatWales and the other journalists, before the one-to-one interviews at Swansea station with panicking Inspector Davies.

Not one of them said, 'Funny, looks like your doppelganger,' except a cock-sure, loud-voiced girl called Cerys who was new at the fire service press office and was sitting in on the interviews, supposedly so she could coordinate the fire chief's statements with ours later. But she spent more time flicking her enormous mane of backcombed blond hair and fiddling with her Blackberry than making notes. I think she was texting someone about something that was not work-related, because every so often she would chuckle to herself in a pleased fashion.

'Ha, ha! Your evil twin,' she snorted, waving the printout of the e-fit at me in between interview slots. 'Quite exciting this, isn't it?'

I returned her smile, pleasantly.

'Everyone singing from the same hymn sheet, eh?' asked Chief Cavendish while he hung around looking serious and responsible and generally getting in the way. He'd come down to 'oversee things' after lunch and had spent the afternoon asking a lot of pointless questions, getting under our feet and saying he was available if any further comments were needed.

'Yes, boss. All in order,' I reassured him.

'Her evil twin, or what?' beamed Cerys at him in a matey, chums-together manner. He looked her up and down but he didn't smile. He didn't know her and therefore expected her to speak to him when spoken to, and to call him Sir or Chief Superintendent when she addressed him.

'Who was that girl?' he asked me later, as I was pouring him some tea from the urn we'd set up for the journalists.

'New fire service press officer. Don't think she has much experience.'

'I'll say! By 'eck,' the Yorkshireman surfacing more fully for a moment as he voiced his disapproval. 'A pink suit, for God's sake. Does that say *professional* to you?'

'It's a fashion statement. Though a statement of what exactly, I'd rather not say.'

'Quite. I've seen less make-up on hookers. Not, that I've seen hookers, of course. Not personally. Well, you know what I mean.'

'Have a biscuit, boss,' I said. And shut up before the next journalist comes in.

At that moment Anne Nolan popped her head around the door. I'd never seen her in person until that afternoon, when she'd been introduced by one of the officers. She did look a bit like me – same height, same build, same blondish hair.

'Hi again, Anne,' I said, waving her in. 'This is Chief Superintendent Cavendish, overseeing while Chief Superintendent Pike is on leave. Inspector Phil Davies will be doing the interview for you, in five minutes. Want some tea?'

'No thanks, Jen. Actually, I'm not going to do the interview. Well, with my name being involved in it we thought it might be better if Jack did it. He's here somewhere. Jack?' she called down the corridor.

A tall, sandy haired guy in specs ambled into the room with a half swagger in his step, pulled off his glasses and extended his hand with an over-charming smile.

'You must be Jennifer. It's nice to finally meet in person, put a face to the name.'

The pleasure's all yours, I'm sure. I smiled back and introduced him to the Chief.

'Right,' said Jack, rubbing his hands together. 'Shall we get started? Deadlines, you know. Can't hang around all day.'

'It's a bloody cheek, pretending to be one of us though, isn't it?' said Jack, as I showed him back to the front entrance from the command room half an hour later. 'Imagine saying you're Anne, of all people? They blame us reporters for everything, though, don't they? We're always the whipping boys for trying to do our jobs.'

You *were* crawling through the undergrowth with a camera at eight-thirty this morning though, Jack. I know it was you, I thought. Who else would be that big a pain in the arse for a few pictures of burnt-out caravans?

'Your lot will be interrogating Anne next,' continued Jack huffily, buttoning the *News-at-Ten* serious-reporter mackintosh he had slipped on and crumpling the press release I had given him into the bin. 'We can get that release on email, right? When are your lot actually going to comment properly on this development war business?' he demanded.

Development *war*. He said it with a newsreader inflection, stressing the word 'war', long and with a warm vowel. Everything was a War or an Outrage or a Scandal in Jack's world. Once a hack, always a hack.

I smiled. 'No comment, Jack. Like the inspector said, we have a number of lines of enquiry and the investigation is ongoing.'

'Yeah, yeah,' he muttered, fishing a cigarette out of his pocket. 'But everyone knows about the land war business. You might as well admit it.'

'Night, Jack,' I said patiently as he allowed me to steer him out of the main door into the car park.

'You will let me know right away, if there're any developments?' He pulled his collar up against the wind and let the cigarette dangle from his lips in what he evidently thought was a raffish, Bogart-ian fashion. 'We want to keep on top of this one, you know.'

'You and me both,' I agreed.

'You will let us know *before* the deadline, right?'

'You'll know when I know Jack, as always.'

'I wish I thought that was true,' he harrumphed, lifting a battered, silver Zippo lighter in his cupped hands.

'You can't smoke that in this car park,' I said, still with a smile, and adding a wave of my hand as I turned back to the doors

'Bloody press officers,' I heard him mutter as he ambled down the steps towards Anne, who was bringing her car round from the rear car park, lighting the cigarette anyway.

'What a rebel,' said Pat the janitor, rolling his eyes as he swept up the porch for the night.

'What a prick,' said Inspector Davies, hastily getting into his car and making a run for it.

Chapter Eighteen

'Jen, the chief super was very impressed with your briefing and input for the arson business today,' said Nige around 7 p.m. that evening, after I returned to the central press office, got an update from Doyle and then updated the press office computer records.

'Oh, really? I'm *so* glad,' I replied flatly. I'm not sure if I or Nige was more surprised to hear the note of open sarcasm in my voice. We both ignored it.

'You know I'm going for the interview for the comms job next week?' continued Nige. I did know. He'd been dithering for ages about whether or not to try for the post of head of force communications. It would mean a temporary raise and good experience. He'd move to the administrative HQ site outside Cardiff and have a 'top corridor' office of his own opposite the assistant chief constable's, currently occupied by Kathy Collier who was swelling at a startling rate and more than ready for her maternity leave.

Personally, I thought he was too nice to get it, not bolshy and melodramatic enough. Sometimes in the force it's not what you say that matters but how loudly and with how much conviction you can say it. Also, I think Chief Superintendent Cavendish, who would be one of the officers taking the interviews, thought Nige was a bit effeminate. He didn't like purple ties any more than he liked pink suits.

'*If* I get it, my job will be open for an acting-up opportunity for six months,' continued Nige, though I was hardly listening. Snow had been forecast again and I, like everyone else unfortunate enough to still be in the building so late, was twitchily eyeing the sky, hoping the sleety showers outside wouldn't firm up into anything more flaky.

'Why don't you go for it? Temporary Media Manager?' Nigel twittered keenly. 'You've been here, what, seven years? (six years, I mentally corrected). You know as much about this organisation as I do and you're my senior press officer. I'd back you. I think we work well together. I could get the application form for you. More money, more exposure, you know – up the old greasy ladder.' (Greasy pole, you mean.) 'I mean, you must be finding it frustrating, still being a press officer. With all your experience, you should be managing. You'd be good at it. All the officers get on with you and value your advice. I mentioned it to the assistant chief constable. He said he'd be more than happy for you to try for it. He likes you after you worked with him on that malpractice scandal last year and he says he's heard lots of good things about you.'

But it's just a stopgap job, the voice in my head said. A six-, soon to be seven-year stopgap job.

Perhaps I would have filled out the application if Justin hadn't happened to me, even though the thought of more responsibility, more bureaucracy, felt like a creeping form of death. What excuse would I have had not to? But I had Justin on my mind and it was impossible to invest time and energy into anything else.

'Yes, I'll probably give it a try,' I lied, eager for him to leave.

Before I clocked off I made one last visit to Bodie's office to see if he had anything further to tell me about the investigation, anything that might develop overnight. He wasn't in the CID room but his phone was on the monitor top, meaning he was around somewhere. On his desk was a pile of evidence bags from the arson site. They were obviously waiting to be properly bagged up, labelled and then entered in the log. Two of the bags contained blackened bits of undetermined electrical parts, but I saw immediately that one clearly contained a charred Maglite torch.

I could see as it sat in the bag, its presence expanding to fill the room, what I hadn't seen when I'd pulled it off the shelf behind the pantry door and taken it to Justin's caravan. Dan's initials and force number were scratched on the underside.

Force numbers are ID numbers, personal to every staff member and officer. The torch was dirty and blackened but I spotted it right away, just as all officers will spot a force number, with its unique digits, a mile off. It's like scanning a list of names – your own always leaps out at you. The higher the force number the older you are in service. Most officers can pretty much tell the year you joined from your number.

Dan's Maglite was an old work one. Torches aren't tagged to a specific officer, but lots of officers will scratch their force number into their property to prevent light fingers appropriating their kit. It's the equivalent of writing your name on the tab of your school jumper. One of the great contradictions of life in the force is that you could leave a ten pound note, or a bag full of diamonds, on your desk for months, and no one would dream of taking them – that would be stealing. But if you leave milk in a communal fridge, force-issue kit unattended or office equipment like pens and staplers in plain sight, it's fair game. I should have released that Dan would be meticulous enough to mark his equipment.

A torch with Dan's force number on it appearing in an arson investigation would be an interesting talking point, wouldn't it? What possible reason would it have for being in the charred wreckage of a caravan, on a case Dan wasn't even assigned to? This was bad enough in itself, but it also made a link between me and the whole business and potentially Justin. What if someone bright, someone like Bodie, cross-checked the names of the caravan owners for previous incidents or for recent searches on our systems? I'd searched for the name Mathry just a few weeks previously on PNN and Nomad. That search might show.

And I'd searched on the camper van's number plate too. That would lead to the report of the RTC ten years ago, also involving the Mathrys. Of course, Bodie's ID would show as the originator of the searches, not mine. But that in itself would raise questions among the professional question-askers of the CID. If Bodie hadn't done it, someone with access to his office had, and for some reason they had wanted to cover their tracks.

The e-fit did look rather a lot like me. Might a penny drop somewhere? This wasn't enough, on its own, to suggest I'd done anything criminal, but how long could I keep evading questions? What if someone had seen me? Someone who might open the newspaper in the morning and respond to our arson appeal with previously unknown facts and figures?

What if someone showed Gwen and Len a photo of Dan or a photo of me, as they tried to answer the question of the mysterious Maglite?

Would one penny-drop be followed by another and another until there was a rain of coins that added up to a deluge of questions? If asked, what excuses would I come up with for being on the caravan site talking to the Nashes and then lying about it when I made the appeal?

At the very least it put me under a cloud of suspicion of professional misconduct, misuse of police resources. And what would I say to Dan? Could I keep lying to him? It was *his* old torch.

I reasoned all this in a matter of moments, while my gaze was fixed like a spotlight on the plastic bag on the desk. Equally quickly I knew I had to take a chance, right away, right at that moment. There might be no other opportunity.

Glancing around, I spotted exactly what I was looking for – a box of plastic gloves. I dashed to the corridor to check all was clear. The whole station seemed locked in silence. It was late. The lights in the corridor were out.

I pushed the door closed, gently pulled the plastic bag to the edge of the desk and eased it open with plastic-gloved fingers. With a pair of scissors from a nearby pot of pens, I quickly, but with infinite care, scraped away the paint on the underside of the Maglite to obscure the last two numbers, and the first, in the sequence. I rubbed out Dan's initials and a patch of paint on the other side so it would look more random. Then I rubbed soot and grime over the patches to hide the freshness of the damage. It looked pretty good. It had taken only a minute, perhaps less.

I resealed the bag and placed it back in the centre of the little pile. I pulled off the gloves and slid them, and the scissors, into my pocket.

In an instant I wondered what the hell I had done. It had taken only sixty seconds to potentially place myself in serious trouble. Now I really *had* tampered with evidence. But the thought of anyone finding Paul Mathry and finding out about

251

the hotel, the cottage, the video, had overridden any sense of legality or reserve, any qualms of right or wrong.

Anyway, it was too late. I couldn't take it back, reel the time in again, wind it up, put it on a spool in my pocket to re-run in the future. I'd acted on instinct, with no deliberation. I hoped, for once, my instinct would prove right.

I listened for the sounds of late workers in the corridor again, then slid the office door open. I heard the ping of the lift doors opening at the other end and saw a dark figure amble in. They, he or she, couldn't have seen me. It was too dark, thankfully. I dashed up the flight of stairs at the far end of the building just in case I was spotted, and headed back to the relative safety of the press office.

At the top of the corridor I heard the lift ping again and, to my alarm, saw Fat Paula hurry out. I don't *think* she could have seen me at the far end of the gloomy stretch of corridor, but I recognised her narrow - skirted silhouette, the thin hang of hair. What was *she* doing in the building so late in the evening?

Quick as a flash of common sense, I decided to hide in plain sight. I dashed to my desk, picked up my phone and dialled the Tannoy number. A second later I spoke at the beep and heard my voice reflected back at me from the corridor outside, like a railway platform announcer, made slightly strange by the electronics.

'If DC Ryan is still in the building, could he please call the press office on extension 26444. That's DC Ryan, extension 26444, please.' The message would be heard throughout the building.

A few seconds later Paula poked her head in through the door.

'So you're *here* are you?'

'Yep, still. It's been mad today. The arson. No time to spit, as usual.' I emphasised the 'as usual'. 'Do you need something?'

'I was looking for you,' she admitted, eyeing me suspiciously. 'I have this expenses form to return to you. You've claimed at the wrong rate. It's twenty-four miles from Central to Swansea, not thirty.'

'Oh, my mistake, thanks.' I stared at her expectantly as I took the expenses sheet, waiting for her to find a reason to stay and harangue me further. She was trying hard, but evidently couldn't think of anything. 'Well, you need to be accurate with these mileage claims, Jennifer. And make sure you sign accurately for your flexi hours.'

'Sure will.'

She hovered for a moment or two then departed with a reluctant, 'Don't stay too late.'

I waited ten minutes to see if Bodie *would* answer my hail but he didn't. He was either elsewhere or too busy to respond. On the way home I stopped at one of the corner shops without CCTV outside. I bought a loaf of bread, posted a birthday card to my uncle Owen and threw the plastic gloves and the scissors into the waste bin outside. I tried not to think of Dan's Maglite torch, in the darkness of the CID office, in its evidence bag.

Chapter Nineteen

Dan was on nights again. By the time I got home he'd already left for the station. A little note was stuck on the fridge saying, 'Hope your day wasn't too busy. Give me a call if you can. x.'

I was on call that night so I had to leave my phone on. Even though I dearly longed for a large glass of wine I couldn't drink in case I had to drive to an emergency. I had a couple of cursory calls from fretting sergeants around eight o' clock when I was half-heartedly steaming some salmon and broccoli and boiling a few potatoes. There'd been a fatal RTC in Butetown, and a teenager had been arrested for stealing a golf cart and driving it down the M4 in a drunken bout of revelry. That would attract some media attention in the morning.

After that I pulled out the wedding manual and looked for a few minutes at what still needed to be done before the rapidly approaching June deadline. There was a long list, not the least of which was buying a dress and paying deposits to a lot of people, but I put it away again after just a few minutes.

The jeweller had left a message on the answerphone to say the wedding rings had been sized and were ready for collection at our convenience.

I tried to watch TV but I couldn't concentrate. My mind

was whizzing around like a pinball machine. I couldn't even read. It hadn't been so bad while I'd been busy during the day, while I'd been on fact-sifting autopilot. I'd detached myself sufficiently to deal with the arson professionally and go through the motions with a competent air of complacency. But then there was the Maglite business. And then I was in the house alone, and the evening swallowed up the house and the street, and all the world was silence and darkness and a sea of implications.

I kept expecting the phone to ring with news of the appeal. Had I been careless somehow? Had someone, not Gwen, seen my car parked off the road down in Aberthin, taken the number plate? As I pushed cold broccoli around my plate I wondered if a call from a curious DC was already bouncing off the nearest satellite and heading for the phone handset next to me.

Would another text come from Justin about the details for the next payment?

I kept seeing 'Surf Sluts' in my head. 'Annie's Ass fun'. Two condoms. Two condoms in the cottage that morning. Would Justin contact me?

Would my colleagues call with, 'Just a few questions?'

Had I done the right thing with the Maglite? There couldn't be any fingerprints on it. Thank God I'd worn gloves. But what if, in the panic, I'd left other traces of myself in the caravan that night? What if someone spotted that the evidence bag had been tampered with? What if someone had already seen the numbers on the torch, noted them down and was now scratching their head as to how they had vanished? I hadn't thought of that – dear God!

But the bag had been dumped in a pile of stuff that needed to be logged, as if it has just been gathered to get it away from the scene. It shouldn't have been left like that, in an unlocked office, but such things do happen after twelve-hour shifts, when officers are hungry and exhausted and desperately need the loo or a sandwich. I just hoped, if this *was* the case, then no one would want to draw attention to it, because that would beg the question of why the evidence was left unattended in the first place.

There were so many unknowns that the slow slide of the evening began to resemble long forgotten childhood weekends in winter – those cool grey in-between days, and damp and silent Sundays, that rolled out endlessly when I was seven, or eight or nine years old.

Heavy grey skies would squat above our neat little house. Time would slowly wind down to a point of infinity where it appeared to stretch away to the edges of the afternoon, as distant and immovable as the vanishing point on the edge of a black hole.

Me, my mum and my dad, were caught on the cusp of every afternoon before or since, my dad always sitting cardigan-clad in the brown and cream armchair mug of tea in hand, slipper-shod and smiling; my mum in perpetual hover near the kitchen sink, tea towel thrown over her shoulder, peeling potatoes and carrots, I, contained in the tiny castle tower of my far-off bedroom, sprawled on the sun-yellow rug, surrounded by books.

On the edge of this afternoon, time would stall in the nothing-to-do-ness and central-heating-ticking quietness. It was not boredom but a hypersensitivity that refined all my senses to unbearable keenness, pulling me out of my book, out of the pictures and strings of words, on to that sun-yellow rug, so I was so much in myself and nowhere else – no castle turret, no pirate boat at sea, just a girl adrift on a Sunday afternoon in the emptiness – that I could hardly bear it.

Every cherry blossom or dew-sparkled wing tip on my Flower Fairy quilt fell into nerve-shredding clarity; the toe scuffs on my catalogue-bought white trainers bawled of dry, tripping, playground ordeals; the smell of the leather from my grandmother's bible, serving as a door stop, protested with clanging insolence of forgotten ghostly-cold chapels where footsteps echoed on stone. And through all this clamour wound the golden-crisp smell of pastry browning nicely and beef juice bubbling meatily below.

Like a human presence in the bedroom was the sense of waiting, only waiting – waiting for Sunday lunch, then waiting for Matey bubble bath and blow-dried hair in blue towelling pyjamas, waiting for bed. But there was also waiting for something else, waiting to be someone older, someone else, *somewhere* else.

It was the same that night, alone in my grown-up house. The waiting – for Justin to call, the police to call, for night to tip inevitably into day and into the life where I was the star of a porn website or the subject of a police investigation. There was the unbearable clarity of Justin's flesh on my flesh, the dust and candle wax smell of the cottage, the mildew-damp of the caravan, the terrible nearness of the hands-free cream telephone that replaced the one I smashed on the day of Sophie's call, the call taken by a press officer and fiancée that no longer seemed to be present.

Sometimes my childhood waiting could be relieved by hiding. I would crawl under my rickety bunk bed, among the discarded soft toys, and bags of unloved board games, right to the back. Sometimes I chose a spot behind the pantry door, under the hanging heap of duffle coats, faintly spidery, smelling of dried rain. The tighter the fit, the darker the space, the more the sense of waiting could be pushed back by the sense of deliberate hiding. There was comfort in the confined gloom and the dulling of the Sunday sounds, comfort in the choice of withdrawing.

Perhaps the same remedy could stop me from suffocating now, I thought. I could crawl behind the sofa, or into one of the larger bedroom wardrobes – we even had a pantry door with Dan's outdoor coats hung behind it, near at hand.

But such things were no longer possible. So, instead of crawling into darkness, I ironed a blouse, cleaned the kitchen sink, filed my fingernails, applied a new face cream with fruit acids for a youthful glow and checked the news. I did this like any other adult in any other house in any other city that night.

Hours later, I was in bed but awake when I heard Dan return in the early hours, heard the familiar sounds of boots being discarded and the fridge opening downstairs. I pretended to be asleep, but I let him hold me when he slid into bed next to me.

'Missed you,' he muttered. 'You smell of oranges.'

Next morning, as I was taking off my coat and switching on my computer, the chief, his rosy, hearty face even redder than usual, hurtled into the press office, tossed his hat on the desk, threw himself into Serian's swivel chair with a weighty thump, and rattled a newspaper in my face. DI Harden was in tow, looking careworn. Behind him was Doyle, hovering with discretion by the door, ready to make a silent exit.

Oh, God! What's the panic now? I wondered, sitting down and waiting for someone to explain, wishing I could crawl into the stationery cupboard and pull the door closed behind me.

'That bloody Jack, whatever his name is,' sputtered Chief Superintendent Cavendish, his pink head apparently about to explode above his tight, white collar. He tugged at his tie. 'He caught me on the way out of the Swansea police station last night. Some rumours had been doing the rounds down in Aberthin because we had the forensics boys down there. I told him it was off the record.'

(There's no such thing, I muttered under my breath, as I did every time I heard that patently false and redundant promise.)

'And we'd let him know if it was confirmed.'

(But he wants to be the one to break it first and their deadline was last night. *Before what was confirmed?*)

'But he's quoted it as an "unofficial source". The little shit.' He waved his hand at the paper he had thrust at me, waiting for me to read.

'I already read this morning's paper, boss,' I said. 'What's the problem? It's what Inspector Davies went through with them in the interviews. We knew they'd fictionalise the rest.'

The article, though sensationally dramatised in Jack's inimitable style, was no surprise. It was the basic story and the e-fit of me in my baseball cap, with Gwen's inaccuracies repeated as facts.

'You haven't seen the city edition, then?' huffed the chief.

'No, I was waiting for the post room to bring it up.'

'Take a look.'

'ARSON MAY BE MURDER HUNT,' screamed the headline. 'Human remains found in caravan wreckage,' said the strapline.

I read the headline and the first paragraph twice before I could speak. 'What? What is this? Is it true? Have we found remains? I was on call last night, why didn't anyone call me? No one called me.'

'We weren't sure what we had. We were keeping it under

wraps until we could put something together for the press today,' said the DI over the chief's shoulder, rolling his eyes and making the recognised sign for wanker, his head inclined towards the boss.

From the door, Jimmy shrugged and waved his hand in a 'don't ask' gesture and sidled out.

'Well, have we? I mean, have we found remains or not?' I demanded. 'Why didn't anyone call me last night?'

'Well, we're not *sure* what we've got yet,' said the chief, blustering a little now. Like many senior male officers, the more he realised he'd messed up the more intransigent he became.

'Like I said to this Jack character, it was some clothing and a few bones, some hair. It's still under investigation. I told that prick it was off the record.'

'Why didn't you ring and check with me?' I persisted. 'You can't ask journalists to hold on to information like that. You pretty much gave him the green light to print the rumours by acknowledging what he said. He hasn't quoted you, not exactly. That's how they work. I would have told you to go "no comment" if you'd run it past me. That way they can't speculate.'

He looked a bit sulky but still didn't relent from his position of personal outrage. 'Like I said, I thought it was clear it was *not* an official comment.'

The DI rolled his eyes again.

'So what *is* the deal with these bones then?' I asked, pointedly addressing the DI now, surprised by my own patience, the steadiness of my voice, while the voice in my head was yelling, *Who's dead? For God's sake, who's dead?* 'I mean the real deal, for my information, not for the press.'

'We're not sure, Jen,' said the DI. 'CSI are there now,

recovering them. 'There's still a terrible mess, looks like part of a blanket maybe and some bones that could be a ribcage and maybe fingers. But it's a total write-off – all the caravan frames fell in, the fabric and fittings are melted over everything. Must have gone up like Roman candles. If you ask me the whole place was a death trap. None of the fire hydrants were connected. We're not sure if they'd been tampered with or just neglected. We're just trying to get an idea of what we're looking at.'

Could it be Justin in the wreckage? Could it? said a soft, hopeful voice, pushing its way up to the left side of my skull. That would make things a hell of a lot easier, wouldn't it? In fact it would be a godsend, a direct and undeniable miracle. Nothing in my head said, 'That's not right, Jen,' Nothing said, 'It's bad to wish someone dead,' not even my mother's familiar warning voice, saying something like 'Do as you would be done by.' It was stubbornly mute. I thought clearly and calmly, 'Please God, let him be dead. Surely he deserves it.' A black prayer, if ever there was one, but a prayer nevertheless.

My reverie was broken by the chief's strident insistence that he wanted to make a complaint to the editor, that he wanted an apology, a retraction in print. I knew this would only make things ten times worse and highlight the fact that he was a fool.

'But you did say it to him, Sir? Off the record or not?'

'Humph,' he said noncommittally, which meant yes.

'There's not much we can do then, I assure you. Let it pass. It's done now.' Earning £60,000 still doesn't guarantee common sense or the ability to keep your mouth shut, does it? 'All we can do now, boss, is correct the errors and issue a fresh release saying where we are with it and that it's not a murder enquiry.'

It may never be a murder inquiry, said my press officer persona. As I had said to Dan, people die all the time, bodies are found, investigations begin. Most of the time it's just accidental, wrong place at the wrong time, bad luck, like Dan's little old lady who was eaten by animals. If she could suffer such bad luck, Justin deserved bad luck. But, thinking all too clearly of what he had done to me, what he might have done to others, including Suzy Milland, I was pretty sure he also deserved worse. Only time would tell.

But I didn't have any for the next eight hours. By the time the headline had been spotted by the rest of the South Wales media the telephones rang off the hook for two hours and the press office tipped into a chaos of barely controlled activity. Nige looked about to have a nervous breakdown. The chief got in the way again, hovering round in a spare chair, pacing up and down and listening in to some of the media calls. Fat Paula wandered past a couple of times, peering in through the open door, and I was convinced she'd now thought of something additional from the previous night to harangue me about, but I don't think she wanted to come in with the chief in residence.

At 11 a.m. I jumped in the car and spent the rest of the day in Swansea, redoing the interviews of the day before with the DI.

The only good thing was that, despite the widespread news coverage, no additional information about the arson had come to light and no one had called in to the incident room with any information about the mystery woman in the baseball cap.

The worst part was waiting for CSI to do their slow and painstaking work with their tweezers, bags of white powder and brushes. It would be at least twenty-four hours before they'd clear the scene and we might know something, anything, about the bones. This waiting was still painful but at least it had a point, like waiting for the governor's pardon while the prison officers next door set up Old Sparky and the hands of the clock inched ever closer to midnight.

It was 8 p.m. by the time I made it home. The sleet had turned into plump flakes of snow again, and the sky had closed in tightly. A deceptively warm-looking orange sodium glow over the roof tops meant the snow was probably going to get heavier. Half the roads in South Wales had promptly ground to a halt again, and I had crawled along the M4 for over an hour on what was usually a twenty-minute trip.

Trudging at last up the shadowy front path of our house, my tread lead-like and my shoulders just as heavy, I longed to be inside and to shut the door on the world.

I must not have been paying attention because I didn't see or hear anyone approach. As I put my key in the door and pushed it open, I felt a hand on my arm and another on my shoulder, pushing me back into the porch, my back making hard contact with the doorframe and a burst of breath curling out into the night air.

'Shush, shush, I know how you like to make lots of noise,' said Justin, grinning into my face, clearly alive, uncharred, and well pleased with himself. 'So little Jen's turned detective, has she? I should have known you'd be trouble, but I couldn't resist you. You looked so damned sweet, so pristine that night in the hotel. I knew you'd be desperate for a fuck if I just twiddled the right knobs, so to speak, and you were. But what part of "I'm not interested" do you not understand?

'First you follow me to Porthcawl with what was, frankly, an embarrassing display of neediness, then, before I know it you're skulking around the caravan pumping that old bitch

Gwen for information. I've heard of bunny boilers, but this is stalking become desperate. If you carry on like this I'll have to apply for a restraining order. It might only be a caravan but I think it's still illegal to break into one. Or burn one down.'

I attempted to speak, trying to push him off, but his grip was as tight as a handcuff on my forearm, the other pinning me to the door frame. The deep Victorian porch screened us from the street and houses nearby. There was no sound of a car or a footfall, everyone was curtained off behind their windows.

'What am I going to do with you, sweetheart, if you won't take no for an answer?' He was clearly enjoying his rant too much to expect an answer. 'Stop squirming, unless you've gone to all this trouble because you just want me to get into your pants again, in which case keep at it, I like the friction.'

'What do you want from me, you sick bastard?'

'Now now, you're the one playing amateur detective. Nice e-fit, by the way. It's not a bad likeness, but you're more attractive in the flesh and I've seen all your flesh, haven't I?'

'I don't know what you're talking about.'

'Sure you do. I admit, I underestimated you. You spooked me, you know, turning up like that at Santos's. How did you find me, by the way? No matter, I didn't think you'd actually track me down, but I thought, better make sure there was nothing, er, incriminating lying round the caravan. Bit of a clean up, you know. I shouldn't have sent that fool to sort it out, but I was dealing with some business elsewhere. If you want something doing, do it yourself. I just didn't want to wait. You must have missed him by a minute when you played cat burglar that night. I knew it was you when he said we'd had a *visitor*, especially when I found a note from that old bag

Gwen saying some girl had been looking around asking for *Paul*.'

'Why did you burn down your caravan?' I asked. There were lots of other questions I wanted to ask at that moment, but this seemed like the one most likely to elicit a practical answer and give me time to think.

'Well it wasn't a plan, I'll give you that,' said Justin, rather amused. 'When that tosser Pootle called and told me we'd had a visitor, I went straight round next morning to make sure he'd cleaned up. The cunt was passed out on the bench, reeking of pot. He never was the classiest guy, nor the brightest lad. He never could understand the finesse, the business end of our business. Rule number one – Don't do your own drugs. And one look at the entertainment snippet he'd been watching and I could see the useless fucker had used the caravan for the extracurricular activities. Rule number two – Don't shit where you eat, right? No doubt his spunk was all over that place and lord knows who else's juices. I knew he was staying there now and then but not carrying out *business* there. I should have realised he wouldn't follow the rules.'

'Business, what business?' I said, though really I had all but guessed.

'Come on, don't be coy, Jen. You've participated yourself. And you found his video disks didn't you? I know you did.'

Actually, I hadn't found any disks. They must have been hidden in the caravan somewhere but I hadn't discovered them. I didn't say this, though. Maybe it was good that Justin thought I had some evidence.

'Yes, I've got some disks,' I said. 'Lovely viewing they make too. "Surf Sluts", wasn't it? Now that's classy Justin. I'd expected more from you.'

'And your fiancé of you, no doubt?' he mused, half-smiling.

'"Surf Sluts" is Pootle's thing. I have my own favourite spots.' He sighed, almost regretfully.

'I shouldn't have tried it on with you, I guess. It was too close to home. I got careless. I was lazy, getting a key for that cottage off one of Pootle's deadbeat mates. I just needed another grand or so, thought it would be easy money. One last gasp before I leave these shores for some fun. You've made it all messy now. *Untidy*. I had to get rid of any evidence of Pootle's exploits, just in case. For all I knew, you were intending to bring the police back.'

'But why Gwen's van?' I knew the answer already.

'Well, I couldn't just do the old man's, could I? Everyone knows Gwen and Len were holding up the sale of that park. Someone was bound to have a grudge. It looked better that way. It muddied the tracks.'

'But the bones, the remains?'

'Pootle was a loose end,' he said with emphasis.

My throat tightened. 'You mean, you can't mean . . .' My horror must have shown on my face, for in the next instant he laughed.

'Nah, don't panic Jen. It *is* weird but it isn't Pootle, I assure you. I was pissed off with him but I wouldn't torch him. I'm not a *monster*, Jennifer!'

'About Pootle . . .' The words died in my throat. I had to ask him something now. I didn't want to. I didn't want to ask him anything, knowing that would be showing my weakness, adding to the power he had over me because I needed the answer.

'Justin, I have to ask you something. That night, at the cottage. There were two condoms. Was that because . . .? Were you the only one there that night?'

He regarded me with something like admiration. 'Well *that*

is a good question, isn't it? You're good at the details aren't you, Jen? Good for you. But maybe you'll have to wait for my next little action sequence to find out who all the players are?'

'You mean, you and Pootle? You can't have . . . You couldn't have.'

'You can't even remember, can you? There could have been half your fiancé's officers pounding away on you in that room that night and you wouldn't have known. That, incidentally is another good reason to get ready for my next payment, Nancy Drew. This time it's going to be more, though, for the inconvenience.

Justin, I can't. I *won't* keep paying you money. I'm not that rich, for God's sake. You've done enough. How long's it going to go on for?'

'That really depends on how much you can convince me you are a good little girl now. You want to keep your nice policeman husband in the dark, don't you? I think the rates are very reasonable. You'll only spend the money on shoes or clothes or something. Think of it as an investment in your happy future.'

'But why are you doing this?' I could feel panic surging up into my throat again. In a moment I might wail, scream or beg, even smash my forehead into his grinning face, anything to make him take his hands off me. 'You don't know me. I don't do this. It was a mistake. I don't do that sort of thing.'

'Right, that's what your type always says. You think it'd be any fun if I picked the cheap sluts? There's plenty of sex on offer out there, darling – practically anywhere, for a few rounds of drinks. Part of the fun is picking the right target. And I'm good at that. You pick the right upmarket location – you have to get the quiet, professional, sensible ones, the ones who think they're a cut above the rest, the ones with the most to lose.

Otherwise there's no shame to make them pay, to make them want to keep it secret from their mummies, daddies and fiancés, is there?'

Genuine distaste must have gathered in my face as the scale of his enterprise, his *business,* as he'd called it, clarified fully, for the first time. There was pragmatism and planning to it, devoid of compassion, a cold obliviousness to the cruelty and carnage he was creating – for fun, for profit, to make some holiday money. I wondered why he was being so honest, why he was telling me all this. I realised it was because he was enjoying laying it out before me piece by piece, because he was arrogant enough to believe there was absolutely nothing I could do, because he was right, I had a lot to lose.

'Don't look at me like that, Jen,' he laughed. 'It sure beats working for a living, doesn't it? And paying taxes? It's just about making the most of what you are good at, seeing the gap in the market. Come on, I didn't *rape* you or anything. You wanted to do it. I was your little holiday romance, your knight in shining armour, wasn't I? I put in the effort – be fair now, I said all the right things.'

'But you *drugged* me, the Rohypnol . . . I found it in your caravan.'

He chuckled softly. 'Yes, it is ironic that you seem to be the first one who's actually followed up and cottoned on to my foolproof little plan, because you were the easiest in the world to scam into bed. You must have been really longing for some attention. A few references about pop groups and poetry, a quick tale or two about travel writing and you practically fell into bed. I didn't even *need* to use the Rohypnol on you! The bullshit and the Merlot was enough. The magic pills are there for insurance, of course, if the deal needs to be sealed, but it didn't this time. So you needn't get all, 'You did it against my will,' on me. You did what you wanted to do.'

I felt bile rise in my mouth. 'Is that what you told Suzy? That it was her fault?' I was guessing, of course, but the shot seemed to hit a soft spot somewhere. Justin's face clouded out for second. Something old and complicated surfaced in his eyes, something damaged. It might have been hurt but it was veiled quickly by anger.

'Don't talk to me about Suzy,' he snapped. 'She was a little bitch. I just didn't want to see it. So holier than thou, always believing she was better than everyone else. She wasn't too damn saintly to start making out with that posh lawyer prick, though, was she? Probably been dicking him for months while she acted like the Virgin Mary. Was I supposed to let her get away with it? She wasn't so virgin white once Daddy had seen the lovely photo spread.'

'And the baby?

'It wasn't *my* baby. I didn't tell her to throw herself off a hundred-foot bridge, did I? That's not the point anyway. The point is – my indulgence has reached its limit. Give me £500, no more meddling, no more visiting and snooping, or I promise you, you *will* be a lot more sorry than sorry Suzy.'

'Fuck you,' I spat, before I'd even thought if this was a good idea. I couldn't bear his hand on me a second longer and tried to wrench myself from his grip. But he held fast.

'Easy girl, easy. I didn't get the impression you were fond of the rough stuff. Maybe you're even more of a dark horse than I realised. Maybe you're getting off on this. Perhaps I do it for you in a way beloved Inspector Dan can't. Perhaps I underestimated you there, too. Are you one of those girls who just likes to *pretend* to resist? What do you say, Jen? Shall we test the theory?'

He shoved his hand up to grab my breast and kissed me hard.

'Getting the juices going yet?' he sniggered, tugging at my trouser waistband. 'No? Disappointing.'

A fire was sparking inside me. It was latent pride, I think, a flicker of rage so dark and molten it was beyond sense and self-preservation.

'What if I tell the police?' I said. 'I know who you are, I know you hurt Suzy. I've got the Rohypnol. I've got the disks. I bet there are other women who will come forward.'

'Right, right – and what evidence do you really have? You, of all people, should know how important *evidence* is. You won't find my face on any of those disks. You won't find Pootle's either. I quality-controlled them from the start. You could have got them anywhere. And I think you'll find 'Surf Sluts' has a few fewer videos than yesterday. You know it's just your word against mine, sweetie pie. In fact, if you were silly enough to try and involve me in your little delusions, maybe I would have to tell my side of the story to one of your sympathetic colleagues.

'Yes, I can see it now. I'm a simple man, I had a one-night stand but the crazy bird is stalking me. She follows me when I'm surfing, she damages my VW, hassles my neighbours, breaks into my caravan and then it mysteriously burns down. I'm concerned for my safety. By the way, I bet you broke a few rules to find me, didn't you? Oh yes, naughty, naughty.

'You should know when you're out of your depth. But if you still think it's worth it, remember you're still just one click away from internet stardom. I bet your friends in the local papers would like to see your feature film debut, wouldn't they? Jack Thomson isn't it? NewsBeatWales Agency? He's very interested in this story, isn't he? He wrote such a lovely, lurid piece today – I saw his byline. And don't forget, I know where you live and work too, sweetheart.'

He let me go, after a moment – a long moment. He wanted me to know that he was 'letting me go', because, right then, he chose to. He knew I was no real threat to him. He knew I was defeated. 'I'll be in touch with the details for your donation,' he said. Then he pecked me on the forehead, pulled up his collar and disappeared into the street full of snow.

I watched him recede, soundlessly. After a moment I unlocked the door and slid inside. I sat on the bottom step of the stair, listening, listening for any sound of Justin. But there was none. I waited in the dark for some time. I was trembling a little.

I tried to think through the implication of what Justin had threatened. The way he had put it, everything I had done could be interpreted exactly the way he described. So there was a sex tape – lots of couples make those these days. How humiliating would it be if he claimed I was stalking him, if he made a complaint against me? It would be round the station and the force in a matter of days, no matter how 'sensitively' it was handled. And it would be doubly humiliating for me because of the standards I had set for myself – the respectable, sensible press officer. I knew how people would see me. Not so bloody aloof now, is she? That would be the gloating comment of the likes of Fat Paula and everyone who thought an inspector's fiancée was fair game.

And what if he tried to take out a restraining order? It would go through the courts. I'd have no anonymity from media reporting because it doesn't apply if the sexual offence is part of another prosecution. Jack NewsBeatWales could take it all down, he could name me, and what a story he would make of it. What poetic revenge he would exact for all the times he felt I had coolly brushed him off, denied him information for his stories, held the moral high ground.

I knew Justin could pull it off. He'd fooled me completely, hadn't he? Only a performance of subtlety and accomplishment could separate me from my Marks and Spencer's cotton low-rise briefs. They'd see what he wanted them to see, a clean-cut guy who had made a mistake and scorned a woman. I could never live it down or survive the chief super's quiet talk that would begin with the treacherous words, 'Of course we don't believe it, Jennifer, but every complaint has to be thoroughly investigated . . .'

My image of professionalism *was* me. Jen Johnson the press officer – efficient, capable, restrained, ladylike, controlled. Not that *thing* in the video, legs spread, panting and writhing.

How I wanted Dan just then, to be in his arms where I knew I'd be safe. But he was working the late shift. It would be four hours at least before he was home. I sagged down the middle as I remembered how I had used to look forward to Dan's late shifts. Other wives and partners complained, but not me. Having Dan there made the place untidy and noisy. Dan always had the TV on just a bit too loud. I was forever asking him to, 'Turn it down just a notch, sweetie,' And he endlessly channel surfed, ten minutes of this, two of that, thirty seconds of that.

If he wasn't watching TV he wandered round with his iPod loudly providing a scratchy accompaniment to whatever I was trying to read.

With the house to myself I could pick a movie or a DVD box set and watch for hours in a single stream of uninterrupted peace, or, best of all, read a book in complete silence, make a lean, slow supper for myself and eat it with the tea towel tucked in my t shirt, washing up right away and keeping the place neat. These were wonderfully unobserved indulgent hours of doing nothing. I had hugged them to myself like a precious cargo of release from having to bite my tongue.

Now the emptiness of the house chided me with silent reprimands. Each room seemed to creak with absence. We'd been living there nearly three years. We'd bought it at a good price because it had been owned by an old man who'd died, and it needed some fixing up. But we hadn't really fixed it up.

We'd bought furniture for the living room and given it a lick of paint, laid new carpets. But we'd never found time to fit a new kitchen. The downstairs rear living room was full of boxes of books, paperwork and kitchenware from our old flat. Dan was no good at DIY and, to be fair, he'd never had the time with his erratic working hours. I would have had the time but I never had the inclination.

But it was now clear to me there was a deeper reason why I hadn't wanted to spend my weekends comparing taps and tiles, kitchen counters and hobs. I'd been hiding – hiding at university in my student house, hiding in my engagement that was not yet a marriage, hiding in my job, hiding in command team meetings behind solid advice and the capable handling of business. I was hiding, because if I came out into the open and embraced the wedding, and the interior decorating, and tried to be comms manager, then it would mean this was my *home*, not just a house, this was my *career*, not just a job, this was my life, not just my life *for now* and this was all there was. This was who I was. Everything I was. *All* I was. And I hated that.

I sat in the dark and cried.

Chapter Twenty

I was still sitting in the dark of the living room when I heard Dan's key in the door. He was startled when he clicked on the light and saw me curled on the sofa.

'What's wrong, Jen? Why are you sitting in the dark? You never wait up for me,' he said. That was true, it had been a long time since I'd waited up for him.

'I just missed you, that's all. I thought I'd wait for you.'

'I left you a message to call me, again. Just like last night. But you didn't call.'

I'd forgotten to check the messages. 'Things have been a bit crazy, that's all. We never seem to get a chance to talk now.'

'That's not entirely my fault any more is it, Jen?' he said. He stayed standing in the door. He did not come and sit with me as I'd hoped.

'What does that mean?'

'Come on, Jen, since we decided to get married, even before the Sophie thing, you've been pulling further and further away from me. I thought we could try and change that. I've been trying hard, I really have. But over the last few weeks, I can barely get two words out of you. You were miles away when we went for the weekend to the Aeron Inn. You won't talk about the wedding or the honeymoon. You don't want to talk about anything at all. I mean, I know part of this is my fault, but I can only say sorry so many times.'

'Maybe there's a few more in you yet. You talk of the wedding, but we haven't exactly been planning this together have we, Dan? You're far too busy with your career to want to be involved,' I shot at him, instantly defensive and then shamed by my petulance. This was coming out all wrong. Why was I attacking him? He was right, I had been distant but this wasn't supposed to be happening. I wanted to tell him I loved him. I wanted his comfort. But the words had become lodged in my throat, expanding to suffocating size, and instead I was voicing the usual sulky, childish complaints.

'Is there something you want to tell me?' said Dan suddenly. 'Is there someone else?'

I was genuinely startled. 'Someone else?' Where had that come from? Surely he couldn't know. How could he know?

'All you do is check your emails, twenty times a day, then check your phone. All very secretive, isn't it? Whenever I ask where you've been you never really say. If I ring you're not home, or not answering. I leave a message but you don't call back. I just wondered if maybe there was someone else, not that I'd blame you, I guess.'

'There isn't anyone else, Dan.'

'Really? Because I often think that you must wonder what it's like. You know, you've never *been* with another man, that I know of. You must wonder if you're missing out on something.' He sounded bitter.

How could he think that? It had been about many things but never about that, about sex, about missing out. But how could I explain?

'I . . . No. I mean, there isn't anyone else, Dan. I promise you.'

275

'Not even someone from work?'

'Work?' He was just guessing, then? He didn't really know anything. 'Like who?'

He paused. 'I did wonder if it might be Bodie.'

'Bodie?' I laughed after a stunned moment, suddenly relieved that Marc might be the extent of his suspicions. But Dan did not see the humour, not at all.

'Don't laugh at me, Jennifer,' he ordered quietly. His voice was flat. He never called me Jennifer. Jen or sweetheart or pet, perhaps, but never Jennifer. The significance of using my full name was a sign of how serious he was.

'I'm not laughing at you,' I recovered hastily. 'Just . . . No, a dozen times no! Why the heck would you think that? Me and Bodie?'

I got up and tried to move towards him, to put my arms around him, but he backed away. I couldn't bear the thought of him backing away, not now. It was too much like backing out. That was supposed to be my prerogative, wasn't it? I was the one with doubts. But they seemed very far off at that moment, as they had two nights before when I'd had the dream about Justin and the first and only name I had instinctively called had been Dan's.

'Well, I've seen the way he is with you in the office,' continued Dan. '"Feel my buns of steel", wasn't it?'

He'd remembered *that*? 'But that's just . . .'

'At the Christmas do, too – he was pretty friendly. You didn't seem to mind too much.'

'But that was . . .'

He was warming to this theme now, his voice rising in volume and also a deepening a notch.

'Do you realise we haven't made love for over a month, not

even at the hotel when we went away for the weekend, weeks and weeks ago?'

I did know. Of course I knew. I'd been avoiding it recently, any opportunity for sex. Not because I didn't want Dan – in many ways I longed more than ever for his touch, but because every time I thought about sex it was somehow a replay of that night with Justin all over again. The act seemed burned on my brain from the video, if not the occasion itself. I couldn't un-see it, un-feel it.

Justin had worked his way into my head and my life so thoroughly, into my every working, sleeping minute, he'd even worked his way into my bed and the increasing space between me and Dan. If Dan and I went to bed he would be making love with that woman from the video, not with me. I didn't want that. I didn't want her inside our house or our life.

'Look, it's just been a tough few weeks, Dan,' I said, trying to be soothing, non-confrontational. 'I *promise* you there's nothing between Bodie and me. He was so embarrassed about being drunk at the Area party he came and apologised to me. He actually asked if you were offended.'

'He called you at the hotel, Jen. Twice.'

'What?'

'I know his number. It was in your phone.'

'You've been spying into my phone?'

'No. Well, I did look at it. It rang while you were in the loos, then when I was at the bar. I heard you say, "I love you". I wanted to know who it was. It was his number.'

Yes, I remembered. Bodie had called, thinking I was on call. I had said 'Love you too.' It had been said sarcastically, but evidently not sarcastically enough for anyone who overheard. Then Dan had taken the phone and put it away. Obviously he'd checked it when I wasn't looking. So I had been right to delete all Justin's messages. I didn't want to think what would have happened if I hadn't.

'Bodie thought I was on call,' I said calmly. 'He rang me instead of Serian, that's all. The control room hadn't swapped our names in the rota. I just said that because he was pretending to have a go at me for slacking off.' It sounded stupid in that context. I didn't quite believe it myself.

Dan looked incredulous, but rather than dignify what I'd said with a response he said coolly, 'Right. So where were you on Tuesday afternoon and then in the evening?'

'What?'

'It's a simple question. It's the question I asked Fat Paula when I popped over to the nick and she said you were apparently *off* somewhere with Bodie, that's how she put it. *Off somewhere.* She also said that's usually where you were when no one could find you. What did she mean by that, exactly?' It was a demand now, not a request for information.

Tuesday afternoon? I'd been in Swansea with Sergeant Stan, then sneaked off home early from there, chatted to Dan in the hall as he was leaving, perused 'Surf Sluts', gone for a run and assaulted a teenager.

'I can't remember exactly, Dan. I think I came home early and then went running.'

'Running? Of course! You should be running a marathon by now, the hours you put in!'

This was getting out of control. I could feel the tension tipping us away from our usual centre of gravity, outwards towards chaos. I made an effort to make myself sound calm.

'I wasn't with Bodie, Dan. Paula's just got it in for me because I don't sign her bloody attendance book like a good little girl. She hates the fact she can't keep tabs on me. I was *not* with Bodie. We do not see each other outside the office. I promise you. I love *you*.'

'Then why was his car in the street earlier?'

'What?' This was too sudden a swerve in yet another direction. I felt a surge of motion sickness.

Dan continued, 'I was called to an incident two streets down, a sudden death. I drove past to see if you were at home. Not that you ever seem to be home now. The house was dark but your car was here, and Bodie's car was parked down the street, that stupid little black convertible he drives. It's there now. At one o clock in the morning. I think it got stuck in the snow. But what was he doing here, Jennifer?'

There was something shifting beneath the planes of his face, narrowing between his eyes, building in his shoulders. I knew at once the origin, though I'd seldom seen it in Dan. He was suppressing the urge to hit something. Not me, he'd never do that, but maybe something else, anything else. If Bodie were here he'd want to hit him. I half expected Dan to stride through the house throwing open wardrobe doors and checking under the stairs to see if Bodie was hiding somewhere, clad in boxer shorts and a general air of guilt.

'Dan, he wasn't *here*. Bodie's *never* been here,' I pleaded, thinking of Dan passing in the street, thinking that some time tonight he had driven by, perhaps while Justin had been kissing me with his hands on me. 'I was probably sleeping. I swear to you, on my life, there's nothing going on with me and Marc.'

'So what is it, then?' demanded Dan. 'What is up with you? Because I know it's something and if it's *me*, and you just don't want me, then I want to know, now.'

This was a demand, an ultimatum. Perhaps this was the Dan, the relentless and stone-voiced Dan regularly encountered by the people he arrested, by the people he interrogated and questioned. This was the Dan who had risen with spectacular speed to inspector by hard work and sheer determination, the half of Dan that was fused to the half I lived with, silently present beneath the face and hands I recognised. It was almost impossible to lie to this man. This was an interrogation. He expected an answer and not an excuse.

I wanted to tell him the truth. I wanted to trust that he would understand but I couldn't believe it. Perhaps in time he might, perhaps in time he'd see it for what it was, if I could explain it all, slowly and clearly. Not just the bare facts – I slept with a complete stranger, he filmed it and now he's blackmailing me. If I tried that I'd never make it past the first few lines before he'd insist that I tell him exactly who and where Justin was.

His urge to express his feelings through striking out was still barely suppressed. He'd want to confront Justin for sure, and in his current mood he might just end up ripping his head off, which would mean the end of his career and an end to my predicament with the worst possible outcome. Then he'd turn away from me and there'd be no chance to explain anything else, because at that point the reasons wouldn't matter.

I couldn't do it. I sat back down on the chair and put my head in my hands.

'Clearly you have nothing to say to me,' said Dan when I offered nothing but silence, 'And, for you of all people, I know that is never a good thing. When *you* run out of the will to reason and rationalise we might as well admit we've reached the point of no return.' His anger was shifting now, focusing itself on me.

'I'm just finding all this a bit much, Dan' I said. 'The

pressure of the wedding, all the expectations – everyone expecting me to be so happy, so thrilled with it all.'

'And you're *not*, are you? Not at all. If you didn't want to marry me you should have said. Perhaps there's a lot of things you should have said a long time ago.'

'Dan –'

'It's too late now, isn't it.' He said it as a statement, not a question. He moved to the door, to go upstairs. I hoped he meant, it was too late at night to argue, not that it was too late in the day to try to put things right. I didn't want it to be too late for that.

'Dan, please.' I grabbed his arm, stepped in his path, but he shook me off.

'It's time for you to decide what you want, Jen. I love you. I always have. But I'm not going to be the guy you just settle for.'

'Dan,' I was still standing in front of him, not wanting to leave it like this, panic growing. But he put his arm up and pushed me aside, not violently but firmly, raising his other hand in front of him as a warning.

'Don't. I'm going to bed now. I'll sleep in the spare room. I have to be up early. You let me know what you decide.'

Being alone in the dark, under the cold bedcovers, with Dan silent in the room next door, I remembered only too well the torture of other nights we had spent that way, other nights following our first few arguments as a couple. That seemed very long ago.

There was never any real shouting or histrionics, just our voices raised a little, throwing accusations or supposed irritations back and forth and then the shut-down of Dan's silence. But for me the dry, sharp-edged shards of those pointed complaints and petty disappointments would lie through the night as a brittle desert between our bodies, in our double bed, their slivers sticking in the skin at the slightest movement.

How long I lay there wanting to speak, wanting to shout, wanting to reason it out, but fearing further angry retorts from Dan's dark shape, feeling the hum of his hurt, strangled by my confusion and teary recriminations. All the while I would replay our exchanges in my head in the hope of resolution, alert in a fabric world of eyeless waiting, fathomless with excuses and justifications. I would listen to his breathing and think, 'How can you sleep at a time like this, when the world is breaking apart?'

But by morning we had always pulled back together, some tidal current ensuring we did not drift apart for too long. Or was it that I was always the first to come round, reach out, hold him?

I had spent a night like that, alone in the Watch-house, the night I fled from home after speaking to Sophie. The last night of what I had come to think of as my old life. The life before Justin.

That night I was safe in my assured victim's shell, knowing for once, with certainty, that I was not at fault. I had not overreacted. Dan alone was to blame, Dan and *her*. In that certainty had been the possibility of grabbing hold of new truths, using them to look ahead, to the suggestion that maybe things had to change – confronting what I felt about Dan, a choice to be made rather than an assumption of who we were, handed down between us through the years.

In the toss and turn of sleep under the Watch-house eaves I had remembered that moment of strange sun-lit unearthliness on the shores of Cape Cod, when all possibilities were opening up. And through my tears there was a bright, humming thread of light, that things didn't have to be the way they now seemed they had to be. Something was going to happen.

Then there was Justin. And he had seemed handsome and well read, fond of novels and poetry, approving of my indie rock and roll. He had heard of Robert Frost, 'The one less travelled by,' he had said, the road I had wanted to try, and it had echoed deep inside me.

But now I could see how truly blinded I had been. I saw from my bed's eye view how what Justin was looking for had been written all over me that night, branded on my skin and down to the bone in the Snug. *Save me, discover me, free me!* – my tell-tale heart beating its tattoo, loud enough for the whole damn hotel, pub and town to hear if they had listened for a moment: *Attractive female, almost twenty-nine, bored and afraid – escapist hero wanted, please apply and ply with booze.*

If it had been just the sex I think I would have been less humiliated. But the promise, oh the promise of something more . . .

It seemed absurdly obvious now, exactly how Justin had done it all so easily. Justin had been casing the hotel that night, with his book at the bar – looking for a target. His gaze must have fastened on me immediately, alone in a hotel full of smoochy, smug couples with a book in my hand to ward off the sight of all that fawning and fondling.

He'd no doubt noted my half glances in his direction. With the blush that bloomed red and ready I'd bestowed on him evidence of my ripeness, he just had to pick the right moment to pluck me.

He'd headed to the pub the next night and led me expertly through the planned revelations of our conversation. From the moment we'd started to chat we had so much in common. But how much of that had I volunteered myself and he'd just agreed with? So he'd said he liked Elbow. But one quick look on the driver's seat of my car in the hotel car park would have revealed battered copies of the band's CDs. There were half a dozen paperbacks on the back seat, too, and several copies of *The Times* travel magazine. You didn't need to be a detective to carry out that simple investigation. I had given so much of myself away.

He hadn't known anyone at the Mochyn Ddu pub, but he'd given the impression of being a local very simply – buy a sandwich there at lunch time and the barman will acknowledge you again when you return; ask some surfer dude where the right lines are likely to come through and he'll oblige with talk of tubes and boards. Instantly you are Carl's old mate – easiest thing in the world, and to the world the obvious assumption? He belongs here.

I'd taken my purse with me to the bar in the Mochyn Ddu but I'd left my handbag with my life in it right next to Justin on the seat, a present to a conman, containing my driver's licence, bits of mail with my home address on, my police ID badge on its strap, my police business cards, my mobile phone – everything he had needed to know at the touch of his fingertips, beneath the table top, while I waited for another round of drinks and he, all the while, smiled. The rest I had simply told him. Then the chase was on.

How many successes could you expect with this game of his? One in three? More? It was easy to see now what he and Pootle had worked out between them. Read the hotel guides, pick one venue each, case them, select a victim, use a false name, try your hand at role-playing seduction, ensure you score – Rohypnol or not – get your video, make some money by threatening to air it. If the women don't bite, move on to the next; if they do, pocket the cash. Keep it clean and simple. Keep it distant. Don't shit where you eat.

Justin had called it a business. It must have had profitable returns.

And I had laid myself open, in every sense, to this production line of opportunity, to the man who appeared to be everything I desired in my fiancé, but was none of these things, and was not even close to the things that mattered.

At no point had I felt coerced, at no point had I done anything I could say I hadn't wanted to, until the point I couldn't remember, and the night and the booze and the suitor Justin created swallowed me whole. I'd never know if he had drugged me or if it had just been the wine that had stolen my memories and my judgement.

Worst of all was that he might have shared me with Pootle. Two condoms, two men? Justin might reveal to me if Pootle had been there, eventually, but he might not, and it certainly wouldn't be anything I'd want to see. Justin would string that little revelation out too, turning the screws to make me wince because I had crossed him – made things *untidy*.

And all this because I'd made the fatal mistake of allowing myself to think a man could carry me away from myself. Not towards a 'happy' ending with a wedding, but away from one, towards an alternative ending, and an imagined romance. It was unfolding entirely of its own free will – like those childhood fantasies of discovering my royal parentage, my entitlement to something better, it would happen and my life would be changed in the wink of an eye.

But romances and love stories aren't necessarily the same thing. I know that now. Romances are bright and shiny and come in clean, candy-cute colours. Love stories, however, can be full of all sorts of things romances can't: jealousy and anger, frustration and regret – dark things, tarnished things – and that isn't necessarily a bad thing, because it's real. You can grab it and tear at it and drag it in close to you, inhaling its smell of fire and night.

Romance evaporates in the hand before your fist can close over it. If you try to grasp it you are left only with the faint smell of boiled sweets, of powdered sugar, a sticky memory already fading.

The fact is, every time I had bitten my lip with Dan, listened to his choice of music because it was easier, taken the holidays he preferred, I had been avoiding the real moments of life, just like I had refused to see them every time Dan brought me an unasked-for cup of tea, or tickled the special spot on my back that he knows makes me laugh.

When I met Justin he seemed to offer an escape into fantasy romance. What he'd provided was entry into a disfiguringly embarrassing time bomb, ready to explode in a welter of groans, thrusts and pale pink panties – a candlelit cliché of homemade adult entertainment. And I knew I wasn't the only one who'd made the mistake. How many other women had, and would continue, to fall for him? How many relationships, careers, lives, had caved in under the cruelty, the demands, the realisation of the tawdriness of the truth?

In one way or another Suzy Milland hadn't been able to handle it. She'd taken flight from a bridge rather than deal with the aftermath, or the uncertainty, or the shame.

In that moment, alone in my bed, I could understand that, the simple relief of the clarity, the removal of the wondering, all the question marks erased. Suzy's eyes bored into mine from the memory of her photographs. I felt she was asking a question, the question I had been asking myself for a number of weeks now. How far will you go to end this?

'I'm so sorry, Dan,' I mouthed in the dark, tears prickling under my closed lids. When Dan and I lay curled up in bed, in our cocoon, after the dusk and before the morning rolled over, warming the blackness with our breath, it was the only place in the world I had ever really felt safe – safe and still. The darkness might rear up and surge round us like the storm of the century but with Dan there it would fail to take me, or to separate us.

As long as Dan doesn't find out, I thought.

I had to take action. But how? How could I preserve what we had? What we were? Freeze it in the moment – unchanged, unsullied, unspoilt? So he would never look at me with disappointment in his eyes?

Something had been flickering on the edge of my awareness for weeks. I just never thought I would take such a step. But we all have our strengths and weakness. We all have our limits. Eventually we have to know when we are outmatched.

I woke early next morning and lay staring at the ceiling for the signs of the dawn. My body felt heavy and my head thick. At 7.30 a.m. I tiptoed past Dan's snores from the spare room, and put on my running shoes. In ten minutes I was jogging on the edge of the common. It was just getting light. One or two early dog walkers hurried by, wrapped up against the March morning chill and the three inches of icing-sugar frost coating the world.

My head was empty of all logical and strategic thought. I padded along in the rising grey light, beside ducks sleeping with their heads tucked into waxy feathers, past early birds pecking at the solid soil, through the twitter-song of sunrise and the slowly increasing sound of distant traffic. In my head I repeated a mantra I sometimes used: *calm, clear, cool; calm, clear, cool –* nothing else. The air was wonderfully calm as the light rays emerged over tree tops, above the smell of cold earth and wet river. My pulse and breath combined in a double heartbeat, synchronised, non verbal, non linear, just drumming, just there.

I passed the playing fields and the rear of the music school, the backs of the sandstone terraces at the edge of the city. A group of boys, perhaps twelve or thirteen years old, heading to school, their black trousers and ties visible under their winter coats, sniggering as I passed, woolly hats pulled down low. One of them shouted, 'Show us your tits, darling', but I was only vaguely aware of their presence, as if they were merely a back projection on a screen nearby, two-dimensional, moving in an unreal winter-white postcard land, flickering back into nothingness as I passed.

As I ran, further than ever before, everything distilled into an instinct, an answer that was beyond justification or simple right and wrong. I'd reached the point where reason ended and a great gap appeared – a wide, black, heavy-eyed gap that had nothing to do with lack of sleep. But that was ok. I'd come this far. There could be no going back.

I stopped running, abruptly. I was winded, slick from head to foot with sweat. Then I saw I was standing at the edge of the bridge near the Whitchurch weir. The angling club lay across the misty stretch of water. The river poured wide and white across the lip of the weir, down the ten-foot slope to an anarchic churn of spray and bubbles.

I walked calmly to the upstream edge of the bank, my feet sucking on the snow-slippery earth. In that water lived something welcomingly clean and bitter cold. I breathed and stared, breathed and stared. In a little while my breathing and the water rush were one in my head. Deep beneath that water would be a cool, calm clarity unlike anywhere else. I started the Count; when the time ran out, I would act.

Chapter Twenty-One

I don't know how long I stood there.

At some point, some time later, long after I had reached zero, I realised a middle-aged man was standing on the bridge a step or two away from me, his eyes wide with anxiety. His right gloved hand was extended, his feet were making little slow, shuffling movements towards me. Beside him a fat golden retriever, head cocked on one side, watched closely, his chocolate-brown eyes fixed intently on mine.

As my gaze aligned with the man's, he stopped his shuffle, wiped his hands on his anorak and smiled weakly.

'Now, now love,' he said softly, raising his hands in front of him in a 'hold on for a minute' gesture. 'You ok?' Not going to do anything stupid, are you?'

I looked back at the water, looked up again at him, realisation dawning. The man looked as white and grey as the churn of spray below. I immediately felt bad – I had given him a scare. I allowed myself a slow, tight smile.

'Maybe I am going to do something stupid, but not right now,' I said calmly. 'Don't worry. Everything is fine.'

Then I pulled out my mobile phone and called a taxi. I was way too tired to walk home, let alone run.

Dan had already left for work when I got back. He'd left me

a note on the kitchen table that said. 'Let's talk tonight. I'm sorry. I love you.' I held the note in my hand for a long time.

I took a shower and dressed. I called Nige and told him I was taking the day off sick. Then I went to Dan's desk drawer and pulled out his address book. I looked up the phone number and dialled it quickly. I didn't even think about doing the Count. That time was long past. The decision was made and I knew I was going to act. The phone rang three times at the other end.

When Sophie answered, I asked:

'Do you remember when you asked me what I wanted for a wedding present?'

On Monday, when I returned to work, the world appeared to rotate as evenly as normal. Nigel asked me if I was feeling better and offered me a doughnut from a big box he'd bought to cheer everyone up. I took a vanilla cream, and Serian made us coffee. I dealt with a sudden death and a car accident and attended the morning tasking meeting.

At about 11.30 a.m. Bodie called me up and asked me to come down to his office when I had five minutes to spare.

'Look, Jen, there's something I wanted to warn you about,' he said, closing the door behind me a touch awkwardly, before sitting down at his new desk, a *sergeant's* desk with a flat-screen monitor and sleek keyboard. His recently framed certificates of achievement were hung on the freshly painted duck-egg blue walls. A pinboard already displayed the Force Customer Charter and Force Annual Plan for the year ahead, printed in breezy, easy-to-read primary colours. Bodie had recently received notification that he would soon be *acting* sarge no more – his stripes were on their way and he was already playing the part as befitted his increased rank.

Here it comes, I thought, seeing the earnestness in his face as I sat down opposite him. It's started. The questions, the inconsistencies. They've noticed the Maglite. They've received some new information. Someone's come forward regarding the appeal. They've made the connections. This was *the talk*, the talk that preceded the friendly questions, then the official questions, then the statements, and then who knew what.

'That bitch Fat Paula was nosing around looking for you on Tuesday again,' began Bodie. 'She came down here asking if I'd seen you because you were supposed to be in Swansea and weren't, or something, because she'd tried to ring you there and they said you'd left. Like I'd know where you were in the middle of dealing with an assault, a mugging *and* an arson. Knowing she has it in for you, I said you and me had been in the station down there going through some appeals, off and on. Not a problem. I got rid of her.

'But Wednesday night she was down here again, saying she'd seen you coming out of the CID room and what might you be doing in here, and where was I at the time?' He looked a bit bashful, and gave an apologetic shrug. 'Between you and me, I was starving and I'd nipped over the Spar to get a beef and onion pasty. I hadn't eaten since noon, this was seven at night. But she made comments about security and some evidence bags I'd left on the desk and them not being checked in properly. Interfering old cow. I don't know what her problem is, but I said I'd been giving you an update on the case, covering my own arse as well, obviously. I know I should have checked the bags into the Swansea evidence room right away but I didn't realise Doyle had put them in the boot of my car until I was halfway here. I was only *gone* for twenty minutes over the shop. I did wonder if she thought we'd been having it away in the store cupboard or something, the way she was looking at me.'

He said this almost wistfully, then covered it with a half laugh and said, 'As if! She said something about find one of you, find the other, whatever the hell that meant. What was *she* bloody snooping about for at seven in the night anyway, I ask you? Anyway, I thought she might try and stir up trouble. I'd already had a bollocking from the super about not locking my bloody PNN again. I've got a mental block about that thing, honestly.

'I knew you were down in Swansea again Thursday so I thought I'd nip round to your house on the way to work on Thursday night and tell you what I'd told her, in case she nabbed you Friday, so we could say the same thing – one story for all, so to speak.'

He shifted in the chair and fiddled with the knob that controlled the angle of the backrest. 'I thought maybe you had a reason for not being in Swansea that you might not want to, um, share with Paula.'

I wasn't sure what he wanted me to say.

'You didn't come to the house though, Marc. I was home all Thursday evening,' I offered. I knew, of course, that he was referring to the night Justin and I had last spoken, when we'd traded threats on the doorstep. Dan had *said* he'd seen Bodie's car in the street. Looks like he had been right.

'Yeah, I know,' Bodie looked sheepish again. He focussed on an imaginary point on the noticeboard to my right and said, 'I was looking for your house. You know I couldn't quite remember the number – the number's fallen off, by the way.' He cleared his throat. 'Well, I was across the street and I er, I saw you and a *bloke* in the doorway.' He looked away at the customer service promise. 'It wasn't *Dan*,' he prompted, when

I didn't speak. 'You looked *cosy*. I thought maybe there was something, *extracurricular* going on.' Bodie, the oracle of the extracurricular!

'I mean, it's none of my business, really, so I just buggered off. 'Course, like a twat, I couldn't get my car out of the street with the snow freezing. I had to park it at the end of your road and leave it. Got a taxi into the station from the main road. What was I thinking? A convertible, in Wales?'

He was trying to make a joke now, trying to look as if he was not hoping I would explain this away. Dan was his mate, his senior officer. I was his colleague and also more. He was offering me an alibi if I needed one – if I was having an affair, if I needed a favour to cover my tracks with Fat Paula. He was also asking me to provide one for his oversight with the evidence. That was all.

'Marc, you dickhead,' I smiled with an excellent approximation of amusement. 'That was an old mate from uni you saw. He'd taken me out for a coffee after work, that's all. He was going home to his *wife*.'

The lie slid out easily, seamlessly, now that I'd had so much practice. 'You know, Dan *saw* your car in the street, when he got home that night. We even had a row about it because he thought you and me might be, how did you put it? Being, *extracurricular*.' I raised a genuine smile this time as the big man blushed from goatee to hairline.

'Oh, God!' moaned Bodie. 'Oh, I'm such a twat. Dan was right moody with me last week. That explains it! You did tell him we weren't, you know . . . right? He knows we're not . . .'

'He knows,' I said reassuringly. 'It was just one of those stupid *couple* rows. It's ok.'

'So, I'm still invited to the stag drink thing then? And the wedding?'

'Of course.' I rose to leave, relieved. At least for that moment I was not being questioned or interrogated about anything else.

'Er, about Wednesday night?' he asked awkwardly.

'Fat Paula hasn't said anything to me about Swansea or about Wednesday. I haven't seen her at all today, actually. But thanks for the warning. As far as I'm concerned you were here in the office logging evidence until I left on Wednesday. We were going over the arson updates together. If she missed you, or was looking for you, I expect you were just in the loo for a minute.'

'Thanks, Jen,' he smiled gratefully. 'No sense walking into trouble, is there?'

'Quite,' I agreed.

We didn't find out until a few days later that Fat Paula wasn't going to be causing trouble for anyone else for a while. Two of the long-suffering admin girls in expenses and overtime claims had made complaints about bullying and harassment. Two more members of staff had then come forward and said they'd been victimised by her, too. Paula had been suspended pending an investigation.

Six months later the complaints were upheld. In the best police tradition she was asked to move on.

Chapter Twenty-Two

I must say, it was a truly successful wedding. I actually enjoyed it and I hadn't expected to. In many ways it was the day I would have hoped for if I had ever hoped for such a day. Dan agreed.

I was glad we'd kept it a quiet affair. In the end there were just thirty-five guests and minimum fuss at the hotel in the nearby picturesque market town of Cowbridge. We swapped from the large conservatory to the little ballroom a few weeks before. It was much less formal that way. The good thing about stalling on paying those deposits and making up my mind was that amending the bookings was easy.

A few weeks before the day I'd bought my 1930s-style blue silk tea dress off the peg at House of Fraser in town. I'd also cancelled the orders with Blooming Marvellous and ordered bouquets of cream roses from the florist two doors down from the inn, one for me and one for Beck, who was unofficial 'bridesmaid'. Izzy had a little corsage. Stephen was not there with Beck. They had split up a few weeks before but, to be honest, I think she was relieved.

Registrar Claire was as good as her word, and the ceremony was swift and simple and more touching than I would have thought possible. My mum spent the day dabbing happy tears from her eyes, gamely persevering with her new high-heeled shoes. Of course, Dan had no family there and my dad served as honorary, unofficial best man, but Bodie and Doyle made up the numbers very smartly on his side, along with Inspector Karen Smart and her girlfriend and two sergeants from his shift.

I smiled until my jaw ached. Dan beamed from beginning to end – a wide, simple grin, both smug and contented at the same time. It hurt my heart, but in a good way.

Everyone praised the hot lunchtime buffet and the no-fuss atmosphere that allowed us more time to get down to some drinking and chatting.

After the meal, while people were drifting off to the bar and to their rooms before the influx of evening guests, I made sure Dan was safely ensconced in boozy camaraderie with my dad and then slipped out the back door of the hotel.

A man was standing at the end of the sunlit grassy garden, by the gate to the rear lane, almost merging with the deep shadow of the oak tree. His suit was dark and neat, as was his hair. He looked like a guest but he was not. Not quite.

'Hello, Jennifer,' he said. 'I'm Vitaly. Sophia said to give you her best.' He offered his hand for me to shake, a surprisingly elegant long-fingered hand. Together we stepped behind the broad trunk of the tree so we could not be observed.

'She's sorry for that first misunderstanding on the telephone,' added Vitaly. 'She apologises again for any difficulty it caused. She was embarrassed by the confusion.'

'That's quite all right,' I answered. 'She has explained herself more than adequately since then.'

We looked at each other in the late afternoon light.

'Daniel has chosen a very beautiful bride,' he smiled. 'And have you had a perfect day?'

'Most certainly, thank you'.

I remember this conversation now, with perfect clarity, as if it is still occurring, as if Vitaly is just this minute saying, 'I wish you great happiness' and again I see him pause and look down into his hand which holds an unobtrusive rectangular box, wrapped in silver paper. A pink bow blooms on top. 'Would you like your gift now?' he says.

I hesitate for a moment, but it is too late to pretend that it contains a surprise, that this is not what I wanted, or what, in a way, I had asked for. I take it, stare at it for a moment and then thank him.

'You are welcome. But don't open it now. Put it away safely – for later, no? Then, after opening, burn it – the gift and the box. You understand?'

'Yes, of course.'

He is waiting for me to speak, to see if there is something I want to ask. He knows there is. I think he knows what people are about to ask or say from long experience. His hair is dark, but there are greying strands at the brow that match the colour of his eyes.

'Did he say anything?' I ask finally.

Vitaly suppresses a smile. 'Nothing very polite. Nothing very coherent. He was not contrite,' he looks at his hands. 'He was,' he searches for the right word, 'rather slow to comprehend his situation at first. He became more amenable when I became persuasive, and then when I asked after his father and his mother's health, he was more *malleable*. I told him that he was, "one click away from losing something that's rather more important to him if he ever tries anything like it again." That was the instruction, that's what I was told to say. That was correct, yes?'

'That was it, yes.'

'There was a little, er, collateral damage, I'm afraid,' he adds after a moment. 'We were *interrupted*. The unexpected does occur sometimes. The information we are given can be a little inaccurate. But I believe it was part and parcel of the same task, so I won't bother you with the details.'

I imagine that I would not care for the details. Hearing them wouldn't change what had happened, so I say, 'You're the professional. I trust your discretion.'

He smiles a little at that. 'Sophia never did say what this was about,' he prompts.

'No? She didn't ask. She asked me what I wanted for a wedding gift. I told her. She didn't need to ask.'

'Then I won't now. I don't doubt you had your reasons.'

'Dan can never know, of course.'

'Naturally.'

I look at Vitaly and he looks at me. He looks like a wedding guest but he is not – not quite. I look into his calm, grey eyes – they give nothing away. I do not want to think about what they might show if they could.

'Do you enjoy your work?' I ask suddenly, in spite of myself.

This is not the question he expected and it brings a full smile to his mouth, a smile that ignites an unexpected warmth. He tips me a formal bow. 'Let's say, I take a pride in it, yes.' His voice is precise, modified, slightly accented. I still pay attention to voices.

He knows I want to ask more and waits. He is patient.

I succumb. 'Are there, perhaps other boxes, I mean other "presents", ones without wedding bows? Ones you've already disposed of?'

He smiles the smile of a benevolent uncle or priest. 'That is business, not appropriate for a wedding day, Mrs *Collins.*" A small crackle of the smile extends to his eyes and he relents,

298

perhaps a sliver more than he ever relents. 'Perhaps there are. I sometimes bow to the creative urge.'

'Good.'

Now I sense approval, as minute half moons at the corners of his mouth dimple further. 'I think you and I understand each other. It is a shame we'll never meet again. You would be an asset to our family.'

'Yes, I believe you are right,' I reply. 'We do understand each other.' I clutch the box to my chest and nod a final farewell, turning back to the rest of my wedding day and the rest of my life. In that life, Vitaly, and all that he represents will once again cease to exist.

Moments later, with my hand on the hotel door handle, I pause to look back, intending to give him a last smile. But the garden is empty and only the shadow remains beneath the tree.

As the months have rolled by I have thought repeatedly about Vitaly, about my wedding gift, about what it meant, but I know that, no matter how much I am tempted, it is something I can never speak of. It is my secret now. It is mine to keep, just as Dan kept his. But I will keep mine much closer and much better.

In a strange way Dan's secret led directly to mine because it was so different to what I had first imagined. When I heard her voice, Sophie's voice, on his mobile phone, on that long ago October morning, I had assumed what all wives-to-be would have assumed there was another woman – he was having an affair. How could he? How *dare* he?

But poor Dan was hiding something else. His real name, for instance. He had changed it because, years ago, he had decided he wanted to be someone else. Since then he had maintained the same lie, a lie that made it possible for him to be beyond reproach, beyond suspicion, to give no one the excuse to suspect he was anything other than who he appeared, least of all me.

I understood this when he explained it, when I finally listened. I'd been too outraged to listen before. All the words he had tried to speak after Sophie's phone call had sounded like lies, like a foolish fiction, concocted to hide his obvious infidelity. But when I really listened I understood lots of things. Not all at once, but as the weeks passed and the months passed.

I understood why he had assumed his great aunt Alice's surname when he moved to live with her in Bristol as a boy. He did it to have nothing to do with his father and his father's family, or their name. He did it so Daniel Collins could eventually apply for a passport and new documents to join the police force, to follow the career he had always dreamed of. The police application vetting procedures are very strict. They search your background and your connections for anything undesirable – previous convictions, debts and, most crucially in Dan's case, dubious relations. Dan knew they'd never allow a young man with a father who was part of a suspected London crime family, with links going all the way back to Eastern Europe (the Ukraine, to be precise), into the ranks.

It wouldn't be appropriate. It wouldn't be transparent.

Even if by some miracle they did allow him inside he'd have to live with the air of others' suspicion that 'the apple doesn't fall far from the tree', that promotions might not be entirely on merit, that dealings might not be completely above board – the rumours, the jibes, the whispers.

His mum, Alice, had been just seventeen when she'd fled to London from Bristol to experience the bright lights of

Britain's biggest city. Young and fatally pretty, she'd started work in a little boutique where she'd come to the attention of Dan's father, Tom. He was twenty-six years old then, tall, dark and handsome, a driver and organiser in the up-and-coming family business, a flasher of cash, a speaker of smooth words, a maker of promises. It had taken Alice about three days to fall in love with Tom, three months to realise she might have made a mistake and the rest of her short life trying to correct her oversight.

The early years of Dan's childhood had been spent in the boomerang curve of her attempts to leave his father, fleeing their flat with suitcases on sudden, anxious taxi trips to cheap hotels in the middle of the night. There would be shouting and broken furniture and sometimes calming intervention by one of Tom's steadier, older brothers, Karol or Josef, leading to Alice's teary promises to return.

Then Dan's mum died in a car accident when he was ten years old. That part of what he'd told me was true. But she had not been married to his dad. She was the mistress, not the wife. Dan soon learned that his dad had a legitimate wife and daughter in Bethnal Green and another mistress in Odessa.

Dan's grandparents were already dead. His nearest relative on his mother's side was his mum's aunt, also called Alice in the family tradition, a not so Lady Bracknell-type widow living in Bristol. She had sheltered Dan and her niece in the past, during some of those brief escape attempts. She had lived up to her family responsibilities, taken Dan in and taken care of him.

Dan's father, always working his way through a string of mistresses, visited Dan several times a year, when he remembered. Occasionally he would take Dan to London to visit his uncles, but towards the end he took to appearing on the doorstep at inappropriate times of the night wrapped in an air of drunken defiance, suppressed aggression and self pity. He knew he was dying, slowly eaten away by an unseen mass in his bowels that left him weighing less than eight stone at the time of his demise.

When he finally succumbed, Dan, now fifteen, had asked his great aunt to officially adopt him. She already felt like his mother and happily obliged. She wasn't particularly wealthy. She didn't leave him a fancy house in her will. But Uncle Karol, who always had a soft spot for Dan, and little time for his volatile brother, wanted to do right by his unofficial nephew. He had provided cash for Dan's needs while his aunt was alive and some money in trust for Dan when he turned eighteen, enough for him to get his education and a place to live.

He helped in other ways, too, at Dan's determined request. Changing someone's name on legal documents and birth certificate, to erase their parenthood, isn't as difficult as you might think. These things can be arranged if you know the right people. With these you can apply for a passport and, once you have that most official form of photo ID, you are effectively someone new. The trick is to make sure you don't forget what your mother's maiden name is supposed to be, years later, when you are about to get married, and need to perform a small deception for the registrar.

With this technical little bit of law breaking, Dan separated himself from the suspicion of his family ties, from anyone who would remember the ill-fated union of the Tomasz Petrovich and Alice Lancaster. He made it into university at a safe distance over the Severn Bridge, then made it onto the police training programme once all the vetting checks on Daniel Collins, son of Alice and John Collins, had come back clean.

All this was hardly something you could explain to your

new nineteen-year-old girlfriend – why would you try, until you knew you could trust her? Then, after some time had passed, and you knew you *could*, how could you find a way to casually mention it? To drop it into the conversation?

The connection would certainly never have been renewed if Uncle Karol, with no son of his own, hadn't died of a sudden heart attack. He inadvertently left the absent Daniel Petrovich, still named as the only heir in his unaltered will, rather a lot of money. More awkwardly, he had left him several endowments from long-forgotten independent investments.

Several arms of the family business were quite legitimate these days, including intercontinental import/export – officially car parts, heavy plant and transport contracts. Beneath these were the other items such as drugs, the occasional bag of weapons, cash, and even people, as time went on, but some of the legitimate staff didn't necessarily know this. This meant there were business lawyers in Odessa and London haggling over Uncle Karol's estate and the whereabouts of Daniel Petrovich.

If Dan hadn't gone to London, to surreptitiously sign the papers offered by the lawyers, they might have come to search for him, asking questions, and who knows what they would have found out?

Sophie, Uncle Josef's daughter, had arranged it all. She was now a prominent player in the company, her father's daughter, the sort of efficient person who could be relied upon to resolve problems and deal with difficult matters discreetly. If it had simply been the matter of the will, there would have been ways to make the arrangements without ever involving Dan. But the endowments were held by companies not connected to the *intimate* side of the family business. They needed a little reassurance that the right man was legitimately signing away his money to Sophia Petrovich. The strong family resemblance of Dan to his father and his uncles, and the production of the original birth certificate Dan had kept hidden, just in case, smoothed the process considerably.

Then it was over – that is, until I had found some things I shouldn't have. Those two receipts from that unexpected 'work' trip to London I knew Dan hadn't claimed on force expenses; the half overheard, hushed late-night conversation with Sophie; the receipt for the lilies I hadn't received – the funeral flowers. Naturally, Dan had carefully paid for everything with cash – the petrol, the hotel, the flowers – he'd left no paper trail. But he *had* left the receipts in the pocket of his best jacket where I had found them. Well, where I had searched.

Then came the call from Sophie to tell him all the business was completed.

When Dan had tried to explain this to me, that sunny October morning, in the face of my hurricane-rage, disbelief had been my natural reaction. *Oh, so she's your cousin, Dan? Of course she is! I've just never heard of her before because, until now you've had no living family!*

What a pathetic fiction.

But it was the truth. I had spoken to Sophie when I'd had time to absorb the information, after my return from the Watch-house, and she'd confirmed what Dan had told me. It was just that one family issue, the will, the inheritance, and so on. Just that one time. Nothing more. An isolated business matter. I had told her never to contact Dan or our home again. She said she would have no reason to call. Of course, I had not thought then that I might have a reason to call *her*.

It is strange how the simplest things can be misinterpreted, confused, misunderstood in a split second or over a longer stretch of time. As we set off on our honeymoon Dan told me he had noticed a definite change in me, in the months before and the weeks after the wedding. He said he liked it.

'God there were times over the last few years when I found myself doubting what you really felt about me, about anything, Jen,' he said. 'You never seemed touched by anything, never really angry, never really frustrated, never weeping, never really laughing. You were so cool, so calm, so logical about everything – it was like everything was a run-through, a test, and I kept failing it. There were times when I wished you would just lose your temper with me, yell at me, smash something. Sometimes I was tempted to behave *really* badly just to try and make you react. But in the end I'd have to walk off because I just wanted to shake you so badly I didn't trust myself.

'There were so many times I wanted to tell you the truth. You've been the only family that matters to me for so long. But I could never find a way. I felt that if you could be less rational, less perfect, then I could be too, and maybe I could tell you the truth. Now, it's like you've resurfaced again – you're my Jen from college, when I met you.'

He's right, in a way. I did rediscover myself. Maybe I have Justin to thank for that, for making me decide to fight for my life, for making me value it. He forced me to accept that I couldn't be an observer. I had to create what I wanted and nurture what was good. So I found my compromise and my courage.

But I also found my cruelty, too. I suppose the challenge now is to close the lid of that hole in my heart again, keep it shut, trap the ills left inside and keep them there, along with the hope that one day, years from now, all this will not come back to confront me, on some sunny afternoon perhaps, when Dan and I are preparing for a romantic hotel trip and the phone rings and the timing couldn't possibly be worse . . .

But I can't worry too much about what I can't control. I'll deal with it when the time comes.

We had a beautiful honeymoon, four months after the wedding. Dan and I went to New England in the fall and marvelled at the crayon-bright colours of the trees and hills. He enjoyed visiting the blue and white sweep of the Cape Cod National Seashore and whale watching at Nantucket Island. He even attempted to read *Moby-Dick* while we were there. He said the half he's read so far is pretty good, but I won't blame him if he never finishes it. It's a bit of a doorstop, to be honest. I never actually finished it myself.

We ended our trip with four days in New York. I'd always wanted to visit New York. I think the architecture is amazing.

Epilogue

I should probably mention that there was still one surprise waiting for me when I returned from my honeymoon that autumn.

From the March of that year, up until the wedding, I had still half expected to receive another message or email from Justin. My eyes and ears were constantly searching for any news of him – in the police records, in the papers, on Facebook. I even checked 'Surf Sluts' from time to time, just in case, but there were no more postings. I said to myself, maybe Justin has taken pity on me after all, maybe he's decided to go straight. Maybe he's seen the error of his ways and become a reformed character. Maybe he's bored with the world of online porn. Maybe . . .

After the wedding, and my present, I stopped looking.

At the end of October, newly returned from New York, I was 'acting up' for Nige as media manager, while he acted up for the comms manager Kathy Collier, who had extended her maternity leave. After morning tasking Bodie barrelled into the office, booming that he wanted help with a press release for a missing person called Paul Mathry, from Swansea.

Paul Mathry's parents were concerned because they

hadn't heard from him for six months. Paul was not a model son, no previous convictions but mostly unemployed, semi-itinerant, into a few dodgy dealings and the odd bit of drugs. His mum and dad were used to him not calling for months at a time, except when he needed money, but the calls had stopped around April. Then they'd had a phone call from a surf travel group he appeared to have been due to take a holiday with in August – he and a male passenger, so the agent said.

It was an eight-week tour of Australia's best surf beaches. Accommodation and transport all in, but, though the deposit had been paid, neither man had confirmed their flight details and the £1,000 balance was outstanding. Mum and dad were surprised that Paul could afford something like that.

'They'll still have to stump up the cash, though,' said Bodie, sighing in a way that said, *bloody kids these days*. 'We'd better go through the motions, Jen, put out an appeal, tick a few boxes. But we'll probably just find him in a drug squat or a ditch somewhere, in a few months, stinking up the place.'

'Quite possibly,' I'd replied.

'It's a coincidence, though,' ruminated Bodie. 'It's the same family that owned one of those caravans down Aberthin. Remember the ones that went up in the arson? It still annoys me we never got anyone pegged for that. 'Course it didn't help that that stupid girl from The Chronicle didn't come forward and tell us she'd been down there badgering the residents the week before, taking pictures, looking for dirt on the development company. We wasted a lot of time with that e-fit from the old woman, before the site manager rang us. We should have prosecuted the paper for wasting our time.

'I'd bet my badge it was one of the other tenants who set the fire. I heard the land sold last month for a real tidy sum— the people left will have made a mint because that old couple lost their van. If that isn't a motive, I don't know what is. 'Course that means the Mathrys can probably afford to stump up for little Paulie's holiday money, but still, a grand's a grand.

'If I didn't know better I'd say Paul Mathry was a heap of ash in his dad's caravan, but forensics assured me those bones we found were definitely canine. Mr Mathry said it was probably one of their old spaniels. Why do people bury their dogs in their gardens and such like? It doesn't seem hygienic to me.'

He handed me the photograph that Mr and Mrs Mathry had given him for the appeal. 'It's an ok pic,' he mused, 'Quite old, though, but it's the only one they had. Not many Kodak moments in that family recently, I think.'

'Kodak moments? What's that mean?' asked Serian, earwigging across the desk.

'Bloody hell, you're making me feel old now, love,' said Bodie. 'You know, "picture-perfect" moments? Happy snaps? Jesus!'

When Bodie handed me the photo my first thought was, *it's a good job it was dark in the porch on the night you saw Paul Mathry on my doorstep with his hand up my shirt, otherwise I'd have a lot of explaining to do.* But I soon realised it wouldn't have mattered if he had seen his face.

The photo in my hand showed Paul Mathry, aged around nineteen, with a pale, dark-haired girl – Suzy Milland. What surprised me was that it wasn't Paul Mathry as I knew him. It wasn't Justin. The photo was of Justin's mate, Pootle.

Come to think of it, I'd only assumed that Justin was

'Paul Mathry' because the Mathrys owned the caravan and I'd seen Justin with Suzy in the photo I found there. Then I'd assumed because Justin was 'Paul', that he and Suzy had been a couple. But had it been Pootle who had taken all those wind-blown shots of Suzy, after all? *It wasn't my baby*, Justin had said, when I'd mentioned her pregnancy. For once in his life had he been telling a small truth?

While Bodie waited, I got to work scanning and digitally cropping Suzy out of the photo, ready to send Paul Mathry's image to Jack NewsBeatWales and the other media. While I worked, Bodie hovered around, doing his best to annoy Serian.

'Does this Paul fella have a vehicle? Transport? Credit card?' I asked after a few minutes, using the usual press release fact formula.

'Well, we found the old camper van his dad said he drives, parked up a few streets away from the house in Uplands. Locked up, all safe. No signs of any damage or anything funny. No credit card, just hand-to-mouth and cash off the old folks.'

'Will they give us a bit of a heartfelt plea for information, give it that human interest angle?' I asked, as usual.

'I dunno this time, Jen. I suppose I could ask, but I got the impression he wasn't the apple of mummy and daddy's eye. Bit of family history there, I think. They're a nice, ordinary couple, you know. Don't mean you don't end up with a scumbag son, unfortunately.'

Then I got to the question I really wanted to ask. 'Do we know who the friend was, the one he was supposed to be travelling with to Australia?' I asked this, casually, careful to seem almost uninterested.

'Nah, it was "plus one" on the booking, until the balance

was paid. We can appeal for him, right? Maybe he'll come forward, though I doubt it. Probably a druggie too. Put my usual bit of a quote on there, will you Jen? I trust you to make me sound sensible and concerned.'

'Will do,' I promised.

So I composed the press release, invented some comments for Bodie to give, tidied up the information and released the appeal on the media template. After a moment's hesitation, I took Paul Mathry's picture and filed him in my Book of the Dead.

In the days that followed, and even now, on occasion, I think back to the call I made to Sophie, the information I handed over, what I told her I wanted. Then I cannot help but wonder exactly who Vitaly confronted to provide me with my wedding present, whose fingers I had looked at, in the box with the pink bow, before I'd burnt it.

The gift I'd asked for was freedom, for a problem to be neutralised, removed. I hadn't specified how I'd wanted that done. They knew far more about that sort of thing than I did. I had just provided a name, one name, and family details.

Vitaly had mentioned something about an interruption though, about 'collateral damage'. On my wedding day he implied he'd had to improvise, and I suspected he was thorough enough to deal with all eventualities. Either way, the end result was the same. There were no more texts, no more emails and no more threats from Justin. My problem had vanished.

As for all the other loose ends, they remained untied and untouched. No arrests were made regarding the arson at the Aberthin caravan site. There were no fingerprints to check, and no unexpected witnesses emerged. No other sightings of the e-fit girl were reported after Anne Nolan owned up to her snooping with her black camera bag. Dan's Maglite still sits on the shelf in the evidence cupboard, the bag becoming dustier every day. Soon it will be buried behind newer pieces of unsolved CID puzzles and then eventually forgotten.

I ran three public appeals regarding the whereabouts of Paul Mathry over a six-month period but, a year on, he hasn't been sighted or found.

So far we haven't traced Paul Mathry's mystery travel companion.

More often than I thought I would, I pull our wedding album from the study shelf, open the black suede cover and flick through the glossy pages. I am still pleased with the result. Dan and I look genuinely happy – he is dashing and clean cut, I appear chic and a touch enigmatic. We both are smiling and respectable. The shot of us under the gnarled oak tree in the streaming sunlight says just what it should say. *Mr and Mrs Collins, Happily Married.*

The Dan at my side may not be quite the same man I courted at college but he is the husband I love and appreciate. The woman in the photograph is not the woman he met, or proposed to, or the woman who fled in a car to a chic hotel retreat in a fit of temporary madness. She vanished somewhere along that windblown road to Gower. Maybe she's still missing out there, somewhere where the sea and sky and land meet, waiting. But Dan adores the woman in the photograph just as much – more, I think.

Suzy and Justin look happy in their photos too. Each of them is full of smiles, each time I draw them out of their hiding place in the Robert Frost poetry anthology and place them next to ours in the wedding album. But people are so much more than the smiles they wear. Don't be so sure you can tell predator from prey at a glance.

If I had remembered this one single thing perhaps I wouldn't have ended up in bed with a stranger and had to do what I did. But if Justin Reynolds, whoever he was, and Paul Mathry wherever he is, had remembered it, they might still have all their digits, and maybe even their lives. Sometimes the sheep's clothing the wolf chooses is floppy hair, flip-flops and surfer beads, sometimes it's a sandy-blond bob, neat suit and a reassuring telephone manner. Underneath the smiles of both there can be teeth. You can never be too careful.

ALSO BY BEVERLEY JONES

Telling Stories

ISBN 978-1-908122-11-7

£7.99

Stories lie.
Truth hurts.
Secrets can be deadly.

The reunion of Lizzy Jones and her three university friends in Cardiff is shattered by the mysterious appearance of Jenny, a girl who seems to know them all. When Jenny's body is found later, it becomes clear that the friends were probably the last people to see her alive.

Lizzy, a cub reporter, is assigned the story and decides to say nothing about her encounter with the dead woman. She also chooses to say nothing about the fact that one of their number, Mike, cannot explain his absence on the night Jenny fell – or was pushed- into the River Taff.

Looking back to her heady student days with her friends in Wales and relating her investigation into the background of the enigmatic Jenny, Lizzy revels in telling their stories – stories that will have life-changing consequences for all.